Excerpts from STAKE THROUGH THE HEART

She seemed so far away and yet
hair was ruffled and then I met her
The red light was coming from h
I tried to scream, but there was
opened over my spread legs and her w............ seemed to drip red.
"First," she finally continued, "there's the devouring."

—**CASTLE WRATH**, Karin Kallmaker

⚰

The woman moaned. Nadia held her tight, kissing her deeply on the mouth, then letting her tongue glide down over her collarbone to the hot indentation between her breasts. If she had the time, she would make love to the woman first, but she was so hungry. It had been days since she'd feasted.

—**RUNNING WITH STONE PONIES**, Barbara Johnson

⚰

She kissed me hard, biting down on my lower lip till she drew blood. She licked my lips and let out a low, rumbling sound like a purring cat. I was excited, but I was also scared. If it had been Driver's Ed instead of sex, she would have been shoving me out onto the interstate when I had only just learned how to circle an empty parking lot. "Sweet," she whispered, licking her own lips, then leaning down to kiss my neck.

—**WE RECRUIT**, Julia Watts

⚰

She played her tongue lightly over my earlobe, down my throat, and then sucked at my neck. She ran her hands under my T-shirt, feeling my skin, making me squirm. "I wonder, sometimes, if she brings me here just so I might find you. God, Rebecca, I want you so badly—"

I pushed her back, sure of one thing as I seemed to straddle vast gulfs in time. "I'm Rhenné."

—**ELSEWHEN**, Therese Szymanski

RAVES FOR THE *NEW EXPLOITS* SERIES . . .

"Good sex and good humor together in one lesbian story is a true rarity!"

—*Curve Magazine*

"Finalist for best erotica of 2004."

—Lambda Literary Foundation

". . . Romantic, funny, thoughtful, and hot. Buy a copy and live happily ever after."

—*Midwest Review of Books*

"Magic both in and out of relationships . . . amusing twists . . . and totally enjoyable."

—*Golden Threads*

"Fun is exactly what the reader gets."

—R. Lynne Watson

"If you enjoy a fun romp between the covers (of a book), then look for this wonderfully racy collection at your favorite bookstore."

—*MegaScene*

"*Once Upon a Dyke* transforms virtually all of the shopworn conventions of the fairy tales we know into fertile ground for a host of adult stories with heroines that are nobody's gender stereotypes . . ."

—Quality Paperback Book Club

"In writing about the rituals of female magic, all four authors managed to conjure up a wonderful strong and real undercurrent of strength and sensuality . . . You'll leave feeling like an associate member of an ancient, lively and mystical coven of bewitchingly smart and sensual lesbians."

—Joy Parks, *WOMO*

STAKE THROUGH THE HEART

BARBARA JOHNSON
KARIN KALLMAKER
THERESE SZYMANSKI
JULIA WATTS

Bella
BOOKS
2006

Bella Books, Inc.
P.O. Box 10543
Tallahassee, FL 32302

Printed in the United States of America on acid-free paper
First Edition

Editors: Karin Kallmaker and Julia Watts
Cover designer: LA Callaghan

ISBN 1-59493-071-6

CONTENTS

FOREWORD

Catherine Deneuve and Susan Sarandon. If those two names don't make erotic visions dance through your head, then hightail it to the nearest movie store and rent a copy of Tony Scott's 1983 lesbian vampire classic *The Hunger*. Once you reach the film's key scene, you'll want to make judicious use of the pause button.

From Bram Stoker to Barnabas Collins to Buffy, vampires have long captured the popular imagination. But even before Catherine and Susan acted upon their hunger, there was a special connection between lesbianism and vampirism. J. Sheridan Le Fanu's novel *Carmilla*, which is said to have been the partial inspiration for Stoker's *Dracula*, is as dykey as anything published in 1872 could get by with being. On film, the 1936 Universal horror film *Dracula's Daughter* has strong lesbian undertones. And later high-camp flicks such as 1971's *Daughters of Darkness* are more frank in their erotic exploitation of the lesbian-vampire connection, sometimes with unintentionally hilarious results.

Of course, all these books and films are examples of mainstream depictions of lesbian vampires, and while enjoyable, can also be troubling in their implication that lesbianism is an evil on par with drinking the blood of the living. Lesbians, these mainstream books and films—as well as countless darkly sexual covers of pulp novels—suggest, are shadowy, sinister predators who must satisfy their perverse lusts under the cloak of darkness.

We, the authors of *Stake Through the Heart*, are not in the mainstream. As a result, we join our sister lesbian writers who have chosen to reclaim and embrace the lesbian vampire for a number of reasons: Because she knows what it is to live a life that is often misunderstood. Because she is the ultimate seductress. Because she is sexy. Whether we long to bite or be bitten—or both—we yearn for her twilight, where the clarity of sunlight and the freedom of darkness intermingle in our fantasies.

We hope that the lesbian vampires you meet in *Stake Through the Heart* capture your imagination, fuel your desire and ignite your hunger.

Julia Watts   Karin Kallmaker
        September 2006

VAMP

an introductory musical passage of two or four measures often repeated several times before a solo or between verses

to piece (something old) with a new part

to practice seductive wiles on

one who lives by preying on others

a woman who exploits and ruins her lover— short for vampire

CASTLE WRATH

KARIN KALLMAKER

CHAPTER 1

*I am an heiress. A dark woman
follows me. Steak and stilton pie.
Arrival in Inverness.*

The important thing is that you believe what I'm telling you because, frankly, it's unbelievable from the get-go. It's not like it's a long story, or anything, and I still don't know how it ends, but it's completely and totally true.

I took this writing class and they said the important thing was to write what you know and leave out the boring bits. That's two important things, I realize that now, but here's what I know and I'm leaving out the boring part about how it all came to pass: I inherited a castle in Scotland!

You don't want to know about my grandfather's great aunt's adopted son's nephew-by-marriage who died without issue and the long series of accidents that led to me being the heir—trust me, it's a forty-part episode of Masterpiece Theatre. But here I am on a train in the Scottish countryside, trying to imagine the fate that caused all those deaths that let this incredible thing happen to me. It's a bit freaky thinking about karma and fate and payback so I'm not thinking about it.

What I *am* thinking about right now is that I can't understand a thing anyone says and I'm hungry. Plus, there's this tall, dark woman who keeps staring at me. I think I saw her at the train station in Glasgow. I had to run for the train and she seemed to be following me because she was running too. She's attractive but hardly my type—too old. Too serious, I'll bet. I trod on her foot when the train started to go and she said "buggery bollocks" and I said I was sorry so I don't know why she's staring at me.

I wonder if she's the other heir.

Sorry, I hadn't gotten to that part. I didn't mean to leave it out as it's not at all boring. See, there are two heirs. We have to live in the castle for thirty nights and then one of us will inherit and the other gets a ticket home.

The other heir, P. Tennielle of Manchester, England, U.K., is some kind of artist. She must be successful—after all, she has a Web page. The "P" stands for Portia, how British is that? The photos of her were badly lit but the staring woman could be her. What a way to start off, me tromping on her foot. But she doesn't know it's me of course as I don't have a Web page yet. Right now, to her, I'm just a clumsy American, not B. Brannigan of Lodi, California, U.S.A. The "B" stands for Brittany, by the way. Maybe when we meet officially at the solicitor's office in Inverness she won't remember me. That is, if that's her.

My best friend, Susie Bling (I know, that's hysterical, isn't it?) is nearly an attorney and she said the will is completely screwed up and would never fly in the U.S. except it was written over 300 years ago—before the U.S. of A. even existed!—after some sixth earl of someplace was "attaindered." I tried to look that up online but after about two minutes I needed a latte, know what I mean?

I'm hoping stilton is a cheese and that food bought on the train isn't going to put me in the toilet for the next 24 hours. But lots of people in business suits are digging in so I'm taking my chances. Shillings and pence aren't troubling me. Even if I don't get the castle, I get ten thousand pounds which will pay for this really *spiffing* trip to England—Scotland's in England, or is it the other way around? I can never remember. Anyway, I can do pretty much as I like, including not counting my cell minutes, and still have a bundle for some necessities when I get home again.

Steak and stilton pie is tasty, and that's a relief. The tall, dark woman got off the train at the last stop before Inverness and that was a relief too. I guess when I edit this I'll just take her out. It's incredible what I see out the window—cows and country houses, stuff like that. If it weren't for the train I was on I'd expect to see Conestoga wagons.

I don't suppose they ever used Conestoga wagons here.

The previous stops taught me that when it was time to get off the train you'd better be near the doors and ready to jump, luggage and all. They barely came to a full and complete stop. As I attempted to alight with some kind of dignity I tripped on the smaller of my two suitcases. A nice older gentleman caught me. Scottish men went up in my estimation after two wearing T-shirts with "Caley Thistle" volunteered to manage my bags all the way to the taxi stand, giving me a chance to get my skirt back into place. I didn't understand a word they said except the invitation for "a pint" which I had to turn down. There was the solicitor waiting, for one thing, and they were cute but not my type. The matching shirts celebrating foliage screamed "gay" to me. Their scruffy ruggedness would turn heads in San Francisco, but I prefer creatures with clits. And breasts. And good fashion sense. And brains. Financially self-sufficient is always a plus, believe you me. But this story is not about my user ex who still owes me rent money.

Inverness sounded so romantic, but my first impression when we reached the street was that I was freezing. The sweater that had seemed oppressively hot when I left home felt like tissue paper. I hoped there was a Target or Old Navy.

"Where to, miss?" At least I think that's what the cab driver said. I read the address for Roderick Macklin Stuart, LLB, off the letter I had carried with me from the moment I had opened it in my tiny studio apartment, which was all I could afford. For what I paid I could buy a house back in Lodi, but there were hardly any theaters in Lodi, let alone film schools. The cab driver responded, I am not making this up, with, "Will you hi-glock-lo-Monday-knee?"

I made a little sound and he said, "Right, then," and off we went. Bang out of the station he made a right turn into certain death. I was a very long way from Lodi, indeed.

Inverness was a charming city, like something off a postcard, and I could hardly believe I was being driven through it in a black cab like Supernanny's. There was a cathedral silhouetted against the afternoon sky and a beautiful river that split the city in two. I had a list of places I wanted to see tonight and in the morning, but I did need to sort out a place to stay and buy my transit ticket to Durness via Wick as well. I tried to get my old camera into position to take some pictures but the cabbie swooped so quickly along the roadway that I knew my cell phone's little built-in digital couldn't cope. As soon as I was paid by the solicitor for the funds I'd already spent to get here, I was going right out to buy a real digital camera, if not here in Inverness, then when my bus got to Wick tomorrow.

My journey included such romantic names, even the ones I couldn't pronounce, like Craig Phadraig, Clò Mór, Kinlockbervie and Tongue. Well, I can pronounce Tongue. I've been told I use it well too. All of the cities sounded charming and somewhat mysterious, but my final destination, the Castle Wrath, at the tip of Cape Wrath, on the Kyle of Durness, chilled the blood in my veins. I'm sure the location is charming—okay, I've used charming three times in two paragraphs. I'm sure the location is quaint, but a bit colder than I expected. I had looked up Cape Wrath on the Internet and it's the heart of walking tours in the Highlands. That just makes me want to put on a tartan and dance. I wondered if there'd be men in kilts.

Then I wondered if Scottish butches wore kilts. It seemed like they ought to, and just thinking about it passed the rest of the scary cab ride. A kilt with a nice big codpiece, only they're not called codpieces on kilts, are they? But then what I was really thinking about wasn't called a codpiece on a butch either.

In a much less stressful state of mind, I paid the cabbie and examined my surroundings. The buildings were quaint (darn it, now I'd have to think of another adjective) and undeniably old. The steps I made my way up, thumping my cases after me, were grooved and worn. On the right was another set of obviously modern stairs, wooden, with a handrail in bright yellow, tacked on to please some building inspector, no doubt. Halfway up the old steps I slipped on the slick stone and nearly bashed my knee. I didn't glance over at whomever was going up the sensible wooden stairs. I just wanted a sense of style. There was a metaphor somewhere in beginning this grand adventure by climbing steps older than the Revolution.

"Are you all right?"

I glanced up and there she was, the buggery-bollocks woman from the train. She *was* following me. But I'd seen her get off the train. Perhaps this was a twin? What was her game? "I'm fine," I finally answered.

"What a coincidence. You were at the station in Glasgow, weren't you?"

"And on the same train." I wondered if she'd admit it.

"Well, if you arrive in Glasgow and are going on to Inverness, there's just the one train. The odd part is you standing here on the same steps as me. Are you a reporter?"

"No." I got back into motion and finished the climb and yet, standing next to her she was still twelve inches taller. I wondered how tall that made her, somewhere around six feet I'd guess, only in meters. "I have an appointment."

"I'm Portia Tennielle." She held out her hand. "You're an American, you're at this address, at this hour, so you must be Brittany Brannigan."

Buggery bollocks, it was her.

CHAPTER 2

*Time for tea. Two pints too
many. An indiscreet question.
Alternative transportation.*

I saw you get off the train," I said, trying to sound casual.

She opened the heavy door of the building for me and I realized I could walk under her extended arm with ease. "Yes, I needed to drop my friend and pick up a car."

"Are you familiar with the area?"

She nodded. The door closed behind us with a dull thud. "My family had holidays in the Highlands when I was a girl."

I really didn't think I'd be the one who got the castle in the end, and her familiarity with the area cemented my feeling. No doubt she would know how to keep ancient boilers running, what to do during a hurricane and which walking paths would end in bogs. I hoped to finish my month without getting bog on my shoes.

I followed P. Tennielle down a long narrow hallway to the very last door, which turned out to be a stairwell. My suitcases grew heavier with each tread, but I made it to the top of the stairs without bursting a vein. I would not show weakness in front of the taller, thinner, older, and undoubtedly wilier woman. She had to be at least thirty-five but she went up the stairs as if they were flat, her steps light and quiet.

That the building was only two stories made my day. The

upstairs hallway seemed to be on a slight downhill slope and my suitcase kept wanting to roll into the wall. There was hardly enough room to make our way between stacks of moldering boxes piled high enough to put me in mind of Miss Havisham's house.

"Come in, come in," a cheerful voice called. I followed Portia around another pile of boxes to find a small man at a crowded desk rising to greet us both. There were two chairs so free of dust and clutter that I was convinced the piles of boxes and papers near them had been on them until the moment our arrival had been detected.

We were offered tea and I accepted, hoping for some of the little cakes I'd had during my brief stopover in London.

"The kettle will only be a few minutes to the boil." Mr. Stuart set his spectacles down on the ink-stained blotter. "So Miss Brannigan—"

"Ms.," I emphasized. "But everyone calls me Brit."

Portia snickered. "How apropos. You could end up one."

"Would I have to become a British citizen to inherit?"

"No, not—"

"I like being an American. We have our messed-up moments, but I'd really not want to change." For a castle of my own, I might consider it, though.

"The land can be inherited by a foreigner, isn't that right?" Portia gave Mr. Stuart a smile I couldn't quite fathom. "The language in the will was meant to allow British and Irish heirs, who were deemed foreigners at the time."

"That's quite right, but—"

"Then that's good news for the California girl, isn't it?" I smiled brightly at both of them. "I mean, if I do inherit, which isn't at all settled, is it?"

"Not settled, no—"

"But the title can only be taken on by a British subject." Portia transferred that enigmatic smile to me. Her Web page had really lousy photos. They had captured her good looks, certainly, but she also gave good brood.

"Title?" I didn't remember anything about a title in the letter.

"The earldom isn't on the roll anymore, of course, not since the Jacobite—"

"Of course not," Portia agreed. "It's more of a prestige claim."

The kettle boiled.

Mr. Stuart bustled about and I was saddened to see no sign of little cakes. There was, however, a package of cookies.

He plopped several teabags into a bright blue teapot. "So Ms. Brannigan, what is it you do in America?"

Susie and I had rehearsed my response. "I'm in retail at the moment, and attending university."

"Oh?" Portia sat still and upright, hardly moving even when she spoke. "What field of study?"

"American literature and filmmaking. I intend to write my own films."

She gave me a nod that could have meant she was impressed, but also could have meant she thought I was full of it. I had no idea what she was really thinking until she said, "How interesting."

It made me want to hoity her toity. Right then I decided I wasn't just going to roll over and play Misty for her. "It's challenging. I like a challenge."

"Living in Los Angeles must be an advantage, then." Mr. Stuart carried a tray over to his desk, which had—I'm sure not coincidentally—a clear space just large enough for it. "Miss Tennielle, would you be mother?"

"I'd be delighted." Portia began fussing with the cups.

"I don't live in Los Angeles. I was born and raised in Lodi, which is in the northern part of the state."

"Oh, San Francisco!" Mr. Stuart beamed at me. "I was there a very long time ago. Delightful city."

I wasn't going to explain that San Franciscans would vote Republican before they'd claim Lodi as part of their mecca, so I nodded. "I'm going to school in Berkeley. Across the bay."

"That's a very good university," Portia said. "Sugar?"

I hoped my hesitation went unnoticed. "Yes."

"One or two?"

"One."

"Biscuit?"

"Yes, please." I was no novice, and I knew that biscuit meant cookie. "Thank you."

"You're welcome." She handed me a delicate teacup balanced on an equally delicate plate. The ritual was repeated with Mr. Stuart, except his tea went into a mug that looked as if it might be washed annually. By the time that was all concluded I had decided there was no need to point out that I was attending the Bay Area Academy of Literature and Film, not the University of California. I hadn't said I was *at* Berkeley, only going to school *in* Berkeley, which was absolutely letter-perfect truth.

Mr. Stuart sipped from his cup, thanked Portia again, and said, "I suppose we'll have to do a spot of business, though it's not often I have tea with two beautiful women."

So much for Scotsmen being dour, I thought. "I can safely say that I've never done anything like this before."

"The terms of the will are quite clear."

I snorted, then turned it into a cough.

Mr. Stuart blithely continued, "Both of you are the surviving claimants along competing lines and therefore must first prove your intent to claim your inheritance by occupying the castle for a period of thirty nights. Time spent elsewhere would constitute a relinquishment of your claim. At the end of thirty nights, you need to present yourself in person, with a statement of intent to press your claim. If you both press your claim, a tribunal of three judges will decide between you, based on your plans for the caring for the family heritage in keeping with the desires of . . ."

He went on for some time. I emptied my cup of tea, refused a refill and another cookie as he continued to read. In the interest of skipping over the boring bits, I'll move ahead to when he said, "If you'll provide me with your travel expenses so far, I am authorized to write a bank draft."

Thank goodness he'd brought it up. I'd not wanted to appear a money-grubbing American by broaching the subject myself, even if it was over twelve hundred dollars so far. It was a lot of rent money. I handed over my neatly organized pile of receipts. "There'll also be a hotel tonight and bus tomorrow."

Portia had only a single page. "Just the rail ticket, single. I've borrowed a car from a mate."

I hoped my needing to spend more wouldn't be held against me later. I'd shopped hard for the flight, and the rail pass I'd bought before leaving the States had been cheaper than flying the entire way to Inverness, honest. I started to explain all of that but Mr. Stuart waved his hand around in a shushing gesture.

"I'm authorized to provide a small advance for the remainder of your journey, to use as you like. You may arrive in Wick too late to drive out to the castle. You could stay at the Durness for the night. I'm told it's a lovely old hotel, and the closest to the cape, only four miles away."

I was a little jolted to think that the nearest civilization was farther from the castle than the whole length of Lodi. I'd lived in a city all my life. Well, some people don't think Lodi is a city, but it is.

Mr. Stuart carefully wrote out the checks to each of us. Portia departed after the appropriate sentiments, then Mr. Stuart told me where to find the bank that would let me cash the check. Fortunately, it was the same bank that would honor my American bank's cash machine card. I rose from the chair armed with the check, Mr. Stuart's map of the countryside near Castle Wrath and a thick folder with a copy of my ancestor's will and other documents concerning the inheritance.

Refusing help with my cases, I got myself down to the ground floor and discovered Portia waiting for me.

"If you'd like a pint, we could make a few plans." She held the door and I tried to look nonchalant as I steered toward the modern set of stairs. "My car is just round the corner. We could go to the bank together first, before it closes for the day."

"That would be wonderfully convenient." I figured a friendly approach was the best approach. "If it's not a bother."

"Not at all. Let me help with that case."

She was all courtesy and charm, but I remained wary. Her "mate's" car turned out to be a dignified but still racy black Jaguar with a "boot" already full of Portia's cases. Mine fit on the miniscule backseat, however, and once they were settled, I gladly oozed down into the passenger seat—on the wrong side of the car—with a sigh of relief. Portia was a less frightening driver than the cabbie, and as long as I didn't watch when she made a right turn, I did okay.

At the bank I cashed the check and the teller helped me figure out the conversion to dollars, then accepted a deposit to pay down my credit card balance for the expenses. That still left me with a nice bundle of very pretty notes. In a month I'd have a whole lot of very pretty notes. Beer and dinner were looking very good to me. My adrenaline was waning, now that I was here and Mr. Stuart had put my mind mostly at ease. I'd had a secret worry that I'd find it was all a convincing joke.

"Have you a preference where we eat?"

"No, not at all. Something authentic, that would be good. I had a pie on the train."

"There's a pub just up Loch Ness way. It's very scenic."

Loch Ness was on my list of things I hoped to see. I didn't believe there was a monster or any silliness like that, but I was curious about a place that could spawn so many juicy stories that in turn inspired a whole lot of scary movies. There'd have been no creature from any lagoon, let alone a black one, without Nessie. "That sounds delightful. Is Urquhart Castle near?"

She gave me a surprised look. "Yes, it is, though I believe it closes for visitors at sunset. It's a ruin, you know."

"I know." The sky was already deepening into twilight.

"I'm impressed you know the geography so well."

The Jaguar purred along a narrow road and I tried not to watch her hands on the wheel. She was very attractive, I had to admit that. But it didn't mean she was gay, though I was getting pings.

"I'm not very well traveled and I might not ever get back here, so I wanted to see as much as possible while I can. My grandmother insists she was told a long-handed-down story about some ancestress losing her virtue to James the Second there. I'm supposed to look for proof that he stayed at the castle at some point, but I'm not all that hopeful."

"Ah, so you're also on a quest as well as in the running for a castle of your own."

"Is this whole situation bizarre to you?"

"Quite. I had no idea I was connected to a former earldom. It's the kind of thing English schoolgirls fantasize about, an affiliation with nobility."

I wondered what else she fantasized about, but it hardly seemed like the time to ask.

After three pints in a loud pub claiming to be the finest in Drumnadrochit, it seemed like a good time to ask.

We were sitting very close because it was quite noisy. The sausages and mashed potatoes were filling, and I think warm beer is more potent than chilled.

"I want my first project on film to be a scary thriller," I was telling her. "The two scariest movies I know are *Silence of the Lambs* and *The Blair Witch Project*. Neither one follows the Hollywood formula for horror films."

"There's a formula?" Portia sipped from her beer and I thought how pale and fine her skin looked in the low light.

"Absolutely. You show the girl's tits or something suggestively sensual, like John Travolta getting a blow job in *Carrie*, and about ten to fifteen seconds later, as the sexual response hits the viewer, the blood slashing spatter begins. Mock ejaculation—catharsis. For the male viewer, that is." I took a large swallow of my beer. It was kind of nutty and golden tasting. Sort of yummy. "But I think women are different."

"Oh, so do I." Portia looked away, but her expression was suggestive.

"Do you?" More pings on the gaydar. "I think we can sometimes be scared by that scenario, too, but we get batbrained terrified when we are given the time to absorb a character's terror for ourselves. So a big blunt thing falls on Travolta. He was a bad guy—who cares? But Jodie Foster shakes like a leaf for fifteen minutes and the tension is unbearable. I want to make a movie like that, one that connects that way with women."

"Do you like connecting with women?" Portia turned her head to regard me directly. Her lips looked crimson, her skin smooth and luminous as a pearl. She smiled broadly when I didn't answer right away and I noticed her teeth were vividly white. "I'm gay. How about you?"

"Me too."

"Thought so." She laughed into her beer. "Well, that's going to put someone in a proper twist. I thought I might not inherit because I'm gay, but now that's moot. The next denizen of Castle Wrath will be a lesbian."

"That's not the sort of thing that English schoolgirls fantasize about?"

"Not this one."

I couldn't help myself. "What did you fantasize about instead?"

"As a schoolgirl? Footballers. I was very hung up on footballers. Then I saw my first girl in a rugby shirt and that was that. Never looked back."

I stared into the bottom of that third pint of beer and wondered where it had gone. "Is that still your type?"

"Oh, I've learned not to be predictable in my tastes."

So I didn't need to be some rugged jockette. I heard the sound of screeching brakes and realized it was my psyche-mobile. I wasn't here to get married, or get laid even, though getting laid had crossed my mind more than once during the third beer. I was here to inherit a castle, if I could. Of course if I could inherit a castle *and* get laid, that would be even better. Married—queers did that here, too.

Even though I thought my mouth had been shut down by the psyche-mobile warning, I heard myself ask, slurring only slightly, "Now that you're all grown up, what do you fantasize about?"

"Drive up to Durness with me tonight and I'll tell you."

I blinked.

"That's what I wanted to talk to you about. Why stay here overnight and drive up on your own tomorrow? Or were you going to take the rail to Wick and then a bus to Durness?"

"I'd planned to get a car in Durness—not so far for me to drive on the wrong side of the road."

"It'd be easier all the way around if you drove up with me, wouldn't it? I'm driving up tonight."

It was a friendly offer, and it made a lot of sense. Truth be told, I was a little scared being so far from home, and getting myself all the way to Castle Wrath using the stop-and-ask directions method was making me nervous.

"Sure," I said. Maybe she wanted a little more of my company too. The thought encouraged me. "That would be great."

CHAPTER 3

*Dark roads. A scare in the
dark. Tea in a castle kitchen.
A surprising dream.*

I fell asleep two minutes into the drive, so didn't get to hear Portia's fantasies that night. I woke with a start and remembered all in a flash my intentions to acquire a digital camera, sightsee and find something warmer than the thick sweater I'd hoped would be coverage enough for the Scottish early spring. There was no sign of a shopping mall outside the window. There, in fact, was no sign of anything but black.

I could use my dandy little laptop to order a camera and a jacket, I supposed. "Deliver to Castle Wrath" would look mighty fine.

My head felt like it weighed more than usual as I tried to sit up. I hoped I hadn't been snoring. Something refined and heavy in violins was rolling out of the speakers—the kind of thing you'd hear in a castle drawing room.

"You were worn out."

"Yeah, I guess so." I ran my hand through my hair, which felt greasy, and wished for a bathroom. The headlights illuminated a pitted road not even wide enough for two cars. "I slept some on the flight from San Francisco, but I haven't been sleeping well overall. Excited about the trip."

"That's understandable."

It felt downright weird to look to my right to study the driver of the car. The dashboard lights cast her face in shadow, but it was undeniable: P. Tennielle of Manchester, England, U.K., was a hottie. She'd look great in a castle drawing room. A rather short, perky and modestly shaped American girl from Lodi, California, had little chance. While I was a couple of steps above "mousey," I was the kind of person people had to be reminded they'd met before.

"How far are we from Durness?"

"We just passed through. Next stop is our new home."

"Oh!" The car's clock said it was after two a.m. "I thought we'd stop in Durness for the night."

"The hotel was shuttered and dark—we can go back if we have to, but it looked as if there was no one awake."

Portia was driving no more than fifteen miles an hour as the road narrowed even more. "How will you know where to turn?"

"If we get to the ferry that takes us across the kyle to Cape Wrath, we took the wrong turn about three minutes ago. But I think we're fine."

She had barely finished speaking when the headlights swept over a stone wall. Navigating carefully, she turned into a narrow entrance flanked by two enormous, square posts. A small building that looked as if it might be an old barracks of some kind was built into the wall to the south, but our lights quickly slid past it as we turned north on a gravel driveway.

I repeated to myself, "Last night I dreamt I went to Manderley again," but the driveway wasn't long, winding and tree-lined. After only a minute of slow driving, Portia stopped the car at the foot of wide steps, then turned off the engine.

It was dark. Dark and windy. Windy enough that something spattered the car with each gust. I'd remember that sound effect for my scary movie, I thought, not wanting to admit I was frightened.

The set was great, couldn't have been better. It didn't matter that I was on the other side of the world from home.

Bravado was the only reason I opened the door. Portia quickly put her hand on my arm.

"Hang on. Let me resettle the car."

She backed carefully so that the headlights were on the front door. The steps *were* steep and old, nearly as treacherous as the ones I'd fallen on this afternoon in front of Mr. Stuart's offices. Not all that deep down inside my inner scaredy-cat was yowling that it seemed like I was on the other side of the world from Mr. Stuart's office as well.

Leaving our bags, we got out of the car at the same time. The wind felt like knives of ice, and it *howled*. Way, way more howling than "Funeral for a Friend" which wasn't what I wanted to be thinking about at all. Funerals, I mean. There's plenty of wind in the Bay Area but it never made this kind of noise. This wind was alive, howling furiously, and it was telling me to go home.

My sweater was a feeble joke. I'd meant to rent a car in Durness regardless, just so I would be able to get things if I needed them. I was betting it was a couple hundred miles to the nearest Gap. I was trapped here and I was going to freeze to death. If I didn't die of exposure, there was always the possibility that the spider I saw scuttling out of sight on the steps would have a lethal bite when it returned, after I fell asleep, with all of its kin.

Portia clanged the heavy door knocker six times. The thuds resonated beyond the door into what sounded to me like an empty house.

"There might not even be beds ready for us," I said. "Or heat and water. A bathroom would be a welcome sight."

Portia clanged another half-dozen times. "We're expected, so the caretaker is here somewhere."

"Caretaker?"

"Place like this there's got to be a caretaker."

I wished I was as certain as she was. I realized I'd no idea what the expenses of owning even a small castle were and how the estate paid them. "We're expected tomorrow."

She tried the large knob and flashed me a brilliant grin when it turned. The door swung open with a creak that belied the idea that there was any kind of caretaker. A stone floor covered by a runner of dark carpet was illuminated by the headlights.

"After you," I said.

"Right." Portia led the way.

The widely flung door let in the car's yellow lighting, but it also let in the howling wind. The edges of the carpet ruffled up, then flapped back down, and the echo did not make me think of snapping bat jaws.

Portia fumbled along the wall to her left while I carefully edged to the right, searching for a light switch. My hand encountered something stringy and soft, threads of some kind, fringe, not webs . . . of course not, and I wasn't thinking about Frodo in the spider's lair, not me.

"Nobody said anything about needing a flashlight," I muttered.

"If we have to, we can empty the boot and see if there's an emergency torch."

I encountered something about half my height and as my eyes adjusted better to the dark I could tell it gleamed slightly. Something highly polished. I bent to try to figure it out just as Portia gave a cry of triumph. Light flooded the hallway and I found myself face to face with a grimacing gargoyle.

Okay, I screamed. Anybody would have screamed.

"Bloody hell!" Portia glared at me from the other side of the open door. "You scared the wadding out of me!"

I flushed. It was just one of those decorative items made out of the creature's body, with the flat of the back serving as a small table. I'd seen them as butlers and pigs but never anything so gruesome as this drool-dripping demon. The tray contained a short stack of cards that said, "Welcome to Castle Wrath. Please stay in the areas marked for public viewing. Your courtesy is appreciated."

Not waiting for any apology from me, Portia stomped down the steps to the car. I hurried after, securing my cases from the backseat and struggling back up the steep stairs with them.

It felt much better to enter my new temporary, but possibly permanent, home with the lights on. The wind seemed less vocal and I could appreciate the stark simplicity of the narrow but high stone hall that ended in a velvet rope with a sign reading "Family only." Beyond was a staircase that disappeared up a turret or something. There were two closed doors on the left and two open on the right.

Leaving my cases, I peeked into the first door on the right. A formal sitting room, not very large, and stuffed with the kind of antiques that looked torturous to use—sofas with large wooden arms and rock-like cushions, chairs with knobby backs, that sort of thing. The fireplace was covered by a grill that was locked.

The next room was a little museum about the castle, featuring a few paintings of previous occupants; some personal effects including a curved sword, a helmet with heavy engraving, an elegant enameled hairbrush, comb and shaving set; a tartan throw that was primarily red, and a placard explaining the Wrath clan affiliations. The far corner promised information about the local dialect and Highlands customs. I'd have to study that myself.

The door slammed shut and Portia stood there, smoothing her wind-ruffled hair. She looked *perfect* against the old stone. I could see her in a suit made of that brilliant red tartan. In my imagination sometimes she wore a kilt with a codpiece only called something different—I was going to have to ask—and sometimes she wore a skirt and very high heels. She seemed like a flexible kind of woman. Regardless, her stance was positively regal.

"I've shut off the lights and locked the car." She strode over to the first door on the left, opened it without hesitation and disappeared within. I was right behind her as she switched on an overhead lamp. A long hardwood table with seating for at least sixteen stretched the length of the room, which was lined with buffets and etageres, all empty. The clan tartan was used as a table runner, and the blue threading in the tartan matched the draperies and chair covers. The end of the table nearest us had an old, deep divot, as if some angry lord had thrust a dagger into it to make a point.

Portia had already walked the length of the room and disappeared into what was probably the kitchen. Sure enough, that was the second roped-off room, and in its far depths were two very welcome sights: a small table for six, nestled into what might be a warm, sunny corner of the kitchen, and a bathroom.

I wasn't proud. I scooted past Portia, found the light, locked the door and took care of my urgent needs.

When I emerged Portia had a kettle in one hand and was waiting at the kitchen sink. "Would you like some tea?"

"Yes, thank you. I'm cold to the bone."

She turned the spigot and I was pleased to see clear water stream out in response, albeit after an initial coughing sputter.

The stove she also quickly mastered, striking a match to light a burner before setting the kettle in place. She easily found mugs and tea.

"How do you know where everything is?"

She shrugged. "Everything is where it seems it ought to be. The kettle was there on the counter, the mugs in the cupboard above, the tea in the drawer below. There's some sugar packets and powdered milk."

Disquieted, I distracted myself by looking into the refrigerator. Only a dish with baking soda was to be found. It was turned on, but set to its least cold temperature. "We're lucky to have tea and fake milk."

"Likely the caretakers count on it being here."

"How many times have you been here before?"

"The castle itself? Only once, to look round inside. But I had a couple of walking holidays, so I've seen the cape, the lighthouse and all that." She excused herself to the bathroom, leaving me to study the clean white paint and simple wildflower drawings that graced the walls. I liked the kitchen, a lot. I could plug in my laptop at the table, surf the Internet and be very happy with some coffee and toast in the morning. Of course there was no coffee and toast. I'd make do with one of the nutrition bars squirreled away in my suitcase.

Morning, I reminded myself as I warmed my hands near the burner lit under the teakettle, wasn't that far off. The long sleep in the car had eased a lot of my exhaustion, and as soon as I had something warm in my stomach I only wanted to find a bed. Given the way I felt I'd be lucky to wake before nightfall.

Portia dropped teabags tagged "Typhoo" into the mugs and poured on the boiling water. The aroma of steeping tea chased away the faint dusty old castle smell. I smiled at the thought—I'd not known what dusty old castle smell was until just a short while ago.

"What's amusing?" She slid gracefully into a chair at the table.

"I know what a castle smells like, now."

"Ah. I was just thinking that I hope there are made-up beds. The sun will be up all too soon." She smiled into her tea as she sipped and I couldn't help but notice how red her lips were against the ice white of the mug.

I couldn't say what it was about her that I found so fascinating. Maybe it was simply that I'd never met anyone like her before. She was unusual in my world—sexy voice, elegant bearing and an unmistakable, at least to me, sensuality. I'd have to visit her Web site again and find out just what kinds of performance art she, well, performed. I remembered photos of live models posed in public places, some painted, some draped, some artfully naked. I'd been more interested in who she was than what she did, wondering what would be judged in her favor as a claimant rather than mine.

Really, I hadn't ever thought I'd be the one chosen. I was just here to collect the second prize. She was so much more suited to it all than I was, but part of me didn't want to give up without some kind of fight.

"Something wrong?"

I shook myself out of my thoughts. "Sorry, I wasn't staring at you, not really. Just . . . very tired." I felt mildly dizzy as a tidal wave of jet lag washed over me.

"Perhaps," she said, with a smile, "we might be entitled to carry a mug of tea around with us while we look for our bedrooms."

"After all . . ." I hoped my smile was as jaunty as hers. "We own the place."

We laughed like conspirators and turned off the kitchen lights on our way out. I grabbed the lighter of my two bags and followed Portia up the stairs. The stone walls were covered sparsely with tapestries and paintings, some of which were so grimy I couldn't make out the subject. There were two small windows with thick, opaque glass, and cold air seeped in around them.

The second floor was noticeably colder than the ground floor. The stairs continued up one more flight, but we headed into the hallway, which, like the floor below, featured four doors, two on each side.

The first two, left and right, were both empty. I opened the second door on the left with a sinking heart, but was surprised by a fully furnished room, complete with a curtained four-poster bed. I guessed the previous occupant had been male, as the colors were predominantly deep blues and browns.

"At least there's one bed," Portia said from behind me. Her breath was warm and I suddenly hoped the last room was empty too. Sharing a bed with her was not an unpleasant prospect.

"We won't freeze to death. I think that's a good thing."

I could feel when she was no longer behind me. Turning, I watched her open the last door and felt slightly breathless when her lips curved in a broad smile.

"What do you think?" She waved at the room with a graceful gesture of one arm.

I joined her to peer in, and immediately grinned as well.

Though the furnishings were similar in quantity and size, this room was all whites and deep red, like a Valentine bower. The bed draperies were ruffled and appliquéd with English roses. It was a little more fussy and girlie than I'd have chosen, but I still liked it.

Sneaking a glance at Portia, who looked very amused, I said, "What do you say I take this one?"

"Bless you," she said emphatically. "It's a little dark, but the one across the hall will do just fine for me."

Just like that it was done. I wheeled my suitcase into my room, and she into hers. I met her coming up the stairs with her second case as I went down for mine. She had at least one more suitcase in her car, but I was so sleepy I didn't care if she needed help fetching it.

To my relief, I discovered I had my own small bathroom, obviously converted from a closet. When I spotted the tiny space heater near the bed all my needs were met. Well, all the needs I was allowing to surface at that moment, anyway.

In rapid order, I switched on the heater, unpacked my toiletries, brushed my teeth, snatched pajamas from the suitcase, scrubbed my face and headed for the bed. Once in, I untied the drawstrings on the curtains farthest from the heater. The little space quickly warmed and, after a few minutes, I knew I was comfortable enough to sleep. I quickly turned the heater off and closed the final set of curtains.

I was awake long enough to think that never in all my life had I thought I'd fall asleep in a castle, in a room I could—for a length of time—call my own. I had surely slipped into some alternative reality or gone back in time. Either way it didn't matter . . . didn't matter . . .

I dreamed.

There was a noise on the other side of the curtain but before I could be alarmed, she said, softly, "It's cold."

She slipped past the curtains into my warm, comfortable bed, her knees bumping mine. I gave her more room but she whispered, "No, no," and put her arms around me, pulling us closer together.

"Portia," I murmured, as the warmth around me intensified.

She glowed as if there were candles in her eyes. "Yes."

My skin was melting and yet my body curved to fit in her arms. Her lips found my throat and I felt her teeth nip me lightly, then they nipped at my earlobe, then the notch of my collarbone.

My sighs were muffled by the draperies, but the thick fabric also seemed to hold us in our own world. Her teeth found my nipple through the soft cotton of my sleep shirt and I couldn't help my little cry of response.

"Is that what you like?" She bit it again, more firmly and I felt flooded with pleasure.

"Yes." It was so warm in the bed now, with my rising pulse and the light in her eyes, her skin.

She threw back the covers and buried her face in my throat as her hands pulled down my pajama bottoms. I felt exposed and vulnerable, which only excited me more. The wind seemed to howl right outside the bed and we were suffused by a soft low light, as if my dream was being lit by moonlight.

She would look so sexy on film, I thought, but nothing remained of coherence when her hands gripped my hips and pulled me down slightly in the bed. Braced on one arm, she pulled up my top, and her mouth found my hard, erect nipple. It was shockingly good and I arched under her, loving the way her teeth roughened my skin.

Raising her head to look at me, she said, "You're perfect."

"Nobody's ever said that to me before."

"I'm not nobody." She gazed at my exposed body, smiling with anticipation. "You look so sexy. And so much like you want to be devoured."

"Yes," I breathed out.

One hand was brushing the insides of my thighs so lazily that it was driving me crazy. I tried to lift my swollen flesh so her fingers would finally touch me, but she laughed low in her throat. "Don't worry, California Girl. I'm going to fuck you. But first . . ."

Her words sent a shiver the length of my body. She inched downward, leaving wet kisses and mild stings of little bites all over my breasts and torso. I was held in place by the pressure of her body and the degree of my lust. I tried to spread myself open, wanted to beg for her to do *everything* but I was mute in my desire.

My pulse was pounding so hard that the light intensified to a sharp red. She held my wrists tight in her hands, pulling me downward slightly again. "Look at me."

Focusing on her face was very difficult. She seemed so far away and yet she was right there. Her dark hair was ruffled and then I met her gaze.

The red light was coming from her eyes.

I tried to scream, but there was no sound in me. Her mouth opened over my spread legs and her white teeth seemed to drip red.

"First," she finally continued, "there's the devouring."

CHAPTER 4

A rude awakening. It drizzles.
I find the top of the castle.
The caretaker's daughter.

ray daylight streamed in through a small crack in the bed curtains. I groaned into it, shading my eyes. My entire body ached and my head felt like a hangover. Had the beer really been that potent?

I shifted slightly and was sorry I had when my thigh and back muscles screamed in protest. I felt as if I'd been toting barges all night instead of having erotic nightmares.

The light felt early, like not much past dawn. I wasn't sure why I had awakened—then I heard a stealthy noise. I mean it was a sound that if louder I'd recognize, I was sure of that, but it was so soft and drawn out that I didn't know what it was, but it was caused by someone who didn't want me to hear it. Maybe the doorknob turning? Was Portia checking on me?

Great, now my heart was pounding, both from the idea that someone might be either entering or leaving my room and from the memory of last night's dream, which had been very nice right up to the point when it hadn't been very nice at all.

Quietly, I slid to the edge of the bed nearest the door, got carefully to my knees and peeked through the curtains.

And found myself nearly lip-to-lip with a complete stranger. She screamed.

I screamed.

"Who the feck are you?"

"What the fuck are you doing in my room?"

She was turning as crimson as her hair and backing away, a pipe wrench in one hand. "I thought you were a crasher—we get those from time to time and this room is for one of the heirs."

I was still clutching the curtains around my face. "Well that's me! One of the heirs. Did you also wake up the other one, or was I just lucky?"

From the doorway, Portia said, "Well, I'm awake now. Your scream is piercing, Brittany."

"Oh, bloody hell!" The newcomer spun on her heel, taking in Portia. "I'm sorry, really, but you weren't expected last night and I thought someone had decided to bivouac here."

"Who are you?" Portia sounded completely calm, civilized, regal even.

"Melanie Drake. My da is the caretaker, but he broke his arm a few days ago and since I'm between assignments, I said I'd help out."

My gaze fell on a small clock on the writing desk. "Is it really only seven a.m.?" The mere thought that I'd only had a few hours of sleep brought tears to my eyes.

"I really am sorry. Why don't you go back to sleep?" Melanie turned back to me, and I wasn't so far gone that I didn't see how striking her blue eyes were.

"All the adrenaline I have left in my body is currently working through my bloodstream."

Portia, leaning casually against my door jamb, said, "Are you going to do a disembodied head impression all day?"

I released the curtain. "I might have been naked, you know."

Portia and Melanie just stared. So, fine, I was wearing my Buffy pajamas. Disconcerted, I added, "I'm not surprised people crash here—the door was unlocked."

"No it wasn't," Melanie quickly said.

"Yes." Portia had on her full Queen Mother demeanor. It was scary. "Yes, it was."

"Oh." Melanie colored again, and I wondered how often she did that. She was probably not a very good liar, not that that was a bad thing. "That was my oversight then. Da will thrash me later, so you don't need to."

"Aren't you being just a bit cheeky to your possible new bosses?" Portia tightened her heavy black silk robe.

"Yes, I certainly am. But as I said, I'm not the regular servant. I'll likely be gone before you know which of you will be the . . . winner. Meanwhile, if something breaks, I'm staying at the guard-house most days."

"Which is where?"

Melanie gave me a withering look. "If you look out a window and you don't see another building, it's not that way."

Well, I thought, Melanie knew a good exit line. Her not very quiet footsteps seemed to echo from all the way downstairs. I stared at Portia, who stared back for a moment, then grinned.

"Local color, she's certainly that. I'm going for some tea. Do you want some?"

"No, I think I'll take a shower and settle in. Call home, that sort of thing."

"Suit yourself." Portia left behind a subtle scent, one which I realized I'd been deeply inhaling in that dream. My body was trying to tell me, just from that scent, that it had been more than a dream, but that was ridiculous. If it hadn't been a dream I'd have bite marks in places where I'd still feel them.

I found what I'd overlooked last night, which was the lock on the door. Sure of my privacy, I got out my little travel mirror. After a little poking and prodding in places that were still claiming it hadn't been a dream, I concluded it must have been. No bite marks. Not that I had expected there to be any.

After a tepid but thorough shower, I found myself exploring the third floor. Instead of four rooms there were six smaller ones, two stuffed with furniture swathed in sheets of various colors, and a communal bathroom. I thought they had once upon a time been servants' quarters. At the far end of the central hallway was a steep winding stair that ended in a heavy overhead door. Still unable to raise a cell phone signal I thought it couldn't hurt to try up on the roof. Three hard whacks later, the latch gave. I had to put my shoulders against the door and push up as hard as I could with my legs, but with a sudden whoosh it lifted, slamming over onto the roof.

That was when I realized it was raining. Well, raining was too strong a word, I told myself. It was drizzling, there, that was perfect. The drizzle went right past me and down the stairs. I hurriedly got out onto the roof. I'd check for a signal and skedaddle back to the dry indoors as quickly as possible.

I'd never given much thought to what the roof of a castle might be like, but the surface felt a lot like asphalt. It was ringed by fortifications of stone—one reason I imagined it was only three stories. Overall, Castle Wrath was less of a traditional castle and more of a keep, the difference between the two being something I'd looked up before leaving home. It sat on a mound higher than the surrounding area, and there was probably a basement where things like ancient sewage systems had existed, along with essential larders. It had been built to house perhaps twenty people in all, along with however many soldiers could fit in the guardhouse. That didn't seem like many, but given the sparseness of the population, twenty to thirty could have defended this place quite well from the average insurgence.

The drizzle made it hard to see any distance at all. Peering through gaps in the uppermost blocks of stone I could barely make out the guardhouse near the front gates. The other three directions had no discernible landmarks. Gray mist blanketed everything. Drizzle was not the right word, I decided. It was raining.

None of which helped with my current predicament. I held my cell phone aloft but the depressing "service not found" display remained. Worldwide coverage, my ass.

It took some ingenuity, but I managed to get the trap door closed with only minor damage to my head and left shoulder, which only reminded me, as I blinked away stars, that the rest of me hurt. I wanted some Advil and breakfast now.

The rain had made the narrow stairs slippery but I didn't break more than a nail on the way down. I'd just set my foot to the nice, solid flooring, when I heard a noise behind me.

"What the feck were you doing on the roof?"

"Trying to get a cell phone signal." I turned to face Melanie with some of Portia's aplomb. This was, after all, my castle. Partly. For a month.

"Right." She stood there in her khaki jeans, heavy boots and thick shirt looking like a curly haired elf who'd borrowed today's attire from her brother the giant.

I waved the device at her. "No luck. I didn't see a phone in my room. Where's the phone downstairs? I can call my friend to let her know I'm safe and log on to drop everyone else e-mail."

"There isn't one."

I blinked at her. "Huh?"

"As I was telling Herself just now, there's no phone. There's one at the guardhouse you can borrow if you like."

"Can I borrow it all the way here for a month?"

She put one hand, dwarfed by the flannel sleeve, on her hip. "The guardhouse isn't on the national registry. So there's a phone."

Evidently that made sense, because she clambered past me up the stairs to the roof, shot the bolt on the trap door—to my chagrin, I'd forgotten—and scuttled back down without another word. She'd have disappeared down the main stairway if I hadn't stopped her with, "Let's pretend I'm a newcomer from a foreign land and explain what you mean."

She brushed red tendrils out of her eyes. The girl needed a haircut. "Castle Wrath is a national treasure, didn't you know? As such, it's on the list. No one's actually lived in it since the early Twenties, and it's not been used for much of anything since World War Two, when it served as a staging area for the local Home Guard."

I wanted in the worst way to tell her that what she was saying was the boring bits a good storyteller left out. "And so?"

"And so it's never been modernized past getting electric and running water. You're occupying the most lavish living quarters the castle has seen in probably a century."

It was a daunting thought. "Not even a phone?"

I'm pretty sure the gesture she made meant *Americans are deaf and stupid* but she said, "If you want to do anything, even spit a new color on the walls, it has to be cleared by a committee. And all the decisions of that committee have to be ratified at a special bi-weekly meeting of the autonomous collective."

It was doubtful that she knew that my hands on my hips and the tilt of my head meant *Scottish caretakers are stuck-up bitches* but I let that message show in the tone of my voice. "Oh. I see. Is that before or after a moistened bint lobs a scimitar at you?"

Then she did a completely unexpected thing.

She smiled. And her eyes sparkled like, I swear, like something gorgeously blue in overripe poetry, only beautiful. "Damn, I'll have to get better material. Herself downstairs completely missed it."

"My friend Susie breathes the *Flying Circus*, and anybody who knows film has *Holy Grail* memorized."

She raised her eyebrows and without a doubt it meant *Americans are unfathomable.*

I pursed my lips for *Scots are troublemakers.*

"Seriously." She turned toward the stairs. "You can't do anything to this place without nine levels of permission. So there's no phone. Da said no one could agree how to string the wires. You can use the one in the guardhouse."

"Okay. I need to."

"Your mum must be worried." She clomped down the stairs ahead of me.

"She and my father died in an accident a couple of years ago."

She glanced back over her shoulder as she reached the second floor. "Sorry about that."

I shrugged. "You didn't know."

"You like films? Movies?"

"It's what I'm studying."

"Right, then. Your girlfriend—" She gave me a sly look. "The Python expert. She'll be worried?"

"Just a friend, and yes, she will be."

"You came all this way on your own?"

"There was nobody I cared to invite."

"Oh." She reached the bottom floor and within a few steps had her hand on a large door at the rear of the main hallway I'd not noticed last night. When she opened it I saw it led to the garden, such as it was. "Right, then."

And that was the last I saw of her for several hours.

CHAPTER 5

An expedition. Berry crumble.
More tea. Disaster strikes.

ortia and I agreed a grocery expedition into Durness was essential. I know I had expected some kind of cook or butler or something, but I didn't want to tell her that. I'd had enough *Americans are stupid* attitude from Melanie. But I think she had expected it as well. I only had a few more breakfast bars, and tea wasn't cutting into my caffeine need. She was certain there was a petrol station—took me a bit to realize she didn't mean a patrol or police station—and I very much needed something warm and waterproof in the outerwear department. Lists made, we set off in the Jaguar.

By watery daylight, the countryside looked forbidding but starkly beautiful. Perfect for a scary movie, one where a group of apocalypse survivors gathered to live out their remaining days until a murderer picks them off one by one.

Sometimes, I have more imagination than is good for me.

It didn't help that the first sign of civilization we came to was a cemetery. A steepled church stood in the distance and beyond that an occasional rooftop hinted at a village.

Taking note of a sign pointing the way to nearby sea caves, I asked, "What's a Smoo?"

"A hole or a cave, in Norse."

"Oh. They named the cave 'Cave'? That's up there with naming the planet after the dirt."

"You look at the world in an interesting way, Brittany."

I glanced at her. "You mean an American way."

"Well, you are that." She threw me a half-smile.

"Guilty as charged—oh!"

We came up over a rise and a narrow lake snaked through the hills for miles. There were white buildings dotted all along its shore. In rapid succession we crossed bridges over burbling streams—I was pretty sure if we had stopped and listened we'd have heard burbling—and I saw at least one fisherman standing thigh-deep in quickly running water. Had the sun been out it would have been idyllic. As it was it was beautiful.

"Lovely, isn't it?" Portia eased to a stop while a small flock of sheep were driven across the roadway in front of us.

"Why is it called a kyle?"

"Gaelic root, *caol*. Which probably means 'a great long thing that takes forever to go around on the way to where a body wants to get to.'"

I laughed. "Does *firth* mean 'dare you to put a bridge over this'?"

Her chuckle was appreciative. "Yes, you're probably right."

"Why on earth did someone build a castle back that way when just a few miles this way it's so gorgeous?"

"Cussedness is my bet." She accelerated again when the road was clear. "Though salmon running in the stream on the other side of the garden might have been an influence."

"A telephone booth!" I pointed it out. "This *is* the twenty-first century."

She laughed and pointed at a mountain just disappearing into the mist overhead. "Ben Hope. It's a stiff climb, but worth it. You can also tramp to the Broch, that's a leftover stone building from the Picts. And that—" She directed my attention to our left. "That is the most northerly golf course in Scotland."

"A village of what, four hundred people and there's a golf course?"

"They invented the thing."

"Okay. I can see that." Wildflowers were spread over the carpets of grass, only absent near what I assumed were the greens. "You're quite the guide."

"Walking holidays bring one into contact with every element of a location. I played a round of golf just to say I'd done the eighteenth hole when the tide was in. I teed off over the Atlantic Ocean, well, after a fashion. I don't golf. So I lost four balls into the surf. Getting the fifth over was so fun I tried for a sixth, and lost two more before I succeeded."

"You don't play by the rules, do you?"

"Not if I can help it. I've always wanted to do a sculpture up here for the annual festival, but I can never convince my mates to make the trip."

"A sculpture?"

Evidently, it was something near to her heart as the smile curving her lips was the most genuine and relaxed I'd seen. "Sure. The Pictish Broch, for example. I've always wanted to drape it in woad blue and paint my mates and pose them."

"Is that the kind of performance art you do?"

"Mostly."

I wanted to ask how she paid her bills, because I was betting that performance art paid as well as being a film student. I couldn't figure out how to ask what she did for a living as if art wasn't doing something.

The narrow road turned into the village and she guided the Jaguar up to a gas pump at the station on the corner. "I also did a fair bit of software design, and bought Internet stocks at the right time. Sold them at the right time." She shrugged. "When the money runs out I might go back to it. But I'd prefer not to."

"I hear you."

She got out of the car to purchase the gas and I studied what I could see of the village. Durness was larger than I thought it would be, but smaller than I'd hoped. There was the hotel, another inn, a pub, a tourist information kiosk and what looked like a municipal utilities building. The nearest building—a small cottage—boasted a homemade sign that promised freshly made cheese.

No sign of a Gap, an Old Navy . . . okay, so I was someplace that hadn't yet been Disneyfied or covered with parking lots and big box stores. I really did appreciate that. But I was cold and after a few minutes outside I was going to be wet. I wanted to rent my own car so if I had to go all the way to Tongue or Wick for shops, I could do so. But renting a car wasn't on the list of things one did in Durness, that much was clear.

When Portia got back in the car, I said, "I don't see a grocery store."

"There's a little market in the pub, which shares a wall with the tea room. Good for tins and a few things made locally."

"Do you think we could go into Tongue? I'd like to rent a car and buy a raincoat. And a digital camera."

"You're free to drive this car whenever you like. I don't plan on using it every day."

"Oh. That's very kind, but I've never driven a stick before."

"Stick?"

"Manual transmission." I pointed at the extra foot pedal. "I'm okay with an automatic."

"Oh—I'm sorry, then. If I'd not been in such a hurry, you'd have taken a car on your way here. I'll drive you to Tongue tomorrow or the next day. I think you could rent something there."

"Okay. And don't be sorry. I'd still be on a bus from Wick if you hadn't given me a lift last night, so thank you."

We raided the little grocery for canned spaghetti, tubes of Vegemite—I said I'd try it—and some freshly baked bread, locally churned butter and homemade berry crumble. A few other items completed the bare necessities. We split the bill, decided tea with cut sandwiches sounded good, and I was happy with a steaming bowl of soup as well. I didn't care what part of the sheep was in it, and I didn't ask. My stomach was pleased and that was all that mattered.

We were most of the way back to the Castle when we passed an older woman walking slowly in that direction with a mesh grocery bag over one shoulder. Portia eased to a stop and rolled down the window and asked if she was going to the castle and if so, would she like a lift. At least that's what I thought she said—her accent changed completely and the conversation was so rapid-fire I couldn't really follow it.

Her offer was accepted, however, and I quickly moved to the tiny backseat so that the older woman, whose picture would not be in the dictionary next to *nimble*, could sit in the passenger seat.

"What business takes you to the castle," is what I think Portia said, once we were underway again.

"The cook. For two fortnights and a bit. Are you the new laird?"

"It's not decided yet. One of us is. We didn't know there was to be a cook."

That was an understatement.

"Melanie herself hired me. I don't do fancy, but nobody leaves Mrs. Dobnail's table hungry. There's old Thomas and his truck. He'll have dropped me supplies."

It took some doing, but Portia was able to squeeze to one side to let the vintage truck pass on the other. The driver, presumably old Thomas, dipped his cap and kept on going.

"We bought a crumble at the grocer," I offered.

"Did you now? That'll be mine. Out of the oven at sunrise."

"It'll be perfect for afternoon tea." Portia gave me some kind of warning glance and all I could think was that I'd need to get out for some exercise if there was dessert at two or three meals a day. Still, that food supplies were taken care of was a big relief. I wasn't that fond of cooking, either, so Mrs. Dobnail could have at it.

Portia drove round to the side of the building on our return, and Mrs. Dobnail promptly disappeared through the kitchen door. Melanie appeared once again from nowhere.

"Been into town?"

"We needed something to eat. We didn't know what the

arrangements were." Portia was using her Queen Mum voice again.

I managed to get myself out of the backseat. "No phone, but food and a cook. Is there anything else we should know?"

"There's a welcoming committee arriving at three. Nobody thought you'd leave direct from Inverness last night."

"Life isn't always predictable." Portia strode into the house, leaving Melanie to stare balefully at me.

"What did I do?"

"Not a thing."

"Fine. Can I come to the guardhouse in about ten minutes to use the phone line?"

"Surely."

I wasn't certain if Melanie was intending to imitate Portia's regal departure, but it was a dead ringer. I would have laughed but somehow I felt as if everyone was mad at me.

The dessert was delicious, and Mrs. Dobnail made very, very strong coffee that I loved down to the last thick drop. It was more than ten minutes before I knocked on the door to the guardhouse, but at least I wasn't empty-handed.

"I brought you some berry crumble," I said immediately, handing over the plate.

"That wasn't necessary."

"I'll eat it if you don't want it. It's tasty."

Her lips twitched. "I didn't say that."

I waited.

After a sniff at the dish she said, "Thank you."

"You're welcome. Where can I hook up? I just want to toss off a few e-mails."

I had no idea why Melanie was grinning. "The phone's in the kitchen." She led the way through the narrow but long room. Three-quarter height stone walls divided the space into three chambers, with the living area first, the kitchen next and the bedroom at the rear. I had a quick look at the Spartan four-poster bed and dresser before turning my attention to the kitchen counter. Melanie rustled in a drawer for a fork, then devoted herself to the crumble as I set down my laptop near the outlet above the counter.

I spotted the phone anchored to the wall and my heart sank. It was a museum piece and I was quite certain there was no universal jack behind it. I'd need one of those huge handset receivers if I wanted to dial up to the Internet, but I'd only seen those in old movies. Still, I'd boot up and see if there was any hope at all.

The electrical outlet was a little differently shaped than I was used to, but my plug fit. I had just pressed the on button when Melanie shouted, "No!"

She snatched the plug out of the outlet, but just after there was an alarming crack from inside my laptop case.

Nothing smoked. Nothing caught on fire. But I knew, I just knew, it was dead.

CHAPTER 6

I find the edge of the world.
Coins and a phone box.
It rains. How not to swoon.

What else was there to do when I woke up the next morning? My laptop was fried, I had to leave my temporary home just to make a phone call, and had no car at my disposal. I might have been on the moon for all the access I had to the outside world. I was in no mood for a pity ride from Portia, who was busy on the phone at Melanie's.

My body was still feeling sore, and I had to force myself to eat some of the breakfast that Mrs. Dobnail had left in the refrigerator in tidy covered dishes. It took forever to heat up without a microwave, but it was delicious, some kind of layered dough with meats and spinach in between. I just didn't feel all that hungry.

It was quite early, so I decided to go for a very long walk. The extra desserts and pastries with savories would catch up to me. I'd feel better for the exercise too. It would get me out of the dusty old castle. It was absolutely the best thing I could do for myself. I was used to walking. Berkeley was a pedestrian city, at least where I lived. Hills didn't daunt me, and my shoes were up to the streets. I had some control over my life, dammit, so I was going for a walk.

What did a little rain matter?

My shoes were not, however, entirely up to the muddy road, but I didn't care. I had credit cards and money in my pocket and four miles was not a long way to walk. Abraham Lincoln had walked five miles to return a book, but then he hadn't known the wonder of online shipping. Not that I was going to be bitter or anything.

The walk was uneventful and quiet. I would have worn my Nano but I was all too aware now that I had no way to recharge it until I acquired a voltage adapter or borrowed Melanie's, which I didn't want to do as that would just underscore her opinion of me as a stupid American. I had inherited a castle in Scotland but I couldn't even go shopping. I wondered if this was how Mary Queen of Scots had felt, forever being held prisoner in castles with no music and only one book to read. I tried to tell myself that a long walk in the countryside would have seemed like heaven to poor Mary.

Yeah, that made me feel tons better.

I reached the telephone box with relief, noted that it didn't accept credit cards and fed in a coin. The operator responded to my question and I walked on into town to get a whole lot more change. If I'd been hungry I might have acquired a serving of mince pie, which had all the earmarks of Mrs. Dobnail's fine work. I wondered if she ever slept.

Mrs. Dobnail had provided a pleasant tea for the welcoming committee yesterday. To quote one of the women who had enthusiastically shaken my hand, "She's a dab hand with a crust." The townsfolk, most of whom were part of the preservation society, had seemed pleasant enough. I didn't follow a lot of the conversation, but enough to know that they were all avidly interested in changing nothing. Portia had done that Queen Mum thing while I'd been weeping inside for my poor laptop.

The grocer gave me change and I bought a container of hot tea—a clever Thermos with a strap I could sling over one shoulder. At the telephone box I talked to the operator again, fed in a great many coins and listened to the phone on the other side of the world ring.

On the fourth ring, the line picked up. "You've reached Susie. Leave a message."

After the off-key beep, I said, "So where the hell are you? You weren't home yesterday and I walked four fucking miles to make this phone call. I'm sorry, I'm so frustrated. I probably sounded like a psycho yesterday. My laptop might not be completely dead, but there's no place within a hundred miles where I can take it to be fixed. I have my backup disks. I suppose I should be grateful for that. Anyway, I think I can pick up messages left on my cell from the phones I have available, so let me know you're okay and you got my messages. I need to know someone knows I'm here. Everyone is nice but I'm so out of place. The only thing I really like is the coffee. The cook makes great food, she left some for our breakfast, and I'm just getting through the day today. I don't think I want a cast—"

The beep on Susie's machine sounded.

I got the operator again, tried to give her a credit card but the concept confused her, pushed in a bunch more coins, and got into my cell voice mail after a few mistakes. To my relief there were two messages from Susie. The gossipy one about who was doing who I skipped over—at a couple of pounds a minute, I didn't care. Her second message was vastly comforting.

"Hey girl, you sound so far away. What the fuck with the laptop? That sucks completely. Electricity is electricity, isn't it? But I'm glad you got there safe and all. Take pictures and write it all on sheepskin with a quill, whatever it takes, because this is the adventure of a lifetime. And call me every so often so I don't send Scotland Yard to make sure that other woman hasn't bumped you off. I miss you. The gang all says hi. Bye."

I wanted in the worst way to call Susie back and tell her that Portia had been in my dreams again, and being around her at breakfast was equally disconcerting. Part of me thought she was dangerously, deliciously gorgeous. The rest of me was intimidated, if not outright scared, by her. The dreams I'd had were so freakish, and if I hadn't already seen her out in the daylight and not catching on fire, I'd have been wondering . . .

I watched too much Buffy, that's all there was to it.

The tea was hot and comforting as I huddled in the phone box. The rain hadn't stopped, but it hadn't gotten worse either. It was steady, relentless and made every minute seem just like the last one. The light never changed and the sky was gray overhead, gray to the north and gray to the south. For a change it was gray both east and west.

A cup of tea consumed, I started out for home again. No doubt Melanie would think my long walk to make a phone call was foolish, but I'd been acutely aware of her there when I'd called Susie yesterday. A little privacy would have been nice. I was betting Portia asked her to leave. I hadn't wanted to cry in front of her, either, but the longer I had rambled on to Susie's answering machine the harder it had been to hold back the tears. I hadn't known about the electricity variance. Nobody had told me I'd need an adapter. I was *not* a stupid American, *not* just another blonde Brittany with the mental acuity of a cotton swab. I knew what *acuity* meant, after all.

Trudging along the muddy road, I realized I didn't want to go back to the castle and read. I was going to burn through the three books I'd brought with me in no time. Given the entertainment prospects I fully understood why someone would walk two hours to have a couple of beers at the pub, and walk two hours home again. Maybe I'd walk to the phone every day.

At the fork in the road I turned toward the lighthouse. No time like the present to see it. People came from all over the world to see it.

It kept on raining. I walked. My crosstrainers were soaked.

The road rose and fell, *rolled* was the right word, I supposed. Even the prospect of writing a juicy story about this adventure or making a scary movie didn't distract me from my wet feet and isolation. The countryside was charming, quaint—whatever. Wet sheep are pungent. The smell is not charming or quaint at all, actually.

There was no lighthouse at the end of the road. There was a ferry station, closed, and some information on how to cross the kyle to Cape Wrath, and then walk to the lighthouse from there. Evidently, there were cliffs worth seeing over there too. It was probably very picaresque—there! Would some California blonde bimbo know what *picaresque* meant? Wait. Did I mean picturesque?

My mind churning nonsense, I stood on the deserted dock for a while. The colorless water was swallowed up by the flat, gray sky so there was no telling which was which. There was nothing out there. Nothing in any direction. Just the edge of the world, and I was trapped.

I sneezed, wiped my nose on the soggy sleeve of my sweater, and mopped at my streaming eyes. I just hadn't expected everything to be so . . . real. This wasn't like a movie at all. Shit still happened, and I got my fair share, as usual.

Pity, party of one, your table is ready.

I'm a happy person. Normally, I have more energy than I know what to do with. I'm always thinking something new and in my opinion, walls were made for bouncing off of. I'd walked a long way, I was cold and wet and my shoes made squish-squish noises with every step. It ought to have seemed a lark, but every step was harder than the last. I knew the castle was not that far away. It felt as if I should be already there, but the road stretched right in front of my eyes.

The stone pillars flanking the drive seemed to pop up out of nowhere. I was leaning on one before I fully realized I was nearly home. I was warm and sticky even though my hands felt cold. I walked slowly up the driveway and it seemed as long as the one to

Manderley. The stairs were very steep, and I was extremely glad to be out of the rain once I closed the heavy front door behind me.

Melanie was in the kitchen, making herself tea. I supposed that was cheeky, as Portia would say. I couldn't care.

"Where've you been? You look like the cat chewed you and dragged you in."

"Just walking." I felt a hard sweat break out under my hair, but figured it was a reaction to finally being in from the cold. "I went to town. And out to the ferry dock."

"Good walk, that. You might have wanted boots in this weather, though."

I looked at her, thinking that I didn't the *feck* have any boots, thank you very much, and no way to acquire any either. I opened my mouth to say that, at least I think that's what I intended to say. But what I said was, "I don't feel so good."

Portia had put something in the beer. I wanted to tell Melanie that, but my mouth wouldn't work. My mouth wouldn't obey my brain, except when my lips were touched with a damp cloth and I would suck on it. I was so thirsty.

"Keep her hydrated."

I don't know who said that. I knew I'd had a shot. My chest was so heavy. Poison, I wanted to say. Portia . . .

She'd been in my bed that first night. I had to tell someone. Then Portia was in my bed again. We were swimming underwater, but it made me cough. She drew me to the surface, kissed me deep and hard. Her hunger for me was heady and I was reckless, wrapping my legs around her waist as she bared me. Her teeth gleamed as she bit my nipple.

"Delicious . . ." She raised her head to gaze at me with her blood-red eyes. "All the nourishment I need."

The cold, wet cloth was against my lips. I sucked from it, trying to moisten the back of my throat.

"I won't be responsible if you keep her here. She should be in hospital."

"She can't leave. If she does she forfeits her claim. It wouldn't be fair. She caught this virus, you said, probably on the plane, and that's not her fault."

Who was pleading my case for me? What virus?

Portia was floating above my bed, her body wrapped in a black cape. I parted it as I pulled her down on top of me, and her naked skin was like fire on mine. Feverish and hot, her hands fumbled under the sheets. She pushed up my pajama top, trapping my arms, and yanked down my bottoms so I couldn't move my legs. Immobilized, I moaned into her harsh kiss. I wanted her to touch me, to have me, consequences be damned. Had she drugged me? Poisoned me? These dreams weren't like me. I felt wild, unleashed.

She was petting my body, enjoying me as her captive. The wet cloth was at my lips again and I sucked at it, then kissed her. I begged, I pleaded, but I heard no words, only her low laugh as she toyed with my nipples. I didn't want her to stop. My body was hot like a wildfire. I was wet like the ocean, an ocean as red as her eyes, with black skies overhead. There was no sun, no moon, just a moistened bint. I ducked the scimitar, but Portia caught it. By divine right, she inherited the castle.

She touched me and I was burning.

CHAPTER 7

Angelic nursing. Satanic rites.
I discover Portia's true proclivities.

There's discomfort, like when the nurse says "just a little pinch" before she sticks an eight-inch needle into your bum, and there's discomfort, like when my mom said "cramps don't hurt" and then there's discomfort, like when it's "oh baby, yeah . . . that hurts so good." And then there's pain.

It was pain that had me sobbing when someone moved me. I could even sense that the hands were gentle and I was distantly aware that someone was making comforting shushing noises.

The soft, lyrical voice I didn't know, that had insisted I couldn't go to the hospital, was saying things like, "Just once more. We'll stop in a minute. Fresh sheets. It's okay."

There was a malignant dwarf inside my chest, twisting my lungs in knots. When the twisting stopped, piercing with acid-dipped needles replaced it. The hands on my shoulders and hips were gloved in fire. I was beyond even being able to pray for it to stop.

"First, there's the devouring," I heard Portia say. I'd fallen into a web of evil and now she was torturing me. Nothing made any sense, but that kind voice kept telling me I'd be fine, which had to be a lie when I hurt so much.

Something cool was against my forehead. The gentle, low voice said, "You've got a virus and it hurts like the devil. But the doctor says you made it this far, you're going to be fine. In a day or two you'll be your old self."

I knew it was all a lie, so I swatted at the voice, at least I tried to, but my hand wouldn't obey me.

"You're going to be fine, Brittany. Go to sleep. I'll be right here."

I tried to open my eyes, but they watered terribly in the light.

"No, no, sweetie, keep your eyes closed. The light will hurt."

Portia had bitten me. The virus was lycanthropy. No, wait, that meant I was a werewolf. Portia had made me a vampire. I couldn't stand the light, and the fire I felt all over was me losing my immortal soul. I had no champion to save me, no Scoobies to come to my rescue. I'd be so pale, and that never looked good on a blonde. Could vampires wear Prada? How did they do their banking before ATMs? Why couldn't I breathe?

"Sleep, Brittany. You'll get better faster if you sleep now."

Kind, considerate voice. Probably the Vampire Transition Nurse. I don't know what all she had injected me with, but it made me listen to her. A tissue dabbed at my eyes and nose, and then I went back to oblivion.

"Her fever broke last night," someone was whispering. "I'm hoping she'll be able to drink on her own."

Queen Vampire—Portia—said, "You've been very good to play nurse."

"Who else was going to?"

I stirred, anticipating the waves of fire, but instead of pain I felt only a bone-deep weariness. Swallowing was difficult, making it impossible to talk. Still, my feeble gesture must have been enough to get some attention, because the bed curtains were pulled back.

I flinched from the light and the curtain was quickly adjusted so I remained in the shadow.

"How are you feeling?" It was the sweet, gentle voice I'd been hearing in my dreams, but that made no sense, because Melanie's mouth was moving and that nice voice was coming out of her.

I wet my lips with my tongue, or tried to, and she briefly left my sight, returning in moments with a mug. Sliding onto the bed near my shoulders, she slipped an arm under me and easily lifted me while holding the mug to my lips.

Water had never tasted so pure, so clean, so perfect and sweet. I swallowed, sipped again, and swallowed. Finally, I was able to croak out, "Thank you."

"All you have to do now," Melanie said softly, "is sleep and drink. There's a bit of sugar in the water and Mrs. Dobnail's got rice mash. You have a rest. Then we'll try more water and a spoonful or two of food."

"What happened?"

"You caught flu and the virus got into the lining around your brain."

"Because I was walking in the rain?" My mother, when I was a little girl, had insisted I'd catch my death from walking in the rain.

"No. Might have sped up the spread. But the doctor thinks you caught it on the plane or just before you left home. Anyone you know been sick?"

I managed to shake my head no and my eyes drooped shut.

"That's right. You sleep."

When I next stirred I wasn't so much thirsty as I was hungry. I hoped that meant I was getting better. Rice sounded kind of good, which could mean I wasn't turning into a vampire. The pain in my chest had eased and I was definitely breathing. The only thing that was making me feel like the undead was my matted hair and grimy skin.

I managed to wiggle up the pillows a little, but my head started to throb. I wondered where my Angel of Mercy was. With all the strength of a newborn kitten I pushed the bed curtains apart. The room beyond my bed was chilly and I was quite alone.

Above and below me, however, I could discern there was activity. Voices rose and fell—there was laughter and banter. The thick windows told me it was night and it sounded like there was a party and I was missing it.

It took a few moments, but I finally got my legs over the edge of the bed. I sat there, catching my breath, and wondered who had arranged to have guests. Probably Portia, lobbying the local hob-nobbery. Whatever had made me sick wasn't catching, I guess. That made me feel a little better.

Using the bed as a support, I got myself to the foot of it, then transferred my weight to the chair at the small writing desk. Clean face and hands would go a long way to making me feel completely human. In spite of my death grip on the chair, I still swayed, so I thought it best to sit down. That's when I saw the note addressed to me and the small covered plate.

Melanie—at least I presumed that she'd penned it, given it was signed with a lavish "M"—had written, "Eat some of this if you can. That's the doctor's orders. I had to go to my father's for the night. I'll be back by lunch tomorrow."

I lifted the little dome to find a bowl of rice scented with nutmeg and cinnamon. There were also a half dozen almonds on the side of the plate and several slices of banana. My hunger button turned fully to on and the first bite was delicious. I had no trouble swallowing it, and I didn't want fresh blood as a chaser. Whatever had made me sick and whatever drugs they'd given me had certainly combined to give me wicked weird nightmares. No doubt the virus had been responsible for the nightmare that very first night and all the aches and pains since.

I felt full after just a few bites, but I made myself eat the banana and almonds. After that I made it to the bathroom. Cold water on my face felt marvelous.

Getting back to bed took the same pit stop at the desk to rest, but I had a little more rice and felt sleepy in a normal, not exhausted way. The party was still going on, but any thought I might have had about joining it was gone the moment I got myself under the still warm covers.

A resounding thud overhead woke me. It felt as if I'd been asleep for several hours. I'd forgotten to let the bed curtain down again, and my nose was cold. Though I was a little annoyed by the continuing sounds of the party—which had apparently moved to the third floor, directly over my head—I felt much, much better. This time I made it to the bathroom without resting, and even found the strength to strip and get in the shower. I didn't exactly have the energy to lather, rinse and repeat, but I felt like a brand new woman when I pulled a T-shirt over my head and slipped into some warm flannel sleep pants.

There had been several more thuds above me, then long periods of quiet, and I admit I was curious. If Melanie was gone, then it meant the party was Portia's. They might have chosen the other side of the floor. More importantly, if they knew I was awake, would I be invited? It was nearly one a.m., so I think I could be forgiven for investigating in my sleep attire.

The hallway outside my door was dark, which disconcerted me. Without the noise directly overhead I could hear the whistle of the wind outside. Like the night we had arrived, it seemed alive, howling and hungry. I crept to the stairs and listened—it had gone completely still on the floor above me again.

Was that a rustle of fabric? The skirts of some long dead chatelaine? I tried to shake off the fancy as goose bumps the size of mosquito bites rose on my skin. The back of my neck was suddenly cold, as if ghosts breathed on me. Another rustle, this time sounding like wings, flapped overhead, going up the stairwell to the next floor. My heart was pounding and dizziness was threatening to overwhelm me.

Laughter and commotion broke out above me again, startling a gasp out of me. My arms were trembling. What were they doing?

My skin was tingling and my head throbbing like it would burst. The sounds were like a siren call now, pulling me toward the party, which sounded like a frat party, though in a dark and stormy castle, *bacchanal* might be the better word.

I crept up the stairs to the darkened third floor. I could hear music now, including a low, raspy saxophone that made me think of long legs and silk stockings. I saw no one—the party was behind a closed door, which put me in a dilemma. I'd have to knock or something.

Reminding myself that this was my castle too, at least for now, I paused at the door. The climb had left me shaking and I wasn't sure this was a good idea. But with all the noise they were making I couldn't go back to sleep either.

Nobody heard me knock and I didn't want to bang. I slowly turned the knob and pushed the door until it was slightly ajar. The music stopped and the room went still. Had they heard me? Was everyone watching the door slowly open? Were there demons with fingers like knives waiting to rip my heart out?

I was paralyzed with fear, then heard low voices. Perhaps I hadn't been detected after all.

Peeking in, I saw several women, apparently watching something farther into the room. It was impossible not to notice immediately that they were all gorgeous—perfect hair and makeup, and exceedingly shapely physiques. They had long nails, long enough to cause a significant ouch in tender places, but not so sharp they could slice me to pieces. One onlooker wore a body suit of red latex that molded her backside to perfection. In fact, it seemed to be a costume party, as her thick blonde curls were capped with a set of devil's horns. The other two women were in T-shirts and jeans, though, leaving me puzzled.

I inched a little farther into the room, trying to figure out what they were studying. The music was loud but nobody was talking, that is, until I heard a woman out of my range of sight say loudly, "Right there!"

Another female voice answered sharply with, "Don't stop."

A hundred thoughts went through my head, especially when I could tell from this angle that the red latex woman's breasts—perfect breasts—were exposed. Another few inches through the door and I could see the whole tableau.

Two black-robed and hooded women, with only their eyes and deep cleavage showing, stood on either side of the head of a black-draped bed. Both grasped battle-axes with blades mottled with red. A third stood at the foot of the bed, her arms raised as she swayed and chanted.

A short-haired brunette, naked except for leather straps at her waist and an upside down pentagram painted in blood red on her back, was on top of an extremely well-endowed blonde. I do mean *extremely*. Her breasts were mesmerizing the way they didn't move at all in spite of the brunette's almost manic motions on top of her. Their pale skin, crimson lips and red nipples, all set off by the black sheets, seemed to blaze in the bright lights.

The rhythmic sound of wet flesh being parted by whatever device the woman on top was wearing finally reached my ears. Their humping frenzy had the complete attention of the other women I could now see, some of whom were as provocatively half-dressed as the woman in red latex. Portia had an amazing group of very attractive friends, if you like women a little on the synthetic side.

The sound of a slap brought my attention back to the bed. The blonde on the bottom slapped her partner's butt cheek again, drawing a cry of pleasure out of her. What kind of sex games involved battle-axes and women dressed as devils? What kind of ritual were they doing? The chanting sounded like Latin and was rising in pitch.

The blonde on the bottom suddenly yelled, "You're mine now, forever." Her hips rose and her breasts finally moved as she grasped the woman on top by the back of the head, drawing her down for a heated kiss. Her hungry mouth moved to the other woman's shoulders, then—like something out of all the nightmares I'd had since I'd arrived at this place—she bared her sharp canines and sank them into the other woman's neck.

The woman on top screamed.

I screamed.

"Bloody hell! Cut!"

I'd know that Queen Vampire voice anywhere. I threw open the door the rest of the way and there she was, standing just behind a very annoyed looking camerawoman. Portia looked icily beautiful in black brushed denim slacks and a shapely, clinging black sweater.

She also had a clipboard and I was pretty sure she wanted to throw it at me. "Brittany!"

There was assorted babble, all of the annoyed variety. The couple on the bed parted and battle-axes were put down.

"How was I to know you were making porn right over my bedroom?"

They were all mad at me. So they'd change angles and film the climax again—what was the big deal? What I couldn't get over was the array of partially naked and naked women around me, including the brunette who was still wearing her accoutrements. They were just standing around like it was perfectly normal in the middle of the night to be shooting an all-woman porn project.

"It's not porn," Portia said haughtily.

"Oh right. Performance art."

"Pornography is all about the male view—"

"Oh, please. Like men aren't going to want to watch this kind of action too."

"It's by women, for women, about women." There was a hint of a smile in Portia's eyes, but otherwise she appeared to be dead serious.

"Whatever!" Portia would have said more, but I suddenly felt very weak—okay, and turned on—and it didn't seem like shouting was a good use of my energy. "It's not like I'm uptight about it. Consenting adults and all that. It's freakin' one o'clock in the morning, I've been really sick and you keep dropping something on the floor. Which is *my* ceiling." Tears abruptly stung my eyes. "I want to sleep."

"Oh!" Those expressive eyes became much, much warmer. "I had no idea of the time. We get into having a scene just so and . . ." She shrugged.

They had certainly looked into it all right. "I understand."

"You're a future filmmaker yourself, so I'm sure you do. Let's call it a night, everybody. Find a bed . . . and we'll finish tomorrow night." She turned to me with one of her most charming smiles. "Let me make sure you're safe in bed. You look like a strong wind would knock you over."

"A weak chicken could knock me over right now," I admitted.

Once we were in the hallway I said, "You might have told me you made movies. I would have been okay about what type. I mean, I live in Berkeley."

"I didn't know how you'd feel about it." She kept with my slow pace, one warm, supportive hand at the small of my back. Cast members passed us, disappearing in pairs and trios into the other rooms. Glimpses told me that beds had been uncovered and trunks with costumes and other, um, gear, were covering most of the other furniture. "I do other kinds of performance art, but this is what pays the bills. People don't understand, believe me, I know. None of our welcoming committee would ever get over the very idea, never mind that this castle was likely the scene of far more graphic and far less consensual activities through its many centuries in the quest for power."

I realized that if Portia's profession were to come out she might not be the one who inherited the castle. It would be a rotten thing to do, no more right than if she'd been straight and outed me to get me disqualified. Sisterhood is powerful and all that, yeah, I know, it's a book my mother owned, but film school was full of guys who think they're the only ones with balls. I mean, they are, technically, but I have ovaries. "No, you'll never convince them that you're in a noble profession."

She paused at the top of the stairs to take my arm. "Lean on me. Seriously, you look wiped out."

I was trembling, and her touch wasn't helping. "Thanks. I'm shaky, yeah." We took the stairs one at a time and I was grateful for her steadiness.

"I know it was a risk to do this shoot here, but the location is perfect, we had fun in the basement earlier, and my mates wanted to see the place, so we thought why not do a vampire scene and some location shots for our latest work? It's about women's fantasies. Most male viewers would find it far too talky and chick focused."

Recalling the vigor of the coupling I'd witnessed—even if it was feigned and big fake boobs did nothing for me—I had to admit it wasn't that far from fantasies of my own. "Do you think women will enjoy the bite part?"

"You didn't see the setup where the consent is clear—submission in fantasy is big with a lot of women. Fantasy is the place where it's always safe."

The bite part didn't exactly zing my buttons though the rest made sense to me. "While I was raving delirious I thought you'd changed me into a vampire."

Her laugh was hearty. "Did you? Sapphic bite and all?"

I flushed. "Something like that."

"I'm flattered that you think me so . . . powerful."

We reached the bottom of the stairs and I had to stop to ease some of the lightheadedness. I wasn't going to tell her that my dream hadn't been about power, but about sensuality. "I was feeling so strange—I didn't realize I was getting sick. I thought you'd spiked my beer even though I knew that was crazy."

She laughed again. "I'd never do that to beer."

I tried to smile through my exhaustion. "Why do I not find that particularly reassuring?"

"Hey . . ." She grabbed me as I faltered. "Come on. Time for bed for you."

"I've never been that sick in my life," I admitted. "Worse than a hangover."

"Encephalitis is dead worse than a hangover."

I blinked. "Encephalitis?" I wish I knew exactly what it was. It sounded so serious. So fatal.

"Virus in the lining of your brain. Painful. Takes days to get over the worst, and you're not going to feel spot on for a couple of weeks, maybe."

I paused with my hand on my doorknob, finally taking in that I'd been very ill. "How long was I . . . out?"

"From when Melanie carried you upstairs? This is . . . the night of the third day."

Melanie had carried me up the stairs? How? She had to be much, much stronger than she looked. It was such a butch thing to do for a little elf.

"And I thought I'd be bored without my laptop." I tried to laugh, but blinked back tears instead.

She put her hand on mine and turned the knob. "Bedtime."

She didn't exactly carry me across the room, which was another reason she couldn't be an immortal vampire—where was the super-human strength for swooning damsels? Her arm was, however, firmly around me. I felt so conflicted. Part of me wanted to bury my face in her hair and take in the subtleties of her scent. Part of me wanted to share a scene with her in whatever movie she'd like to make. Part of me wanted to cry. The rest of me wanted to sleep.

What was it about her? Why did I feel so helpless? She wasn't a vampire putting some spell on me, but I felt bewitched.

She pulled back the covers and gently pressed me down to the mattress. Our hands tangled, caught, my arms were around her neck, and all I could think was that the dizziness and exhaustion were not dampening my libido in the least.

"That was some scene you were filming," I whispered before I let go of her neck.

She remained leaning over me. "Dee's boobs were hogging the screen, as usual, but Faye won't do a movie unless she gets one scene with her honey, so . . . They get some great chemistry, especially when Faye plays the submissive."

"Do you like submissive women?" I didn't mean my voice to sound quite so breathy, but it was and if I'd had the strength I would have blushed at my blatant come on.

"Yes. That's why I direct and don't act." She was staring into my eyes and I was liking what I saw there.

"You never act?"

"No."

"So if you were with someone it would be because you wanted to be?"

"That's the only reason I'm ever with someone."

My heart was pounding and I didn't know what to say or do next. She slowly looked down my body, then sought my gaze again. Her expression was intense and yet withdrawn. I should sleep, I thought. I didn't have the strength to have sex, certainly not the kind that Portia seemed to prefer. The kind that Portia was somehow creating the need for in me. I'd never wanted . . . I'm not vanilla, but . . . I'd never thought about . . .

There was a fever in my brain, all right, and I thought my head would explode when she leaned so close our lips were nearly touching, and said, "Get naked for me."

I exhaled as if I'd been struck. I was weak and vulnerable . . . and I liked it. I shimmied out of my sleep pants, hiding how dizzy the effort made me. She never lifted her gaze from mine and it was intimate and knowing. Did she really know me the way her eyes suggested, or was I like so many others she had little doubt she could rock my world?

"Naked," she repeated. "Everything off."

Still looking into her eyes, I got my arms out of my T-shirt and slowly pulled it up to my neck. I didn't have Dee's boobs, not by at least two letters of the alphabet, but I'd always thought they were nicely shaped. The other women who'd seen them tended to be appreciative.

She hadn't even looked down yet. I broke our eye contact to pull the shirt over my head, and her gaze was still on mine when I looked again, like she was already inside me.

The T-shirt joined my other clothes on the floor next to the bed. It had barely fallen from my fingertips when her body slid on top of mine.

The moan I let out I felt all the way down in my toes. Her brushed denim jeans were soft between my thighs and the light-weight sweater she wore caressed my breasts.

"Nicely done. I had a feeling when we met you might enjoy this," she murmured. "You've never done this before, have you?"

"I'm not a virgin."

"No, I mean let yourself be taken and enjoyed because it excites you to be in someone else's control for a while."

I shook my head. "No . . . not quite like this."

"Do you want me to make love to you? Take you?"

"Yes," I admitted. "I don't know why."

"Because you want it is reason enough. You're a long way from home and it's been scary." She brushed her lips against mine. "To be taken care of by someone else feels safe. I won't hurt you."

I was trembling, remembering that first dream and her lethal red eyes. How did I know she wouldn't hurt me? What exactly did she want to do?

"Stop thinking, Brittany." She pushed herself off of me, settling on her knees between my thighs. She pulled me toward her, firmly, so my legs were spread over her thighs and I was completely exposed to her. "No more thinking. Just feel."

She stroked my shoulders, my arms, my tummy. Her fingers pressed into my hips and thighs, then lightly brushed over my face and throat. She petted and touched me until I was writhing under her hands. My breasts ached to be noticed and touched and I could smell how wet I was. I felt as delirious as I had during the night-mares, but it was better, so much better, with real hands.

"That's right. I love getting a woman all worked up. You want me, don't you?"

"Yes."

"You want me to fuck you, don't you?"

"Please, yes."

"Touch your nipples. Show me," she ordered with a lustful edge to her voice. I think, I'm not sure, but if I hadn't heard and seen how flushed she was, that she was panting slightly, I might have stopped. But she was turned on too, by what I was doing and what I was letting her do.

I wondered if this was what sex drugs would feel like—I felt drunk but very aware of every sensation. X was supposed to be so commonplace, but never at the parties I went to. I brushed my hard nipples with my nails, then took each between finger and thumb and twisted, slowly. Just enough. I used my nails again, a little harder, then twisted and pulled and felt my hips jump in response.

"God, yes, show me. Get yourself really hot for me."

"I'm on fire," I managed to say. I gulped for air and added, "I might pass out, I'm so high."

"Oh no, I can't have that. You stay wide awake. And wide open."

I watched her lick two fingers, her tongue sinuous, and I wanted those fingers inside me. "Please."

"Don't stop playing with your nipples. I want to watch."

I moaned, loudly, and realized I was toying with my nipples the way I would my clit, but she hadn't told me I could touch myself there. Was I that close to climaxing? She hadn't touched me at all, except to position me. If I touched my clit I'd come. If she touched it I'd come. If she put those fingers inside me, I'd come.

"Oh, you are so sweet, so delicious." Her eyes were glittering with arousal. "You like being told what to do."

I did tonight, I wanted to say, but she was reaching for my hands and I couldn't have spoken right then to save my life. She put my hands on my spread thighs, then slipped her own under my ass to massage me.

"Your clit is so swollen. Put one finger on it."

I did as she asked, touching myself, and I wondered if I should be ashamed to be so open to her, embarrassed to give her some, if not all, of my secrets. She was watching my finger circle, rub, dip, tease as if she'd never seen anything like it before. She was hungry for it, starved for it, and I realized that while she was giving me what I wanted tonight, that was exactly what I was giving her.

My voice low and intense, I asked, "Do you want to watch me come?"

Her jaw went slightly slack, then she gritted her teeth. "Yes. Fuck yourself."

I was quicksilver slippery, lightning fast, both hands on my cunt. Fingers plunged in, while others tapped, pulled and circled my clit. I arched to her unrelenting gaze, and I showed her, showed her . . . showed her. I was tight and wide open and I felt her intense gaze as if she was the one moving my hands.

Finally spent, I gave a little cry and slumped to the bed, my heart pounding and my mind in a blue, easy haze.

She put my wet hands on my breasts. "Stay like that. It's my turn to enjoy you."

The haze shifted from blue to red when her mouth covered my clit. She fed on me, fed on my cunt, drinking, licking, sucking, and if she was a vampire, I didn't care. She drove her tongue into me, then trapped my clit between her lips while her fingers went inside me.

"You liked coming for me, didn't you?" She wetly kissed my clit again. "A show like that deserves a reward."

She spread her fingers inside me, and I cried out. She was touching places no one had really paid attention to before and I was so dissolved, so weak, that all I could do was yield. Yet it was still a choice, to open myself, and open, and take her in.

She enjoyed me, and her lust for it had me finding the strength to respond. I moved for her, ground myself on her fingers and mouth. I climaxed again, and maybe a third time, but by then my brain had said enough. Whether I was fainting or dying, I didn't know, but if the latter, my last conscious thought was *what a way to go.*

CHAPTER 8

Angels fear to tread. Meeting the
crew. I try new things.

ell. I see you've had some personal nursing."

I managed to get my eyes open. "What time is it?"

"It's after lunch." Melanie was glaring at me. "The rest of this lot is still asleep too. Did you enjoy their little show?"

I crimsoned, recalling the show I had very much enjoyed the night before. I didn't remember Portia leaving, but she obviously had. "They woke me up in the middle of the night. Not that it's any business of yours."

"You're right, it's not my business. You do whatever you like, but the next time you faint dead away at my feet, I will not be spending the next three days making sure you don't die."

She was gone in a sparkle of red hair before I could take in that she looked very trim in a sweater and slacks that fit her. Bloody hell, to quote Portia. For heaven's sake, whose castle was this, anyway? I was nearly an heiress, and given the way real rich people and so-called nobility behaved these days, a private, consensual tryst was tame. How dare she judge me, even if my behavior last night shocked me a little bit too? I'd walked in on a really hot sex scene, no matter how staged, and a girl has needs. I was an adult, wasn't I?

God, it had felt so good. I slumped on the pillows for a few minutes, enjoying a languid doze.

I felt badly when I spotted the bowl of soup on the writing desk, and saw that my dishes of last night had been taken away. Melanie had taken care of that I would think before she saw the note on my bedside table, reading in hard-to-miss lettering, "It was a pleasure to bite you last night. I hope you wake this morning having enjoyed pleasant dreams as a result."

It was signed with a stylish "P." All things considered, it was quite discreet. But bad enough that combined with my sleepwear scattered on the floor, Melanie had figured it out. And she had spent a couple of days taking care of me and then I'd gone and potentially exhausted myself. But I felt so much better this morning—sex was good medicine. Right, Melanie would want to hear all about that theory.

It took a while, but I managed another shower, ate the soup, was pleased I had to use the bathroom in the normal course of things—that was progress, I recalled from Susie's experience. I found clean jeans, but they were my last pair in that condition, which begged the question of what happened with laundry in a castle that didn't even have a phone. My three-quarter sleeve pullovers, which served me well in the chilly Berkeley summers, would keep me warm here, if I were near a roaring fire. Though I knew I wouldn't have the strength for it for several days, I fully intended to get to wherever I needed to go and buy some appropriate clothes and rent a car. Maybe, now that we'd become—well, *intimate* was the right word, I guess—Portia really would drive me all the way to Tongue.

A vision of her tongue licking greedily left me feeling weak. I had never experienced anything like last night, and that included a one-night thing after a party in Berkeley with ropes that had seemed more silly than exciting. Part of me thought I was having a psychological breakdown and the other part of me was loudly insisting I was finally learning to live. A long way from home, yes, but this could become home. This could be who I really was.

Looking in the mirror, where my reflection was most definitely visible, I said aloud, "The question is, do you like who you are here?"

I still had three weeks to find out.

Mrs. Dobnail was busy at work on something redolent of bacon and pepper. She bustled around me like a hen, quickly poured me tea and served up a slice of mutton pie, which was actually delicious. I could only eat a third of what she provided, but she seemed pleased when I thanked her.

"Is it a lot of extra work, cooking for the house guests?"

"I can cook for twelve as easily as two, simple fare. Yon pie is left from last night."

We agreed on the usefulness of microwaves and that the castle's electrical system likely couldn't support one. The dryer in the basement—I hadn't realized there was a floor below this one but supposed every castle had a dungeon—ran on a propane supply.

"A girl is coming in tomorrow to do the rough, and laundering sheets and towels is on her list. I'll have her get your things. The washer is a wee bit basic, so you might be wanting to rinse your smalls yourself."

I nodded as if I understood and thought I'd sneak down later to look at the machine.

We were joined by several of the cast, including Dee of the breasts and her girlfriend, Faye. They good-naturedly made up sandwiches and drank large quantities of tea, asking after my health and quizzing me about life in San Francisco. My status as a film student added to common ground and I felt welcome.

"You should watch filming tonight," Dee said. "Portia is really good with lighting and mood and she's very organized. I've worked with some who thought anything was good enough."

Faye smooched Dee on the cheek as she rose to put her dishes in the sink. "If you're in a film, any frame with you makes it great. But Portia's brill."

"Oh, how you all flatter me." I turned with everyone else to see Portia in the doorway, looking vibrant and well-rested. Slacks and sweater, both in a deep foresty green, once again brought out her pale skin, red lips and intense eyes.

I wanted her to take me back up to bed and the strength of my desire left me breathless. "Dee thinks I should watch the filming tonight. That I'd learn a few things."

Her eyes said she would enjoy teaching me more new things while her mouth said, "That could be fun."

I was getting that lightheaded feeling again. Her effect on me was ridiculous, I chided myself. She didn't have to drug me, just being near her was a drug. "I think I'll go back to bed for a while. I just ran out of strength."

She didn't offer to help me to bed, not then.

I wasn't really sleepy, but the quietness of my room was welcome after the hubbub in the kitchen. I sat instead at the writing desk and decided if I couldn't type on my laptop I could at least write some notes, just as Susie had suggested.

I quickly grew frustrated at both the slowness and quality of my penmanship, but I was able to jot down impressions and thoughts. As I wrote there were slamming doors, the tramp of feet and the echoes of laughter. I heard male voices, briefly, and I peeked out the window in time to see a group of hikers with walking sticks departing. I realized I felt more like I was living in a boarding house than a castle I might some day call my own.

Eventually my hand wearied and I was ready for a nap. When I woke again it was after dark, and my stomach was growling. Still feeling weak I brushed my hair and made my way downstairs to find dinner underway. Portia quickly pulled out a chair for me and Faye filled a plate from the dishes on the sideboard.

"What was hilarious," the camerawoman of the previous night

was saying, "was the way those hikers were watching all of us. Their first thought, being guys, was they had just won the lottery. All these women and apparently none of them with men in tow."

Dee, her distracting cleavage in full view, said, "Then their poor little faces fell. They looked like street urchins with no money for the candy shop."

"I think," Portia observed, "that it was you and Faye making out that broke their hearts."

"Good," Faye said, setting a plate in front of me. "They were being nosy, going past the ropes. We were just protecting your castle, Port."

"It's not mine yet," Portia said quickly. "I gave Brittany encephalitis, but she survived it. Who knew Americans were so tough?"

I endured some good-natured ribbing before I said, firmly, "Most Americans are mutts, mixed breeds and offshoots of people so intractable they got kicked out of every place they tried to settle. We're tenacious, to say the least."

"Even when you're dead wrong about something, you don't ever give up, that's for certain."

The discussion turned to politics and I let it ebb around me as I slowly ate a sizeable helping of Mrs. Dobnail's onion and potato casserole, capped with thick, crumbled bacon, and a large helping of string beans boiled with tomatoes and ham. I wasn't going to argue that of late our government hadn't been spectacularly inept and undeniably stupid. I was more concerned, perhaps selfishly, in whether Portia would ever glance at me so I'd have a clue what she was thinking. They preached to the choir for a while, then turned to discussions of the night's work ahead of them.

"We'll take the bite again," Portia said, not looking at me, "and then go on to the group scene with the acolytes and the devil. Jennie, I hope you don't mind another night in latex."

"When have I ever minded?" Jennie, I surmised, was the woman in the devil costume the night before, though I didn't really recognize her. Admittedly, I had not studied her face. When she got up to get seconds from the sideboard, her jean-clad back-side confirmed my identification. I could have bounced a quarter off her ass and given how lustful I was feeling around Portia, I wouldn't have passed up the chance to do so.

I was jarred out of my contemplation of how well a woman's hips can fit into her thighs by Melanie's arrival. If any of us had wanted the time of day it was clear we weren't going to get it. Clad once again in the oversized flannels and denims of some large member of her family, she stomped through the dining room with a rolled packet of tools under one arm. "Sorry," she muttered. "Mrs. Dobnail's got a blown fuse."

She had disappeared into the kitchen when Dee said, "What's with those trews?"

"I like a femme dressed up all butch," Jennie said, "but that's just wrong."

I rose to help myself to the scones and cream on the sideboard. Okay, so I didn't like Melanie's prudish attitude and general bad temper, but she was filling in for family and instead of a nice, quiet castle with the occasional hiker crashing for the night, she had a houseful of people to fix up after. Being catty about her clothes didn't seem nice to me.

I might have defended her but the lights went out.

From the kitchen, Melanie's voice called, "Sorry!"

The room erupted into startled babble. Abruptly, I was aware of someone behind me. I knew the cologne. She pressed me forward, her hands sweeping around me to firmly grasp my breasts. Her crotch ground into me from behind as she whispered, "I want to have you again tonight. Enjoy you all over again."

I shoved back against her, beyond rational thought, and moaned.

"Quiet. This is our little secret." Her hands grasped my inner thighs with her thumbs pressing into the seam of my jeans. So much for them being reasonably clean. She laughed in my ear. "If the answer is yes, work *pineapple* into the conversation."

She was gone, apparently at complete ease in the dark. From

farther away than I would have thought possible, she said loudly, "How much longer, Melanie?"

"Not much," was the answer, and, within a few seconds, the lights came back on to scattered cheers.

I finished splitting the scone and slathering it with strawberry jam, then somehow managed to return to my seat with something like grace. I was sodden and my breasts felt swollen and heavy, so much so I felt off-balance. To Portia I said, "Is strawberry jam what one always has with scones?"

"Sometimes there's grape, but strawberry is common, yes. Is there something you'd like better?" Her lips quirked to one side, as if she was anticipating my reply.

"I think they'd be tasty with orange-pineapple marmalade is all."

She didn't wink. I didn't either. I upgraded my condition from sodden to soaked.

With everyone else heading upstairs to do the filming, it seemed the thing to do to trail along. Easily winded and fatigued, I also had basic aches and pains, even after some ibuprofen. Still, the intrigue of watching a film shoot had me climbing the stairs. It had nothing to do with Portia or the subject matter, nothing at all.

In spite of their apparent casualness, the crew was briskly professional. In rapid succession Portia filmed devil Jennie coaxing a fantasy out of a dreamy-eyed Dee, Jennie then ordering her acolytes to their knees so she could strip them of their robes, and brief reaction close-ups of the three acolytes. Then the next tableau on the black-draped bed was set up.

With half of my mind, I could watch dispassionately. These were actors, and the action scripted. The lights, onlookers and camera all broke the spell that the movie itself would potentially weave on later viewers. The camera recorded the acolytes, now naked except for red latex thongs, tying their mistress to the bed with purple cords. Once done, the action stopped so that Jennie could get completely comfortable and the ties redone so they wouldn't come apart during the next scene. This was movie making. Start and stop. Film this, break, film that. Only in the director's mind was there cohesion and a sense of story. It wasn't sex, it was make-believe.

Then, when the acolytes took turns running their tongues up and down, thoroughly, completely, wetly, between Jennie's legs, and Jennie's nipples hardened, her skin flushed . . . my heart began to pound. When they had to stop because an acolyte accidentally tripped up in the sheets, Jennie gave a groan of frustration. The camera rolled again, and Jennie's moan when the attentions resumed sounded very real to me. There was no doubt in my mind that everyone enjoyed every aspect of what they were doing.

Every once in a while I would tear my gaze from Jennie's spread legs and watch Portia at work. Her gaze rarely left the monitor, but sometimes she looked up at the live action and I swear I saw her body tighten. My own responded, remembering the feel of her on top of me.

At one point she caught me looking. The look she gave me, searing hot, sent a shiver down my spine. She was going to do something to me later, and I didn't care what.

"You did so well last night, touching yourself for me." Portia backed me across my bedroom until my shoulders were against one of the bedposts. "Will you do what I ask again tonight?"

I felt molten inside, steeped in desire. "Yes," I breathed out.

"Strip."

It was a relief to take off my sweater and bra. She would touch me soon, and put out the burning fire.

"That's enough." She reached into her back pocket and I could hear blood rushing in my ears when I saw the short length of purple cord. "Is this okay?"

What else could I say? I never thought I'd do this, but I wanted her to have me, enjoy me the way she had last night. I had never realized how complicated it was, and how sensual, the awareness that as I took pleasure I could give it. I told her the truth, which was another whispered, "Yes."

Her eyes glittering, she pulled my arms behind me and loosely tied me with the cord. I didn't know if I could free myself, but I didn't try either. The position left my breasts vulnerable and with each passing moment my jeans felt smaller and smaller.

She used her lips, her teeth, her fingertips, nuzzling and playing with my ear lobes, my lips, my throat. With a playful grin she bit down slightly on my neck, then said in my ear, "That's not the fluid I'm really after."

The clock was not within range of my sight, so I have no idea how long she spent teasing my breasts and nipples. My breathing was ragged and I squirmed uncontrollably against her before she was done teasing me.

"God, please," I panted when her fingers finally went to the top button of my jeans. My arms were starting to ache and I wanted to ask if we could move to the bed, but she was so obviously turned on and I liked having that kind of impact on her if the discomfort didn't get too distracting.

The sound of my zipper made my knees buckle. My arms were forgotten. The seam moved against my swollen clit and I shuddered, very close to what I knew would be the first of several orgasms. With a primal growl, Portia dropped to her knees and bit into my crotch through my jeans.

"Come now!" She rubbed her face into me and my extreme arousal immediately responded. I cried out and she said hoarsely, "That's right, give us what we both want."

I bucked against her face, stunned that it felt so good to come and yet so frustrating, because she wasn't touching me, wasn't inside me.

She rose to her feet and in the same motion pushed my jeans down past my thighs. Leaning into me she again played her lips over my throat, her teeth over my lips.

"Just think, if someone opened that door right now, what a luscious, delicious sight they would see."

I realized then that, for her, part of the excitement was visual. She was turned on by the picture we made, my arms bound behind me, body curved in surrender and not quite nude, suggesting her seduction of me was still not complete. She was completely clothed and in total control of me.

Surprising both of us, I said, "I only want to share this with you."

"I'm sorry," she said quickly. "I wasn't suggesting otherwise. We're not there . . . yet."

I wasn't sure I ever would be. I was so turned on, but I didn't want to think about anything but her and what she was doing to me. "Right now," I paused to try to catch my breath. "Right now, just us."

Her hands cupped my hips as she ground against me. We were writhing in a sensual dance and for a while I think I was leading as much as she was. She pressed my ass into the post, spreading my legs as far as they could go with my jeans still above my knees.

"This is what you want, isn't it?" Her hips churned against mine as she licked my neck. "Do you like this?"

"Yes," I answered, and it seemed as if she was touching me everywhere at once. She asked every few seconds if I liked it, and I groaned yes, and we repeated that over and over while her hands found skin that I had never realized could feel so much sensation.

"Does that feel good?"

"Yes."

"Do you like this?"

"Yes."

Back and forth, question and answer. I said yes so much that when the question changed I could say nothing but yes.

"Do you want me to put you on the bed?"

"Yes."

"Fuck you?"

"Yes."

"Until you scream?"

"Yes!"

My arms were free, but the numbness and ache in them were nothing compared to the other sensations rocketing through me. She threw me onto the bed and I was swamped with dizziness and exhaustion but that too went out of my mind as her fingers slid into me.

"You're like a river. I want to swim . . ." She kissed my clit, then shoved into me, hard.

"Yes, oh please."

She kept fucking me as she stripped my jeans off, then split my legs apart and shoved into me even harder. She was on top of me, holding me down as I writhed and met her strokes. I didn't realize I was coming until I already was, as fiercely as the way she was taking me.

"That's right, I'm not stopping. You are going to come until I'm done with you."

I was babbling yes, moaning it, breathing it, pouring it over her. Every time I said it, she seemed to drink in more of me, eyes shining, skin gleaming, until her entire body seemed to glow.

CHAPTER 9

I fail to secure transport.
Phoning home. A geography lesson.
Laundry in a dungeon.

Slamming doors woke me. I looked out my window, through yet more rain, and saw several cars, all filling with crewmembers and equipment. Where had the cars come from? Had they been behind the building? I realized I hadn't been outside since my long walk, but my illness didn't seem any excuse for remaining so unaware of what was going on around me. The longer I was here the more my world seemed to shrink. Any minute now I'd disappear for a hundred years and I wasn't that fond of Gene Kelly.

Any crewmember could give me a lift into whatever the next large town was they passed. I scrambled into my clothes from last night, even though the jeans were soggy in places, and ran a comb through my hair. The result was disastrous, so I pulled on an Oakland A's cap.

"Hi," I said to Faye as she headed for the door with a box of what looked like microphones.

"Hullo. We're just about off. Thanks for the loan of your castle."

I followed her outside. "You're welcome. I enjoyed it."

She gave me a coy, knowing look. "I might have heard something to that effect in the wee hours."

I blushed furiously. "I don't suppose I could get a lift to a town big enough to have car rentals."

Dee, looking slightly less bodacious than usual in a thick sweatshirt, helped Faye get the box into the last square inch of the car's trunk. "We're full up. I think everyone is."

Faye called out my question to the general gathering and to my dismay everyone explained they'd used every last inch of space. They all had jobs to return to, so no one could stay, even if I offered to return for them and drive them wherever they needed to go. Several had a long car trek ahead of them, and five people to a car had been far cheaper than rail tickets.

Dejected, I was ready to pout until I heard Portia say behind me, "Tomorrow, for sure, we'll drive to Tongue. It'll be a fun day out after you've been so sick."

My mood instantly reversed. I felt like the queen of my own castle, standing on the steps next to a beautiful and passionate woman, waving goodbye to our guests. When we went inside, a teenager with a resemblance to Mrs. Dobnail was washing up many plates and pots while Mrs. Dobnail herself layered ingredients carefully into a baking dish.

"I've got yer dinner just here. An hour in a medium oven and it'll be nice."

"Thank you," we said in unison.

Portia continued, "You've worked so hard these last few days, and I really do appreciate it."

"You've been more than generous, ma'am. My girl just has a few things to finish, and we'll get the last linens from below and be off."

I realized that meant the laundry had been done. Dang, I'd just have to manage it myself. And I was perfectly capable of doing so, I reminded myself. I wasn't a castle-owning dilettante yet, and nobody who grew up in Lodi had ever had someone other than their mom do their laundry for them.

Given that the casserole looked rich and filling, I helped myself to some plain cold meat from the refrigerator and a handful of nuts from the bowl on the table. Portia watched me nibble with a look in her eyes that raised my temperature.

"Just building my strength," I said.

"Good." Her lips curved in an suggestive smile as if so say "You'll need it."

"I feel as if I've not really explored anything," I admitted. "I haven't even read the displays in the other room."

"It won't take long. There's a few photographs that are interesting, from the last years the castle was occupied."

"Do you think it's possible to really live here these days? Given the restrictions and isolation?"

She nodded. "With money. There's no reason a carefully planned, compatible addition can't be added for a modern kitchen and to house a generator, satellite dishes—"

"Now you're talking." I would never have that kind of money. Portia, however, might . . . and she had the personality to gain agreement from the local historic site committees. She really would be a better owner of the castle. I watched her hands, her lips, her body, and, yes, I'd enjoy the rest of my stay before signing away my claim.

After Mrs. Dobnail and her daughter left, we gazed at each other across the table.

"I need to wash some clothes or I'll have nothing to wear," I admitted.

"Don't do that on my account. I find you quite entrancing with nothing on."

I blushed. I mean, what else does a girl do in response to that kind of compliment? "It's a little cold to be naked."

"Not in my bed."

"And people walk in here all the time."

"Yes." She nodded. "You have a point there. Melanie doesn't know how to knock, for one."

"She did take care of me, and I haven't thanked her."

Portia smiled slightly. "Perhaps you should do that. I have to make some notes about the filming, and write up a number of letters. I can send them tomorrow—I'm sure Tongue has an Internet café. It's a nuisance not having a phone."

"That," I agreed heartily, "is an understatement. I think I'll walk down to talk to Melanie's and make a phone call. My friend Susie has to be worried."

So that was what I did. Making use of one of the ubiquitous umbrellas in the stand by the door, I went out into the afternoon rain, wetting my feet, but nothing like I had on that long walk.

Melanie didn't answer the door, and finally I tried the knob. It wasn't as if she knocked before entering my room, even if she had been checking on me. If she wasn't home I would be glad of the privacy.

I managed the string of country codes with the old-fashioned dial phone, and much to my relief Susie answered, sounding sleepy.

"Girlfriend!" Her enthusiasm instantly warmed me. "I was getting worried. How are you? What have you been doing with yourself?"

"I'm getting over the flu," I allowed. "I'm sorry if I worried you."

"Yeah, I was definitely—" There was a slight commotion as the phone was muffled. I heard Susie say "all the way from England so you can just wait" and then into the phone she said, "I was definitely worried."

"Who's in bed with you?" I demanded.

"No one you know yet, but that might change. If he behaves." There was a swatting sound.

"I feel so far away." And homesick, I wanted to say. I missed

Susie and classes and Berkeley and yet I didn't want to go home, either. "I've met someone too."

"Oh, that's great! I mean, you can't stay there or anything like that or else I'll never forgive you but I hope you're having fun. Even with the flu."

"I am having fun. A lot of fun."

"Maybe she'll decide she wants to live in the States."

"Um . . ." I didn't quite know what to say. I hadn't gotten my brain past the bedroom to U-Hauls. Susie was the quickest U-Haul renter I knew, straight girl or not. "It's not like that. Yet. Might never be."

"Oh, just romping in bed, huh?"

Recalling the previous night, I said smugly, "Not always."

"Wicked thing!" Susie laughed and I remembered why I loved hanging out with her. "I hope whoever she is, she fucks your brains out."

"Oh yeah, there's been plenty of that." I heard a noise behind me and there was Melanie, hands on hips. She looked a little tense, but nodded and went about making herself tea.

I don't know why I said it, and it was childish. "Not just that, but she sucks my brains out too."

Melanie's back stiffened and some of the sugar on her teaspoon spilled onto the counter. I instantly regretted my crudeness, but Susie's laugh was nearly worth it.

"Keep that up and you'll get as dirty-mouthed as me."

"I don't think I want to excel at it, but knew you'd appreciate the pun." Melanie still had her back turned, and she kept her back to me the entire time Susie and I chatted and she drank her tea.

I finally put the phone down, saying to her, "Will the bill for that go to the estate or will you let me know what I owe?"

"The estate."

"I don't know how much a call from Scotland, England, is to Berkeley, California."

She slowly turned around, her eyebrows so pulled down they almost touched. "Here's an essential clue. Scotland is not in

England. Scotland is a *country* and has been since Eight-Forty-Three. It's located on the island of Great Britain and is part of the United Kingdom. We are self-governed and jointly governed, a state of complexity I thought an American would be able to grasp, but alas I am once again underwhelmed by the American education system."

Stung, I could only think to say, "Scotland is the size of Maine."

"Is that supposed to mean something to me? You've got an idiot for a leader, and you picked him. Most of the idiots in our history at least we inherited."

"Have you ever heard of inbreeding, then?"

"I've seen *Deliverance*, yes."

Ouch. "What is with your attitude?"

"I don't have one, but yours is so American—"

"Whatever! I can see you think I'm just another person out to annoy you." I stomped to the kitchen doorway, then looked back. "Thank you for taking care of me!"

"You're welcome," she snarled back. That soft, kind voice while she'd been nursing me, whoo-hoo baby, it was long gone.

"You could have let them take me to the hospital, you know. If you hate me that much. That would have ended my claim."

"I thought you were the lesser of two evils. That you might just have a brain, but you're just another bird all gooey-eyed over tall, dark and dangerous. You think she's going to make you some kind of star?"

"No," I answered, surprised. "I want to make movies, not star in them."

"That's what the world needs, moresomes on film, heaps more porn."

"I don't want to make porn. I want to make all sorts of movies, movies that women really connect to. Like a horror movie that really gets to women especially."

Her expression grew slightly less mulish. "You mean like those movies with scenes where some tart with a really big pair is rubbing soap all over herself? I never knew tits could get that dirty, but it's fun to watch."

"Now who is wanting some good porn?"

"Fine."

"Whatever."

I had gone three paces from the kitchen when I turned back to confront her again. "What do you call that thing on a man's kilt? In front."

Her eyebrows up to her hairline, she said, "A sporran. Why?"

"I knew it wasn't a codpiece, that's all."

I stomped outside and instantly regretted it as mud soaked my pant legs. Oh well, I was going to do my laundry next and then I fully intended to let Portia get that foul-humored Melanie out of my head. You would think someone with such a perpetual wicked bad mood couldn't possibly look so harmless and pretty.

"You forgot your brolly."

I turned back to snatch the umbrella from her and headed for the castle. I honestly didn't know what a bint was and if I'd been a hundred percent sure it was a pithy insult, I'd have called her one. As it was I just hoped she didn't see me slip in the mud.

After a refreshingly hot shower—I still didn't feel as if I'd ever get my hair clean from the days it had gone unwashed—I found a box to load up with my dirty clothes, and carried it carefully down the stairs and through the kitchen to the basement door. I had to rest for a bit as I was still easily winded, but a snitched morsel of a berry crumble loosely covered on the counter restored me. A blast of cold air whooshed through my hair as I opened the door and peered into the dark. Fumbling, I found a light switch finally, and descended the narrow stairs with relief. The room was so utilitarian it was prosaic. The washing machine was no mystery and within a few minutes my darks were swishing in water and suds.

Looking around, I couldn't see how Portia and crew could have filmed anything down here. It was a basement, nothing more. I was about to leave when I saw two doors under the stairs. The first, ordinary wood, opened into a large closet full of janitorial equipment and supplies, like mops, brooms and bottles of wood oil cleaner.

The second door was oversized, and was so cold to the touch that I realized it had to be made of metal, long painted over. There was a heavy bolt, which lifted easily, and I eased the door open, expecting as loud a creak as the front door had let out the night we'd arrived.

To my surprise it swung open noiselessly, and I found myself in a poorly lit room that had at some point been used as a wine cellar. Empty racks lined two walls. The other two were exposed stone with remnants of those things that hold torches—great, now I knew what a sporran was but I'd forgotten the basic elements of a scary dungeon set design.

I shivered and decided to go back to the warmth of the kitchen, but hadn't even turned around when Portia said, in a low voice, "Dee and Jennie were freezing down here."

"I believe it." She'd changed her clothes—it was hard not to notice the leather vest and pants immediately. Her hair was slicked back and she'd taken on a James Dean swagger. With an intrigued smile, I said, "Did you dress for me?"

"No," she said promptly. "I dressed for my date later."

"Someone I know."

"I don't think you've met, no."

She advanced on me, her steps making no sound at all on the floor. She looked very good with a touch of butch, though the unmistakable swells under the vest would never let anyone mistake her for anything but a woman. My eyes fell to the tight pants and my heart began to pound at the sight of another unmistakable swell.

"If you were wearing a kilt," I said, "that could be a sporran."

"Only if I were wearing it on the outside. And I like it inside." She backed me up to the wall. "Do you like the dungeon?"

"I would have expected you to have implements of torture."

Her crotch pinned me to the wall as she slipped a hand into her vest. "Who says I don't have a few on me?"

The handcuffs caught me by surprise. For the first time with her, I felt hesitant. "I'm not sure—"

"We're all alone," she murmured in my ear. "You're so vocal when you're getting it the way you obviously love it, and down here you can scream. Just one wrist . . . cuffed to the cresset."

That's right, the torch thingies . . . cressets. "It's a little cold."

"Not for long." She nibbled on my ear as her hands began a tantalizingly slow exploration of my body. "You'll be able to tell people you were a captive in a dungeon and fucked within an inch of your life."

"I think I was within an inch of my life already this week."

She made a little growling noise in my ear and it made me a little weak in the knees. "I thought after the fun we've had that this was a natural next step."

"I know, it's just . . . I mean . . ."

She bit my lower lip and her hands were under my sweater. The warmth of her body compared to the cold stone against my back brought out of wave of prickling goose bumps. "Give me your wrist."

Aroused, but afraid, I slowly extended my wrist.

"Are you sure? To do this you have to invite me in, all the way in."

"I'm sure." I blushed at the quaver in my voice.

She ratcheted the handcuff around my wrist and lifted my arm above my head. Briefly on tiptoe she hooked the other cuff on the cresset's supporting arm. Stepping back, she said, in a deeply pleased voice, "Don't you make a wonderful picture."

"Do I?" I felt awkward and yet my body was swelling and starting to ache for more of her touch.

"Yes. If everyone hadn't left I'd film you. I love how you flush, how you moan . . . and how you scream."

She pulled up my sweater to unhook my bra and raw, sensual feelings swept over me. Vulnerable to her as I had been last night, clearly, there was no reason for either of us to be here except to have sex. It was that simple. No pretense at affection, she'd never even kissed me. We were going to fuck.

Briefly, for one last moment, I realized how far I was from home. Not just Berkeley, but Lodi, where crops grew, nothing happened, and there were no dungeons. I had inherited a castle—okay maybe I wasn't going to but right now it was partly mine. A woman's home is her castle, and she ought to be able to get laid any way she wanted. Right now, I wanted it this way.

Portia had my jeans off me within a few minutes and paused, kneeling at my feet, to push her tongue between my legs. I shuddered in response and tried to open myself to her, but she was already pulling away. "I'll be back to taste you again."

She rose to her feet, the leather outfit rubbing slowly up the front of me. "That's where I'm going to bite you. That's where it won't show."

I giggled. "You're a gorgeous vampire, did you know that?"

"So I've been told." Her lips were curved in that enigmatic smile I'd first seen in Mr. Stuart's office. "Do you feel that?"

"Oh. God, yes, I can feel it." The bulge in her pants was pressing into my thigh.

"You want it, don't you?"

"Yes."

Her hand cupped me between my legs and squeezed. "You're wet for me."

"Does that surprise you?"

"No." She grinned broadly. "Not given the spell I've put on you and various substances I've slipped into your food."

I giggled until I heard her zipper. Then, all I could think about was her fingers opening me, and the heat of her skin as she peeled down her pants. I couldn't see what she was wearing because she was pressing so hard into me, but I could feel it. Ample, heavy—it was the kind of item I'd lusted after but never had the guts to buy for myself. It bumped against my clit and I jerked against the handcuff.

"I wish I could really tie you to this wall. Manacles, ropes, really make you my prisoner."

"Believe me." I panted into her ear, trying to catch my breath. "This is quite enough to get me really high."

"Good. I need you high. I want your blood hot and full of all those good chemicals, the ones we make naturally, when something feels . . . this . . . good."

She pushed inside me, slowly, firmly, and without stopping.

"Oh, dear God." I'd never felt so full and the sensation was incredible. I wanted to wrap my legs around her but it didn't seem possible with only one arm to hold on to her as well.

She pinned my shoulders to the wall and moved her hips. "It feels good, doesn't it?"

"Yes."

"You are so fun to pleasure, such an easy fuck." She was biting at my neck as she moved faster and faster. "It's okay to scream. I want you to scream."

I gritted my teeth. "Then make me scream."

She laughed, her eyes glittering, and began to pump against me so hard my back was scraping on the wall. I'd be bruised tomorrow, but I didn't care.

Abruptly she stopped, pulled out of me.

I groaned, loudly.

"Do you want more?"

"Yes, you know I do."

"Beg."

She brushed my clit and I shuddered on the edge. The nearness of my release was excruciating. "Please don't stop."

"You'll have to do better than that, Brittany." Her fingers played over my nipples. "Right now, you belong to me. Nothing happens to you unless I want it to."

"Fuck me." I closed my eyes, getting lost in the feelings that were drowning my senses. "Fuck me, please."

"That's better. I'm not going to, but that's better."

My eyes flew open and I watched her back away from me. In disbelief I said, "I . . . what more do you want from me?"

"I want everything." She smiled at me as if I were a child. "You're too close to the truth, you silly little fool. And since you've proven so incredibly easy to prime, your blood will be the best I've enjoyed in a long while. The only thing that pumps it more than sex is fear."

She reached for my free wrist as I said, "Portia, I'm not . . . this isn't funny. I mean, I want to finish and I don't mind some playacting, but—"

I don't know where the other set of cuffs came from in her clothing, but one was around my free wrist and she moved so quickly she'd secured me to the other cresset before I realized she wasn't joking.

Stepping back, her eyes aglow, she said, "Simply delicious."

"Let me go." I wavered between agonizing arousal, disbelief and fear.

"You want me to fuck you, don't you? You were just begging for it. This will be even more exciting."

"Yes, I know, but—"

She was against me again, slipping inside me again, and she was right, it was more exciting. My body felt absolutely unreal and my inhibitions seemed completely gone. I begged her for more, I begged her not to stop again, I pleaded with her to enjoy my body, to pleasure herself until my hoarse words reached a crescendo.

I screamed and she gave a cry of triumph, grinding into me.

"That's right, that's right, you're mine now."

She pulled my legs around her waist and I winced at the pressure against my wrists from the cuffs, but her fingers on my clit as she continued to move inside me distracted me. We writhed against the wall, with her saying things so earthy and hot I could feel my blood reaching a boil.

One hand slipped behind my head, cushioning it as she fucked me so hard I was bouncing against the wall. "This is what you are, California Girl. This is what you were made for. Mine to use."

I screamed again, orgasm tightening every muscle, firing along every nerve. I hadn't thought she would push me this hard, hadn't known I would let her, and I'd never felt anything like that release in my life. Every bit of energy I possessed drained out of me and I slumped against the wall, on the edge of consciousness.

She slipped out of me. It took all the strength I had to raise my head.

Too numb to scream again, I saw that her eyes were glowing red.

"And now," she said, in a conversational tone, "the devouring."

CHAPTER 10

Transformations.
I am a poor bairn.
The inheritance. Scottish women.

She bit me, on her knees, sank her teeth into my most tender flesh and she drank with wet coughing sounds that turned my stomach, and I was helpless to stop her.

"Delicious," she said. "I am so looking forward to my next meal. I'm sorry it'll be your last because I do have a date tonight, and I've offered to share you."

She left me there. Half-naked, both wrists slowly going numb, my arms shrieking for a change of position, she left me there. The dungeon door was closing behind her as I tried to find another scream, something someone would hear.

"Please don't do this," I pleaded through tears. "Why are you doing this to me?"

She paused briefly. "I told you. Fear on top of sex is the best blood."

She closed the door and the darkness was absolute.

I was having a nightmare, that was it. I was still delusional from being sick. I'd wake up in a few minutes to find I was tangled in the ropes she'd used last night, but otherwise safe in my own bed. There were no such things as vampires, and Portia was not one anyway. She had a reflection, her body was warm, and I'd seen her eat plenty of food.

In spite of the cold, I was sweating profusely. When had I developed such a longing for rough sex? What had happened to me since coming to this place? I wanted to go back home, go back to being B. Brannigan of Lodi, California, U.S.A.

I was all alone in the dark. My eyes wouldn't adjust to it and now I could hear the furtive movements of four-legged creatures. I desperately wished I'd never seen *The Tower of London* because right now Vincent Price with a rat by the tail would shred what was left of my mind.

The pain was intense. I hurt . . . every bit of me ached. That wet, coughing sound was still filling my ears, sounding like death. The terror was spreading all over my body until I couldn't breathe. Portia had used me and somehow managed to get me to say yes. I'd invited her in. I'd given her everything.

There was a flicker of light and I flinched from it.

She was back, her hands were all over me, and they felt as if they were gloved in fire. How long until she bit me again, how long until she drank every ounce of blood in my body?

"Stop," I whimpered. "Please stop."

"Just one more," a voice answered, strangely soft and kind.

"I can't. Please let me go." I coughed, and it sounded thick and wet.

"It's okay." Shushing noises, from far away.

I couldn't feel the wall against my back anymore. All the nerves in my body seemed to be dead. Had Portia done her work? Was I in heaven? I wasn't sure I believed in heaven and if it really existed then I guess I'd pretty much feel like a fool.

"Don't open your eyes. There . . . now you can relax."

The hands were no longer on my body and I felt tears on my face. My wrists were free. A tissue came out of the darkness to dab my face and something wet was against my lips.

"The poor bairn," someone else said. "I'll leave the mash right here. And there's some fresh tea for you, love."

"Thank you. I think her fever has broken. I hated moving her— she was crying. It must hurt like the devil."

I could feel the voice drifting away, a rowboat on the ocean tide, or was it me drifting? Perhaps. I was floating now, still in the dark, but at least the pain had stopped.

When I opened my eyes the first thing I saw was Portia in a chair near my bed, reading. Her hair was pulled back in a simple ponytail, and with glasses slipping down her nose she hardly looked like a pornographer, and even less like a vampire. Then the memories washed over me, including the terror in the dungeon. I made a little sound as the echo of my screams filled my head, and she looked up from her book.

"Hullo there, sunshine. You're back with us."

I tried to crawl to the far side of the bed, but my arms weren't in the mood to obey me. Melanie was suddenly there too, wiping sleep out of her eyes and yawning.

"There you are. I knew you'd wake up just before the doctor got here. But that was quite a scare you gave me last night."

Portia said, not looking at me, "I'm so glad you woke me. That was far too much worry for one person. At least you got some sleep, finally."

Melanie shrugged. "I was going to fall asleep on her, and the way she was thrashing around—I really thought she was having a seizure, like the doctor warned."

What on earth were they talking about? Was Melanie in on it? Was she a vampire too, the date that Portia had mentioned was going to share in my blood? I hurt all over. Everywhere. But when I looked at my wrists there were no marks.

"Hey." Portia leaned over the bed. "Are you all there?" To Melanie she added, "She looks terrified."

Melanie, still using that soft, kind voice, said, "If I were this far from home I'd be scared too."

There was a knock at the door and Portia admitted an older man with a black bag. I didn't understand a single thing he said, but he grunted at my temperature, looked in my eyes and listened to my breathing. Whatever he said after that made both Melanie and Portia smile with relief, and after a hearty, "hi-glock-lo-Monday-knee" he left.

"Eat a little something," Melanie urged.

I couldn't even find my voice. Portia was moving around my room and I kept track of her out of the corner of my eye. My wrists weren't even bruised.

"The doctor said we need to get your kidneys functioning again. That means you need to eat, drink and visit the loo." She spooned up a small amount of something that smelled faintly of cinnamon. Rice? I had a small bite and she gave me a pleased smile.

Another two bites, several swallows of water, and she pressed me back into the sheets. "Sleep now. If you feel like you can stand up later, a shower could happen."

Portia turned from my writing desk. She looked at me like she wanted to . . . devour me. I had only one thing I wanted to say to Melanie. I whispered it as she leaned forward to tidy the sheets over me.

"What was that?"

Carefully, not wanting to go to sleep with Portia anywhere near me while she still had a reason to hurt me, I said, "I relinquish my claim."

"You don't have to do this," Melanie said.

"Yes, I do. I know you think I'm still irrational, but I want to go home."

I saw her expression go carefully blank before she feigned interest in the book she was reading. She sat some distance from the heater, but I was still easily chilled.

She'd kept me company for the past week, reading to me in her soft, lilting voice, and bringing me meals. My eyes were finally back to normal and I could read on my own, but even today she'd offered to entertain me. "You could at least stay the whole month."

"Not here. I really don't want to stay here a day longer than I have to. I'm glad Mr. Stuart could get up here so quickly."

She didn't answer and I blinked back tears. I knew I was totally screwed in the head—you try having nightmares like I'd had and not think that a change of venue was welcome. I wanted to go back to a world where the freakish and outlandish were within my control. "I'm sorry. I wasn't going to be the one selected anyway. Portia has the money to help preserve this place. I don't. And I don't speak the language."

Melanie had a glimmer of a smile. "It's English."

"*Buggery bollocks* is English."

"Do me a favor—stick to American curses, okay?"

I pursed my lips at her. "No fucking way is that English, what you all talk to each other."

"Maybe not the Queen's English," she allowed. "But you were thinking we were something out of *Brigadoon*."

I'd grown to love the sight of her hair and the sound of her voice, but part of me argued that if I was feeling attachment it was because I was scared to death of Portia. A red-headed elf was better protection than my own meager strength, that was for sure. "Maybe. I surely feel as if I've landed someplace lost in time."

"The modern world is just past the next glen. You can visit it whenever you like. I'd take you there myself, if you stayed. The rest of the month, I mean." Her eyes were trying to say something and I wanted to receive the message, but I still felt too weak, and too unlike myself to be certain of anything I felt.

"When your dad is better, you're going back to Glasgow." I had to remind her that I wasn't the only one leaving.

She sighed. "Yes, a living must be earned. And it's a good job for someone who's only studied history and doesn't know a lick about programming computers."

"At least it's teaching."

Her shrug was eloquent. "I wasn't thinking I'd settle down to teaching quite so soon. I've not seen as much of the world as I wanted."

"You could visit San Francisco. I'd be happy to put you up."

She gave me a quizzical look, then said, with transparent nonchalance, "You mean a place to stay?"

"Yeah. It's the least I can do."

Her smile was somewhere between relieved and excited. "That would be a bit fun, yeah."

The sound of tires on the drive outside brought us both to our feet. I didn't want to leave the warmth of my room, but the sooner I signed the papers, the sooner I'd stop having waking flashbacks of Portia's teeth sinking into my cunt. Freud would have a field day.

Portia gave me a curious and puzzled look, as I joined her in the main hallway, a look much the same as she had given me for the last week. We all met Mr. Stuart at the door.

He shook water off of his umbrella and glanced around the entry. "I do believe this is one of the smallest castles I've ever seen, but a castle it is, with a great deal of history. I'm a lucky man to be visiting it with three lovely ladies to take care of me."

Melanie took his arm and we all sat down at the table in the kitchen. In short order Mrs. Dobnail set down a tray laden with her wonderful little cookies, sugar and cream. A second delivery provided a teapot, cups and saucers. Portia played mother.

I couldn't help myself. I watched her hands like a hawk. As far as I could tell, she didn't have a chance to add anything.

Mr. Stuart explained to me what it would mean when I relinquished my claim. He went on for some time and I didn't really listen that closely as I figured I understood the basics. I signed the papers, Portia got the castle, and I was just another American with ancestral roots in Scotland.

He showed me where to sign. I scrawled my signature and added the date.

Portia gave a little sound. "I really don't know what to say, Brittany. I'm so sorry you got sick."

"Why prolong it? You belong here and I don't." I gave her a sweet smile. I knew I was nuts, but I could not shake the nightmare memory of her calling me a silly little fool who knew too much. Well, this silly little fool was getting out of Dodge.

Melanie turned to say something to Mr. Stuart and for a moment I felt alone with Portia. Her eyes suddenly sparkled and she grinned at me, victorious.

When Melanie looked up to see why I'd spilled my tea there

was nothing to point at, no reason to say more than, "How clumsy of me."

For as long as I lived I would never forget that grin of victory when Portia bared her teeth and lovingly ran her tongue over her fangs.

Melanie drove me all the way to the train station in Inverness. The sun was up and I saw the countryside at last. Ruggedly deserted highlands eased in the deeply green valleys with rivers, lakes, and wildflowers as plentiful as the blades of grass. I'd come back someday, when I wasn't so frightened. Maybe with a guide of my own. I glanced at Melanie and felt lucky to be alive.

"I was supposed to visit Urquhart Castle, to make my grandmother happy. But I don't think I can face another castle."

"What about Nessie? Did you get a chance to hunt for her?" A road sign flicked past; we would be in Inverness in another fifteen minutes if Melanie kept tearing along the road. I liked the way she drove. I wondered if she did other things the same way, all fire and speed. I wondered what it would take to slow her down, sometimes.

"No. I guess I'll regret going home after seeing so little."

"You really were quite ill. It's a small wonder you want home."

"You've been very kind to me."

Melanie shrugged, the same way she'd shrugged the last time I'd thanked her. "Do you want a bite to eat before the airport?"

"Sure." I wondered when I'd stop flinching every time someone used that particular noun.

She coasted into the next tiny village, and turned in at a pub. Once we'd ordered our food—steak and stilton pie for me, thank you very much—we carried beers to a little table near a window.

After a few sips, I reached into my backpack and drew out an envelope.

"What's this?" Melanie took it from me with a wary look. "You best not be trying to pay me or some nonsense like that."

"No, nothing like that. It's a gift. I recently came into some money, and when I made my travel arrangements . . ."

She opened the envelope and then gave me a cautiously hopeful look. "An air ticket to San Francisco?"

"Open booking, from Glasgow—you pick what date you want. When you can . . . stay for a while." Like as long as immigration would allow.

"I shouldn't accept this, but I do try to use the brain I was born with."

"In the States we'd say that our momma didn't raise no fools."

She grinned at me, every tooth absolutely normal. Maybe I'd never know for sure if I'd seen fangs on Portia or if I'd just wanted to see them to excuse being a spectacular quitter. But Melanie was human and cute, sharply funny and knew more about movies than the average elf. Plus the hair and the voice and . . . I was running away, but giving her a chance to chase me, I guess.

The train station was busy, but Melanie found a place to pull in so she could help me with my bags. We stood awkwardly at the curb and she said something about the weather and I don't know what I said, and it's a good thing I try to leave out the boring bits.

Imitating her soft burr, I asked, "So you'll come to America sometime soon, yeah?"

"Wise ass," she answered, grinning again. "You Americans are all alike."

"Scottish women are *such* bitches."

Here's the thing about a good exit line. After delivering one, don't fall over the suitcase you forgot was behind you.

After Melanie picked me up, she kissed me. Thoroughly.

Running
with
Stone Ponies

Barbara Johnson

Chapter 1

The autumn morning dawned clear and bright, though the temperature dipped below normal. Snuggled in a fleece jacket adorned with the images of running ponies, Celine Ashton leaned against the fence and surveyed the paddock where her prized thoroughbreds grazed contentedly on stacks of fresh hay or on still-green pasture grass. All of the horses wore colorful Navajo-made blankets to protect them against the cold. The chill air made the breath from their nostrils visible. She laughed softly, thinking it made them all look like they were smoking.

It had taken her a long time and lots of hard work to get to this point, though she'd had a good foundation to start from, thanks to her late father. Now one of the country's top breeders of world-class racing thoroughbreds, Celine, unlike most breeders, made sure none of her horses ever ended up in a slaughterhouse—not before, during, or after their careers as racers. Anyone buying a horse from Ashton Ranch had to sign an ironclad legal agreement that they would return any horse to her before having it destroyed for any reason other than an untreatable medical condition, and she even had approval authority over any future sales of the horse or any offspring thereof. She'd vowed that none of her animals would end up in some disreputable roadside zoo or circus or shipped off to some country where horsemeat was still considered a delicacy. One would think that almost four decades into the twenty-first century such practices no longer existed, but the sad fact remained that it was so.

She fingered the sugar cubes in her pocket and clicked her tongue. The horses raised their heads and looked at her, their ears pricking up, but one broke from the herd and trotted over to her. He was a magnificent animal, with a gleaming black coat and matching mane and tail. He was as black as the stone for which he'd been named: Obsidian. After having won his share of races, he'd sired more winning racehorses than any previous champions combined, even the legendary Secretariat and Seattle Slew. Celine stroked Obsidian's soft nose, smiling as she remembered the offer she'd recently received from a Saudi crown prince. Twelve million dollars! It was always easy to say no to offers like that. Obsidian was not for sale at any price. And though she could have made a lot of improvements to the ranch with twelve million dollars, Celine was certainly not hurting for money.

"Would you have liked to have lived in the desert?" she asked the horse as she ran her hand along his smooth, muscular neck.

Obsidian snorted and nodded.

"Ungrateful beast," Celine said, taking the sugar from her pocket.

He took it gently from her, then she patted his flank to send him back to the field. She watched as he took his stride, still capable of displaying the awesome power and speed that had made him the envy of the horse-racing world. Many a jockey had practically begged to ride him, and those lucky enough to do so invariably finished the race in first place.

Some of the other horses took off running too as Obsidian raced by. Galloping across the green pasture land, they reminded Celine of the wild ponies of the West, ponies whose days were numbered as a ruthlessly anti-environment administration increased its stranglehold on the nation—more ruthless even than the Bush administration early in the century. Celine rested her arms along the fence, feeling the tears in her eyes as she thought about the plight of those wild mustangs. And she remembered too the first time she'd seen Obsidian's mother—as a gangly filly cruelly taken from her mother and destined for the slaughterhouse.

"Daddy," she had pleaded, "you have to buy her."

Her father had looked at her, pity in his eyes for the fifteen-year-old girl who wanted to save every living creature.

"Darling, we can't take another horse."

"I promise I'll take care of her. I'll work extra hours after school to pay for everything she'll need. Please. She'll be a great racehorse. I just know she will!"

She hadn't had to beg long. Following the death of Celine's mother, it was rare that he could say no to their only child, so he'd given in once again. And no, Athena had not become a great racehorse, but some of her offspring had. Then Obsidian was born—to become a legend. However, in the cruel irony that life sometimes throws at us, Celine's father had died the very night Obsidian came into this world.

In the middle of the night, she'd run up to the house, thrilled at the birth of the shiny black foal. Bursting into her father's bedroom to wake him, she'd been surprised to find him not in bed. She found him in the bathroom, crumpled at the foot of the sink, toothbrush still in his hand. She'd screamed long and loud, bringing the stablehands running. And so it was that at the age of twenty she'd inherited Ashton Ranch and all the tradition that came with racing horses. Vowing to make her Daddy proud, she'd built the ranch into one of the premier thoroughbred ranches in the world.

"Are you out here daydreaming again?"

Startled, Celine whirled around, her annoyance quickly turning to joy as she beheld Jason Black, her favorite cousin. Slinging her arms around his neck, she hugged him tight. "When did you get back?"

"Day before yesterday," he said, hugging her too.

"And you waited until today to come see me?"

"You know how Mom gets."

Celine nodded. "How is Aunt Julia these days?"

"Same as usual," Jason said as he put his arm around her waist, then led them along the path back to the house. "She didn't curse you out first thing though."

Celine raised her eyebrows.

"No, she waited until dinner time."

"You would think after all these years, she'd get over the fact Daddy left everything to me. I mean, it's not like she had anything to do with the running of the ranch."

"Ah, but she could have sold it and made tons of money. Then she wouldn't have to settle for a Cape Cod on ten acres of land. She could have a penthouse in the city."

Celine sighed in frustration. "Is it really still the money?"

"Yes, and don't offer to give her any like you did a couple of years ago. That only made you more of a demon in her eyes, like you thought she was some kind of charity case."

"I wonder sometimes if Daddy and Aunt Julia were really brother and sister. That two siblings could be so different . . ."

They reached the house and settled onto a porch swing. Jason wrapped a blanket around both their legs. As if on cue, an elderly woman came out bearing a silver tray laden with steaming mugs of hot chocolate.

"Maria," Celine said, taking one of the mugs, "you must be psychic."

"Nope," Jason said as he took the other mug. He took a long drink and smacked his lips loudly. "When I came looking for you, I told her we'd be here in fifteen minutes."

Maria laughed. "You should have let her go on believing I was psychic. Now she'll never listen to me when I tell her not to go out."

"So, Jason, how was your trip?"

Unknown to Jason's mother, he sometimes worked for Celine, acting as her agent in the sale of some of her horses, when time allowed from his job as deputy sheriff. Theirs was not a high-crime county. With some potential buyers, he had an uncanny ability to ferret out the more unscrupulous ones. If anyone was psychic, it was Jason, for he would tell Celine when he should go meet the buyer and when it was safe for her to go herself.

"Well, you definitely don't want to deal with Mr. Anderson. I did some snooping around, and he's not a very pleasant fellow. A lot of the men working for him say he's got a mean streak. And last year three of his horses died suspiciously. I don't know how he's managed to stay under the radar for this long, which also makes me think he's not who he says he is."

"You think Anderson is an alias?"

"Wouldn't surprise me. I could do some more checking if you'd like."

"It might be a good idea. If you find out anything, we can kind of spread the word around the community," she said, thinking about times past when he'd helped her expose crooked folks in the horse-racing industry.

"I did meet someone else interesting though."

Celine grinned. "Tell me about him."

Jason smiled back. "Not him. Her."

"What? Have you gone to the other side?"

"Not for me, silly. For you."

Celine rolled her eyes. "Are you still trying to play match-maker? Who is it this time?"

"Don't give me that look. You'd really like her."

"That's what you said about—what was her name—Sandra?"

He used his foot to get the swing moving. "How was I supposed to know she was a klepto?"

"Um, maybe 'cause you're in law enforcement and should know these things."

"Oh come on, if I ran every one of your potential suitors through the system, you'd be mad at me."

"Guess you're right. Okay, tell me about her."

He took another sip of hot chocolate. "Her name's Nadia Peters, and she's the president of some microchip company that has the U.S. military as a client."

"Why would you think I'd be interested in a woman like that?" She made the swing go faster. "Besides, anyone helping out that fascist in the White House, even in a remote way, is not someone I'm interested in meeting, let alone dating."

"Hey, she sells microchips, not guns."

"She should sell microchips to anyone but the military."

"Why don't you meet her and tell her that? Your powers of persuasion can be quite irresistible."

She gave him a look.

He shook his head slightly. "Okay, maybe you're right."

Celine threw off the blanket and stood up, effectively changing the subject. "Thanks again for checking out that Anderson fellow. And for going to the auction for me. It would have been hard to come back and then take off for the equestrian show right after. I did decide to take Obsidian."

Jason stood too. "I know when I'm being tossed out like a stale sandwich. Let me know if you need more security for the trip. Travis is looking to make some extra cash, what with a new baby on the way and all."

"That would be great. Is he off day after tomorrow?"

"I can arrange it." He stepped off the porch, then stopped and looked back at her. "She's quite a looker, this Nadia Peters. Just your type too. Tall, dark, and handsome ring any bells?"

She threw the blanket at him. Of course, it missed. He laughed.

"Jennifer was blonde," she said.

"Maybe that's why it didn't last."

In answer, Celine went into the house, letting the door slam loudly behind her. She grinned as she heard Jason chortling as he walked away. He loved to tease her, and she liked to let him think it bothered her. But she knew that he probably knew the truth. And who knew? Maybe he was right—maybe she and Jennifer only lasted two years because Jennifer was a blonde. As she headed up the stairs to her bedroom, she decided her next girlfriend should be a redhead.

Preparing for the five-hour drive to the Prince George's County Equestrian Center, Celine was startled to see military airplanes flying low overhead. It wouldn't surprise her as she got closer to the Center, for it was near Andrews Air Force Base, but she didn't see them much here in western Maryland. Low-flying military aircraft were a common sight these days near the nation's capital, and many other big cities for that matter. For the first time in more than twenty years the threat of nuclear attack was very real again.

She yanked at a bridle, making its metal pieces clatter loudly against the wall. Stalking into the barn, she kicked at a bale of hay, feeling her anger build up.

Unlike most of her generation, Celine took the threat seriously. The masses dismissed it, laughing at the sight of old news clips showing children hiding under school desks. The Cuban Missile Crisis of the 1960s and the nuclear showdown with North Korea in 2012 were nothing but forgotten chapters in a dusty old history book, along with the Cold War threat that had died in the 1990s with the breakup of the Soviet Union. The majority of the population had an unwavering belief that no nation would dare attack the United States, a belief that had grown as the memory of 9/11 faded, as first the Iraq war and then the Iran war came and went. They even got over the terrorist attack on Chicago that came a scant fifteen years after the attacks on New York and Washington and then the one on San Diego five years after that. No one paid attention as one by one, India and China and Pakistan and Kazakhstan all tested nuclear weapons. Then, the most shocking of all—Argentina and Panama, followed by a united Korea.

In the tack room, Celine jerked open the lid of a storage chest and withdrew two horse blankets. She slammed the lid down, but the action did nothing to alleviate her fury. How could a country like the United States be so blind?

No one fretted when all the former Soviet republics quietly joined forces again, becoming the United Republic of Russia, and their nuclear weapons program, never completely dead, was re-energized. Europe was fractured, the European Union an ambitious yet still unfulfilled dream as dozens of squabbling countries all vied for power. Who knew what capabilities they had?

Walking outside again, Celine studied the aircrafts' path across the sky for as long as they were visible, reflecting that now, yet another power-hungry President was alienating the rest of the world, determined to keep the Superpower name all to himself. Ten years ago, Congress had changed the law so the president could be elected to two six-year terms, a change orchestrated by an unknown young senator from Mississippi. That ultra-conservative senator had gone on to become elected to the nation's highest office, and Celine was convinced that he intended to make the White House his permanent home.

A couple of hours later, Celine and Travis finalized preparations for the trip. As Jason had suggested, Travis had easily agreed to be extra security for the trip, and she was grateful for his thoroughness as he checked the latch on the horse trailer one more time.

"Kinda scary, huh?" Travis asked, pointing as yet another plane flew overhead. It was so close, they could clearly see the military numbers on its underbelly.

"They probably figure us country bumpkins won't mind as much as the city folks."

"They spooked all the horses this morning. I coulda swore they did it on purpose. You know, like in those old war movies when the planes would swoop low to scare the people."

"You're probably right. The horses were okay though, right?"

"Yeah, but they took off running and headed into the woods. It took me a while to calm Obsidian down." He paused as the horse trailer shook a bit. "He's still pretty restless. He don't usually make such a fuss."

"I'll see what I can do. Be ready to leave in about twenty minutes."

He touched his fingers to the brim of his cowboy hat. "Yes, ma'am."

Celine unlatched the lock and entered the trailer. Obsidian turned his head to look at her, then nickered softly. Walking to the front of the trailer so he wouldn't have to look backward, she took a carrot from her coat pocket.

"It'll be okay, fella," she said as he took the carrot and munched loudly. His eyes had a slightly wild look to them. She ran her hands along his body, starting at his neck and working her way down to his tail. She could feel a trembling in his body, but her fingers seemed to soothe him. She wrapped her arms around his neck, breathing in the strong horse scent of him. His hair felt both rough and soft against her cheek.

Standing beside him, she matched him breath for breath, until she literally felt the tension ease from his body. Checking his tethers once more, she exited the trailer, locking the door and checking it three times. Right on cue, Travis appeared.

"Maria packed us a lunch," he said, holding up a basket covered with a blue-checked towel.

"Well then, let's get started. I want Obsidian to have some quiet time down there before the crowds arrive."

Chapter II

think this is a reason to bring out the champagne, don't you?"

Anna laughed. "Oh Edwin, you'll use any excuse to drink Nadia's Dom Pérignon." She nodded to her secretary. "There's a bottle chilling in the fridge."

"You don't think the acquisition of a major defense contracting company is more than a mere excuse?" Edwin asked. "What do you think, Nadia?"

Nadia Peters turned from the window to face her two top executives and best friends. "You've both outdone yourselves," she acknowledged. "None of this would have happened without you." She looked out the window again. "And I know you each think you deserve to become President of TechChip."

Anna and Edwin looked at each other. Then the sound of the champagne distracted them for a moment. There was silence as the secretary poured out three glasses.

"Have a glass yourself, Claire," Nadia said.

"Thank you, Ms. Peters." Claire poured a fourth glass, then brought one to Nadia. "Your champagne."

Nadia took the glass from her and smiled. Claire blinked. Even though she was straight, she couldn't help but be affected by that dazzling smile and those brilliant blue eyes. She'd overheard Anna say more than once that Nadia Peters was a lesbian goddess. Claire also knew her boss was still not over the end of her relationship with Ms. Peters, no matter how many other women she dated. And sometimes, like now, Claire could understand why someone would never get over a woman like Nadia Peters.

Claire closed her eyes for a second. When she opened them again, Nadia had turned to the window again. Anyone who knew Nadia recognized it as a sign that something was bothering her. She could stand for hours just looking out the window, almost with longing, as if she couldn't be a part of the world outside. And since the windows were tinted to diffuse sunlight, Claire had come to suspect Ms. Peters had some sort of condition that made her intolerant of direct sun.

"Nadia?" Anna asked. "What is it?"

Nadia turned from the window to raise her flute. "To the acquisition. And to two of the best employees anyone could wish for."

They raised their glasses, then sipped their champagne.

"I have decided to take the President position myself."

If Anna and Edwin were disappointed, they were both well-trained enough not to show it. Claire, however, was not so well-trained. "Oh," she said, looking at her boss. Anna's face was expressionless.

"I know you both worked very hard for months to acquire TechChip for me. It was not easy. And it is only fair that you would assume one of you would become president." She took a sip of champagne. "But to tell you the truth, I have been at loose ends for quite a while now, and I think this is something I need." She smiled again. "And besides, how can I choose one of you over the other?"

"What roles do you see us in?" Edwin asked.

"CEO and COO, of course. You will both report directly to me. And I promise, I'll let you run the company as you see fit, for the most part. I will only insist that I have final say in any major contracts or acquisitions." She put down her glass and went around her desk to sit down. "Now, I'm sorry, but I have work to do."

☩

It was a typical dismissal. Anyone on the outside would think Nadia was displeased with them. The other three, however, simply stood up, then walked out. "How could she do this?" she heard Claire say as the door closed. Nadia assumed the question was directed to Anna. She knew the two women, and maybe even Edwin too, expected Anna to get the President position because of her and Nadia's previous relationship. But Nadia had learned long ago not to let personal feelings interfere with her business decisions.

Contrary to what she'd told them, she didn't have any pressing business. Instead, she opened the newspaper, bypassing the gloom-and-doom headlines in favor of the entertainment section. A headline caught her eye: *Champion Racer Obsidian to be Star Attraction at Maryland Equestrian Show*. She wasn't surprised that her local Connecticut paper would feature such a story. The horse was a legend not only in the racing community, but throughout the world. It was rare indeed that he would appear in public. Obsidian's owner, Celine Ashton, was proving even more elusive.

Nadia too admired the thoroughbred. He was so like a horse she had once owned many years ago, back when she lived in the Old Country. The memory of Lucifer brought a smile to her lips. What a thrill it had been to ride him across the fields and meadows of her homeland. If she closed her eyes, she could visualize the sun glinting off his jet-black coat, feel the warmth of him between her legs, the wind tossing her long hair behind her as they raced through the countryside in the afternoon sunshine. Ah, but that had been before . . .

She shook her head to rid herself of the memory. It did no good to remember what had been. It was one of the reasons she'd emigrated to America all those years ago. It was the reason she prowled the dark streets of the night, looking for solace where she found none. And it was the reason why none of her relationships lasted more than a few months. A horse asked no questions, and while her beloved Lucifer was gone, she'd already put acquisition of the beautiful Obsidian into motion by visiting an auction a couple of weeks earlier. The entire evening had proven well worth her time.

Hoping to meet Celine Ashton, she had immediately headed to the area where the Ashton Ranch horses were exhibited. As usual, they created the greatest interest for the buyers who'd come from all over the world. Ashton Ranch had had eight animals there, two of which were Obsidian's offspring. They had fetched an unbelievable price.

"Beautiful animals, aren't they?"

Nadia turned to see a handsome young man with a smile that would drive most girls crazy. Yet she realized instantly it was not the fair sex he would most likely be interested in. "Yes, they are," she said.

He stuck out his hand. "I'm Jason Black. If you're interested in purchasing one of them, I'm your man."

"Nadia Peters," she said as she shook his hand, trying to hide her disappointment. "I was expecting Ms. Ashton herself."

"Not this time. She had pressing matters at home."

"I see."

He looked at her as if appraising her. "Say, would you care to have dinner with me?"

Surprised, she didn't answer. Could she have been wrong about him?

As if sensing her confusion, he said, "This isn't a come-on. I'd just like to get to know you a bit better. And if I may be honest, I think I might know someone just your type."

She couldn't help but laugh. "A matchmaker, are you?"

"That's just what Celine says. C'mon Ms. Peters, let me take you to dinner and you can tell me all about yourself."

"Oh, why not?" she said. It had been a long time since she'd been out for a purely social occasion. No strings attached. Besides, anything Jason Black could tell her about Celine Ashton could prove useful in negotiations for Obsidian.

A short time later, Nadia studied Jason as he raised a glass of ouzo.

"So, what do you like?" he asked. "Besides Greek food, that is."

"Lots of things. Museums. The theatre. Horses, of course."

"Ah, horses. That's what I like to hear. Do you go to the races?"

She frowned. "No, I don't like horse racing."

He raised an eyebrow. "Then why would you be interested in buying one of Celine's?"

"Because they're beautiful animals. I want one for riding."

He bit into a dolmades. "Did you see one today you're interested in? I might be able to have it removed from the auction."

"You would do that for me?"

"Sure. But it would still cost you."

"I can afford it."

"Old money, or do you work?"

She should have been offended at his line of questioning, but she was not. "Both." She dipped a piece of pita into hummus and took a small bite. "I inherited money, but I also make investments. About a week ago I acquired TechChip. They make microchips."

"Hmmm, microchips. Doesn't sound too exciting."

"Maybe not, but it makes me the president of my own company."

The waiter came with their mousaka and spanikopita. "And who buys your microchips?" Jason liberally sprinkled his mousaka with salt. "Phone company maybe?"

"Actually, the U.S. Air Force mostly. For their planes."

He made a face.

"I know. The whole potential war angle. Do you really believe we're in danger of a nuclear confrontation?"

"I make it a point never to discuss politics," he said, taking another sip of ouzo. "Especially with someone I want to get to know. We don't want to destroy a potential friendship before it even gets started, do we?"

She smiled. "Certainly not."

"You did not like the spanikopita?" the waiter asked more than an hour later.

"It was delicious," Nadia said. "I'm just not very hungry. But you can package that to go."

"Very well." He took her plate away.

"You hardly touched your food," Jason said.

"I'll eat later. So, what time is the auction tomorrow?"

"One in the afternoon. I can expect to see you there?"

"Oh dear, not at that time. If it was early in the morning . . ."

The waiter came with the check. Nadia reached for it, but Jason snatched it away. "I'll put this on my expense account." He winked. "Actually, my cousin's account."

"Your cousin?"

"Celine. Her dad and my mom were siblings."

She stood first. "It was great meeting you."

He scrambled to his feet. "Ditto. I hope we see each other again. And I'm serious. I think you'd be perfect for Celine," he said as they walked to the parking lot.

"Somehow I think your cousin would prefer to pick her own dates."

They stopped at his car. "So she always tells me. Where can I drop you?"

"I think I'm going to walk around town a bit." She held out her hand. "Thanks again for dinner."

He shook her hand, then got into the car. "You be careful."

She waited for him to drive away, then dropped her leftovers into a trashcan before she started walking. She'd not gone far when she spotted a woman alone, and an attractive one at that. Her potential victim strolled casually along the street, stopping here and there to window shop. Her pale flaxen hair and milky-white skin identified her as possibly Nordic. She was slender, yet pleasantly muscled. It was obvious she worked out. Nadia guessed Pilates or yoga.

Though the woman walked alone, there were still plenty of

people on the street. Nadia would need to be patient for an opportunity, but her hunger was strong. The time came sooner and easier than expected. As they turned a corner, the street became deserted. In her hesitation, the woman tripped on a piece of broken sidewalk.

"Here you are," Nadia said as she handed the woman her purse.

Startled, the woman turned, fear in her light-blue eyes. She visibly relaxed when she saw Nadia. "Thank you. How careless of me. It just slipped off my shoulder."

Nadia smiled at her. "You're very welcome." She placed a hand under the woman's elbow. "Come with me?"

The woman fell easily under Nadia's control. She smiled back. "Has anyone told you that you have the most amazing eyes?" she said as she allowed Nadia to guide her into a deserted alleyway. Nadia led her more than halfway down, out of hearing range of any passersby who might appear on the street.

"One or two," Nadia said as she pulled the woman to her, brushing aside long, blonde hair to expose her throat. "You have such soft skin," she said as she nuzzled the woman's neck, feeling the pulse of her blood beneath her lips.

The woman moaned. Nadia held her tight, kissing her deeply on the mouth, then letting her tongue glide down over her collarbone and down to the hot indentation between her breasts. If she had the time, she would make love to the woman first, but she was so hungry. It had been days since she'd feasted. She brought her lips once more to the woman's neck. After one long breath, she let her teeth sink into the tender flesh. The woman moaned again, deeply. Nadia moaned too as she tasted the blood spurting warmly into her mouth. She sucked and swallowed greedily, feeling the blood run down her chin and onto her own neck.

She drank until she felt the woman go limp in her arms. Reluctantly, Nadia stopped. It was not her wish to kill tonight. Temporarily unconscious, the woman would have no memory of what had happened when she woke for Nadia had become a master hypnotist over the years. She gently lowered the woman to the ground. It wasn't very sanitary, but that could not be helped. Nadia took a handkerchief from her jacket pocket, wiped the blood from her mouth, and exited the alley. A man and woman walked up the street, their backs to her. Good. They'd neither seen nor heard anything from the alley.

A few feet away, she flagged down a passing police car. When the officer rolled down his window, she turned her body slightly so he couldn't clearly see her face. "I think a woman's been injured," she said, pointing toward the alley.

Before the officer could get out of the car, Nadia had turned the corner and disappeared into the crowd.

Yes, she thought as she remembered every moment of that visit to the auction, the trip had most definitely been worth it. Sighing, she picked up the paper again. The article went on to say Obsidian's owner, Celine Ashton, would be in attendance. At last, Nadia thought. It would be the perfect opportunity to meet her when she wouldn't be concerned with business. She picked up the phone.

"Claire, I need you to make flight reservations to Baltimore. I'll be bringing my chauffeur, so make arrangements for a rental car. A Rolls, I think."

She looked at the news photo of Obsidian, so much like Lucifer. It seemed like only yesterday that she was a young girl of twelve, racing him across the farm fields of her native Bulgaria. When had she last been home? She closed her eyes, letting her mind carry her back, feeling the wind against her face, breathing in the scent of mown hay and freshly turned earth.

She opened her eyes and touched the photo. She'd make Ms. Ashton an offer for Obsidian that she couldn't refuse.

Chapter III

"That's a magnificent animal."

Her attention focused on the object of those words, Celine felt a flush of pleasure warm her cheeks. To her surprise, her reaction was not only at the compliment extended to her pride and joy, but also because the voice that had spoken was low and sensual. It was a voice that made her feel like she was wrapped in velvet. Giving the silky, black mane one last brush, she then turned to the owner of the voice and felt her cheeks warm even more. The deepening shadows of twilight could not hide the fact that standing before her was the most gorgeous woman she had ever laid eyes on. Jason's clichéd words—tall, dark, and hand-some—immediately came to mind. Yet the slender woman was more than that. Pale skin contrasted sharply with coal-black hair, which contrasted in turn with eyes as blue as a spring sky. High cheekbones and lustrous lips gave her an exotic, somewhat ethnic look. She exuded a confidence that gave her tremendous strength. Momentarily stunned speechless, Celine could only gaze into those dazzling blue eyes. The woman smiled broadly and stuck out a hand.

"I'm Nadia Peters. You can call me Nadia."

Finding her composure, Celine took Nadia's hand and tried to salvage her pride. "Sorry. You startled me. I didn't hear anyone come in."

"Yes, I've been told I need to wear squeaky shoes."

Self-consciously pushing a lock of hair behind her ear, Celine turned back to her horse. "You've seen Obsidian race?"

"No, but I know his reputation. I have to admit though, I don't really like horse racing."

"So, what brings you here?"

"Simple. I want to buy him from you."

Celine laughed. "You and a half dozen others. I'll tell you what I tell them. He's not for sale at any price."

"Everything has a price."

Celine looked at Nadia. Her blue gaze was almost hypnotic. She shivered. As if he too felt the intensity of that stare, Obsidian snorted and pranced nervously in his stall. It almost seemed as if he was trying to back away from them. Celine turned her attention to the animal, running her hand soothingly along his powerful neck while she whispered words of comfort. He bowed his head to her touch.

"I don't know why he's so nervous," she said. "I think I need to shut him in for the night." She gave him one more pat, then closed the upper portion of the door. The nighttime security guard she'd hired to relieve Travis would be here in ten minutes. When she turned once again to Nadia, the woman had moved deeper into the shadows of the stable. It was almost unnerving.

"Perhaps you'll let me try to convince you over dinner?"

Celine shivered again, but this time with pleasure. That velvet voice made her feel like she would do anything Nadia Peters desired. She felt the warmth of blood rush to her face again, then course through her veins, giving her the sensation she was on fire. She stepped quickly from the stable and into the cool night air, welcoming the sudden chill from a mild breeze.

"I'd love to have dinner with you," she said, "but it will be a waste of time. I won't sell at any price."

Nadia took her arm. "Dinner with you would never be a waste of time. Do you like seafood?"

Celine almost jerked when Nadia touched her. The feel of Nadia's fingers on her bare skin was electric, and deeply unsettling. She closed her eyes to quell a momentary sense of vertigo. Why did this woman, this stranger, have such an effect on her? "Yes, I do," she said, opening her eyes and hoping her voice didn't tremble.

Nadia led her to a Rolls Royce gleaming darkly in the harsh electric lights of the stable yard. A chauffeur smoked a cigarette while leaning against the polished hood. He quickly threw down the cigarette as he stepped forward to open the back door. Nadia waited while Celine slid inside, then followed. As the door clicked shut, Celine couldn't help but feel she had taken a path from which she'd not be able to turn back. And in the close confines of the backseat, she was acutely aware of Nadia's body next to hers. As Nadia bent forward to speak to her driver, her hand brushed Celine's thigh. Celine gasped. Nadia leaned back and looked at her.

"Are you all right?"

"Yes. I just . . . Well, I'm a bit surprised at myself for getting into a car with someone I don't know."

Nadia laughed. It made Celine feel tingly all over.

"I can assure you I am not a serial killer. I had dinner with your agent, Jason Black, not too long ago." She took out *Forbes* magazine and pointed to her picture in an article. "There I am. You can read the story if you'd like."

"I think I'll just rely on my instincts," Celine said with more confidence than she really felt. But she was fascinated with Nadia Peters, so she brushed her doubts aside. "Jason did mention your meeting," she admitted, while telling herself Jason would be insufferable if she told him he'd been right about her probable reaction to Ms. Nadia Peters. "Now tell me, why are you so determined to own Obsidian?"

"I'm a collector of all things perfect and beautiful. There is no horse as extraordinary as he is, and I would spare no expense to make him comfortable."

"That's your reason? Because you're a collector? I've never heard of anything so absurd." She frowned. "And I don't believe in collecting animals."

"Perhaps collector was the wrong term to use."

"I had a Saudi crown prince offer me twelve million dollars for him. Can you believe it! I turned him down flat without even thinking twice about it. And I certainly can turn you down."

"You've not heard my offer."

Celine looked at Nadia, ire beginning to overtake any other feelings she might have felt. "Please, just respect my decision and don't bring it up again. I think it might be best if you drop me off at my hotel."

"Very well." She knocked on the window separating them from the chauffeur. When it rolled down, she gave him the address of Celine's hotel.

Celine should have been surprised that Nadia knew where she was staying, but she wasn't. However, she was surprised that Nadia had responded to her request without even a tiny argument. For some reason she couldn't explain, she'd assumed Nadia was interested in her too, not just her horse. Positive she'd felt a connection between them, she couldn't help but feel a little deflated. She felt her face grow warm again and was grateful for the darkness. How could she humiliate herself so?

"I have to ask," Nadia said as she leaned back against the seat, "aren't you ever worried someone might steal Obsidian when he's off your property?"

"I've hired a security firm. They are extremely reliable."

"Like I said, everyone has his price."

Angry now and just a trifle alarmed, Celine said, "Are you warning me or threatening me?"

Nadia's eyes glowed. "I didn't mean to frighten you." She

patted Celine's hand. "I just mean that even the most reliable security service can have people willing to look the other way if they're offered the right amount of money."

"Well then, with that theory, it could happen on my own ranch as well as anywhere else."

Nadia took her hand. Her touch made Celine dizzy. Absurdly, brief thoughts of a magical spell flashed through her mind. She shook her head to dispel the feeling. Most likely, she was merely overtired.

"We started off on the wrong foot. I've been told I can be rather imperious. Let me try again?"

Surprised but pleased, Celine nodded.

"Ms. Ashton, my name is Nadia Peters. I have admired your line of thoroughbreds for many years and am looking to acquire two or three for my personal use. Might we discuss business over dinner?"

"It would be my pleasure."

Nadia rapped on the window again. "Take us to Captain Jack's please."

Again, Celine was surprised. Captain Jack's was a local hole in the wall—one with the best seafood around, but certainly not the type of restaurant she would have expected a woman like Nadia Peters to frequent, or even know about.

"You must be local then, to know of Captain Jack's."

"No, I split my time between New York City and Connecticut, but I make it a point to find the best restaurants wherever I go." She smiled. "As I'm sure you know, décor and ambiance don't always equal delicious and tasty."

Celine laughed. "How true," she said, while thinking the same could be said of women. She wondered just how delicious Nadia might be under that affluent and reserved exterior, then felt herself blushing at the thought. Nadia looked at her and smiled again—a knowing smile, almost as if she could read Celine's mind. *This is nonsense*, Celine thought as she shook her head again to rid herself of such ideas.

Neither woman spoke further the rest of the way to the restaurant. Celine couldn't see outside the tinted windows, but she knew the traffic would be light at this time of day. Sighing, she leaned back against the soft leather seat. She was more exhausted than she realized. In that respect, it was good to be going to Captain Jack's. It was no nonsense and quick. They'd be in and out within an hour.

The driver pulled into the parking lot, then got out and opened the door for them. A couple of scruffy motorcyclists gaped at the fancy car, then swaggered to the front door ahead of them. Just as the two women got there, the men let the door slam shut.

"Rude bastards," Celine muttered.

Nadia called out to her driver, "Take care of things for me."

"Yes, ma'am."

Nadia opened the door, letting Celine walk in first. Celine glared at the motorcyclists, who smirked, then licked their lips suggestively as they let their gazes travel up and down her body. One of them cupped his crotch. She felt immediately creeped out.

"Would you like to leave?" Nadia asked.

"No, it's okay." She led Nadia around a corner to a small alcove. "We don't have to look at them from here."

A gum-cracking waitress whose nametag identified her as Sue came to take their order. "What do you recommend?" Nadia asked.

"Crabs are real fresh today; scallops too. The catfish is one of the cook's specialties."

"I'll have the catfish, blackened," Celine said. "Baked potato, no sour cream, and steamed broccoli."

"Ditto."

"Anything to drink?" Sue asked.

"Beer," Celine said. "Whatever you've got on draft."

"That sounds good," Nadia said.

As the waitress walked away, Celine looked at Nadia. "You are quite a surprise."

"In what way?"

"Well first, I wouldn't take you for the kind of woman who'd be comfortable in a place like this. And I would also expect you to make up your own mind about what to have for dinner."

"And why do you think I didn't?"

"Just a feeling."

Nadia steepled her fingers and rested her chin on them. "I could point out that you too would seem to be much more comfortable in a fancier restaurant. After all, you are a self-made millionaire several times over."

"You have me at a disadvantage then. You've obviously studied up on me, but I know nothing about you. Other than the fact you've been in *Forbes* magazine."

"It's not a long story. My family came from Europe many years ago. I didn't want to just be yet another idle millionaire so I recently bought a company that makes microchips for military aircraft."

Celine raised her eyebrows. "Well, you certainly are blowing all my stereotypes to hell. And I suppose with the current state of affairs you are making money hand over fist?"

Nadia grimaced. "Yes, having a president who is in a tense standoff with another nuclear superpower does make the military order lots of planes, and they all need microchips. I've only seen the dollar figures on paper at this point."

"Does it worry you? All this talk of nuclear war?"

Nadia leaned back in her chair as the waitress delivered their drinks. "I suppose it should, but I've seen it all before."

"You have?"

"Well, not literally. I mean, I've read all the history books too. And of course all the latest specials airing on the History Channel."

Celine looked at her. Nadia had recovered well, but Celine was convinced she had meant her statement literally. Perhaps something had happened in her country? She scanned her memory, trying to recall any recent nuclear incidents. "Where did you say you were from?"

"I didn't, but my family originated in Bulgaria. Well, what used to be Bulgaria anyway. We came to the United States about sixty years ago."

"Nadia Peters doesn't sound very Bulgarian."

Nadia shrugged. "My real name is Nadezhda Pendareva, but no one knows me by that name anymore."

"Oh. I can see why you'd pick something simpler."

"Something like that. But enough about me. I want to know about you."

Over dinner, Celine gave her a brief rundown of her life. It wouldn't do to tell everything all at once, for if Celine had her way, she'd be seeing more of this fascinating yet secretive woman. And she sensed that Nadia Peters was the kind of woman who liked a challenge. Celine could not appear too eager, yet the hunger she felt for this woman seemed to grow with each passing minute. A sudden vivid image of Nadia kissing her neck made her break out in a sweat. She stood abruptly and picked up her purse.

"I have to go to the ladies' room."

Nadia stood, too. "Are you all right?"

"Yes, yes. I'll be right back."

Nadia smiled as she watched Celine hurry away, She would be an easy conquest, she thought, yet dismissed it even as she thought it. No, there was something different about Celine Ashton. Nadia realized in that moment that this woman would not be just another conquest, very disquieting indeed.

Her smile faded as she caught her chauffeur's eye. Purposefully, she walked outside of the restaurant and around to the back. Behind a row of hedges that separated the restaurant from a farm, the two motorcyclists lay face down in the dirt, their throats torn open. Despite her disgust with them, Nadia couldn't help but kneel down and drink thirstily of the blood that still flowed from their wounds. She grimaced slightly at the taste; men's blood just didn't agree with her. Sated, she nodded curtly to her chauffeur.

"You know what to do."

He nodded.

She wiped her mouth and went back into the restaurant, arriving at the table just as Celine returned from the ladies' room. Well familiar with women's habits in restrooms, Nadia had known Celine wouldn't be out in a flash, especially if there was another woman in there with her.

"Feel better?"

"Yes, much. Guess the fish didn't agree with me tonight."

Nadia signaled for the waitress.

"You either," Celine said.

"What?"

Celine pointed to Nadia's plate. "You hardly ate anything."

"Guess I just wasn't hungry." She paid the bill. "I hope we see each other again," she said as she led Celine to the Rolls.

Chapter IV

"I met that woman you told me about," Celine said to Jason one late afternoon several days after she'd returned to the ranch. She was in the stable, brushing the deep russet coat of a pregnant mare.

In tight jeans and a shirt unbuttoned halfway down despite the chill in the air, Jason lounged across a stack of hay bales, looking like he was posing for *Blue Boy* magazine. He chewed on a long piece of hay. "I've told you about so many."

"Not in the last couple of weeks. No, it was the rich one. Nadia Peters."

He sat up. "How did you meet her?"

"She came to the exhibit." Careful not to look at him, she said, "You were right. She is quite attractive."

"Do I know your type, or what?"

"Yes, you do. And there was something about her . . ."

She stopped brushing as she remembered Nadia's mesmerizing blue eyes and the black hair that brushed her shirt collar, curling up slightly at the ends—an arresting combination indeed. And who could forget the long, tapering fingers that Celine just knew would please a woman? She would have let Nadia kiss her that night, but not wanting to seem like an impatient high school kid, had resisted making that known. Although, riding in the car, sitting so close, feeling the heat between them, she had felt herself inexplicably bound to this stranger. There was no doubt in her mind they would be together some day. Had she found at last her true soul mate?

"So, her line of work didn't dissuade you?"

She resumed her brushing, not answering right away as she wrestled silently with her conflicted emotions. It was true that war profiteering was abhorrent to her, but could what Nadia did truly be defined that way?

"We didn't really talk about that," she said finally. "She steered the conversation away from her and to me. I get the feeling she's a very private person."

Jason laughed. "Like you're not? Getting information out of you is next to impossible. That's one reason Jennifer left."

Celine turned to look at him. "Jennifer told you that?"

"Well, not in so many words. She used to confide in me some. You were so reticent about talking about your feelings. I know you lesbians like to do all that processing, and you refused to process."

She brushed more vigorously. "I have nothing to process."

Jason came over and took the brush from her hand. "You're going to make her bald," he said. "C'mon, let's go have some of Maria's great hot chocolate."

As they walked up from the stables, she said, "She asked to buy Obsidian. Told me she was a 'collector' of beautiful things. I told her I didn't believe in collecting animals."

"She doesn't strike me as the kind of person who takes no for an answer."

"Maybe not, but in this instance she'll have to."

At the house, they were surprised to see a hired car with tinted windows parked in front. Maria came quickly out the door. "You have a visitor," she said. "A Ms. Nadia Peters. I tried to put her in the sun room, but she preferred the study."

"It's so dark in there." Celine stripped off her coat and tossed it on the porch swing. "No matter. Bring us some coffee, please." She turned to Jason. "Are you coming in?"

Grinning, he shook his head. "No way. I'll not interfere with the path of true love."

"Oh, you . . ."

He kissed her cheek. "Besides, Mom's probably got dinner almost ready. I expect a full report tomorrow."

He bounded down the steps. Celine waved, then came into the entryway. She paused to look in the mirror, wishing she'd had some notice that Nadia would be visiting. She shook her hair free of its ponytail, liking the way her curls fell just below her shoulders. She'd often wished for blonde hair rather than her rather plain light brown, though she'd been told more than once that it complemented her green eyes. Her cheeks were pink from the walk, and her lips looked swollen, as if she'd been kissing.

She brushed some horse hair from her striped cotton shirt, then walked down the hall to the study. She pushed open the door. Nadia stood near the window, holding back the dark blue drapery. She let it drop into place as she turned to face Celine. Dressed in tight, black jeans and a blue suede shirt that complemented her blue eyes, she took Celine's breath away.

"Hello, Celine," she said. "I hope you don't mind my dropping by unannounced."

That voice. A surge of desire coursed through her body. She couldn't speak. Those amazing blue eyes captured her gaze, holding her like an animal caught in headlights. Stinging blood rushed to her cheeks while her heart thumped painfully in her chest. She put a hand to her throat, feeling her pulse strong and hard against her fingers. She licked her lips. Nadia took a step toward her.

Forcing herself to look away, Celine walked around her desk so she could sit down. "Not at all," she managed to say as she switched on the desk lamp. She indicated the chair where Nadia should sit. "But I am surprised to see you."

"I just wanted to tell you again how much I enjoyed our dinner the other night."

Celine smiled. "A phone call would have sufficed, but thank you. Can you stay for dinner tonight? Maria makes a mean paella."

"I'd love to stay." She paused, letting her words take on a deeper meaning. "Would I be able to talk you into giving me a private tour?"

"Of course." Celine stood. "Would now be a good time, or do you prefer to wait until after dinner?"

Nadia looked out the window. The sun was low in the sky and mostly obscured by clouds. Darkness would fall within the hour. "Now would be fine." She rose from her chair.

Celine pushed the button on an intercom. "Yes, Miss Celine?" Maria's voice answered.

"Ms. Peters will be staying for dinner." She looked at Nadia. "And her driver too?" Nadia nodded. "Yes, her driver too. Can you please make your paella?"

"Of course. Dinner will be in about two hours then."

"Good. Thank you." Celine came from around the desk. "Would you like to walk or ride?"

"Let's ride."

A stablehand helped saddle up two horses, one of them a dark gray flecked with silver and the other a chestnut with black mane and tail. Celine could tell immediately that Nadia was an accomplished rider. She looked as if she'd been born in the saddle.

"You're riding Diamond Dust," Celine said as they turned their horses toward the south pasture. "She won only three races in her career, but had lots of second- and third-place finishes too. She's had several foals, but last year I retired her." She patted her horse. "And this is Winston. He's always been purely a pleasure horse. He suffered an injury when he was barely two years old, so he never raced."

"None of the other breeders can even hope to compete with you. I don't think I've ever seen such perfect creatures."

Pleased at the compliment, Celine felt a flush of pride. "I just wish my father could have lived to see it," she said. "It was his dream. I think that is what motivated me. I believe that wherever he is, he knows and is proud of me." She urged Winston into an easy trot. "But you don't want to hear all that sentimental stuff."

"On the contrary," Nadia said as she too spurred her horse into a trot. "I want to know everything about you."

"You said that before. Why is that? You hardly know me."

"What better way to get to know you?"

"Why me?"

"If I may be totally honest . . ."

Celine nodded, then held her breath.

Nadia continued. "I felt an instant connection with you when we met. It was as if I had found what I've been looking for my whole life."

Celine felt a shiver go up her spine. It was exactly what she had felt herself. How could two people from totally different worlds find each other and know immediately? Feeling too overwhelmed to respond, she set Winston into a gallop. She could hear Nadia close behind. It wouldn't take long for Diamond Dust to overtake Winston. Sure enough, the former racer passed them by. Nadia looked magnificent on a horse. Posture perfect, knees tight against Dust's sides, she rode far ahead, pulling up only when she got to the fencing around the paddock where most of Celine's valuable horses grazed contentedly.

She sat watching Celine approach. It was getting darker by the minute, but Celine could still see the brilliant blue of her eyes. Hypnotic was the only term Celine could think of. She slowed Winston to a walk and came up beside them.

"You're an excellent rider." She jumped down off her horse. Nadia followed suit. They tied the reins to the fence. "You must own at least one horse."

"I have a full stable, but none of my animals can match yours."

A high whinny caught their attention. Obsidian had realized Celine was there. He galloped across the field, almost fading into the blackness of the coming night. The other horses took off running too, their outlines etched against the last light of the day. Obsidian stopped at the fence, the breath steaming from his nostrils. Celine wrapped her arms around his neck, inhaling the strong horse scent of him. It was one of the best smells in the world. He nuzzled her breast pocket. She reached in and took out some sugar cubes.

"I can see why you won't sell him," Nadia said, her velvet voice coming out of the deepening twilight to wrap Celine in its seductive spell.

Celine leaned against the fence, her face tilted up. Nadia moved closer, but this time Celine did not move away. She closed her eyes as Nadia approached, her lips tingling with anticipation. Nadia's lips brushed hers, ever so softly. Nadia's hands felt warm, even through the sleeves of Celine's corduroy jacket. "Nadia," she said, her breath becoming ragged.

In answer, Nadia kissed her deeply, her tongue playing with Celine's. Celine felt her knees go weak, but the fence supported her. Then Nadia's mouth was on Celine's throat. Her teeth grazed ever so gently, yet something made Celine's heart jump with fright. She fought the urge to push Nadia away. Nadia kissed her way across Celine's neck and down over her collarbone. Celine groaned, her fervor make a fire in her blood. She wrapped her arms around Nadia, pulling her in closer. Nadia thrust her leg between Celine's, pushing up against her woman's heat. Again, Celine felt the prick of Nadia's teeth. She gasped, her eyes opening in alarm.

Nadia felt the blood pulsing in Celine's jugular. God, she wanted this woman. It would be so easy to turn her, to make her one with the night. But she'd vowed that when she found her true soul mate, she would turn her only with full consent. Searching for more than four hundred years, she'd left a trail of death and broken hearts behind her, always eluding those who would destroy her. She'd surrounded herself with loyal guardians willing to give up their own lives to protect her. She'd never understood until the moment she'd met Celine why anyone would give their life for another.

Nadia held Celine tight, the strength of her fingers bruising Celine's arms even through the thickness of her jacket. She ran her teeth along Celine's sweet-smelling neck, wanting to taste her, to drink the life's blood that sustained her. But she also wanted to make love to this woman—to bring Celine to heights of passion she'd never had before. Celine gasped. Nadia sensed her fear. She looked deep into Celine's frightened eyes, smiling as Celine relaxed into her arms.

"I want you," she whispered into Celine's ear as she lowered her to the ground. She unbuttoned Celine's jacket, then her shirt. Nadia trailed her tongue along Celine's collarbone, then down between her breasts and farther still, across her warm belly and to the satin barrier of her underwear. A slight touch and Celine raised her hips, letting Nadia slide her jeans and panties down, leaving her exposed to the evening air.

Nadia dropped to her knees, letting her fingers run up and down Celine's body. Celine moaned softly, moving ever so slightly at Nadia's touch. Nadia traced the fine blue veins beneath Celine's pale skin. She pulled Celine up into an embrace, leaning down to kiss Celine's soft lips. She loved the feel of a naked woman in her arms. Supporting Celine's back with one arm, she brushed her other hand over Celine's breasts, liking the way her nipples responded. Rosy and erect, they beckoned her mouth. She sucked in first one, then the other.

"Oh . . ."

Celine moaned and arched against her, her hands twining into Nadia's hair, urging her on. Nadia bit the nipple in her mouth, making Celine cry out, but when she tried to pull away, Celine held her head in place. Grinning, Nadia sucked and bit harder, feeling Celine squirm beneath her, listening to her deep groan of pleasure. Her free hand moved over the hills and valleys of Celine's body, stopping only at moist curls between Celine's legs. Her fingers played through the hair, stroking the sensitive flesh between vulva and leg, liking the way Celine opened her legs to her. Her fingers caressed the folds of her labia, sliding deep into warm heat, becoming coated with sticky wetness.

"Nadia, please . . ." Celine moaned, arching against Nadia's hand.

"You like that?" Nadia whispered. "You want to feel me inside you?"

"Yes, dear God, yes!"

Laughing, Nadia said, "So eager, my lovely Celine."

She kissed her fiercely then, letting her tongue plunge deeply into her mouth, claiming her. Celine sucked greedily on her tongue. Nadia pulled away suddenly so she could stretch Celine out. Celine moaned again, then cried out as Nadia's fingers thrust inside her. Nadia's teeth nibbled ever so lightly along her neck, before she moved down over Celine's body until she lay between her widespread legs.

Breathing in the scent of her, Nadia licked and sucked Celine's clit, her fingers keeping up a steady rhythm. Celine bucked beneath her, her body raising off the ground again and again. Nadia grabbed Celine's ass with her free hand, tempted to take Celine to what she suspected would be an untried new pleasure.

As if sensing Nadia's intent, Celine clenched her ass cheeks tight. "No, not now," she breathed. "Not yet."

Nadia couldn't help but moan herself as she continued to lick, then suck, then lick again. She plunged her fingers ever deeper inside Celine, loving the feel of tightness surrounding them. Nadia's already acute senses heightened even more as Celine journeyed toward climax. She could literally hear the rush of blood, the sound of Celine's beating heart. She couldn't help but nip the swollen lips she sucked into her mouth. She groaned at the taste of blood. Sweet. Intoxicating.

"Yes, Nadia! Oh yes!"

Nadia held tight as Celine thrashed beneath her, loving the feel of Celine's hands grasping her hair, then the sharp prick of nails on her shoulders. Celine raised her knees up just as Nadia tasted the gush of fluid in her mouth. Oh that it could nourish her the way she needed.

"Oh God, oh God!"

Nadia almost laughed out loud as Obsidian lowered his head and snorted. Had he never heard two women making love before? Withdrawing her fingers, she continued to gently lick Celine's clit until she felt her final trembling release.

Celine sighed. "Oh woman, you should package that mouth."

Nadia did laugh then, deep and long. The sound sent Obsidian into a gallop. "I am glad I could please you."

"I can't move."

"That's the idea."

As the night surrounded them, Nadia took Celine into her arms, finding unexpected joy at the feel of the heat from her mortal body, breathing in the woman smell of her, pleasingly pungent and strong. Her skin tingled where Celine gently stroked with her fingers. She couldn't remember the last time she'd felt something so . . . so human.

Celine fingered the buttons of Nadia's shirt. Nadia stopped her fingers and kissed the tip of each one.

"Not this time, my love," she said, smiling at the instant disappointment she saw in Celine's lovely green eyes.

And at that moment, she knew she'd found the one.

Chapter V

Has it really been five months?" Celine asked over dinner at the ever-famous Tavern on the Green.

"Five wonderful months," Nadia said with a smile. She reached into the pocket of her jacket. "I have something for you."

Celine took the unmistakable pale blue box. Inside was another box, this one covered in black velvet. "Oh Nadia," she said, taking out a diamond tennis bracelet, "this is beautiful."

"Not as beautiful as you. Do you like it?"

"A diamond bracelet from Tiffany's? I love it." She leaned across the table to kiss her. "Thank you so much. But I don't have anything for you."

"Nothing expected. Don't think of it as an anniversary present. I bought it for you simply because I love you."

Celine held out her wrist. "Put it on for me?"

With a smile, Nadia obliged. The touch of her fingers made Celine flush with desire. Her skin tingled. Grinning ever more broadly, as if she knew exactly the effect she'd had, Nadia leaned back in her chair. "So, tell me. How do you like New York? With all your traveling, it's hard to believe this is truly your first time."

"Just never got around to it. I'm not a city girl, but I enjoyed myself immensely today. I'm just sorry you couldn't do the sight-seeing thing with me."

"An urgent matter came up at TechChip that I had to take care of. Orders for our microchips have tripled in the last month." She took a sip of wine. "But Anna loved getting the day off to act as your tour guide."

"You're sure it's not that you're not feeling well? You've not been yourself the last few days."

"I'm sure. Things have been very hectic at the office, that's all. A little rest and I'll be fine."

"You're more of a night owl, aren't you?"

Nadia nibbled on a slice of bread. "Why do you say that?"

Celine shrugged. "It just seems like we always do things at night. I can't think of a single date where we've done something during the day."

"It's a little difficult to take time off work."

"Well, but what about the weekends? How about we pack a picnic lunch this Saturday and spend the day at Central Park? I've been dying to see Strawberry Fields, the tribute to John Lennon."

"I thought you had a big auction?"

"Darn, you're right. I leave for Kentucky on Friday morning." Celine took Nadia's hand. "Come with me."

"Maybe next time, darling." She pointed to Celine's nearly empty plate. "Are you about ready to go? We need to hurry if we're going to get to the theatre on time."

"Let me just go to the ladies' room." Celine leaned over to kiss Nadia before she headed toward the back of the restaurant.

Nadia called the waiter, shaking her head at his query to package up her leftovers. Smoked salmon was not what she was hungry for. In fact, her true hunger was becoming once again almost uncontrollable. And the weakness was upon her. It had been days since she'd had human blood. Her thirst was so strong, she imagined everyone in the restaurant could feel it too.

It was time to tell Celine the truth. So many times in the past weeks, Nadia had nearly lost her resolve. It was torture to make love to Celine, to feel the blood flowing in her veins, to see it pulsing in the hollow of Celine's throat. Her mouth and teeth ached every time they brushed that soft neck or that moist spot where leg met torso. It would be so easy to make just a little nip on the inside of Celine's thigh during the heat of passion when pain didn't register.

Nadia groaned. Just the thought of it made her crazy. But she was afraid she would lose control . . . would devour Celine until she died. The blood flow from the artery near a woman's sex was more powerful than any other. A drink from there could sustain her for several weeks. She put her head in her hands. Tonight. She would have to tell her tonight.

The hand to her shoulder made her flinch.

"Nadia? Are you all right?"

She smiled at Celine. "Yes, darling. Like I said, just a bit tired."

"We don't have to do to the show. Let me take you home."

Nadia stood up. She could see the concern in Celine's beautiful green eyes. "No, I'll be fine. You've been wanting to see this play."

Outside the restaurant, her chauffeur was waiting. He silently nodded toward the back of the limo. Getting in, she instructed him to take them to the theatre. Once there, she gave Celine her ticket. "You go on in," she said. "I'll be with you momentarily."

She watched until Celine was safely inside the building. Without a word, the chauffeur drove to a nearby parking garage, where he drove to a nearly empty level and then got out to open her door. Nadia climbed into a compartment hidden behind a false wall at the back of the limo. It was a smaller version of where she'd been sitting with Celine, and completely soundproofed. Only a keen observer would realize the inside of the limo was smaller than it appeared from the outside. She stroked the cheek of the frightened woman waiting there for her.

"You are so lovely," she said, staring into eyes as black and luminous as the night sky. "Don't be afraid. I won't hurt you." The woman sighed and visibly relaxed as Nadia continued to caress her. She melted into the power of Nadia's mesmerizing gaze. When it was all over, she would have no memory of what had happened, starting with her abduction. "You smell so good," Nadia said as she kissed the woman gently on the lips, then her eyelids. She'd already deftly unbuttoned her shirt and unzipped her jeans.

Nadia briefly wondered what her chauffeur had done to get the woman into the limo, but she didn't really care. All that mattered was that she was here now, but there wasn't much time. Nadia kissed the woman again, all the while tracing her fingers over her dusky skin. The woman whimpered just a bit, grabbing Nadia's hair and urging her downward. She was responding faster than most of Nadia's victims. Nadia smiled against the luscious mound of her breasts. It didn't matter. Gay or straight, all women wanted one thing—that most powerful of all releases.

"Patience, my beauty," Nadia said as she kissed her again, then tore her bra aside to take first one swollen nipple then the other into her mouth. The woman moaned long and loud, then gasped as Nadia's fingers dipped into her already overflowing sex. Fear could be a strong aphrodisiac, Nadia knew, turning to lust in mere seconds. As long as you had the right partner.

"Help me," Nadia whispered. "Lift your hips."

The woman did as she was bid, letting Nadia pull her jeans and panties down. "Please," she said, once again grabbing hold of Nadia's head.

Nadia went down, feeling dizzy herself as she breathed in the incomparable scent of a woman ready for sex. She buried her tongue into her, all the while squeezing her nipples. The woman was squirming beneath her, her breathing becoming shallow and ragged. She was good and ready. It wouldn't take long for her to climax.

"Mmmm, you taste so good."

"Oh yes, right there. Oh dear Lord, please don't stop."

Nadia licked and sucked on the woman's clit, faster and faster as her movements indicated her quick rush to release. And when Nadia thrust fingers deep inside her, she screamed.

"Oh fuck! Yes!"

Nadia could feel the rhythm of the woman's orgasm as she squeezed Nadia's fingers tight. She gushed like a hot, bubbling spring, her hips bucking against the seat while her legs gripped Nadia's head. Swiftly, Nadia turned and bit deep into the woman's thigh. The woman screamed again and again as Nadia's fingers continued to thrust ever deeper into her. Her blood streamed into Nadia's mouth, red hot and metallic. Nadia felt its powerful energy flow into her, replacing her weakness with strength.

The woman's movements stilled, yet she groaned softly. Nadia drank her fill, then released the coagulant that would stop the bleeding. It was always easier to feast when her victim wasn't thrashing about. Leaving the woman sprawled naked on the seat, Nadia sat up and looked in the mirror. Contrary to common superstition, she could see herself in a mirror, but only at night. And now she saw a woman with blue eyes turned a glowing red, teeth sharp and face smeared with blood. Her dark hair was completely disheveled. She hadn't intended on taking her victim this way. It was supposed to be just a quick fix—an easy bite to the neck—but her thoughts during dinner had taken on a life of their own.

Using pre-moistened cloths, she cleaned the blood off of herself. There was more than usual, for it covered her hands and arms, as well as her face and neck. She'd been careless. Oh, for a shower.

"Damn," she said as she noticed the red stain on her clothes too. She opened a small storage unit and took out a change of clothes. How to explain that to Celine? She glanced at her watch. The play would be starting in mere moments. It would be dark. Maybe she wouldn't notice? She changed quickly and exited the limo.

She spoke to her ever-silent chauffeur. Having rescued him five years ago from a drunken mob of fraternity boys out for some vicious gay bashing, he'd become her most loyal protector. His uncanny ability to know her needs, sometimes before she herself knew, made her wonder if he too was an immortal creature of some sort. She wasn't arrogant enough to believe she and her kind could be the only anomalies of nature.

"Take her to the park, then call nine-one-one. And make sure all her medical expenses are taken care of." She smiled. "Anonymously, of course," she said, knowing full well she didn't need to tell him that.

Celine shifted in her seat, looking at her watch for the hundredth time. Where was Nadia? The play would be starting any minute now. At least they had an aisle seat. Celine hated it when people arrived late and made everyone stand up while they went to their seats. She inevitably was in the row behind so her view was blocked. Nadia slid quietly into the seat beside her.

"Where have you been?" she whispered. "I was getting concerned."

"Sorry." Nadia took Celine's hand and kissed it. "An important business call came in just as I got to the lobby. I took it outside."

"Is your cell phone off now?"

"Shhh," a patron behind them hissed as the lights went down and the orchestra started.

Nadia leaned over. "I have something important to tell you later."

The same irate patron smacked her on the shoulder with his playbill.

"Sorry," she said, resting back in her seat, holding Celine's delicate hand in her own.

Sitting on the sofa in Nadia's penthouse apartment, Celine said, "You are absolutely joking, aren't you?" She set her wineglass down so hard, some of the golden liquid spilled out onto the glass-topped coffee table.

"I've never been more serious."

Celine laughed. "I don't believe you for one second. There are no such things as vampires."

Nadia blinked. Laughter was not what she had expected. She got up from the sofa, killing the urge to pace and instead stood looking at Celine. "Yes, there are. We do exist. We have for hundreds of years."

Celine laughed again. "Well, I'm sorry. I just don't believe you. Creatures of night drinking people's blood and all that malarkey? You've been seeing too many Hollywood movies." She picked up her wineglass again. "Frankly, I am kind of shocked that you, of all people, would say such a thing. You're such a brilliant, smart woman."

"Celine, please—"

"I know, you belong to one of those weird societies. Like the one where they dress up in animal costumes and have sex." She shook her head. "Do you all get together and watch those old movies and TV shows, playacting out parts?"

"No, it's nothing like that. I can prove it to you."

Celine stood up and took Nadia's arm. "Okay then, prove it." She marched her over to the entryway where an oversized antique mirror hung on the wall. Gazing at their reflections, she smiled. "Well, look at that. I can see you in the mirror. Hmmm, guess you're not a vampire tonight."

"That's just a myth."

"How convenient." Celine went back into the living room. "Five months we've been together, and I've never seen this side of you." She faced Nadia. "I don't think I like it much."

Nadia frowned, but then wondered what she had really expected. "I don't usually tell the women I'm with the truth, but I care about you. No, I love you. Madly. You are my soul mate. I want us to be together forever."

"Oh, so you want to bite me and turn me into a vampire too."

"In a word, yes."

Celine laughed again, but there was no humor in it. "Oh God,

I've fallen in love with a lunatic. I find the woman of my dreams, and she's certifiably crazy." She went over to the bar. "I need something stronger than wine," she said as she poured a whisky, neat. She gulped it down, then poured another.

Nadia couldn't help the feeling of joy at Celine's words. "Am I really the woman of your dreams?"

"You were."

"Are you telling me you've fallen out of love with me just like that?" She snapped her fingers.

Celine poured yet another whiskey. "No, I still love you, but I think our relationship is over."

Nadia walked over and grabbed her arms. "No! I won't let you go!"

Celine squirmed away. "You're hurting me." She put the coffee table between them. "What did you expect me to do? Embrace this fantasy you have? Tell me, do Anna and Edwin play along with you?"

"They protect me."

"Ah, so they do play along. Well, I've heard of weirder things, I suppose. There was that Congressman a few years back who allegedly liked to be flogged while he had his toenails painted in ten different colors."

Nadia came around the coffee table and took Celine's arm again, gently this time. "I swear to you, I am telling the truth."

"Okay then, go ahead. Turn into a vampire. Let me see your teeth."

"I can't. I already feasted tonight." *Damnation, I should have waited.*

"You just have every convenient excuse." Celine went to the hall closet and collected her shawl and purse. "Please have your chauffeur take me to a hotel. I don't care which one or where. I just want to leave."

"Very well." She picked up an intercom phone, trying not to show her anguish. "Joseph, please bring the limo around. Ms.

Ashton will be going to a hotel tonight. No, I don't know which one. You can use the cell phone in the car to call and find out who's got a room available. Just make sure it's one of the best."

"I'll be going back to the ranch tomorrow. Please don't call me."

As the door slammed shut, Nadia was overcome with a crushing sense of despair, something she'd not felt since the last time she was human. She clenched her fist. She could take Celine against her will. She dropped to the couch, clutching a pillow in her arms.

"No," she said.

Chapter VI

It wasn't until two days later when she got back to the ranch that Celine really cried. She couldn't believe that her whole life had changed in the course of a couple of hours. After the play, Nadia had made love to her in the back of the limo on the ride to the penthouse. If she closed her eyes, she could still feel Nadia's mouth against her throat, feel the thrust of her fingers. It was an exquisite agony to think about it now.

Having sent Jason to the Kentucky auction to take her place, Celine saddled up Obsidian and took off for a ride around the ranch. She had to do something to take her mind off Nadia. It had been a while since she'd done a thorough check of her property. She trusted her ranch hands completely in making sure all the fences were in repair and the No Trespassing signs were honored. She didn't allow hunting on her land, but there'd been times when she or the others had discovered hunters' blinds deep in the forest. It gave her great pleasure to tear them down, but it was a never-ending chore.

She spurred Obsidian into a good gallop, liking the way his powerful muscles felt between her legs. With the wind in her hair and the sun on her face, she could pretend for a moment that she didn't have a care in the world. They galloped across fields and over streams and along dirt roads, racing through the forest and then meadows filled with butterflies. She finally pulled him to a stop near a small pond, both of them breathing heavily and covered with sweat. A lone willow tree offered some shade. She removed Obsidian's saddle and gave him a pat on the rear. He took a long drink from the pond while she did likewise from a bottle of water. Throwing a blanket under the tree, she settled in the shade to eat a peanut butter and jelly sandwich.

It was utterly quiet. It seemed as if it was too hot for even the birds. The tall meadow grasses swayed gently in the light breeze, playing tag with butterflies and bumblebees. Leaning back against the tree trunk, she gazed out over the pond. Sun glinted off the water, giving it a silvery sheen. She could see turtles sunning themselves on a floating log. Now and then a dragonfly flitted into view and out again. The peacefulness here drained the tension from her body. She sighed deeply, thinking of her last conversation with Nadia. What Nadia had told her should be funny, it was so absurd. But it wasn't funny.

As Celine sat there watching the pond, she couldn't help but recall that she'd never been anywhere with Nadia during the daytime. They always went out in the early evening or later, and it was the same if she came to visit Celine at the ranch. Come to think of it, every window where Nadia lived and worked and played was tinted. Celine bit into her sandwich, remembering now how Nadia always seemed to have a lot of food leftover on her plate. What did she always tell the waiters? *I guess I'm just not hungry tonight.* The mirror thing didn't seem to be part of the whole vampire equation, although the antique mirror in the penthouse was really the only one Celine could remember seeing, other than the smaller one in the guest bathroom she always used.

Could it really be possible? She remembered times, too, when Nadia seemed listless and tired, then suddenly would be her usual self. It was not all that odd for someone to be tired, but thinking back now, to Celine it seemed as if with Nadia it happened frequently. Was it a meal of blood that gave Nadia her energy back?

And how did she get it? Did she prowl the streets at night, attacking unsuspecting humans? Or did she have minions who procured blood for her? Just how much "protection" did Edwin and Anna give her? Come to think of it, her chauffeur had always seemed a bit peculiar.

Celine shivered. It was too gruesome to think about. Could she really have been sleeping with—making love with—such a monster? She raised a hand to her neck, thinking back to all the times Nadia had kissed her there, had grazed her ever so lightly with her teeth. She shuddered again.

But oh God, the things Nadia had done to her—the way she'd made her feel, especially the hypnotic effect of those incredible blue eyes and the caress of that velvet voice. No woman had ever captured her the way Nadia had, or loved her like that. Celine moaned aloud just thinking about it. She couldn't imagine not having Nadia Peters in her life.

And she thought too about loving Nadia, remembering the taste and scent of her, the way Nadia responded to her caresses, how she arched into Celine's mouth. She moaned again.

As Celine reached for her water bottle, the sunlight caught her diamond bracelet, igniting its brilliant fire. She scrambled to her feet and quickly saddled Obsidian. She owed it to herself to at least talk with Nadia again.

After giving Maria the night off and telling Roy, her ranch foreman, to keep the other ranch hands away from the house, Celine paced nervously as she waited. The slamming of a car door made her heart beat faster. She felt her resolve crumbling as Nadia strode into the living room without knocking, for she'd never looked so handsome and desirable as she did this night. The flash of those blue eyes and the pout of her full lips were irresistible. Celine looked away.

Nadia was beside her in two seconds, lifting Celine's chin so she had no choice but to look at her. She kissed Celine, deep and hard, taking possession. Celine gasped at the sensation of Nadia's tongue in her mouth, feeling the rush of desire overwhelm her. Nadia crushed Celine tightly to her. Celine wrapped her fingers in Nadia's hair, moaning as Nadia's leg came between hers and pushed against her.

"I want you," Nadia said, "and you know you want me. We belong together. It is our destiny, our fate."

"I thought so too." Celine fought against the temptation, but she was losing. "Oh," she gasped, as Nadia's hands went beneath her shirt. She couldn't help but arch her back to Nadia's touch. Her nipples strained against the confines of her lace bra, aching for Nadia's mouth, and yes, even her teeth.

"Let me have you," Nadia murmured against her neck, her breath hot against Celine's skin.

Breath. How could that be? Weren't vampires supposed to be dead? And soulless?

As if she'd read her thoughts, Nadia said, "You've seen too many Hollywood movies." She unbuttoned Celine's shirt, then pressed her lips to Celine's cleavage. Celine groaned and threw her head back, pressing Nadia's mouth against her. Nadia unclasped the bra, pulling it roughly from Celine's body. She took a swollen nipple into her mouth, sucking and biting hard.

"Sweet Jesus," Celine moaned, flinching at the piercing pain that quickly dissolved into exquisite pleasure. Then she was up against the wall as Nadia's hand pushed her skirt to her waist and ripped her panties off. Celine felt a flood of liquid down her legs, then Nadia's fingers probing her, sliding into her, fluttering against her clit. "Nadia," she said. "Nadia."

Celine slid down the wall and onto the floor, feeling the scratchy wool of the rug cut into her back and buttocks. She didn't care. All she cared about was Nadia. Nadia, whose mouth kissed her lips, then her cheeks, then her throat, trailing down to suck first one nipple then the other, before continuing on across her belly. Celine spread her legs, giving Nadia access to all of her. She held Nadia's head, felt the way it moved as Nadia played her tongue across Celine's clit while her fingers squeezed her nipples.

Celine moaned and arched her back as Nadia licked and sucked her labia before thrusting her tongue deep inside. "Oh yes," Celine cried out, pushing against Nadia's mouth. "I want to feel you inside me."

"Mmmm, I want that too," Nadia said. She pulled back just long enough to put her hand where her mouth had been.

"Please," Celine begged. She thrust her hips forward, urging Nadia's fingers to take possession of her.

With a sense of gratitude that she was once again allowed to touch Celine, Nadia eagerly gave in to Celine's pleas. She needn't have worried about not having lube. Not this time. Celine was plenty wet. Nadia's fingers slid easily inside her, slurping as they went. Celine squirmed beneath her, alternately moving her hips back and forth, then pushing forward. Her fingers grasped Nadia's hair, pulling it tight against Nadia's skull. Celine was alternately moaning and sighing now, her words incoherent.

Nadia moved her tongue rapidly across Celine's clit, taking turns licking and sucking. She could feel Celine's vaginal walls clench and unclench around her fingers. She thrust another one inside, wishing after all that she had lube. She knew how Celine liked sometimes to have Nadia's whole hand inside her, but it would be too risky now.

"Oh God," Celine said. "You're driving me crazy."

And still Nadia played with her. It was too early for Celine's release. She wanted to savor every taste, every smell. Nadia knew just how to bring Celine to the edge and back again. Celine whimpered now with frustration. Nadia smiled, licking her ever so slowly, letting her fingers move in and out. With her other hand she stroked and squeezed Celine's nipples.

Celine's body was flushed deep red. Nadia could literally smell the blood running through Celine's veins, could hear every beat of her heart. The rushing of the blood grew louder and louder to Nadia's ears, like the flood surge of a river after a heavy rain. She could feel her canines forming, feel the saliva in her mouth mingle with the juices of Celine's desire. The blood lust was upon her. She growled softly, plunging her fingers ever deeper inside. Celine was almost screaming now.

"Oh, oh, oh!"

Nadia held tight as Celine thrashed beneath her. Celine's fingernails raked across her shoulders and back.

"Oh God! Nadia! Yes, oh yes. God, don't stop!"

And as Celine shuddered with the force of her orgasm, it took every ounce of self-control Nadia had not to plunge her teeth deep into Celine's thigh. Wanting to give Celine more but unable to continue, Nadia wrenched away with a deep guttural groan. No! She would not take Celine without her consent. Breathing heavily, Nadia crawled away, fighting the roaring in her ears and the instinct that made her want to tear open Celine's throat. Collapsing onto the welcome coolness of the tiled floor in the entryway, she concentrated on breathing slowly.

What seemed like hours later, she felt a tentative hand on her shoulder.

"Nadia? Are you okay?"

Nadia shook her head. She didn't yet trust herself to look at Celine.

"Nadia, please look at me. Tell me what's wrong. Let me help you."

"You can't." Even to her own ears, her voice sounded strange. Strangled.

Celine's hands were gentle as she made Nadia look at her. Her small gasp and wide eyes were the only reaction to what Nadia knew must be a frightening sight. And certainly not an attractive one. Sure enough, Celine used the skirt she still wore to wipe the spittle from the corners of Nadia's mouth, and then the sweat from her brow and cheeks. Nadia felt her teeth retract as Celine smoothed back her damp hair and caressed her forehead.

Wrapping her arms around Nadia, Celine said, "I want to give you what you need."

Narrowing her eyes, she wondered briefly if she should make certain Celine would not remember this night. "Are you sure?" Nadia whispered.

In answer, Celine swept aside her hair and tilted her head. The pale expanse of her beautiful throat beckoned. With a groan, Nadia sat up and took Celine into her arms. She kissed her neck, softly at first; then with a sigh, she bit deep. Celine cried out, her fingers clutching Nadia's arms. She struggled at first, then relaxed as Nadia drank from her. Nadia stopped only when Celine lost consciousness.

In total control once again, Nadia lifted Celine into her arms and carried her to the bedroom. Grinning, she took off the skirt and cowboy boots Celine still wore, leaving her naked on the bed. Her body glowed ghostly pale in the moonlight, the inside of her thighs still glistening with moisture. Staring down at the woman she loved, Nadia could only dream about the day when they would truly be as one, for though Celine had given herself willingly tonight, it was not yet true consent. Nadia dampened a towel from the bathroom and carefully wiped the blood off of Celine's skin before going to the living room to quickly straighten things up. It would not do to have Maria come home in the morning and find Celine's clothes strewn about. And yes, there was blood to clean up there as well.

In the shower afterward, Nadia let the scalding water rain over her, watching as it turned from bright red to pink to clear.

Chapter VII

A few days later, Celine woke to the rumblings of low-flying aircraft. Though not an unusual occurrence these past few weeks, their number seemed to be greater. She got out of bed and went to the window, pushing aside the curtains. She counted at least twenty planes in the sky. Pulling on a robe, she hurried to the kitchen, where Maria was brewing coffee.

"Maria," she said, "have you heard anything on the news this morning?"

"Yes, ma'am. They say the hostilities have escalated. The President has put all branches of the military on full alert." She poured a mug of coffee and placed it in front of Celine. "They say he's even considering imposing martial law in the major cities."

"Martial law! That's crazy." She took a sip of coffee, scalding her tongue. "Damn it, Maria! I've told you not to brew this so hot!"

"Sorry."

"No, I'm sorry. I shouldn't yell at you like that."

She left the kitchen to go to her study. Once inside, she grabbed the phone, then set it down again as she decided not to call Nadia, not sure whether she'd be in Connecticut or New York. She touched her throat. She'd hardly had time to process their reconciliation, but that she loved Nadia was not in doubt. She smiled. Nor was Nadia's love for her. She shook her head, then picked up the phone again.

"Hi, Aunt Julia. Is Jason home?"

"He was called in to work early this morning."

Celine glanced at the clock. It was barely six a.m. "Do you know if it has something to do with the news this morning?"

"He didn't say."

"Thanks. Bye." Celine hung up the phone. Like hell he'd not said anything. She should have known better than to call her Aunt Julia.

Not really one to watch news broadcasts all day long, she nevertheless turned the TV on to CNN. Despite the early hour, the newscasters already looked nervous as hell, talking about escalating tensions, suspicious activity at foreign military bases, increased military visibility throughout the United States, lack of communications with other world leaders, and the movement of U.S. nuclear submarines and aircraft carriers. Could so much have really happened overnight? The news cameras brought live clips of mayors and governors alternately calling for calm from their citizens and an explanation from the President. Then came the news that the President and his Cabinet had been evacuated from the nation's capital to an undisclosed location. This time, the newscasters looked downright frightened.

"Oh dear God, this is it."

Celine hurried from the study to her bedroom. Throwing on clothes, she returned to the kitchen. "Maria," she said, "I want you and the others to gather all the food you can and take it to the basement. Fill anything that will hold water and take it down as well. Then fill all the bathtubs and sinks." She stopped for a moment to collect her thoughts. "We need to clear out the basement of all the furniture. Bring every blanket and sleeping bag you can find, anything that can be made into a makeshift bed."

Celine jumped into an old jeep and drove down to the stable. Of the six men and four women who worked for her, most of whom slept in quarters near the stable, two were already up starting their early morning chores. She could tell the horses inside were spooked already. How were the ones out in the paddocks?

"Roy. Jack. I need you to go to the house and help Maria. I don't know if you've heard the news this morning, but I think we're going to be attacked. We being the United States."

"You don't really believe that, do you?" Roy, her ranch foreman, asked.

"Yes, I do. Now go. I'll get the others up to take care of the horses."

The two men took off running toward the house. Celine banged on the bedroom doors of the others. Dressing quickly, they gathered together in the stable.

"I don't have time to get into the details now, but the news this morning is not good. I think the United States is on the verge of being attacked by Russia and its coalition. The President and his Cabinet have evacuated Washington."

There was a collective gasp from the others.

"We need to bring all the horses in from the fields to the stables. Fill all the water troughs and any other containers you can find. Fortunately, we just got a hay delivery so the barn is full. I want two of you to check every lock on every structure. I don't want anyone to be able to get into any of our buildings."

"Do you think we'll need more hands?" Amy asked.

"Yes, because I'll want round-the-clock security. There will be two of you on each twelve-hour shift in each stable, more if I see the need. Call any of your friends who need work. I'll pay top dollar, but let them know they'll be fired at the least little infraction." She pointed to Sandra and Andy. "You two go into town and get any supplies you can find. Of course, water is the most important. Get as many cases as you can. Snack foods, like protein bars, are good. First aid kits too."

The roar of planes overhead drew their attention. "This is really serious," Mike said.

"Thank God we don't live closer to Washington," Sam said. "I'll bet those people will be evacuating out our way."

It was true. Garrett County in Maryland was a good six or seven hours from the city. As the world political situation had deteriorated over the years, Celine had wondered sometimes if it would be better to live near what would be Ground Zero in the event of a nuclear attack. Wouldn't it be better to be pulverized right away? How long would it take for a radiation cloud to drift out their way? She'd even seriously considered moving her operations to the heart of the Midwest, but it was even less safe there given the fact they had all those bunkers and missile silos.

"I'm sure you're right," Celine said. "Which is all the more reason to be prepared. It can get ugly." She looked at their worried faces. "I will do my best to take care of you all, but we'll need to really be together as a team. If any of you are uncomfortable for any reason, you aren't obligated to stay."

"I think we're all just worried for our families," Harry said.

"Of course you are. And like I said, no one is obligated to stay."

The remaining ranch hands shuffled their feet, not looking at her or each other. Then they sort of huddled together to talk. Celine waited patiently. Not coincidentally, none of them had family close by. Celine had deliberately hired non-locals, bringing them in from as far away as Alaska. And though some of them were in semi-serious relationships, none were married and none had children. Celine had known that could change with any of them, but so far she'd been lucky. It had been her way of minimizing turnover. Hiring only the best, she'd paid outrageous wages to keep their loyalty.

It paid off when Taylor said, "We're with you."

Celine wasn't surprised Taylor had been chosen the de facto spokesperson. She'd been with Celine the longest, nearly eleven years.

"Thank you. Okay, the rest of you go round up the horses. And be sure to take a rifle with you. I'm not taking any chances."

"Me and Sam will check the locks and fill the water troughs," Harry said.

Andy and Sandra took off for town, while the others saddled up. Celine wanted to go out with them, but she knew everyone would be counting on her to make sure all went smoothly. Preparing to become a nation under siege was not something she'd planned on. Sam was right. Hordes of people would flee the cities and suburbs, heading for the illusion of safety to the few remaining rural areas. Her own worst enemies could very well be her own countrymen.

Her cell phone was ringing when she got back to the house. Before she could even say hello, Nadia asked, "Where are you?"

"At the ranch."

"Thank God. Don't you dare leave. I think you'll be safest there."

"I know that. Where are you? Did you leave the city last night like you'd planned?"

"No, but we're in the car now. They've already grounded non-military flights, so we couldn't use the helicopter." There was a pause. "The roads are already clogged. I don't know how long it will take to get to my country estate."

"Maybe you should come here."

"It would take longer."

"Maybe not. Think about it. You're traveling north from New York, same as everyone else. If you travel south toward Washington, everyone here is also traveling north and west. I think there will be less traffic. Who wants to come to DC knowing it's a prime target?"

"Hold on."

Celine could hear talking but not what they were saying. Finally, Nadia came back. "Okay, we'll give it a try. Hope to see you soon."

"Me too. Nadia?"

"Yes?"

"I love you."

"I love you too."

In just a few hours, the ranch hands had managed to get all the horses in from the paddocks and to the stables. Some horses had to be doubled up. If nothing came of all this, Celine resolved that she would build another stable. She walked from stall to stall, giving a carrot or an apple to each horse. She felt her throat grow tight at the thought of losing any of them, yet she knew it was a good possibility. If the United States did indeed come under nuclear attack, it would only be a matter of time before she and the others felt its effects. Besides the obvious biological hazards, there would be marauding bands of desperate people. Her horses would become a commodity—transportation or even food. And their food supplies would not last forever.

Coming to Obsidian's stall, she put her arms around his neck and sobbed. As if he understood her fear, he stayed perfectly still until she stopped crying. Sniffling, she stroked his soft, velvety nose. "It must be nice sometimes," she said, "not to understand what's going on."

Suddenly, Andy came running. She turned and gasped. "What happened to you?" She reached out. "Your eye . . ."

He was breathing heavily. "Me and Sandra . . . We ran into trouble in town. People are crazy. Some fellas tried to hijack the truck." He grimaced and pointed to his ever-swelling eye and bruised face. "I had to fight them off before Sandy managed to get a rifle from the truck and shoot one in his leg."

"Oh my God, is she all right?"

He grimaced again. "Got a bloody lip for her trouble, but once I got a hold of my rifle too, they scattered." He grinned. "But we got thirty cases of water from old Mr. Johnson, and all the rest of his protein bars. We cleaned up at the farmer's market too. Guess not many people thought of going there yet."

"You did good." She turned to Obsidian. "We got all the horses in too."

"I hope all this turns out to be unnecessary."

She turned back to him. "I do too, Andy. I do too."

At that moment, they heard sirens. It seemed as if every siren in town was going off. They ran outside. The roar of plane engines got louder and louder, until dozens of them appeared in the sky. From inside the house came screams. Celine and Andy ran, only to be met by Sam and Roy. Celine had never seen them so frightened.

"Those bastards have gone and done it!" Sam yelled.

"We're going to finish locking up the stables," Roy said calmly, though he could not hide the panic in his eyes.

"Yes. Be quick." *Oh my God, where is Nadia?* Celine hurried to the house. Inside, her people were glued to the TV set, most of them sobbing as they watched horrific images of something no one had imagined they would ever see—Hiroshima and Nagasaki replayed on American soil.

The grim-faced newscaster was blunt. "The United States came under nuclear attack thirty minutes ago. Several major cities, including Washington DC, have been hit. There are no reports as yet of casualties, but they are expected to number in the millions."

"And there never will be any reports," Amy said. "Those cities are gone!"

"Where are these people reporting from? I'd have thought they were in the very cities being attacked," Taylor said.

"Our affiliates in those cities are most likely dead." Visibly shaken, the anchorman paused before continuing. "The images we bring you are satellite images that our station here in Des Moines is still able to—"

The TV screen suddenly went blank. Taylor snatched up the remote to quickly flip through the channels. Nothing but static. Then she found one with a grainy picture and faded sound.

"I don't know how many viewers out there are able to get this broadcast, but I and my camera crew are ten miles west of Baltimore," the reporter said. The camera panned to a view of the clogged highway. "You can see that no one is going anywhere. There have been a few instances of violence along this road, but so far most people seem to be remaining calm."

"Only ten miles from Baltimore," Celine said. "If that city is struck, they are goners. I think I'd leave the car and run."

"The U.S. has retaliated," the reporter continued. "Nuclear strikes were initiated against targets in the United Republic of Russia, as well as several Middle Eastern states. The President has declared martial law. He is expected to speak to the American people within the next half hour."

"Lord, how many will be left to talk to," Betty said, her voice trembling.

The picture on the TV glowed with a sudden brilliant brightness. Then calm turned quickly to chaos. The sound faded in and out, but Celine and the rest watched in horror as people ran screaming from their cars. The images jumped, as if the person holding the camera was running, then, nothing but blackness.

"Baltimore's been hit," Celine said.

Chapter VIII

No! No!"

Celine ran toward the stables as a National Guard unit moved in, ordering people from the house and off the property.

"This property is being confiscated by the U.S. military by the authority of the President of the United States. You've got thirty minutes to collect your belongings and vacate," said a soldier who appeared to be in charge. He raised his automatic weapon as Roy and Sam approached. They backed away.

Celine burst through the stable doors, screaming again as soldiers released her horses. "No!"

A melee of horses and people surged through the barn, the horses bursting through the doors and disappearing. Some of the animals refused to leave their stalls, then struggled as soldiers grabbed their bridles, forcing them out. Frantically searching for some of her own men, Celine pushed past two guardsmen. She saw Roy and headed toward him.

A soldier pointed his weapon at her. "Stop right there," he ordered.

Behind him she saw Obsidian struggling against another soldier who tried to pull him out of his stall. In the confined space, the horse reared up, his left front hoof dealing the soldier a glancing blow. Other guardsmen ran toward him, pulling the man away just in time as Obsidian's hooves slammed against the floor.

Ignoring the gun-wielding soldier, she tried to brush past him, but another man grabbed her arm to hold her back. She screamed and struggled, trying to get to Obsidian. He'd managed to escape his stall, but surrounded by soldiers, he reared up again, his dark eyes wild with fear and panic. Powerful hooves slashed through the air, their deadly sound against the floor reverberating through the barn repeatedly as he reared up again and again or kicked backward. Men's bodies thudded against the walls and floor as they scrambled to get out of his way. The sound of Obsidian's scream filled the air. A frightened soldier raised his weapon.

"Please, no!" Celine cried.

She felt as if her heart would burst from her chest. Her ears felt filled with cotton, but she heard others shouting, saw Roy and Jack running and wildly gesticulating. The blood roared in her head. Then through the blur came the pop-pop-pop of several gunshots. As if in slow motion, she saw the great black body of Obsidian come crashing down, the splatter of blood arcing through the air.

Celine screamed and screamed.

"How could this have happened?" Nadia asked Jason angrily. "You're the damn deputy sheriff. You couldn't have stopped it?"

Jason walked along quickly with her through the twilight. Leaves and twigs crunched beneath his boots. "The President has declared martial law. The military takes charge over local law enforcement. But we don't have time to argue about this. Where is my cousin?"

"We've got her in a tent in the woods. She's been out of it since . . ." Nadia took a deep breath. "I wasn't there when it happened, but Roy tells me she saw Obsidian shot and killed."

Jason's face blanched. "Oh Lord . . ."

"Yes, Roy told me the horse became really spooked. He was

fighting against being forced out of the stable." She sighed. "I think he just frightened them. The soldiers, I mean."

"That horse was her life. They all were." He pounded his fist against a tree. "Damn them."

Jason pulled his gun at the sound of branches crackling. Jack emerged from the shadows, a rifle held firmly in his hands.

"Oh, it's you," Jack said.

"I'm so sorry," Jason replied. "I would have been here if I could. You must know how crazy everything got." He fell into step with Jack. "How many of you are there?"

"Roy, Sam, Mike, and Taylor. The rest grabbed horses and took off. I don't blame them."

Nadia caught up with the two men. "I got here with my driver about two hours ago. We loaded up the car with as many supplies as we could and left before the soldiers could commandeer the car." She frowned. "Not that it will be any good to us. It's almost out of fuel, and I doubt we'll be able to find more."

Through the trees, firelight glowed softly. The three approached a makeshift tent. Taylor stepped out, her expression grim. "Celine's awake. She's very distraught."

"Let me take care of her," Nadia said, pushing past the woman.

Celine was lying on a sleeping bag, her eyes red and swollen. She sat up and reached out as Nadia came inside. "Nadia," she sobbed.

Nadia knelt beside her, wrapping her arms around her, letting Celine cry. She stroked Celine's soft hair. She couldn't help but notice it smelled of roses. "I'm here now," Nadia said. Celine sobbed quietly. Nadia held her tightly, wishing she could take away her pain. Then Celine's shoulders stopped shaking and she pushed away to look into Nadia's eyes.

"I can't believe you're really here."

Nadia smiled. "Where else would I be?"

Celine took a deep, trembling breath. "You heard what happened?"

"Yes. I am so sorry about Obsidian. About everything."

"We thought we'd prepared for everything. Who knew the military would kick us off our own property and confiscate our supplies?" She clenched her fist. "And there was no reason to harm any of the horses. Or release them."

"It might be best. They'll have a better chance of survival." Nadia paused. "It's going to be terrible out there."

"What did you see?"

"It wasn't pretty. The closer we got to the DC area, the worse it got. Everything's gone. It looks like Hiroshima all over again."

Celine grabbed Nadia. "You really *have* seen it all before, haven't you? What are we going to do?"

"We'll need to keep moving. Stay away from the urban areas. Those were the most likely targets." She looked away. "If you haven't been already, you'll be exposed to radioactive fallout."

Taylor poked her head into the tent. "Don't mean to interrupt, but Jason and the boys want to talk to you."

Celine pulled on a warm fleece jacket against the chill of the night, then she and Nadia exited the tent. The others had made a campfire. Most of them sat around it, huddled in horse blankets. Something smelled awfully good.

"How you doing, Miss Celine?" Roy asked.

Lying through her teeth, she said, "I'll be fine, Roy. Thank you." She looked around the small group. "Thank you all." She licked her lips. "Now, what's that smell?"

Everyone spooned the hearty stew into mugs, then sat on blankets around the fire. "Does anyone have any idea what happened?" Mike asked. "Well, of course I know we've come under nuclear attack, but what's left?"

"You can forget the major cities," Nadia said. "I drove down from Connecticut. We took the side roads as much as possible, but saw nothing but death and destruction. Only static on the radio. Our best hope is to move further inland, to the Midwest."

Taylor snorted. "You don't think the bastards targeted our farmlands?"

"Maybe they did," Nadia replied, "but first they'd want to

destroy our infrastructure—the government, our financial centers, ports, airports. Roads."

"They probably targeted military bases too," Mike said. "And our missile silo sites." He grimaced. "Doesn't bode well for the Midwest either then."

"How do we know if they're done? Maybe more attacks are coming," Sam said.

Celine stood. "We just need to stay together and watch out for each other. We have some supplies. We'll need to ration them, especially the water. We're strong and healthy. We can walk."

As the others debated their best course of action, Nadia unobtrusively poured her untouched stew back into the pot before stepping away into the shadows. She was feeling lightheaded. It had been days since she'd feasted. Her chauffeur appeared at her side. She shook her head at his unspoken query. She'd not use any of Celine's people, but if she didn't get blood soon, she'd be of no use to anyone.

Celine suddenly stood beside her. Her gentle fingers stroked Nadia's arm. "You okay?"

Nadia pushed back a strand of Celine's soft, brown hair. "I haven't eaten in days." She looked into Celine's beautiful green eyes. "I hate to ask you this—"

Celine touched her fingers to Nadia's lips. "Yes."

Leaving the others laughing around the campfire, the two women melted into the darkness of the forest. The canopy of leaves overhead shielded them from the light of the moon and stars. The air smelled deceptively fresh. Somewhere in the night, crickets chirped and an owl hooted. Nadia couldn't help but wonder how much longer such sounds would be heard. It was only a matter of time before the radioactive clouds from several atomic attacks drifted across the whole country. Though almost a century had passed since she'd personally witnessed the destruction and its aftermath in Japan, the passage of time had not diminished her memory of the horror. It had come not long after she'd turned a fellow traveler in Kyoto. She couldn't help but smile at the recollection of the lovely blonde Swede with eyes of ice blue and the body of a Norse goddess.

"Where are you?"

Celine's voice brought her back to the present. "Just remembering another time." She stopped and took Celine's hand. "I think we're far enough away from the others." She leaned down and kissed Celine's soft lips. "I am happy to be with you."

Celine wrapped her arms around Nadia's neck. "I love you," she whispered into Nadia's ear. "Take me."

Nadia growled at her words, feeling the blood lust take hold of her. The urgency of her need precluded any kind of foreplay. She grabbed hold of Celine's hair and roughly forced her head back to expose her neck. She could see—feel—the blood coursing through Celine's arteries and veins. Celine whimpered in fear, but Nadia didn't care. Celine's hands clutched at her, but Nadia forced her back against a tree, pinning one arm against it while she grabbed the other with her free hand. She could feel Celine's fast-beating heart, hear her gasping breaths. All good, for it would make her blood more potent. And in that dark forest, Nadezhda Pendareva became a true creature of the night. Sharp fangs pierced tender flesh, and as the warm blood flowed into her mouth, Nadia could hear the howl of wolves span the distance of time as she was transported back to the primeval forests of her youth. It made her want to throw back her head and howl with them.

Chapter IX

Celine's body was wracked with coughs. She'd thrown up her lunch again. And though she had no mirror, she could feel blisters forming on her face, see them on the backs of her hands. It was as if the fever burning inside her was trying to burst from her body. Something was terribly wrong, but she was afraid to admit what it was. It had only been a couple of weeks since the country had come under nuclear attack, but she and the others had been getting progressively sicker. She didn't want to say the dreaded words—radiation poisoning—but what else could it be? Nadia had alluded to it on that terrible day, but Celine had chosen to ignore her, falling into the fantasy that the countryside was safer than the city. Shivering, she huddled deeper into her jacket. Though her small band of people had ventured farther into the woods and found a cave with a nearby stream, she wondered how long they could realistically survive. She shuddered, remembering them coming across the body of one of her horses. She'd thought it was Diamond Dust. Feeling the nausea rise up, she focused on a bush full of bright red berries in an effort to stop the image of Jack and Roy dragging away the body to butcher it. She couldn't stop it.

After another bout of retching, she leaned back against the rough trunk of a tree. The sun warmed her face. Above her she could see a brilliant azure sky through the spring green of new growth, though if you looked closely you could see the green already turning to brown. How could the sky be so blue? She heard nothing except the sound of her own breathing. When had she last heard birds singing or squirrels searching through fallen leaves? When had a raccoon's eyes glowed at her in the dark? Where were the animals? She sobbed quietly, thinking about all she had lost, thinking of all the country had lost. Was it all even worth living for? Might it not have been better to be near Ground Zero? Any Ground Zero?

The sound of branches snapping made her heart beat faster. Nadia emerged from around an azalea bush bright with purple blooms. With a blanket around her shoulders, she stayed carefully in the shade afforded by the trees. Celine couldn't help but smile at the sight. It had been tricky finding creative ways to protect Nadia from the sun and the suspicions of the others. Except for her chauffeur, of course. Celine's smile faded. He had died three days earlier, the first of them to succumb. It had pained Nadia deeply. Celine couldn't remember a time when she'd seen her so despondent. And Celine couldn't help but wonder who would be next.

"I'm worried about you," Nadia said, her deep yet gentle voice sending shivers of pleasure through Celine.

Celine knew she should get up and join Nadia, but she felt too weak to move. "You look marvelous," she couldn't help but say.

"What?"

"You look marvelous."

Nadia frowned. "What does that have to do with anything?"

"The radiation, it doesn't affect you."

Nadia laughed, but there was no humor in it. "Guess that's one advantage to being a vampire."

Celine suddenly felt silly sitting in the sunlight while Nadia lurked in the shadows, covered up with a blanket like some hoodlum. She struggled to her feet, then doubled over as another wave of nausea swept through her. She coughed violently, gasping as she first tasted blood, then saw it bright red in her palm. She staggered over to Nadia, who caught her in her arms and dragged her deeper into the woods. An outcropping of boulders formed a tiny cave. Nadia quickly spread the blanket down and laid Celine upon it. She held her tight as another coughing fit overtook her. When it was over, she bent down and kissed Celine's damp forehead.

"I can save you," Nadia said.

"How?"

"If I turn you, the sickness will stop. You won't die." She smiled. "At least, not in the way you think of dying."

Celine felt her blood run cold. Was it really possible? But then she would become what Nadia was, a creature dependent on drinking the blood of others. Hiding from the sun and skulking about at night. Like a rat. She closed her eyes. No, not like a rat. Nadia was not some filthy animal. She felt Nadia's fingers caress her cheek, then her neck. Unlike her usual reaction to Nadia's touch, the sensation made her hair stand on end. She could feel the panic rise in her.

"I can't . . ."

Nadia kissed her softly. "I know I promised I would never turn you against your will." Her fingers brushed against Celine's breast. "But I don't know if I can bear to lose you, and it's the only way I can save you."

"I'm afraid," Celine whispered.

Nadia kissed her again. "Don't be."

She looked into Celine's eyes. Celine felt herself falling to Nadia's spell. She really did have a hypnotic effect. Celine couldn't help but smile. Hollywood had gotten that part right. "Will it hurt?" she asked.

Nadia nuzzled her throat. "Only a little."

As Nadia touched her, Celine felt her body relax. It seemed like she was floating in water. The tightness in her lungs, the sharp pain of every breath—all gone. Nadia's mouth was hot against her skin, her teeth sharp. Her hands both soothed and excited her. She couldn't help but arch against Nadia, pushing against the thigh thrust between her legs, wanting the exquisite release only Nadia could bring.

Fuzzy headed, Celine became vaguely aware that she was naked, and that Nadia was naked too. Their slick bodies slid one against the other, a tangle of arms and legs and tongues, yet she felt no pain from her blistered skin. She ran her hands over Nadia's breasts, liking the way her nipples immediately responded. Taking one into her mouth, she sucked hard.

"Oh," Nadia said, her fingers curling into Celine's hair.

She let her hands roam over Nadia's body, enjoying the ripple of muscles beneath her fingertips. Celine stroked Nadia's thighs, urging them to open to her. Nadia groaned loud, pushing against Celine's fingers as they glided through tangled curls and swollen lips before plunging deep into her core.

"Celine!" she cried out.

Celine smothered her cry with a kiss before letting her lips travel over Nadia's body, kissing and licking down her smooth skin. Nadia barely moved beneath her, but her breathing grew shallow. Celine could feel her tight around her fingers. She trailed kisses across her belly as she wriggled down between Nadia's legs. Nadia groaned long and loud again when Celine took her clit into her mouth, sucking then licking up and down, back and forth. Nadia trembled, barely breathing. Celine wiggled her fingers deep inside Nadia, searching for her elusive G-spot. Nadia suddenly gasped. Her body stilled. Then she was rocking against Celine's mouth and squeezing Celine's fingers, calling out Celine's name again and again. Celine moaned too, breathing and tasting her sex, like an overripe peach bursting juicy and lush inside her mouth. Nadia's trembling body relaxed, but she still pulsed gently around Celine's fingers.

"Come here, you," Nadia said, tugging slightly on Celine's hair.

With one final lick, Celine withdrew her fingers and complied. She wriggled her way up Nadia's body, smiling when their eyes met. Nadia's blue eyes blazed like sparkling jewels, then suddenly turned red. Celine felt an uncharacteristic panic overcome her. Overwhelmed by a razor-sharp fear, she tried to turn away, but Nadia caught her in a strong, painful grip.

"Where do you think you're going?" Nadia growled.

"Let me go," Celine said, pushing against Nadia's chest.

Nadia threw back her head and laughed. The sound sent chills up Celine's spine. Nadia looked at her again, her eyes burning with a hunger Celine had never before seen. Once again, she felt the panic rise in her, but also a terror she'd not known before.

"Let me go," she repeated.

In answer, Nadia pulled Celine to her, then kissed her long and hard. Her tongue possessed Celine's mouth, demanding a response. Celine fought against her, but Nadia grabbed a handful of hair and yanked her head back.

"God, please—"

"God can't help you now."

Nadia's teeth grazed along her throat. Celine moaned, waiting. Her stomach lurched. Dread fighting desire.

"Not yet, my love," Nadia said as she pushed Celine to the ground, forcing her legs apart.

It seemed like Nadia barely held her down, yet Celine could not move. Her body literally felt on fire, but whether from the fever raging within her or the heat caused by Nadia's mouth and touch she knew not. The flames licked her skin, made her blood feel like molten lava. She felt caught in a maze of light and heat. She moaned again as Nadia's mouth trailed hot kisses down along her collarbone, over her breasts, across her belly, and to her sex. She felt the wetness flow from her as Nadia's tongue stroked the inside of her thighs, her labia. Her teeth nipped Celine's tender skin.

Fear gave way to want. "You're driving me crazy," Celine said, grabbing hold of Nadia's head. "Suck my clit. Please."

Nadia laughed. The vibration of the sound made Celine squirm even more. She was gasping now, holding Nadia's head tight against her.

"Oh," she said as Nadia's tongue flicked across her clit. Nadia's fingers plunged into her. "Oh God, yes."

Rocking back and forth, following the rhythm of Nadia's fingers, she lost herself in the whirl of emotions and sensations. Nadia's mouth and tongue and hands sent her rising and falling, to the mountain top and back. Then Nadia's fingers thrust ever deep inside her, making her scream while Nadia sucked her clit, hard.

"Nadia!" she called out as her orgasm crested. "Don't stop. Oh please, don't stop."

Her body trembled as she came once, then again.

"Mmmm," Nadia moaned.

Celine's face wet with tears, she softly brushed Nadia's hair, liking the silky feel of it. Nadia stayed between her legs, her lips and fingers gentle once again. Celine couldn't remember a time when she loved Nadia more.

"I love you," she said.

"I love you too," Nadia said.

Celine felt a calmness descend over her, one that took away the horror of the last two weeks. She closed her eyes, her fingers still entwined in Nadia's hair, then opened them wide and screamed as Nadia's teeth ripped open her thigh. Gasping from the intense flash of pain that almost made her lose consciousness, she struggled to break free of Nadia's strong grip but could not. Lightheaded, and with her strength deserting her, Celine dropped her hands to her sides, feeling almost like she was hovering above the ground. Nadia devoured her, tearing at her flesh. Celine felt her own blood, hot and dripping against her thigh. The black rock ceiling of their shelter faded into darkness.

Nadia felt Celine's orgasm tight against her fingers. She flowed warm and wet into Nadia's mouth.

"Mmmm," Nadia moaned, loving the taste of her.

Celine's fingers played with her hair, making her scalp tingle with pleasure. Trying to ignore the sensation, she prepared for what she was about to do. She felt her teeth sharp against the inside of her lip.

"I love you," she heard Celine say.

"I love you too," Nadia replied, then pierced Celine's inner thigh with her fangs. Celine screamed and fought against her, but the blood flowed swiftly and she knew it wouldn't take but a few seconds for Celine to lose consciousness. When the blood flow was no more than a trickle, she moved up to Celine's throat, her own hunger making her rip open the jugular and lap up Celine's life's blood. Just before Celine took her last breath, Nadia tore open her own wrist and pushed Celine's mouth against it. Instinctually, Celine drank from her, weak, yet urgently. Then her head fell limply back against Nadia's arm.

Nadia leaned over and kissed Celine's smooth forehead. "Your old life is all over now, my love. We can be together for all eternity."

Cradling Celine in her arms, she crept deeper into the rock alcove and pulled the blanket over them. Night would fall soon, but she didn't want the others to find them before that.

Chapter X

Celine stretched, feeling the blanket tight around her. Nadia lay beside her. Smiling, she kissed the top of Nadia's head.

"You're awake," Nadia said.

"What time is it?"

"Around eight thirty. The sun's just about down."

Celine threw the blanket off. "I am ravenous. I think I could use a juicy steak right now."

"It's not a steak you need, my dear."

Celine looked at Nadia. Her eyes glowed, wolf-like, in the eerie dusk. She shivered. "Something's happened, hasn't it?"

"I had to save you," Nadia said. "It was the only way."

Celine gasped, the full extent of what Nadia was saying dawning on her. "Oh my God, no. You didn't."

Nadia took her hand. "It was the only way," she repeated. "And you did give me permission."

Celine began to sob. "I don't know if I can live like this."

"It's the only way you can live. How *we* can live."

"What will we tell the others?"

Nadia grabbed hold of both her arms and looked directly into her eyes. "You can tell them nothing. Nothing. We have to leave them, travel on our own."

"But they're all that I have left."

"They're part of your past life. A life that no longer exists. They would kill you. We have only each other now."

Celine pushed away. "No, I can't believe they would hurt me."

"They wouldn't understand." Nadia's voice grew harsh. "You need them now for only one thing. The blood they have to sustain you."

Celine shrank back in horror. "Never!"

Nadia reached up and stroked Celine's hair. Her touch was gentle. "I will teach you how to drink without killing." She kissed Celine, then rose and held out her hand. "Come, let's go back to camp. We can leave later tonight after they've all gone to sleep. I'm sure they're wondering where we are now."

Celine stood. The weakness that had plagued her for days was gone. She felt strong again. She reached up to touch her cheeks. They were smooth. She looked at her hands. The blisters were gone from them too. How would she explain that to the others? She took Nadia's hand.

"Let's go," she said.

"Where the hell have you been?" Taylor asked as Celine and Nadia walked back into camp. "We were ready to send out a search party."

"Yeah, you've been missing all day," Roy said.

"Sorry," Celine said. "We just needed some time alone."

"Jack and Mike have gone looking for food. They thought they saw rabbits." Taylor grimaced. "They're probably contaminated, though."

Ray laughed harshly. "Like we all are." He pointed to his arms, red and raw where the skin was peeling away layer by layer. Blood stained the strips of T-shirt he'd wrapped around the worst of it. They'd long ago run out of the meager first-aid supplies they'd had. And what good was Neosporin and aspirin against saucer-sized blisters and cracking skin?

Tugging her sleeves farther down her arms, Celine looked away, feeling guilty. She had saved herself, but at what price? Or, more precisely, Nadia had saved her. "Maybe if you travel farther inland? Away from the cloud?"

"We're already exposed," Jason said. "While you were gone, the rest of us decided we should try to make our way south, toward Fort Detrick or any city. There's got to be medical help of some sort."

The bushes crackled, and Jack and Mike burst into the clearing, two dead rabbits held triumphantly in their hands. The poor, scrawny things didn't look like they could feed a small fox, let alone eight people. Celine turned her head away. Nadia took her hand.

"I'm not hungry," she mumbled and hurried into the cave. "I've got to get out of here," she told Nadia, who'd followed her inside.

"As soon as they're asleep, we'll go." She nodded toward the others. "But you'll need nourishment first."

Celine shuddered, but she knew Nadia was right. She could already feel the stirrings of an unfamiliar hunger. She ran her tongue along the edges of her teeth. They felt sharp.

"Come with me," Celine whispered as she shook Taylor awake.

"What?" Taylor mumbled.

Celine took her arm, urging her up. "Come," she said again.

She led her out of the cave, careful not to wake the others. In the stillness of the forest, Nadia waited. The two women led Taylor deeper into the woods. She stumbled, still obviously sleepy.

"Where are you taking me?"

"Don't be afraid," Celine said.

Nadia stopped abruptly. She guided Taylor into Celine's arms. If Taylor thought it odd that her boss was now coming on to her, she gave no sign. Instead, she stood quietly. Celine realized that Nadia had used her hypnotic ability to lull Taylor into an easy acquiescence. Celine gently tipped Taylor's head back, exposing her throat. She could see the blood pulsing beneath the surface of her skin, smell it flowing in her veins. She kissed Taylor on the mouth, gliding her tongue along her chin and down her neck. Taylor moaned, leaning against her. Celine held her tight, yet knew Nadia also held her.

"Taylor, you like me, don't you?" Celine murmured against her ear.

"Yes, ma'am."

"You know I would never hurt you."

Taylor nodded. Her breathing was slow and steady. No indication yet that she was afraid. Nadia pushed Celine's head down. "Now," she commanded.

Hesitating only momentarily, Celine bit deep into Taylor's neck, feeling the skin rupture and the blood flow into her mouth and down her throat. Taylor groaned, sagging against Celine as her knees buckled. Nadia held her arms firmly, preventing her from falling. Celine drank thirstily. Suddenly she felt Nadia's hand pushing her away.

"You need to stop now or you'll kill her."

Celine stumbled back. Nadia held a drooping Taylor in her arms. Celine could see the blood glistening bright red against Taylor's skin. She licked her lips, running her tongue along the sharp points of her new teeth. She was still so hungry. As if she'd read Celine's mind, Nadia shook her head and picked Taylor up in her arms before striding back to camp.

She laid Taylor gently on the ground just inside the mouth of the cave. Using a shirt she'd found hanging on a tree limb, she wiped the blood from Taylor's neck. She examined Taylor's wounds, then stood. She took Celine's arm and led her outside.

"A little messy," she said, "but Taylor will be okay. She'll be weak and disoriented, but won't remember what happened." She kissed Celine on the mouth. "Let's go, my sweet."

Traveling by night, finding shelter during the day, Celine and Nadia headed toward a city, any city. Though the death and destruction they found was horrifying, they knew they needed to find people. The dead animals that littered the countryside were of no use to two hungry vampires. The crops growing on the abandoned farms were not the kind of nourishment they needed. At one farm, Celine found a battery-operated ham radio. It crackled when she turned it on, relentless in its static until one station came in very faintly. She held her ear close to hear what was said.

The man's voice was low and emotional. "Though the President continues to run the country from his secret bunker, one has to wonder what country is left. Most of the major cities in the U.S. were attacked, leaving us with very little infrastructure. The National Guard and the military are trying to maintain order, as looters and other criminal elements take over." He took a deep breath. "The medical establishment continues to struggle, plagued by lack of personnel and supplies, as well as any working facilities."

Celine pounded her fist against the table. "Damn him!"

"Who?"

"That no-good president. He brought all this on with his arrogance and disdain for others. He refused to see that his actions turned other nations against us. And now, who will help us? Who *can* help us?"

Nadia pulled Celine into her arms. They listened while the commentator continued. "Other world leaders have condemned the attack, and have pledged to help, though the coalition of countries who attacked the United States has threatened retaliatory action against any nation who attacks them."

"Did we even get any of our own weapons off?"

"I'm sure we did," Nadia said, kissing her.

Celine felt the familiar stirring between her legs. As if reading her mind, Nadia smiled and shook her head. "We have to keep moving. It will be light soon, and I think we're near an inhabited town. We'll find our way there and hole up somewhere until dark."

"How can you tell?"

"I can smell them."

The two women left the farm, following the road for miles. Overhead, the moon shone brightly, covered occasionally by clouds.

"Look, a car," Celine said. She hurried toward it. "Maybe it still runs."

Expecting to find dead people inside, she approached slowly. It was empty, the key still in the ignition. Briefly wondering what had made the occupants desert the vehicle, she climbed in and turned the key, cheering as the engine roared to life.

"Oh my God," she said, "it works." She watched the fuel needle move to half full. Ethanol or gas, it didn't matter. Nadia got into the passenger seat. They took off down the bumpy road, and it wasn't long before they found paved highway. It was eerie to be driving and not see another car. Celine felt like she had stepped into a watercolor painting. Wasn't there a movie made once with that very theme?

Suddenly, the countryside turned urban. They passed a strip mall, then a car dealership. Or at least, what was left of them. The buildings were flattened. Cars were strewn all over as if tossed by a giant hand. They came across the remnants of a church; all that remained was a tilting bell tower.

"This was probably caused by shock waves from the blasts," Nadia said. "I don't believe that downtown-whatever-this-is was a target."

Houses and businesses lay crumbled and empty. Papers and leaves blew across deserted streets. Celine drove slowly, trying to avoid debris and broken glass. She stopped the car. Nadia looked at her.

"Why are you stopping?"

"There must be people here. You said you could smell them."

"I doubt anyone we would find here is still alive. Most people would have left as soon as possible."

Celine glanced out the window. "It's going to be daylight soon. Don't you think this is as good a place as any to find shelter?"

"Yes, you're right." Nadia pointed to the left. "That house over there seems in the best condition."

Celine pulled into the driveway. The whole right side of the house was gone; the left slanted precariously to the left.

Miraculously, a grove of tall oaks remained standing all along the back property line. They got out of the car and cautiously approached the house. Their shoes crunched against the crumbled, shattered remains of the structure. From within, they heard a faint noise.

"Oh my God," Celine said, recognizing the sound. She grabbed Nadia's hand. "There's a dog in there."

They scrambled over the debris until they were in what used to be the living room. Celine listened closely. She heard the barking coming from behind a door to the left. Moving aside a table thrown against the door, she snatched open the door and saw nothing but a dark abyss. As her eyes adjusted to the total blackness, Nadia must have seen the look on her face.

"Yes, that's one advantage you now have. You can see in the dark." She smiled. "It comes in quite handy."

Celine walked confidently down the rickety wooden steps. At the bottom, she looked around, searching for the source of the barking. She spotted the German shepherd cowering in a corner. It was tied with a chain to a pipe. Immediately angry, she hurried over to the animal, but her anger evaporated when she saw that the owners had tried to provide for their pet. The remnants of a forty-pound bag of dog food lay scattered near the blanket on which the dog rested. The plug from the utility sink was unstopped so water from the faucet trickled from the hole and down to the floor, where enough of it pooled before it ran down a drain in the floor.

"It's okay," Celine said as she knelt down, then held out her hand. The dog licked her fingers and began thumping its tail on the floor. She managed to unlatch the chain. The animal practically leaped into her arms and began licking her face. She fell back, laughing.

"What's your name, sweetie?" she asked.

"Wolf," Nadia said. Celine looked at her. Nadia pointed to a dog dish with WOLF emblazoned on it. "Not very original."

"Oh look, the name's on his collar too. Why do you think they left him here?"

"Probably evacuated."

Outraged, Celine said, "But they could have taken him. That law was passed the year after Hurricane Katrina and the whole New Orleans fiasco. It allows people to bring their pets in the event of a mandatory evacuation."

Nadia shrugged. "Who knows what the circumstances were?" She looked around the basement. "We may as well stay here. No windows. That's probably why Wolf is still alive and relatively healthy." She stroked his head. "It'll be quite safe. And we have our own watchdog now."

Celine looked around a bit nervously. "You don't think the house is in danger of collapsing?"

"I think we'll be okay for a day."

They found a closet containing blankets and pillows, and took them to the basement. Pulling cushions off of a ratty old sofa, they made a makeshift bed and snuggled into it, arms around each other. Wolf lay next to Celine, refusing to leave her side.

Chapter XI

The need for blood awakened Celine and Nadia before sunset. It was a gnawing, desperate hunger. Without a word, Nadia grabbed hold of Wolf. Celine looked at her, startled. Surely she wasn't going to do what it looked like?

"We have no other choice," Nadia said. "An animal's blood can sustain us for a short while, but we need to find human blood soon."

Celine averted her eyes as Nadia bent over him, and tried not to listen to Wolf's whimper of fear or the sounds of Nadia drinking. She almost shrieked when Nadia touched her arm. Celine hesitated, but the rich smell of blood compelled her to lean down and lap up the liquid nourishment that flowed from the animal's neck wound. She felt her strength slowly returning. Nadia let her drink for a bit, then stopped her.

"He'll be okay," she said. She patted the dog. "Won't you, boy?"

His tail thumped weakly on the floor.

Both women stood. As if reading each other's mind, Celine grabbed the bag of dog food while Nadia scooped Wolf up into her strong arms. They carefully climbed the stairs, then headed for the car. There wasn't much fuel left, but they hoped it would get them to Frederick. They'd passed a sign saying it was twenty miles ahead. Frederick's closeness to Fort Detrick didn't bode well for its inhabitants; the military facility was a probable target because of its biological weapons research. It had been an open secret for decades that it housed some of the world's deadliest viruses.

Laying the dog gently in the backseat, Nadia then climbed into the driver's side while Celine took the shotgun seat. Driving with the windows down, Celine let the wind whip her hair back and forth. About a half hour later, they saw lights ahead, then they entered Frederick city limits.

"Look out!" Celine screeched as ten figures darted out into the road ahead of them.

Nadia slammed on the brakes. Instantly, the figures, all men, swarmed over the vehicle. Some of them carried what appeared to be lead pipes; one had a rifle. The largest of them wrenched open the driver's side door.

"Get out," he ordered.

Another man opened Celine's door and grabbed her arm, yanking her from her seat. "Let go of me," she demanded.

Another man had opened the back door. Growling, Wolf immediately jumped out and attacked the man holding Celine. The man raised his pipe. "No!" Celine cried, shoving her attacker with all her might. To her astonishment, he went flying several feet. Nadia was at her side as another man came toward her. Nadia's hand shot out to grab him by the neck. With one quick jab of her fingers, she crushed his windpipe. As he crumpled to the ground, the others stood stunned.

"Forget about them!" the ringleader shouted. The rest crammed into the car and took off.

"Let's get out of here," Nadia said. "There's less than an eighth of a tank left. They'll be back for us."

The two women and their canine companion took off running. They didn't stop until they'd lost themselves amid the rubble of what was left of downtown. Amazingly, some of the street lights still worked. Here and there, fires dotted the landscape. And then, at last, they encountered people. People still shell-shocked by what had happened—vacant eyed and moving zombie-like through the dimly lighted streets. They took no notice of the new strangers among them.

"We'll have no problem finding nourishment here," Nadia said matter-of-factly.

Celine shuddered. It would take a while for her to adjust to her new life. But could she? Did she even want to? Really? She looked at the people around them, which made her think of the friends she had left behind. Was it only little more than a week ago? Would they live long enough to find their way to safety? What of her cousin, Jason, who'd been her inseparable companion since they were toddlers? He must be sick with worry. Or worse, maybe he knew somehow that she had abandoned them and hated her for it.

They came to the middle of town, where a park similar to Central Park in New York but nowhere near its size stretched before them. A lot of the trees were down, but some still stood, though they'd mostly been stripped bare of leaves. Several makeshift tents were scattered here and there. Suddenly, Celine gasped and stopped walking, grabbing hold of Nadia's arm.

"What is it?" Nadia asked, concern lacing her voice.

"Look. Up there."

Nadia followed the line of Celine's finger. At the top of a slight hill and silhouetted against the night sky were the outlines of running horses, several of them. Celine's hand trembled even as she discerned the creatures were not real, for they didn't move but stayed frozen in perpetual flight.

"They are so beautiful," she said, feeling the tears well up in her eyes.

She started running. Nadia and Wolf ran with her, winding through the trees and bushes until they reached the hill. Looking for a set of stairs but seeing none, Celine clawed her way up the grassy embankment until she stood among the life-sized statues. Lovingly, she ran her hands over their cool, smooth granite bodies.

She started crying quietly. Nadia put her arm around her, while Wolf cocked his head and gave a low whine.

"I can't believe all this has happened," she sobbed. "Everything I worked for." She turned to Nadia. "And they killed Obsidian." She fell to her knees with a deep, guttural sob.

Nadia knelt beside her, smoothing her hair as she would a child's. "I know, Celine. I know."

"I don't think I can live like this. I really don't. I love you so very much, but I just can't do it. I can't."

"Don't say that. I know you can. I have, for more than four hundred years."

Celine sat next to one of the larger statues and leaned against a leg. Wolf crawled over and lay his head in her lap. She absently stroked his soft fur. Nadia stayed silently beside her, her hand resting on Celine's thigh.

"But have you been happy?"

"Of course I have."

Celine smiled at her. "Be honest. Please."

Nadia shook her head. "Okay, then, no I haven't. Not always. But I am now. Now that I've found you. You're what I've been searching for my whole life."

"But what do we have to look forward to?" Celine made a swooping motion with her hand. "Preying on these people who have suffered so much? Hiding by day and hoping no one finds out what we really are?"

"It's not what you think."

"No, it's worse than I think. Your life is not what it was either. Your livelihood is destroyed. Who's buying microchips now? Who's even alive to buy microchips? We have no homes, no friends." Celine laughed harshly. "Who even knows how much of the world is left?"

Taking her by the arms, Nadia made Celine look at her. "I don't care about the rest of the world. I only care about you, and I will do anything to make you happy."

"Anything?"

"Yes."

Celine ran her fingers gently down Nadia's cheek and along her jawline. God, how she loved this woman. "Tomorrow morning, when the sun comes up, I want you to be here with me. Here, among these running ponies."

Nadia pulled away. Wolf raised his head, then laid back down following a soothing caress from Celine.

"You want to commit suicide?"

"I don't think of it that way. I think of it as freedom."

"Celine—"

Celine put her fingers to Nadia's lips. "Shhh. Don't say any more. My mind is made up. You can be with me, or not. Your choice. I will love you no matter what." She stood up. "Let's go back down now. I want to find a private place for us."

Silently, they made their way down the hill, Wolf following close behind. When they got to the bottom, a little girl about seven years old ran up to them. She threw herself in front of the dog and wrapped her arms around his neck. "Wolfie," she sobbed.

He was licking her face, his tail going a mile a minute. Seconds later, a man joined them. He also knelt down. The dog, in turn, leaped on him and began licking his face too. "Where'd you find our dog?" he asked, his voice husky with emotion.

"Where you left him, in the basement," Celine said, trying not to let her disapproval show.

He glanced at her, then smiled wanly. "We didn't want to leave him, but the National Guard troops who evacuated us said they'd shoot Wolf if we tried to bring him."

Celine felt the anger build in her at the unfairness of it all, but forced it away. It would change nothing. "It was clever of you to keep the water running like that," she said. "And there was plenty of food left, but we lost it when our car was stolen."

"Daddy, can we go show Mommy now?" The little girl tugged impatiently on his hand.

He stood. "Yes, Princess." He turned to Celine and Nadia. "I know it was unintentional, but thank you for reuniting us with our dog."

Celine's throat tightened. "Promise you'll not let anyone take him from you again."

"I promise." He held out his hand. "God bless you."

Celine shook his hand, holding on a little longer than necessary. "Good luck."

He nodded, then took his daughter's hand and headed away. Wolf sat beside Celine. The man turned and whistled. Wolf got up, then hesitated, looking first at Celine, then the man and his daughter.

"C'mon, Wolfie," the little girl called.

"Go on," Celine said, gently pushing the dog toward them. He trotted over to them, then turned and gave Celine one long, last look before disappearing into the trees.

"It's better this way," she said, her throat tight, before Nadia could say anything.

Nadia took Celine into her arms and kissed away her tears.

Somewhere, incongruously, a rooster crowed. Celine stirred, wrapped in Nadia's arms. The air felt chilly against her bare skin. They'd found refuge inside a house with only two of its four walls remaining, but luck of all lucks, it had a bed inside. They'd even discovered a blanket stuffed underneath a broken dresser. Their lovemaking had been slow and gentle, not the wild passion of previous nights. Celine closed her eyes, remembering the feel of Nadia's mouth and hands, the smell and taste of her. She moaned softly.

"Are you all right?" Nadia asked sleepily.

"Thank you for last night," Celine said, kissing her forehead.

"I can give you many more."

Celine didn't answer. Would it really be so bad living as a "creature of the night" as the gothic novels and movies called them? The world would recover from this horrific event, and they would be around to witness it. To help in any way they could. But what kind of world would it be? An environmental disaster. People fighting like animals to survive. Disfigurement. Birth defects. Nations at war. And she and Nadia constantly on the move, never safe. Maybe forced to kill. Always hungry. Preying on innocent people. She pushed away from Nadia. No, she refused to live that way.

"I haven't changed my mind," she said. She stood and threw on her clothes. Looking out the window, she noticed the barest tinge of gold beginning to appear in the sky. She didn't have much time. "Are you coming with me?"

Nadia too rose. She stood, naked and glorious, before Celine. Her blue eyes had never looked more brilliant, nor her deep black hair more lustrous. Her lips beckoned. For a moment, Celine's resolve faltered. Forcing herself to look away, she left the room. She could hear Nadia dressing. Silently, they walked out together, holding hands as they made their way along the ruined street and back to the park.

"Will it hurt?" Celine asked.

Nadia laughed softly. "I don't know, my love. I've never done this before."

Celine laughed too. "Guess that was a silly question."

Entering the park, they could hear people beginning to waken. The hill loomed above them, the dark forms of running ponies forever caught in stone. As Celine made her way up the grassy slope, she heard Obsidian whinny, felt him nudge her hand for sugar or a carrot. The faces of her family and friends flitted through her memory: Jason laughing at one of her sad jokes; Taylor and Roy arguing good-naturedly over which one of them built a better fence. Harry and Mike and Sam. Sandra and Betty. Loyal Maria. And even bitter Aunt Julia.

She held Nadia's hand tight. Her soul mate. They would be together forever.

As the sun illuminated the ponies, they seemed to come alive—manes and tails flowing behind them, eyes flashing, hooves thundering across the ground. The sun crested, glinting off the polished stone.

Nadezhda. Celine. The wind picked up the faint whispers and carried them away in a swirl of dust and ash.

ELSEWHEN

THERESE SZYMANSKI

I: RHENNÉ

Two days before Halloween

It had been a long day, filled with many criminals. I was totally and utterly exhausted. On top of all the regular crime that happened in Warren—which, as the third-largest city in Michigan, just north of Detroit, always had its share of crime—there were also now a few gangs terrorizing the Detroit metro area's convenience stores, gas stations and mom-and-pops.

But I didn't have anything in my apartment for breakfast, and I knew I wasn't going to want to go very far in the morning before eating—so a quick stop at my local, neighborhood 7-Eleven was definitely in order. And who knew? Maybe while doing so, I'd run into Fattie, Shortie, or one of the other members of the crime sprees. My partner, Chuck Gertz—one of the few detectives in the squad who didn't mind partnering with a woman as long as she pulled her own weight—had been joking yesterday about how lucky catching the baddies in the act would be. That might make our jobs a lot easier. But things were never that convenient.

Or at least, not usually. This time, I pulled into the lot and immediately saw them: two men, one lying on the sidewalk in front of the store, apparently unconscious, with another leaning over him. *Leaning over his neck.*

I slammed on my brakes and leapt from the car, pulling my gun. "Freeze!" I yelled, using my door as a block. The crouching one sat on his haunches and looked directly at me. His lean and compact frame reminded me of a jungle cat's—ready to attack at any time. For a moment he really did seem like a panther, what with his black clothing, bloody fangs and sleek, dark looks.

Chuck is so never gonna believe this. I almost pulled the trigger, but froze even as I realized I was imagining things—I mean, there was no way he had fangs that were dripping blood—and he was also . . . strangely familiar.

I don't know how long we were caught, stopped dead, staring at each other. I was the good guy, he was the bad guy, and it felt as if I ought to be a lover, not an enemy. I tried to remember where I knew him from, but couldn't. I couldn't place him, identify him, or remember him. But my whole body shook and I almost fell to my knees when I experienced a vivid, whole-body remembrance of gasping in ecstasy while he held me close.

He finally looked down toward the body at his feet, breaking our connection. He sighed as he rose to his feet. He wasn't very tall. Not tall at all, in fact. To be honest, he was rather short.

"I said freeze or I'll shoot!" I yelled as best I could over my suddenly dry mouth.

"No, actually, you didn't. You just said 'freeze,' " he said nonchalantly, wiping his mouth. He had a slight accent I couldn't place. He was dressed all in black—black jeans, black boots, long black leather trench coat and untucked polka-dotted black shirt. But his sense of style didn't matter as much as the fact that he now held his hands out to his sides in a non-threatening way, as if he was surrendering.

I took a deep breath, still trying to calm myself, and inched around the car door toward him, keeping my gun up. Trying to keep myself focused on what was actually happening—and *not* on—

The feeling of him picking me up in his strong arms and carrying me to safety, no matter how many times I told him I did not require his assistance . . .

Him leaping up onto my windowsill and looking across the room at me as if he was about to eat me in a very good way . . .

His tongue—his body—between my legs as he made me come from the inside out . . .

How much I just wanted to touch him and be with him and in his arms and . . .

The images flew through my mind, leaving me breathless and wanting, craving and reeling—

He kicked the limp arm of the guy on the ground. "He's the one that you want." He nodded toward the store—indicating the clerk, I guessed. "She'll tell you everything you need to know."

"You have to stay."

"No, really, I don't. And I can't," he said, smiling sadly at me.

"You have to give a statement." I kept my gun trained on him, but it didn't really seem to bother him in the least. It was rather disconcerting.

He raised an eyebrow and shook his head slightly. "You're not her." He looked me up and down. "She's gone now. Forever. I just have to accept that." He looked right into me again then sighed. "And I have things to be and people to do." He said the phrase, in his dark low voice, as if he'd coined it. It's hard to explain how, but it sounded different than when someone was just using the same tired old cliché.

Then, before I could say or do anything, he was gone, leaping on a motorcycle I hadn't even noticed—carefully ensuring the tails of his coat were tucked under him. He moved so swiftly it was as if he flew.

It was only when I heard the sirens approaching that I came back to reality and stopped staring after his bike.

Great. I didn't mind some dead perp, but I *did* mind a new problem on my beat. Nobody likes a vigilante.

"I knew I shouldn't have agreed to work this shift by myself. No way, no how, I said." The clerk, a short, black woman who seemed powerful and sure of herself—the sort of small, black woman you know can get even the biggest, baddest dude in line and saying, "Yes, Mama,"—came out to stand next to me and smoke a cigarette. "See, Georgie was sick and they couldn't find anybody to replace her, so I said, sure, no problem, just so long as you pay me overtime. After all, I'd be working for two. I mean, I'm only working here to pay my way through school. I'm pre-law at Wayne State and all." She kicked the guy on the ground. "And this guy is *so* the asshole I want to make sure gets locked up forever."

"What the hell are you doing?" I said, dropping to check out the guy on the ground. I had entirely forgotten about him somehow! *He cackled gleefully as he ripped open the carriage doors to pull me from it and throw me onto the hard ground. I feared for my very life at the hands of these swarthy highwaymen.* No, I thought, this was not a good time to relive the worst of my nightmares.

"I talked 'em into time-and-a-half—" she continued.

I shook my head, not knowing why I felt so dizzy. "What the hell happened here?" I asked. The guy on the ground was pale, with a rapid heartbeat and shallow breathing. He had two pinprick-sized marks in his neck and bruises were rapidly appearing on his visible flesh, but he didn't appear to be shot or stabbed. I couldn't figure out why I was so sure he was about to croak, except maybe he was suffering from internal bleeding, and that was why he was so pale.

"This dirtbag," the clerk tried another kick, but I stopped her with my hand. She satisfied her urge by flicking ash on him. "He tried to rob me. Or *was* robbing me when that . . . that . . . invincible, super-strong, *short* dude came in and saved me. Man, that guy kicked this dude's ass good!"

A patrol car swerved into the lot, lights flashing. Two armed officers jumped out, aiming their guns at us and the store.

"Shh," I told the clerk. I stood, raising my hands over my head and making sure she was behind me. "My name's Rhenné Leon, badge three-eight-two," I nodded down to my badge and name tag. "I'm off-duty Warren. We need an ambulance." I indicated the downed perp.

"I called for an ambulance once Superdude threw this guy outta the store," the clerk said from behind me.

"Oh," I said, hands still up. "An ambulance should already be on its way."

"I know Leon," one of the cops said. "She's Gertz's partner." Then, to me, "Is he the only one?" He was checking out the store and surrounding area.

Fuck me and the horse I rode in on. My head still wasn't on right from that guy with the dark, soulful eyes. I hadn't even thought of securing the scene and ensuring there were no other perps or civilians present.

"Yes," the clerk said, saving my butt. "He's the only one."

I lowered my hands and knelt again. "Looks like he's lost some blood," I said. "And the only wounds I can find are right here." I pointed the marks out to the other cop I now recognized as Hardy. George Hardy. And his partner, Chris O'Keefe.

George and I checked out the store, inside and out, to ensure no one else lurked about—that there wasn't an accomplice waiting for us—while Chris kept an eye on the perp.

I was sure these crime-spreeing types worked as teams, so this guy must've had an accomplice, one who'd gotten the hell outta Dodge as soon as Superdude had shown. Or else I was totally barking up the wrong tree. The paramedics came and picked up the perp, whose ID said he was John Francis Peterson. I was willing to bet it wasn't a fake, since no low-life convenience store thug would put the name Francis on anything he'd chosen for himself.

George and Chris interviewed the clerk and I stuck around since I was wondering about the clerk, what happened, and, well, the Man in Black. I convinced myself I was just checking to make sure all my theories about the crime-spree guys were correct, but really, I was hanging around because I was more than a little curious about the vigilante.

The clerk's name was Sheryl Montgomery. She was 28 and lived in Detroit with three roommates. She worked way up here in Warren since it was a lot safer and she could make better money working here than in the cheap, close-to-campus neighborhood where she lived.

"I'd just finished restocking the shelves," Sheryl was saying to George, "and was standing outside the store, having a smoke and thinking there was something in the air. I mean, it was like a storm was brewing or something—but there wasn't a cloud in the sky. The breeze was almost cool and it really felt strange. It had an . . . ominous . . . feel to it, the feel that it gets when something's gonna happen, and you just hope it's gonna happen to somebody else." She shrugged. "As they say—famous last words and all, y'know? Anyway, so I was just standing there, smoking, and running through a bunch of dates in French history in my head."

"Huh?" That was George. Man, was that George, always ready to call people on things that didn't make sense.

"I'm in college, pre-law, y'know? I already told you that. Anyway, so I was standing there smoking and running a mental review in my head for a test—French history—and a beat-up old Chevy—one of those ancient two-door types with the huge-ass hoods and an engine that'll blow you away—pulled up. And this dude got out of the front passenger's door, gave me a look and went into the store. So I dropped my smoke and followed him in. He went to the back cooler and grabbed some beer. I went behind the front counter. And that was about when I realized that bad feeling in the air was for *me*, and not some other unlucky son-of-a-bitch. Sometimes you can just tell, y'know?" Her preciseness with facts gave me some hope for a possible future for her as an Assistant D.A. I hoped she was in it to prosecute and not defend.

"Yes ma'am, I know," George said. "So what happened then?"

"He came up to the counter, carrying a thirty of beer. I asked for ID, even though he looked like he might be old enough. That's one thing you gotta be careful of in this line of work is making sure they're old enough. Unless they look thirty, I ID 'em. No exceptions. So he reached inside his jacket, like he was grabbing his license, but pulled out a gun instead. He told me to open the register, put all the money into a bag and give it to him. He was totally cold, ruthless and straight about it."

"What made you think that?" I asked. Chris and George both looked at me, reminding me they were on duty and I wasn't. I nodded my understanding with a single, subtle nod. Some rob-and-runs ended with beat cops filling out the paperwork, but I was sure detectives were on their way, since this was sounding an awful lot like one of our gangs.

"It was like he had a plan," Sheryl said. "I've been held up before, by guys on drugs, and I know way too many addicts. This dude was straight—as in, not on drugs." She paused, looked up at us, and said, "Did you know you're more likely to die on the job by working as a convenience store clerk than as a cop?"

"Yes, ma'am, we know," Chris said, apparently realizing how she liked to wander about in her narrative. "So he came in, pulled a gun and tried to rob you. Then what happened?"

"I recognized this M.O., but still I didn't believe he'd just take the cash and run. I mean, really, no telling what he'd do to me once I gave him the money. Scum like this are the reason I'm getting into criminal law—to make sure those like him never, *ever*, see the streets again once they've been locked up. Anyway, then he told me he was gonna take the beer, too. So I told him I was going to grab a bag—a paper bag—to put the money into, and I did that. *Just that.* I tried not to make any sudden moves. It was when I was emptying all the money from the register into the bag that I realized I was never going to see another sunrise in my life. And that was when *he* walked in. *Superdude.* The short guy. I didn't know what to make of him. I mean, he walks into the middle of a hold-up . . . what do you do with that? Really?"

"So we're talking about the guy who came in, beat up Francis, and took off?" Chris said.

"What did he look like?" George asked.

"About five-three, five-four," Sheryl said. "We got that tape measure by the door, so we can give better info about bad guys, and I'm sure that'll tell you just how short this guy was. When you see him leaving on the vid and all. Dude was short."

"Then what happened?" Chris said, again putting her back on track.

"Well, it was . . . It was weird. Beyond weird, really. The bell over the door tinkled when Superdude came in, asking for a pack of Newports, and hold-up dude aimed his gun at Superdude like he was *so* gonna shoot him, and I was all thinking that this was my chance to do something. So I hit the silent alarm."

"Hold on," Chris said. "Who aimed at who?"

Sheryl faced off with Chris. "Superdude came in and Bad dude aimed right at him. Said, 'Don't move,' and Superdude said, 'Or what?' And was practically next to the jackass—Bad dude—before Bad dude pulled the trigger. The weirdest thing was that it looked almost like Superdude hypnotized Bad dude or something."

I kinda knew the feeling. "What do you mean by that?" I asked.

"Well, it was like Bad-dude-Francis-the-Man looked at Superdude, aimed, and . . . had to struggle to actually pull the trigger. Like he wanted to but didn't want to at the same time. Y'know?"

"So the gunman shot this mysterious customer?" George said, obviously trying to bottom line all this jackass, code-name bullshit.

"Well, yeah. First he was all like, 'Stop, or I'll shoot,' and Superdude was just about daring him with, 'Really?' And then Francis shot him. A bunch of times. All direct hits. I saw the bullets hit Superdude, and I saw Superdude jerk backward when they did. I *so* thought he shoulda been dead!"

"Hold on," I said. "You're saying the robber shot this vigilante at close range, and yet the vigilante was still able jump on his bike and ride outta here? After beating the bad guy up and all."

"Yeah, that's exactly what I'm saying. Superdude shoulda been lying dead on the ground, but he beat the crap outta Bad dude. He fuckin' slugged Bad dude so hard Bad dude went flying. I mean, how the fuck d'ya think those cooler doors got smashed? Superdude hit Bad dude outta the ballpark, even though Superdude was like chock full of lead and all. It was like something outta the movies and all, I'm tellin' ya."

"Then what happened?" I asked.

"Superdude picked that jackass right up and carried him out-side. He must've took six shots before he took that guy's gun away, but he picked him up like it was nothing. I just wished he'd a come back inside for his goddamned cigarettes, 'cause I'm tellin' ya, that was a man who seriously needed his nicotine fix."

I suddenly realized that what I'd seen on Superdude's—the vig-ilante's—shirt wasn't polka dots, it was blood. Blood 'cause he'd really gotten shot. Repeatedly. And then drove away on a motor-cycle.

"I gotta tell you," Sheryl said. "When I finally went outside, I was glad Superdude had taken out that asshole—as in, knocked his ass out cold, 'cause . . . well . . . that poor mother-fucker got the crap kicked outta him. I know I'd hate to be beat up like that and still be conscious. He was all bloody. I heard him scream a couple of times, but, out here, nobody would've cared. It's all good."

"When did the car leave?" Chris asked.

"Which car?" Sheryl said.

"The getaway car," Chris said.

"Fuck if I know. I was kinda distracted and all."

The only explanation was that the vigilante had been wearing a bulletproof vest. At least, that was the only logical reason for why he hadn't been killed by the shooting. As for everything else . . . There was just something very much not right with him. He really kinda spooked me out, actually.

Which was why I needed more beer.

Funny, I thought, as I ran into the kitchen table—all right, despite my large alcohol consumption, but my feet seemed to be broke. On my trek back to the couch, the phone rang.

"Yeah-lo," I said, answering it.

"Leon! What the fuck's going on?" Chuck said.

"Oh, Chuck, my buddy, my partner. Thanks for the call back. I think he was wearing a bulletproof vest."

"Rhenné," Chuck said with the same tone he'd use on a two-year old. "Are you drunk?"

"Three sheets, baby. Three sheets."

"What happened tonight?"

"Coincidence. The impossible. I went into a Seven-Eleven when it got robbed, and, man, you got to see the surveillance vids, 'cause it's all wicked whacked."

"Wicked whacked?"

"Yeah. Huh. Say that three times fast. So when can you get over here?" Wow. My beer. It was empty already.

"Leon," Chuck said, "it's the middle of the night. You're not hurt or bleeding. You're just really drunk."

"Yuppers. That I am."

"So there's really no need for me to leave my wife and children in the middle of the night to see you just a few hours after we just got off our seventh twelve-hour shift in a row."

"You think more clearly than I do. And you're the only one I can really talk to about this shit. I sure as shit couldn't talk to those morons there tonight. George and Chris."

"Aw, Leon, you're gettin' soft on me," Chuck said, yawning.

"Go to sleep, bud. I'll fill you in on . . . in two . . . three . . . when we see each other again."

"Call me if you need to."

"Gotcha," I said.

"Like you should've a few hours ago," Chuck said, just before hanging up.

Fucker didn't even let me say good-bye.

I leaned against the wall for a moment, resting my head, before grabbing another beer to take with me back to my lounge chair. After all, I wouldn't want to just sit down before needing another refill.

"Who the fuck was calling at this hour?" Paula said.

"Fuck, don't do that!" I'd forgotten my little sister was crashing at my joint tonight.

"I was trying to sleep through all your noise." She made the Paula Grumpy Face as she pulled a beer out of the fridge.

I stumbled to the table to sit. And missed.

"You're drunk," she said. "You're really stinking drunk. What the hell happened tonight to make you freak out so much you needed to kill a . . . twelve pack?"

Oh, yes. It was because of the freaking and the drinking that I was forgetting so much. Even as drunk as I was, I couldn't admit everything about tonight—about why I suddenly knew reincarnation—the wiggiest fruit loop theory ever—was real and all that. *No, not know so much as believe.*

I could only hope that in the clear light of day, and hangover, reality would return to my universe.

"The impossible happened," I said from the floor. "Never happened. None of it. But you . . . You came here because . . . because . . . something happened with your . . . boy . . . boyfriend . . ." I slurred as I stumbled to my feet and toward her. "I need another beer."

"You really don't," she said. "But here, have this one." She thrust a can into my hand. A full can. Oh, glory. "And that wasn't the question."

"Goddamn you," I said, after swallowing. "This is . . . this is water!"

"Runner, you've always been the sober and obedient one. What the hell is all this about?" With a wave she indicated me and the twelve brave, empty, little soldiers.

"I already told you—you, oh she who does not live with me but moved in nonethe . . . nonethe—"

"Nonetheless. Got it."

"I was coming home tonight after work . . . No food here, so I had to stop to get something for breakfast—some breakfasty yumminess . . ."

"And . . . ?" Paula asked.

"I stopped at Seven-Eleven. The one right up the goddamned road at Thirteen and Hoover. And it'd just been robbed."

"Yeah, I got all that before," Paula said. "From when you were wandering around, talking to yourself while I was trying to sleep."

"I don't talk to myself."

"You always have. Go on."

"So all this shit went down, and I got there right after, and there was this mesmeric guy. This incredible dude. But he took off. And then we—me and George and Chris—talked to Sheryl, the cashier, after we packed off John Francis in the ambulance . . ." I kinda wanted to sleep. Really rather needed to, in fact. And my kitchen floor looked really nice and cool.

"I still don't get what happened that freaked you so," Paula said, sitting across the table from me. I saw her morph through three different looks and outfits: First she was a nun, which worked for her with the grumpy face she does; then she was some sort of renaissance harlot (or maybe a renaissance witch?), which also worked for her 'cause when she's not grumpy she's a hottie; and then it was like she was some la-di-dah Jane Austen high-buttoned lady.

I really needed to finish drinking my water. I was way too drunk.

"From what the clerk said, this guy got shot—repeatedly—and still did incredible, unbelievable, shit. I mean, I saw him after, and thought his shirt was polka-dotted—but it was really splattered with tons of his blood!"

"Oh, god. Did he like die in front of you?"

"No! He got on his goddamned bike . . . and . . ." I suddenly remembered something—somethings. I found a pad and pen and tried to write, but couldn't. "Here," I said to Paula, "write this down—he jumped on his *bike*, a *Harley*, with *California* plates, and took off!"

"Okay, and this is important why?" she said, writing.

"From what the clerk said, he should be dead, but he wasn't, and he nearly killed someone, and then disappeared and we don't have a lot to go on!" I got up, again excited by this, and grabbed another beer from the fridge. "Y'know, Sheryl—she's a real bad ass, did I mention that? I think she's gonna be a French Perry Mason some day."

"Uh, yeah." She took the beer out of my hand before I could even open it.

"She talked about Superdude a lot. And then we—Chris, George and I . . ." I remembered how this vigilante made me feel, and I slowly slid to the ground.

"No, no, Rhenné," Paula said, stopping me as I tried to lie on the kitchen floor. Grunting and cussing at me, she hauled me to my bedroom. "Your bed is a lot more comfortable. C'mon now. Walk with me here."

I could never say no to my baby sis. Neither could most guys, what with her being so attractive with long, blonde hair and green eyes. Plus, she sometimes did this flippy thing with her hair that I could never quite get down right. People thought we looked a lot alike. But she was younger and . . . bouncier. "You thought I was . . . always . . . moving . . . running so fast. Always running. When we were younger. Plus, you couldn't say my name."

"Yes? So what happened, Runner-who-will-regret-the-last-six-beers-tomorrow?"

Yeah. Like I was gonna tell her 'bout how this vigilante looked at me and made me pudding. Like I'd admit I didn't want to sleep 'cause I knew I'd just dream about him and pasts we never shared. Fruit Loops, cuckoo for Cocoa Puffs.

Then I realized she was just wanting specifics, things I could point my finger at and say, "There, this is why I'm drinking myself silly tonight."

So I said, "We watched the surveillance tapes. And we saw the bad guy entering and trying to rob the joint and all. And we even saw him flying through the air like that nun, on that TV show— d'ya remember that?"

"Yeah, yeah, I got the memos and the speeches and all the rest of it, Runner. Got it all already. Except one answer."

"And, uh, yeah. Right. Which one's that?" I was on my back in a dark room and it was nice and peaceful. Restful. Oh, my. Closing my eyes felt quite nice. And stopped the room from spinning.

"Why the fuck did ya get home and drink yourself under the table?"

"Because nothing made sense," I said, rolling over and burying my head under a pillow. "Plus, well, I couldn't reach Chuck."

"Oh. Okay. Fine. And, by the way, my darling, loving sister—I'm fine staying here as long as I'd like, right?"

"Huh?" I sat upright.

"You got here all scared shitless. Nothing's ever scared you before. So what happened? Give me the truth and I'll move out quicker."

"Paula, I already told you that you can stay here as long as you . . . want. Need. You're my sister."

"So tell me what happened tonight already. Why you needed to come here and drink yourself stupid."

"We watched the surveillance tapes, to get more on this mysterious vigilante."

"And . . . ?"

"Nothing." I said. "I saw this guy, face-to-face, and then, we looked at the tapes and he wasn't there. You've heard it all, honest. Just let me sleep already."

"Hold on, what do you mean he wasn't there?"

"We looked at the surveillance tapes from the store. Repeatedly. Several times. And . . . He. Wasn't. There. *I saw him*—California plates on his Harley-Davidson bike. It was big and black, just like everything he wore. Well, actually, since he wasn't too big, everything he wore was small and black. But the bike was big and black." How could I tell her—or anybody—that I saw him and he got inside me, somehow, or maybe he was already there, and it's like he took something out of me when he drove away?

"So what did you see on the tapes?"

"Our perp just flew across the joint, got smashed, smushed, smunched and tossed away like bad white trash all on his own. Nobody done him wrong. In the least. Where vigilante Superdude ought to have been—nothing."

II: DARON

. . . meanwhile . . .

C an I help you?"

"I have a reservation. For a week. Silvers, Daron Silvers." I handed the clerk my driver's license and credit card. It was handy to have appropriate identification for several different countries in unlife. Any vamp who planned and thought ahead had that aspect covered.

"Yeah, I can guess which group you're with," the clerk said, his disgust clearly showing through. His little white-trash ass must not have cared too much for the large group of lesbians staying there this Halloween. I really wished we could stay someplace a little classier some time.

"I hate traveling these days. I just can't wait to get back home. To my castle," I said, filling out the paperwork lightning fast.

"Yeah. Whatever. Room two-ten," the clerk said, handing me my keys. Evelyn kept stressing that we stayed in these cesspools because we were trying for anonymity. Mostly.

"It's in England," I said, letting my English accent flow freely. I reached across the counter and thwapped his shoulder so hard he flew backward. He'd annoyed me with his homophobia and I wanted to make sure he wouldn't even think of messing with us further. "Cheerio, mate." I smiled, winked at him, and went up to meet with my so-called friends. We'd have this last weekend. Next year, at Evelyn's little get-together, they could mourn me.

The lodging was adequate—your basic $69-a-night motel with two double beds; a bathroom with white towels, shampoo, conditioner and soap; and a Bible in the bedside table between the beds. The carpet and walls were beige and the paintings were mass-produced. It looked just like it had every year that Evelyn had been convening us here, except for the placards making the dubious claim of hi-speed Internet.

I put out my do-not-disturb sign, ensured no one could open the door without waking me, and laid my body bag out on the bed. I didn't need a coffin, or body bag, even, but the latter kept out the light. I could get the same effect sleeping on the bathroom floor, but the bed was a lot more comfortable. Additionally, because I didn't need to breathe, I often found being sealed in an enclosed space comforting, and after all the years I'd lived through straw beds and no plumbing, I'd take all the comforting I could get.

I looked out into the night. I remembered the sweet woman I met the last time I was in this town—Victoria. I'd just been out for a little fun, and briefly, only briefly, convinced myself that she could be Rebecca, come again to me.

I was lonely. I wanted my Rebecca. Her and the release she offered.

So I used Victoria and left her. Because she wasn't Rebecca. No one ever was. Whenever I thought a woman *might* be her, she wasn't, or she disappeared.

I'd often dreamt about reuniting with her. My Rebecca. It'd become a fantasy that ran through my head, more elaborate every year. These days, it was us, running toward each other in the surf as the sun set. You know the one.

But then, of course, I'd remember I was a vampire and would expire in such a setting. Running toward each other in a cemetery is really not quite so romantic.

I hadn't even had sex since that last time I was here in Warren, a nothing suburb of Detroit. I'd had thousands of girls, women, through the years, but I no longer cared. About women. Sex. Orgasms. Sometimes it felt as though I just had to perform, and I just wanted . . . something lasting and whole. Someone to love.

And someone to love me back.

I'd found that someone, hundreds of years before, and I'd let her be killed.

I wondered if other vampires felt this way, because it never seemed as if they did. Maybe they'd just never enjoyed real love, and without experiencing it they couldn't know what they were missing. Or else they went through unlife always thinking they'd have time, some day, to experience it, so never looked for it, never found it and never missed it. Sometimes, I wished I could still be like the others—able to run around and use women left and right. But for the last few decades I'd realized the love I'd known made all else cliché.

I needed to go to sleep.

Somebody knocked on my door. Even from the bed I recognized the scent. "How'd you find me?" I asked, letting Marguerite in.

"Evelyn," she said, sitting next to me on the bed. Her long red hair streamed about her, falling below her ample cleavage. Attractive, yes, but I'd already been there and done that and it wasn't worth revisiting. Not yet again. Once more.

"The sun's coming up soon," I said, lighting a smoke. "You should go back to your room." Seeing her so shortly after the dust-up at that convenience store—complete with two men who reminded me of the bastards who'd killed Rebecca, as well as this year's Rebecca look-alike—made me wonder briefly about coincidence. I knew coincidences happened all the time, but that didn't mean I couldn't find them suspicious. I wish I'd been able to drain the getaway driver, too.

"I was thinking," Marguerite replied, leaning back on the bed, "that maybe I could spend the day with you."

"It's a body bag built for one."

"You used to rest with Rebecca."

"I had a coffin back then. And she had a bed."

Marguerite sat up. "Oh, we both know you no longer use a body bag. Or coffin. They're so passé."

"The curtains sometimes open in these cheap motels during the day, and I really hate waking up on fire." I unzipped the bag and opened my duffel so I could pull out my toothbrush and other toiletries. Nobody wants to live forever with bad teeth.

"Oh, baby, you're always on fire," Marguerite said, wrapping her arms around me from behind. With a little show of strength, she whipped me onto my back on the bed and straddled me. "Daron, my sweet demon lover, you cannot forever remain chaste to the memory of your dearest Rebecca."

"I've never remained chaste to her." I stood, dumping her onto the floor. "But I loved her. And will always."

"If you really loved her, you would have changed her."

"Maybe I wanted to give her a choice—*really* give her a choice. Maybe I don't think it's all that to be a vampire, and so didn't think I should just bring her over to satisfy my own urges and wants, y'know?" I pulled a handkerchief from my pocket and used it to prop the Bible from the bedside drawer against the curtains to keep them shut.

"When are you going to realize that we are the superior race? That those we changed are actually blessed? Honored?" She followed me around, as if she thought she was going to get somewhere with me by doing so. It wasn't a totally misguided thought, since I sometimes did give in and fuck her. Some old habits die hard.

And then what she'd said struck me. "Marguerite, you haven't been changing people again, have you?"

"Not above what I'm *allowed*. These days."

"So then you're feeding. And killing."

"Only those who need it. I follow every one of the *laws* we've set for ourselves. Even though I don't agree with them."

"Look, Marguerite, I'm kicking you out—literally, if I have to—and going to sleep. And you know I'm not kidding."

"Some day you will give up all hope for your beloved Rebecca. Just hope that occurs before I've totally given up on you."

"You give up on *me* twice a day, but you go through women like others . . . Oh, for fuck's sake, I drove nearly a thousand miles tonight and just can't come up with any amusing similes here. Please forgive."

"I love the way you speak—I love how you adapt your speeches to fit the words and slang of the current day. For the most part."

"What can I say? I'm ever-evolving. It's part of how I hide." Part of me wanted to want her, after all she was attractive enough—but I couldn't stop thinking about the police officer I'd run into tonight. Victoria hadn't looked much like Rebecca at all—but that cop tonight had. She'd been an almost-exact replica of her. I wondered if she had a slender, green-eyed, Wiccan, blonde younger sister who looked almost exactly like her. If she did, she'd be a dead-ringer for my girl.

"Why can't you just learn to let go of all mortal encumbrances like the rest of us?" Marguerite asked, caressing my cheek. "It would all be ever so much easier for you if you did."

I dropped my toiletries in the bath and turned back to Marguerite. "You make it sound as if changing who I am is as easy as changing diapers. It's not as if what sets us apart from regular folks is as tangible as a soul, demon or something." We're just really old, practically immortal humans suffering from a blood virus that changes us—mutates us. And as we got older, the virus became more powerful, as did we. It changed our physiology, making us stronger and faster. It made us heal quicker and extended our lifetimes, making us nearly unkillable.

"And we can have fun, or sit and brood. I choose fun. As do most of us. After all, that is what it is all about," Marguerite said, trying to guide me back to the bed.

"Haven't you yet realized just how tired and drunk I have to be to fuck you?"

"But you *are* tired."

"And you just want me for a meaningless fuck. And yet you wonder why I keep avoiding fucking you."

"You're in a foul mood, aren't you?" She pushed me down to the bed and straddled me again. She brushed her lips softly over mine. "Till the night is upon us again." And then she left.

I took a shower, brushed my teeth, set my alarm for just before sunset the following eve and zipped myself into my body bag, hoping for quick, dream-free sleep.

But I just knew I'd dream of my years with Marguerite, and the dalliances I'd had with her since.

When you've been around as long as I have, it's actually rather a bit of a surprise to be wrong.

I raced down the street, fleeing from the fine lady whose purse I'd just nicked. I wasn't so afraid of her as her I was of her lackeys. No way could she keep up with me—I was amazed she herself had even started giving chase to me.

But then I was down an alley and there was no place left to run, so I ran toward a wall, intent on running up it, but I wasn't as tall, strong or fast as I ought to be. I looked down and realized in horror I was dressed as the street urchin I'd been before the Bubonic Plague had struck.

It was only then that I realized it was daytime. A murky, stinky day, but day nonetheless. I turned about, to run back the way I'd come, but with a whoosh! *Evelyn stood before me. I knew who she was and that as the thief, pickpocket and criminal I was then, I didn't stand a chance against her. I remembered that back then, for my age and size, I was strong. She was stronger. Stronger than any such fine lady I'd ever met before. Stronger than* anyone *I'd ever met before.*

She twisted my arm till I fell to my knees. The sound of horses and carriages going down dirt streets was replaced by a faint buzzing.

"You have potential . . . lass," she said, immediately seeing through my until-then impenetrable guise. "If you dare see what you can become,

join me here, tonight." She slipped a piece of paper into my hand before releasing me.

"I don't need your stinkin' help," I said, tossing the paper to the ground. The buzzing grew louder.

"If you can't read it, don't ignore it," she said. "You'll simply have to follow me till our appointment. I am positive you are most talented at following people, so you should have no trouble at all with it. I'm sure anyone not my equal would never even notice your presence, in fact."

She knew I was illiterate, and gave me the solution I'd obviously come up with on my own.

"You're going to have to give a statement," the cop from earlier tonight said, stepping up next to me. She was in her uniform. Her squad car, with lights flashing and sirens buzzing, was just behind her. She seemed a lot taller than earlier.

"I don't have time," I said, pointing off toward Evelyn. "I have to follow her."

"You have to give a statement. I can't let you leave until you give a statement."

"No, no. I have to follow her because I can't read this note she gave me and I have to muck out her stables." Why did I want to go muck out her stables? I couldn't control a thing I was doing or saying.

And as I turned around to once again address the copper, everything morphed so I was mucking out Evelyn's stables. This was ridiculous. I tossed my shovel down.

"If you leave now, you'll never know what could be," Evelyn said, bringing me my supper just as she had that first night I began working under her employ. She ran her fingers lightly over her décolletage. I couldn't take my eyes off her, especially when she ran her tongue over her lips.

The lights started flashing again, complete with sirens wailing, and I turned around . . .

"You have to give a statement." But this time it was my Rebecca saying it.

⊕

I bolted upright in my body bag. Though I had been dreaming, I could sense it was still nighttime. There were as yet several hours to go before daybreak. I wondered if I could go back to that 7-Eleven and track her scent from there to her home.

Or else, I could Google her based on the name I'd seen on her badge and all that—Rhenné Leon. Find out where she lived that way. Maybe go pay her a visit.

The second surprise since my arrival was that the Internet connection actually worked. I Googled as I pulled on a black T-shirt, new-rinse jeans and my trench and boots. I picked up my helmet and Mapquested on my way out. Some of my kind found modern technology too anachronistic for their taste, but I thought Wireless was as useful as the internal combustion engine had proven to be.

"Hey, d'ya know where the ice machine is?" a fellow asked soon as I stepped out of my room.

I barely glanced at him before I vaulted the second-floor railing to land next to my bike.

"Dude, how'd you do that?" he asked, running over to the railing to look down on me.

I thought about quickly thralling him into forgetfulness, but it wasn't worth my time or effort. "I'm springy."

I gave no thought to the gathering I left behind, our entire gang of Evelyn's children, grandchildren, great-grandchildren, et cetera. The annual gathering could convene without me.

Mapquest directed me to Rhenné Leon's apartment and I circled the building, sniffing till I was sure I knew which apartment was hers. After a quick, quiet leap to her balcony I perched lightly on the railing to peer inside, focusing on all movements and voices.

I needed to catch her by herself. That was the only way I'd know if she really was Rebecca.

So, for now, I waited. I waited, watched, listened and perched.

When her sister took her to her bedroom, I leapt over to the barely there window ledge, grasping the bricks of the building to hold myself in place. Just call me Spider-Vamp.

And, as soon as her sister left—a sister who resembled her so much I had to look twice to discern one from the other, just like old times—I tried to jimmy the window.

It didn't move an inch. It was locked.

III: RHENNÉ

The next morning, before dawn

I *slipped between the curtains on my bed, crossed the room from the four-poster, parted the heavy draperies and opened my window.*

"You must grant me an invitation into your abode," she said. She'd saved me, I knew this, before and again. She meant no harm to me or any other who dwelt within.

"You are always welcome wherever I might dwell." As soon as I said it, I also knew I shouldn't have. I hurried back to the safety of my bed, pulling the bed curtains tightly closed. I no sooner secured them than they melted to nothing and everything in the room changed, except her. She was leaning over the bed, now, and nothing in me offered any kind of resistance to her tender touch on my cheek.

This was whacked. This was weird. I didn't talk like this. Glancing down at the filmy gown that was rumpled from sleep, I knew I sure as shit didn't look like this. Well, maybe a little.

She gazed down at me. "I can't help but hope you're her."
"Who?"

She eased me onto my back, then lay on top of me, grinding her thigh against my cunt, pushing up against me and making me arch beneath her. She ran her lips lightly over mine, until I opened to her, allowing her tongue to enter me.

She kissed my lips. Sucked them lightly while she ran her hands down my arms, feeling my body beneath hers.

She played her tongue lightly over my earlobe, down my neck, and then sucked at my pulse point. She ran her hands under my T-shirt, feeling my skin, making me squirm. "I wonder, sometimes, if she brings me here just so I might find you. God, Rebecca, I want you so badly—"

I pushed her back, sure of one thing as I seemed to straddle vast gulfs in time. "I'm Rhenné."

"Yes. You are." She stared at me. Right into my eyes. "Lie down. I want you."

I wasn't so easily swayed. I didn't follow her instructions. "My dear sir, I cannot so flaunt the ways of propriety. I should not have even allowed you into my bedchamber thusly. It is not right." Wait. I thought she was a woman. Was she a man? Or was that simply my wishful thinking? And what was with me, talking like something out of a bad horror flick?

Meanwhile, she touched and caressed me. She ran her fingers lightly over my torso and down my leg, even as she pushed herself against my cunt. "Get naked. You're not her, and this isn't happening—it's just a dream—so give yourself to me. Forget everything except the now. Don't worry about anything but desire. You want me, I want you. Let's do this for now."

I struggled out of my shirt and bra, and then lay down again, terror and arousal overwhelming my swimming senses.

"Oh yes," she said, running her hand over my nipple, over my breast. Then she leaned down to run her lips over my other nipple, toy and play with it, then bite it. Hard. "Get naked for me."

I couldn't do anything but listen to her. Obey her.

And it felt so good.

I shimmied out of my panties and dropped them to the floor beside the bed. It wasn't as if it was real, or as if I had any choice in the matter, after all. I lay back on the bed, my hands and arms covering my nudity.

"Relax," she said. She reached down, pried my limbs from across my body, and pressed them into the bed next to me. "You're beautiful. Every *last inch of you." She said this last part cupping my cheek and looking directly into my eyes. "Take a deep breath."*

I did so, and as I did, it felt as if my body was filling with a wanton sexuality. I let my legs fall open just a little bit. Cool air from the open window stroked my wetness, causing me to gasp slightly.

"That's my beautiful girl," she said. Her gaze traveling slowly, appreciatively, down my body felt like a caress. And then her fingers stroking between my legs caused me to moan and open my thighs further, behaving worse than any lady of the night. She brought her fingers up to her lips and sucked them. "Mm. I could live off this sweet nectar for an eternity."

I shuddered. I couldn't remember ever being so turned on, wet and open. My nipples were rock hard. I liked her looking at me, touching me, slipping her fingers inside of me and tasting my skin.

I'd never felt so good even when I masturbated, or thought I'd come with a guy, and as soon as her tongue touched my clit, I knew I was going to come hard, in her mouth.

"God, yes, please!" I screamed, bucking and arching against her as she flicked her tongue across my clit while sucking it and running her hands up and down my body, over my breasts, my nipples . . .

"Yes!"

I wasn't quite sure if the aroma seeping into the bedroom smelled good or made me want to throw up.

"Yo, Runner," Paula said, "I've got some grub on the table—but here's some coffee to get you started."

"Oh. Coffee. Good." I sat up, decided that was taking things a little too quickly, so laid back and focused on just trying to open my eyes. Slowly. "Mornings wouldn't be so bad if they came far later in the day."

"Or, I imagine, not at all with the way you were drinking last night."

"Oh, god." I really deserved to feel this way. "I am *so* glad I don't have to work today."

"The entire city is, I'm sure. I'm thinking extremely hungover cops just don't do the trick."

"That's about the size of."

"Come on, sis, get some food in. It'll make you feel better. That and a shower and all."

"Paula?"

"Yeah, Runner?"

"Last night, it was just the two of us here all night, right?"

"Whaddya mean?"

"I mean, nobody else came here last night, right? During the night or anything?" I had a more-than-vague remembrance of someone visiting me during the night. Coming in through my bedroom window. I looked over and saw that it was unlocked. I wasn't sure what had, or hadn't, happened the night before.

"Well, you were obviously dreaming about something really interesting last night—and talking in your sleep the way you always do. In a really funny accent—like you were in medieval England or something. I almost came in, especially when it sounded like someone else was in here with you . . . but it sounded as if you were having a *really* good time. I didn't want to interrupt . . . anything."

"It was a dream."

"So you don't remember anything about it? It sounded kind of like those nightmares you had when you were a teenager. I mean, I thought you'd grown out of them."

"No. Nothing." Just the feel of lips and fingers and skin . . .

"Rhenné, if there's anything—"

"No. There's not." Paula stared at me for a few moments, as if assessing whether or not she ought to press the issue. "It was nothing," I insisted.

"Tell me."

How could I tell her I needed to remember what was, apparently, just a dream? Such a vivid dream I wasn't sure it hadn't actually happened?

But then I realized I'd never had curtains on any bed I'd ever slept in. Not even at that really nice B&B where Robert had proposed to me. And the guy who came to me in the dream—when I was in the curtained bed—looked a lot like the guy from the 7-Eleven. Superdude. The guy in my dream even wore a long, black cape that resembled the black trench Superdude wore, but why was I thinking it was a woman?

"Paula, I had a whacked weird night yesterday, drank *way* too much and . . . Well, had a bunch of really trippy dreams. That's all. Really. Honest Injun." And then I picked up the morning newspaper and saw a picture of last night's John Francis. For an instant, just like at the 7-Eleven last night, I could feel his rough hands on me as he grabbed my dress and pulled me from my carriage.

A cold chill ran down my spine as someone walked over my grave.

That night, when I was finally over my hangover—mostly— Paula insisted we go out. When I tried to beg off, she said, "Okay, fine. Let's just stay at home watching DVDs of the *X-Files* or *Buffy the Vampire Slayer*—"

"Sounds great." Popcorn and old favorites was a good night in my book.

"I was teasing."

"Oh." Damn.

"You and your entire hermit deal and all that. You see, the point is that you're well on your way to becoming an old maid—what with being obsessed with your work, staying home all the time, and this new obsession with vampires . . . Old maid, definitely."

"Like your love life is successful—and I'm not going to be an old maid!" I was definitely realizing why I lived by myself. My life was my own business.

"How many dates have you had lately?"

"What constitutes *lately*?"

"Past month."

I thought about my midnight dream visitor, and then about

Superdude from last night. Which were the last guys I was interested in. Which I would never, ever, admit. Ever. "Then, Paula, that'd be none. But hold on—what's this with me being obsessed with vampires?" You'd think that having to run from an abusive S.O.B. of a boyfriend would get her to lighten up on my dating, but that apparently wasn't so.

She tossed the evening paper down on the table in front of me. *Murderer—or Vampire?* screamed the headline.

"What sorta crap you readin' these days, kid?" I asked, flipping the paper to read the masthead. Oh. It was one of the city's major, respected, dailies, *The Detroit News.*

She straddled a chair. "C'mon, everything you said last night added up to one thing: Superdude," she made with the air quotes on that, "is a vampire. Just like they say here." She tapped the paper.

"The problem, sister dearest, is that vampires *do not exist.*" Except, of course, my irrational inner self pointed out, for the one I'd perhaps invited in through my window and into my bed the night before.

"Yes. You are correct. We both know that. But has anybody bothered to share that piece of intel with the vampires themselves?"

"Um. *Again,* there's no such thing as vampires." Was I saying that for her benefit or mine?

"Then come up with a logical, *rational,* explanation for what happened last night. Thing is, you got absolutely shit-faced, so get off telling me you weren't thinking something supernatural wasn't happening. Why else were you drinking yourself into a stupor?"

I was in no mood for her to explain me to me. "Listen, Paula, I'm hungover, upset and not in the least having a good day. I know you have a point, so why don't you get to it already? What do *you* think happened last night?"

She paced. "Okay, so get this. That guy last night—the perp— was on drugs and just threw himself around like you saw on the video. For absolutely no reason at all. Except he was crazed on drugs."

"That makes no sense at all," I said, realizing Paula'd been watching more TV than she'd admit to. This *perp* crap was obviously coming from too much *CSI* or *Law & Order*. Spare me amateurs, even my own sister.

"No, hold on. It all comes together, see—for instance, the clerk was overly excited, so she, after the fact, just said whatever you wanted to hear. Regardless of what actually happened." Paula faced off with me, raising an eyebrow and openly challenging me.

God! Little sisters sucked! "But what the hell reason would she have to do that? None of this makes sense, sister dearest." Nor did me having the vivid dreams and hallucinations I'd been having the last twenty-four hours—erotic and fearsome both. One minute I'm getting beer, the next I'm mesmerized by a suspect, then I'm dreaming Bram Stoker. It wasn't just the hangover leaving me feeling as if my world had turned to quicksand.

"As if anything you were postulating last night—any bit of what you were obviously afraid of last night—made any sort of sense at all."

"So then what the hell are you on about?"

She crooked an eyebrow with a smirk. "I'm showing you just how stupid you've been. How you're all whacked about the wrong stuff and got completely wasted for no reason at all."

"You're playing devil's advocate." I was either still too hungover or not drunk enough to bear Paula's District Attorney imitation.

"Just like I've done all my life. You see, it makes perfect sense. I *was* listening last night, after all. And I *have* been reading the papers. Bad enough the tabloids call this guy a vampire, I can't have my cop big sister thinking it as well. You scared me last night—heavy drinking is not your thing," Paula continued. "So Superdude met the bad guy at the door, grabbed him and threw him down outside. Then he either used knives, a fork, or barbecuing implements of some sort to puncture his neck and the bad guy bleeds to death."

"That really doesn't make a lot of sense. The guy I saw wasn't the type to travel with barbeque on his mind."

"You're right, it doesn't make any sense told that way, and it makes no sense that there are vampires running around Warren, of all places. I do have a theory, and if you tell me more maybe it'll start to make sense." She opened up my closet and began, well, ransacking it, pulling out articles of clothing, one by one, and discarding them onto my bed. That is, except for the occasional piece she tossed at the trash. She'd always been a mysterious creature.

"Fine. When you want to share that theory of yours, feel free." I gave an annoyed sigh which she completely ignored. "There is more than one robber. There's one guy who goes into the store, and another who drives the getaway vehicle. Plus, the description of the thief varies, so there's no reason to think all, or any, of these events are related. So I'd say there's at least two groups—at least four guys. Now. Not including the two who have already been killed."

"What about the vigilante? One or more?" She held a blouse up to me, then tossed it on the bed.

"Only one. And he just showed up last night. I don't like vigilantes."

"Okay," Paula said, "so what happened to all the blood that seemed to disappear last night?" She hung first a blue blouse then a green one on the closet's doorknob.

"What do you mean?"

"Well, the article here proclaiming there's a vampire on the loose says that the perp from last night was—oh, really Rhenné, this is so Eighties." Now we were to trousers and skirts and most of them seemed headed directly for the trashcan. Relentlessly, Paula continued her recitation of facts as reported by the infallible newspapers. "He suffered massive blood loss. Pretty much, all the blood was drained from his body. You really need to get a little more inventive with the colors, by the way, sis."

"Yeah, so he bled out, what's the big?" I asked, getting us back with the focus.

"If he'd just bled out, then the blood would be there. In his clothing, on the pavement, somewhere. But it was gone. That doesn't make sense. Like a bunch of other shit that happened last night." She reached into the very back of my closet. "Ooo, leather," she said with a grin, holding up a skirt she'd talked me into buying years before. "Anyway, the lack of blood makes no sense."

"There are countless reasons someone might collect the blood of someone else. Satanic rituals, for instance."

"Bingo! Big sister finally buys a clue!" Paula gave me one of her patented you're-an-idiot looks, then held the leather skirt up to my waist. "Does this still fit you?"

Unwilling to admit she had come up with a not too-unbaked theory to explain the lack of blood, I said carefully, "I know there are medical conditions that are made better through the ingestion of blood. And I can guess at many other reasons someone might harvest blood. But not a single one of them requires the close pin-prick holes in the donor's neck that occurred last night." I yanked off my jeans and put the leather skirt on. Anything to get her to stop fussing with it.

"Are you sure you're a cop? Did you skip detective school or something?" She stood there, hand on hip with her best *duh* gesture. "You're likely dealing with a vampire worshipper or someone who thinks he—or she—*is* a vampire. That looks good on you. I think it works."

Superdude as a vampire wannabe? It could explain a lot. I desperately wanted it to explain everything. She didn't know how I'd stood there, frozen, feeling like I wanted him to drag me to bed. "For what?"

"This rockin' club—maybe we can hook something-something up for you."

"Paula, you're white, you really need to learn to live with that."

"I may be white, but I also got something extra, y'know?"

"You think I should've stuck with Robert." It was like I suddenly understood. She was trying to get me to hook up with someone because she didn't really like how long I'd been single—which was ever since Robert. I followed her into my office, where her gear was. She was digging through her suitcase, apparently looking for an appropriate outfit for herself—now that her fun with me was concluded.

"Runner—Rhenné," she began, "I know a lot of women who would kill for a guy like him. Not me, though. But you're not them, and they're not you. You need to do what's gonna make you happy."

"But Mom and Dad are pissed they don't get to say 'our son-in-law, the doctor' at church socials."

"They'll get over it. Some year. I think they just want grandkids, and they've probably figured out that I'm not getting hitched until I have a lot of fun first."

"You little slut!"

"Hey, I figure as long as it's safe, and we're consenting adults, anything goes."

Consenting adults? We? Was there something Paula wasn't telling me? I thwapped my hands over my ears. "TMI! TMI!"

I kept chanting as I muscled her out of my room. I desperately wished that the vampire-wannabe theory explained how I'd frozen at the crime scene, failed to remember key details and other things that were so unlike me. I looked at my bed and felt a hot flush. Getting drunk and that erotic dream of last night was also so unlike me. I needed a diversion, something more normal than hearing and seeing myself in some past life, in bed with Superdude.

Not all that reluctantly, I put on the black silk blouse she'd chosen and steeled myself for a night on the town. When she came at me with the thigh highs from her own suitcase I agreed just to get it over with.

She took me to this new hot spot that was a total meat market, full of men who were all but slobbering after any attractive woman around, that is, any woman but me. Not that I wanted slobber, but still, it was no help to my ego. It made me feel as if maybe my breasts weren't on public-enough display.

Fuck, I felt conservatively dressed here in spite of the leather-silk-and-stockings outfit Paula had selected solely for the purpose of attracting members of the opposite sex. And I almost couldn't believe I could walk in the four-inch spikes she'd shoved me into.

I felt ultra sexualized, and it did upset me that as far as the men at the bar were concerned, I probably could have shown up in a burlap sack and attracted just as much attention. I was going through a lot of pain and suffering to look like this, and they weren't appreciating it at all, they were hitting on me just because I was a woman as far as I could tell.

"Is this really what it takes to get a date these days?" We were walking around the outer edges of the bar, trying to avoid more of the same sleazy come-ons we had already experienced.

"Bet you're wishing you hadn't dumped Robert right about now," Paula answered with a twinkle in her eye. I hated my sister. And that was such the understatement—I hated her worse than—

Someone slammed into me, all but knocking my drink out of my hand. "Hey, sorry about that, babe," a tall, dark-haired man said. "How 'bout I buy you another?"

"No, thanks," I replied, grabbing Paula and dragging her to the exit. *Babe.* I so did not want to be *babed* again. This place was madness.

"I know of another place we could try," Paula suggested as we settled in the car. She didn't start it, though.

"Is this the sort of place you usually go to?" I asked. "I mean, really?"

"This? Well, no, but I thought you might like it."

"So you've never been here before?"

"Yeah, that's about right."

"Um, so why the hell did you bring me here?"

"I thought this would be the sort of place for you. I thought maybe you'd find someone here. And, well, this is what you'd expect of me."

I leaned my head back against the seat. I was tired. At least the bit of alcohol I'd just downed had gotten rid of the very last remnants of my hangover. "Listen, it's been a long day, and I'm sure tomorrow will be even longer. Why don't we call it a night, and then tomorrow you can take me to someplace you actually like and have been to?" I'd already had more than enough of her riddles and all for now.

"Big sisters can be such a pain."

"Nothing compared with little ones."

Paula looked sideways at me. She was up to less than no good. "Sure you're up to going to my sort of bar, especially on the Saturday before Halloween?"

"Don't tell me you've taken to hanging with bat-head-eating psychos or anything."

"Nope, they're fairly normal folks, all things considered. But it's a date."

She finally started the car and we were quiet in the dark as she drove back to my place. I let myself feel the little bit of alcohol I'd consumed and thought about the past twenty-four hours.

. . . then . . .

I was on a darkened street. I wasn't supposed to be alone. Something must have happened to my father to keep him from bringing the carriage to pick me up. I had never been out alone so late at night before.

I glanced about for a hansom, but seeing none, I kept walking, wondering where I could go to seek refuge during the darkness. How had I let myself get into this position? I was sure my father would be waiting for me when I exited the theatre—just as he told me he would. There had been several mysterious deaths in London of late, and his concern for my safety was justified.

I picked up my pace, wishing for lighter skirts and boots that did not pinch my toes.

I felt as if I was being watched. I looked about and saw nothing, but yet I felt someone's gaze upon me. I turned and ran as fast as I could—I wasn't sure to where I ran, but I knew I had to get away. I paused, glancing about and listening . . .

I heard a swooping of wings above. I ran in the opposite direction, running until my sides and legs ached, until I could no longer breathe and my corset seemed to be squeezing the air out of me. I leaned out of sight against a building, my heart pattering away in my chest.

When I heard nothing and saw nothing, I tried to regain my composure and tidy my disarrayed clothing and hair.

Then everything went black and I was thrown to the ground. A large figure hovered over me, ripping my clothing aside. I screamed, but there was apparently no one to hear.

I knew what was happening and fear paralyzed me.

But then the figure was gone. Dizzied, I pulled myself out of the dirt. The massive figure that just threatened me was now lying prone on the ground. Even as I watched, he groaned, rolled to his feet and fled.

It was only then that I realized someone else was there, with me. This one held out a hand to help me up. I didn't take it. Even though I realized this was likely he who had saved me from the first man, it didn't mean he was safe, either.

"Then go on. Be as you were—heading toward home, or wherever you find shelter now. But know, I will be watching you. I will ensure you are safe."

"Rhenné, Rhenné? Have you heard a word I've said?" Paula asked, reaching over to shake me.

"I'm sorry," I said, trying to bring myself back to reality. I'd not had these nightmares since I was a teenager and now I was having them wide awake. This was not of the good. "I must be more tired than I thought. What were you saying?" I couldn't believe I'd tuned out. I wanted to blame it on so many things—the ever-increasing dreams, last night's vampire, et cetera.

"It's not important, you'll find out sooner or later anyway."

"No, really, I *am* interested." I knew I'd had these dreams before, when I was younger, but they felt déjà vuey beyond that—it wasn't déjà vu from previous dreams, but from another life. I was back to Fruit Loops.

"Have you ever wondered how our folks came up with two such totally different names for us? I mean, isn't it kind of strange?"

"Um, left field?"

"Not so much if you'd been paying attention. There'd been this entire build-up to this. Well, not so much build up as topic climbing to me thinking of this."

"Mom said the names just popped into her head when she first saw each of us. Kind of like it was meant to be."

"Really? She said that?"

"Yeah, why?"

"She just never seemed the sort to believe in all that crap," Paula said, staring straight ahead at the road.

"What crap?"

"Pre-destination, things 'meant to be.' Destiny. Tarot cards, palmistry, fortune telling."

What the heck had I missed when I'd zoned out? Paula was into new heights of conclusion jumping. "I didn't say she was into all of that—just that our names came to her like they were meant to be."

"Yes, but one thing leads to another."

"Leaping to conclusions like always, I see," I said. "Next thing you know, you'll say she's into reincarnation."

"Why do you bring that up? Reincarnation?"

"It was right in line with everything you were saying, so I just figured I'd check in on your thoughts on that, too."

"So nothing at all to do with last night?"

"Superdude and Bad dude?"

"No, when you were sleeping. Dreaming. Inviting someone into your room, talking about your father and his horses and . . ."

"What the hell are you talking about?" I asked.

"You were obviously dreaming about something really interesting last night—and talking in your sleep about it all as well. I heard you talking and listened for a bit. I wasn't sure you were okay."

"For the last time, it was a dream." I wanted to scream. Why did she keep bringing it all up? What was I supposed to say, that I'd invited a man . . . woman . . . vampire . . . something . . . into my bed last night and even now I was so hot with lust I couldn't think? And I needed to think, that was clear. I knew like I'd never known anything in my life that before this business was ended I would need my brains.

IV: DARON

Later that day—the night before Halloween

Vampire slayer or not, I'd like to get Buffy alone in my coffin!"

"Oh, no, Xena's my gal."

"Oh c'mon, I think Gabrielle is way hotter."

The girls were really at it tonight as we prepared for the first of several nights of seeming debauchery here in our annual celebration of immortality. I didn't find their silliness worthy of my attention. Instead, I was thinking of the night before, and how much I'd wanted to go in, but Rhenné was asleep and dreaming and I wasn't sure she would've let me in if I'd asked. I'd really wanted to go in. But I wasn't invited. Not yet.

"No accounting for taste."

"Speaking of taste, Charlotte, where the hell'd you get this stuff?" I said, taking another sip of what was posing as food tonight. Charlotte, as our local host, had provided us with this evening's meal. We'd end up having to scavenge for ourselves sometime this weekend, but tonight we were being particularly discrete. I was glad I'd had a proper meal on that petty thief.

"You don't want to draw attention, so I did the best that I could," Charlotte replied.

"Let me guess, you didn't clean up the streets," Maura said.

"The rules don't say we always have to go for the lowlifes. I have a connection at a local blood bank. She gives me blood that's about to go out of date." She tossed her dark hair with a dismissive glare. "Mortals can be good for something."

"Ugh!" Marguerite said, holding her own mug away from her. "That's it—this one's out of date."

"Aw hell, bottoms up, as old King Cole used to say," I said, downing the rest of my mug like a shot of tequila. Better to get it over with, after all.

"Did you know him?" Jennifer asked, wide-eyed. Her cheerleader costume was short and tight, showing off her lithe figure to perfection. I wondered if she'd wear the same costume all the nights of our celebrating, like I would, or if she'd change costume each night, such as most newbies tended to. Her apparent vapidness made me tired.

"Jennifer, darling," Evelyn said, putting an arm companionably around the much younger woman's shoulders, "King Cole is a nursery rhyme."

"Oh." She looked at Evelyn and almost pulled away, but then cuddled up close enough to get under Evelyn's cloak, literally and figuratively. Living or not, they were all alike—bloody bimbos just trying to hook up with someone of import.

I winked at Evelyn and pulled out a cigarette. I loved her, even though she'd killed me. It's a funny sort of unlife I lead. Kinda like a lot of dykes, actually—always being friends with the exes and all.

"Don't you know those cause cancer?" Jennifer asked.

I lit my fag with my Zippo and blew the smoke in her face. "What I'm wondering is who invited teen vamp?"

"I'm sorry, but it's not my fault I'm so young. I mean, especially compared with you all."

I reached over to run my fingers through Jennifer's long, dark hair, then cupped her cheek. "Just joking around with you, kid." I draped my long black cape around me and faced the others with my best glower. "Well, girls, tonight's our night, isn't it now?"

"Not quite, but it will do for now." Marguerite stood to claim my arm, as if she were anticipating more to come between us later in the night.

"Evelyn?" I said, holding my arm to her as I pulled away and turned my back on Marguerite. "Shall we?" I couldn't shake the niggling suspicion that it was no coincidence Marguerite had appeared so soon after I had drained the modern-day spitting image of one of the black hats I'd tortured and killed for murdering my Rebecca. Plus, she was being terribly clingy.

"Your ride or mine, stud?" Evelyn tucked one slender hand under my arm. I ignored Marguerite's angry hiss.

"I'm kinda likin' my independence these days," I said with a wink. "Let's go separately, shall we? And just hope Teen Vamp doesn't do the urban-surfing-on-a-van-roof thing. It's so over."

"You're bad as ever," she replied.

"So who brought in the youngster, anyway? I thought we were practicing some form of population control?" I asked Evelyn once we were out of the earshot of others. I opened the door of her Jag for her, waiting for her answer.

"Emily. You know how she likes those young'uns." She frowned in such a way that I was sure she would like to be the one punishing Emily for siring another child.

"Never fear! Emily is here!" Emily said, jumping down from the second-story railing of the motel. She was wearing a Superman costume, but instead of a big "S" on her chest, she had a big "E" emblazoned across her breasts. She always had a way of overdoing it.

I climbed aboard my Harley and led the way to the haunt we'd chosen for the night. I anticipated boredom. Again, it was a surprise to find out I could be wrong.

V: RHENNÉ

. . . meanwhile . . .

The Rainbow Room?" I said, when Paula parked and turned
to me. "I hope this place has a slightly lower testosterone
level than that club last night. You said you've been here
before?"

"Yes. Yes, I have. Look, Rhenné, before we go in, there's something I ought to tell you . . ."

"Yes?"

"Well, there's something about me you should know . . ."

"Then tell me already."

"It's not that easy."

She was whacked nervous and on edge. I figured the best thing
was to get on with the night, and let her tell me in her own time.
"So tell me later."

The place was noisy, smoke-laden and dark. Just like I figured
it'd be. We showed our IDs, paid our covers, and went to the bar
to get our drinks.

It didn't take long for me to realize we were almost the only
ones not in costumes. I'd felt out of place the other night, 'cause
I'd been dressed so unlike me. Tonight, my more demure white
silk blouse tucked into a simple pair of jeans was just as out of place
since I was surrounded by cats, cheerleaders, gypsies and cowboys.

"What'll you have?" The bartender, a spunky brown-haired girl, tossed a cocktail napkin on the bar in front of me.

I didn't answer because I couldn't. I had to look at the dance floor. I felt like a moth and when I looked, I saw the flame. Her movements were sleek and graceful as she led her partner about the dance floor. They were the epitome of elegance, almost as if they were from another time.

I felt as if I'd seen her before. Dressed as she was tonight, and dancing as she was tonight.

I'd seen her twirling and leading and dipping another before, and I'd been just as jealous.

It was déjà vu squared. I'd watched her then. I watched her now, and neither time was it the first time.

She was dark and brooding and dressed immaculately as a vampire. Not just any vampire mind you, but Count Dracula—*the* ultimate, the first, vampire. She wore a perfectly tailored tuxedo, complete with a black vest and four-in-hand tie. Her cape was a black so deep it seemed to swallow all light around it—but the inside was blood red, and it was created entirely out of a rich, thick velvet.

Her black hair was slicked back, in the classic Dracula style, and her red lips stood out against her pale skin. Her teeth were those obvious vampire ones you can get at CVS, Meijer's, or wherever around Halloween. Hallowe'en. All Hallows.

And I'd never referred to the holiday by either of those last two names. Ever. So that was strange.

What was more strange was that I looked at her now and realized immediately she was female. I also realized I wouldn't have been able to make that leap so quickly just a few nights ago.

That was when I realized that, in fact, everyone in this bar was female.

Paula had some 'splainin' to do—or maybe I needed to be a more patient listener. What had she been trying to tell me in the car?

And then I realized, as I continued looking, Dracula really was *Superdude*. Not a man. A woman. It seemed so obvious now, but as with every time I tried to think clearly about Superdude, my brain simply wouldn't connect the pieces. Like recalling only hours later that the Harley had sported California plates.

Reality just took a major turn for the weird. I knew I should just go ahead and arrest her, 'cause I was sure we could get an ID on her from district-attorney-in-training Sheryl Montgomery. But I had no backup and no way to call any, and given that I'd just realized I was in a lesbian bar, I didn't think anyone was going to lend a hand. Superdude—Superdudette? Anyway, Superdude could do a lot of damage to a lot of women if cornered. Keeping an eye on the suspect and getting in touch with my lieutenant as soon as I could was the best choice I could make at the moment.

My reluctance to confront her had nothing to do with the fact that she was the "man" I'd let into my room last night in that intensely erotic dream. Nothing to do with the fact that from the moment our gazes had met in the convenience store parking lot I'd wanted her, and known that for a very long time, I'd been hers. Or so I told myself, as I stood there, frozen in place.

The woman Dracula was dancing with was wearing an elegant gown that made me think she was dressed like a courtesan— another word I had never used before.

Her gown was a gorgeous, rich, dark-green velvet, with a sweetheart collar that revealed generous cleavage. Lace trim completed the outfit, along with a simple locket that brought attention to her wonderfully soft-looking, pale breasts.

Looking at her, with her long, beautifully dark locks about her face, made me tremble in fear. There was something about her that scared me nearly to death. My heart was beating so hard I couldn't even stop to wonder how it was I knew what the hell a sweetheart collar looked like.

Dracula led her off the floor, but just at the edge Dracula stopped and joined with friends, one of whom look awfully familiar. Then Dracula glanced around, as if looking for someone in particular. And then she looked at me. Looked right into my eyes. And . . .

A string quartet was playing a waltz, and my dark lover led me with a sureness and skill that was unknown to me before. It seemed as if all the other couples who had earlier crowded the floor now stood back to watch our graceful maneuvers as I was dipped and turned.

My dark lover had everyone in the room mesmerized—myself included.

The skirts of my flowing gown with its white ruffles and lace billowed around us so we were dancing in a cloud of light blue. I caught a glimpse of us in a mirror—or, more correctly, I caught a glimpse of myself, alone, in a mirror, and I momentarily worried that others might notice my bold lover's lack of reflection, but their eyes were on us, not the mirror.

Dazzling jewelry bedecked my ears and throat, and I could only imagine the elegance we displayed as a couple.

This was the dark lover who haunted my dreams all of my life. Again, the truth seemed obvious: a woman, not a man.

The same one who had saved me, long ago. But how did I know that?

I yanked out of her grasp, trying to figure out what had just happened. She looked at me, and I realized a group of people had indeed cleared the floor for us, and were now all looking at us.

The woman Dracula/Superdude had been dancing with stood a few feet away, her arms crossed in front of her. She stared at us—at me—as if she wished I were dead.

I had no idea how I had ended up in Dracula's arms.

I broke out in a cold sweat and did the only thing I could think of. I ran.

Shoving my way into the women's room, I headed right into a stall. I used it, then went to the sink to wash my shaking hands. It was like I couldn't control myself, and inside I wanted to die even while I was jumping up and down and dancing and wanting to throw up all at once.

I was so confused. I bent over the sink, resting my head on my crossed arms. I couldn't cry, because I wasn't sorry. I couldn't scream, because I wasn't angry. And even as I knew I didn't know what I was feeling, I also realized I was frightened.

I felt soft lips on my neck. "I've been waiting for you for a very, very long time." Her arms twined around my waist.

"That's a good line," I said, washing my hands and standing up straight. Dear sweet lord, Paula'd brought me to a gay bar. Well, not just any gay bar—but a *lesbian* bar. The truth finally sank in. My little sister was gay. I felt my pulse quicken and thought I might break out in a cold sweat at any moment.

She was touching me intimately, and I was *enjoying* it. Trembling, even.

"It's not a line."

Trying to maintain anything like control, I looked into the mirror to fix my hair, and noticed I was alone in my reflection.

Somehow I wasn't really surprised.

I turned and looked at the woman who had stepped back and away from me. She was a powerful woman, I could practically smell it. "Well, I'm sorry, but I'm not a lesbian. So if you'll just excuse me . . ."

The woman didn't move. Her eyes really were black as midnight.

Weakly, I tried for conversation. "That's a really nice costume."

She smiled. "Thanks, I've had it a long time. Lifetimes, even." She had a beautiful smile, and she'd taken out her cheap, plastic vampire fangs so I could really see her phenomenally white teeth.

"Do I know you from somewhere? It *was* you at that convenience store, wasn't it?"

"What convenience store?"

"You know the one I mean." I wanted her hands back on me. I wanted her to touch me again. But she kept her distance.

"Not for the life of me."

"Are you even alive?"

She raised an eyebrow. "I'm here hitting on you, aren't I?" She finally, thankfully, ran her fingers through my hair to pull my head back, roughly. "You know we belong together. That is, if you *are* her."

I grabbed her wrist. "I'm not. I'm really not even a lesbian. Really, I'm not. Honestly." I tried to peel myself from her. "I'm just here with my sister who's probably worrying about me right now." I edged around her and finally made it out the door.

Paula handed me a drink as soon as I found her. "Wow, Rhenné, I didn't know you could dance like that!"

"I didn't either—I mean, I can't, I can't really dance like that." If you put me in a court of law, I wouldn't be able to swear to exactly how, or with whom, I'd been dancing that night.

"You could've fooled me."

"Really, Paula, I don't know what that was." I took a long sip of my drink, trying to steady my nerves. Then I took another so I could collect my thoughts and say something that at least vaguely resembled a complete sentence. "Paula, you said this is a bar you come to frequently?"

"No, no—I just said I'd been here before." But then she became suddenly somber and serious. "But yes, yes I do. I come here quite a bit in fact."

I did a slow look-over of the bar, making sure I was right in that it was a lesbian bar. Then I looked around again, so Paula got what I was noticing—what I was thinking. Then I looked at her and said, "Is there something you need to tell me?"

"Rhenné . . ." Paula smiled sadly at me, then turned away.

"I've done the math, Paula. Now I just need you to tell me." I knew what was going on. And I couldn't help but wonder how my reaction might have been different had she told me even a week ago—before I'd begun to realize that maybe vampires were real, and maybe I was in l . . . lust with one. Superdude was no wannabe. And she was a woman. And my brain would implode if I tried to analyze this any further.

"Runner, I'm a lesbian," Paula said, not looking at me. "I've been wanting to—no, needing to—tell you for years. I kept chickening out, but now that my girlfriend and I broke up, I thought maybe I should tell you and just get it over with. Me living with you—now that you've given me asylum—gave me the time and space to do it."

I took a deep breath. "So why'd you bring me here tonight?" I should've figured it out years ago—about boyfriends I somehow never met and all that, but . . . I was Catholic. Denial was in my blood. It was what I did. That and feel whacked guilty about stuff. And be a cop.

"I was still chickening out, so I figured I'd just bring you here and let you—as you said—do the math."

Her throwing my thoughts back at me made me realize *again* how much we were alike. And thinking about Dracula made me think there were even more ways we might be alike. "Oh, shit," I said.

"Runner . . . Rhenné . . . please don't be like this . . . please. You're my sister and I need you."

It really wasn't that surprising, all things considered. I really should have seen it. What was worrying me more was the thought I'd just had about Dracula/Superdude. A woman. Another woman. Like me.

"Runner, I know the folks can't deal with it," Paula said. "Please don't shut me out as well. I need you."

Oh shit. My sister was talking to me. She was worrying that I'd cut her off because she was gay—but I loved her. No matter what. "Baby sis, it's all good to me. And I'm glad if you left a relationship that wasn't good, and I'm glad you knew you could come to me—and trust me enough to tell me about it. About who you really are."

"Oh god, thank you Runner! I've been so worried about how you'd take it." She looked up from her drink and at me. "I should've known you'd be okay with it."

"Really, what's the big?" I couldn't believe I was thinking of another woman the way I was thinking about Dracula/Superdude. I wanted her to kiss me, touch me and . . . I wanted last night to happen in reality. Unless it already had. Then I wanted it to happen again. And I couldn't believe I was thinking about another woman like that. This. That was enough to fry my synapses. I wasn't going to touch the vampire thing at all.

Paula leaned over to give me a great big hug. "Thanks," she whispered into my ear.

"Thank you. Now I've got to work tomorrow. Why don't we call it a night? Go home." I stood.

"Runner, what's going on?"

"I just . . . I need to get out of here."

"Is it because of that woman you were dancing with earlier? The one who is so checking you out right now?" Paula said, looking over my shoulder. "It feels as if I know her from somewhere. She looks familiar."

"In a good way or bad way?" I asked, heat rushing to my face at the very thought of her. I knew I ought to stick around to follow Dracula home, get some more intel on her. But I needed even more to be elsewhere.

"I don't know," Paula said, with a slight smirk. She must have seen the flush come to my face, the way I shifted my stance.

It all sent a chill through me. There was something terribly, terribly wrong here, and I didn't want to explore it at all, because I knew what it meant and I just didn't know how to deal with it. I couldn't think, like my brain had a very real short-circuit. There were things I should be doing, and I couldn't remember what they were. "We need to leave. Now." I grabbed her by her elbow and led her out to her car, noticing en route a motorcycle with Cali plates on it. A bike exactly like the one I'd seen—my head pounded—like I'd seen . . . somewhere.

"What's going on, Rhenné?" Paula asked, noticing me noticing the bike.

"I haven't the foggiest," I said, climbing into the car. Then I said nothing at all for several minutes, mostly because my brain couldn't form words.

"That was all a lot easier than I thought it'd be." Paula hung a right onto 8 Mile, then pulled a U-ie at the light to head east.

"Yeah, well, I like making things easy. Hey, can we stop over there? I don't think I'll be able to sleep right off, and I'd kinda like some beer."

"Yeah, I could go for some of that myself," Paula said, pulling into the lot.

"Wait here," I said. "Miller Lite good for you?" I couldn't help but hope I'd again see Superdude in yet another convenience store tonight. And the fear of running into another criminal raised my adrenaline and served to make me even more excited; even as I told myself that was all too much coincidence for one week, heck, it was too much for one year. And I didn't even believe in coincidence, not really.

"Yeah."

As soon as she stopped, I hopped out and headed in. I didn't want her arguing over who was going to pay. The chilled air from the cooler felt wonderful as I grabbed a six-pack. Then I put that back and grabbed a twelve, then realized my sister had just come out to me—in a gay bar—a lesbian bar—immediately after a woman massively hit on me.

And I was interested.

I swapped the twelve for a thirty and carried it to the front counter.

"This is a holdup," a man said, entering and training a gun between me and the clerk. He wore a black stocking over his face, looking just like the perps I'd seen in vid footage of other crime scenes during our daily briefings. He was very tall. Rather slender. And had his collar turned up around his face, with a knit cap covering most of his head. He was so tall, I guessed he'd have to duck to leave the store via the door. Bet he got called Stretch by his grandma, and that was exactly what we cops called him as well.

Oh fuck me, I thought. I didn't have my gun on me. It was locked in my glove box, just as it always was when I went out and imbibed. Had I really just wished for this? I was losing my mind.

"Raise your hands," Stretch said.

I put the beer on the floor and raised my hands even as the clerk did the same—put up her hands, that is.

I hoped Paula saw what was going down and went somewhere and called the cops—and didn't do anything stupid. Just got out of there.

"You," Stretch said, pointing to the clerk, but keeping an eye on me. "Empty the cash register into a bag. Don't do anything stupid."

Anything I could try would be stupid. I wasn't armed, but Stretch was. Given the usual M.O., he had a driver outside. I didn't know if the driver would take off—as Wednesday night's accomplice had done—or would join the fray if we fought back. Bottom line, it wasn't worth it. These idiots weren't killers unless they felt threatened.

I worked through all this in my mind even as I played the part of the poor innocent with my hands up. "Please don't hurt me," I said. I saw Paula was still parked outside. And then another car pulled up next to hers.

I hoped it wasn't some idiot who'd get her/himself killed.

The clerk was dropping the few bucks from the register into a bag. The front door opened, and the buzzer squalled.

Stretch turned to the front door. If I'd been armed, I might've been able to draw my weapon and take control of the situation. God, I really was a fuckbrain!

"Oh, yo, dude, so sorry." It was a woman. Size, shape and voice all indicated this. She had a ski cap covering her face and was directly addressing Stretch. "Didn't plan on pissing on your turf." Something about her was familiar.

"Get down on the floor next to her," Stretch directed the newcomer, pointing his gun toward me.

"No. I don't like that idea so much. Tell you what—you give me your gun, and I'll let you live," the new woman said, with a very, very slight and light British accent. At least I thought it was British. It was some sort of accent, one that wasn't from this country if my guess was right.

Stretch raised his gun.

Newbie raised hers, Stretch fired—right at her, even as Newbie leapt to take his gun.

I saw bullets hit Newbie. I saw her get hit and jerk in reaction to them.

But still, she flew through the air in a circle, grabbed Stretch's gun, threw it and her own, hit the ground, completed her circle, came up to her knees and grabbed that fuckin' asshole and tossed him out the door.

And without stopping, she leapt out through the front door after the guy.

I scrambled to my feet and raced outside. Newbie pulled up from Stretch's neck when I showed, ran to a fire-engine red, late-model Mustang and zoomed off.

I looked down and saw twin puncture wounds on the perp's neck.

I knew beyond for sure that this vigilante wasn't Superdude, of course. And not just because this "vampire" would've bled Stretch dry if not for me—but also because I just felt it. And knew it. Deep down inside. Yeah, and that was admissible in court.

So we now officially had two vigilantes active in the area. Two blood-sucking vigilantes, and I'd let both of them get away.

I reached down, pulled the ski mask off the perp, and looked at a face from a nightmare: One of mine. *This was the one who had pulled the blade across my throat, allowing my life's blood to flow freely from within me . . .*

I looked up from the corpse and into the eyes of my sister. She was about twenty feet away, staring in horrid fascination from the driver's seat of her car.

When the police showed, I knew I'd get harassed the next day on duty. I knew they didn't like my responses, statement or evidence. Especially since, again, the woman who threw the perp through the front door wasn't visible on any security-tape footage. They really loved my insistence that tonight's vigilante was a different woman than the one from two nights ago—who was a woman, by the way, not a man as I'd previously reported—especially when I could not explain how I knew.

When we got home, I put most of the beer in the fridge, leaving two out for me and Paula.

"Cheers," I said, toasting her.

"So is that what you go through every day?" Paula asked.

"It's usually not quite so life or death." I cracked my beer and took a long swig. "But yeah, kinda."

"Rhenné, I need to know you're really okay with what I told you tonight."

"Paula, realistically, truthfully, you coming out to me is one of the lesser things my mind is whacked on tonight."

"So me coming out to you was no big?"

I shrugged and finished my beer. "Paula, to be honest, if I'd ever opened my eyes, I'd have known you were gay. Also, I'm a cop in this area, and enough of my peers have enough hang-ups on race, religion, orientation and everything else they can be prejudicial on, so I really work on *not* being prejudiced. Plus, well, we both almost got killed tonight, and that really puts things into perspective." That, and seeing someone from one of my worst nightmares, a nightmare that'd been haunting me for as long as I could remember. Seeing that evil man dead and being glad.

"Yeah," she said, finally drinking. "I saw what was happening and part of me wanted to freeze or flee—"

"I'd been hoping you'd leave. Flee. Get out of there."

"What? And leave you? I called the cops."

I raised my can to hers in a toast.

It wasn't long after that I lay in bed, staring at the ceiling, just trying to sleep. My room had never seemed so large before. I heard a light tapping at the window and turned toward it, sensing the shadowy figure just beyond. Every inch of me tingled with anticipation, and I'm sure I didn't tell my feet to go to the floor and carry me across the room to the window.

I know I didn't want to open the window, or unlatch the screen and pull it out.

This was all a dream. That was the only explanation.

But this dream was unlike any of the others I'd had of late. For instance, none of my other dreams featured modern-day conveniences, such as screens.

And none of that made any difference to how hot, needy and wanting I was.

Fucking dammit, I was horny and needed to come—and no man had ever done me good enough to make me really scream. I always pretended with them. Faked it.

But last night's dream made me come so hard I was still soaked in the morning.

And I really wanted to feel like that again. Not just the wetness, not just the coming—but also all the excitement and anticipation that went into it beforehand.

I stared up at my bedroom ceiling and thought about all the sexiest guys I'd known. I then went into Brad in *Troy*, David brooding in *Angel*, and every big-dicked guy I'd ever seen in a porno.

No man had ever done me the way I needed. No one had ever satisfied me totally. No man had ever turned me on so much as Dracula did in my dreams. Or even in our dancing or my imaginings.

When I looked out the window, I saw the mysterious woman from the bar, still dressed in her costume, and, impossibly, hanging in mid-air from the second-story window by merely her fingertips.

I slammed the window shut and dove under the covers of my bed. I stayed that way until I was past dreaming.

VI: DARON

Halloween morning

When I returned to the motel just before sunrise, Evelyn was watching for me. "You think she's your beloved Rebecca, don't you?" she asked, greeting me at my bike.

I climbed off and removed my helmet. "She might be."

"Daron, even we are unsure whether or not reincarnation exists, because sometimes we can hope hard enough that we see what simply isn't there." She was tired, much as I was—tired from our many centuries of undeadness. In today's vernacular, it could perhaps be conveyed by *tired beyond the telling of.* "With all of those who have walked the earth throughout the years, there are bound to be similarities between different people, and those similarities might make one leap to certain ideas of reincarnation."

"So you're telling me—for the hundred-and-fiftieth year in a row—that my Rebecca is gone forever."

She sighed, her patience clearly strained. "I've seen you at many highs and lows, and I'd rather not see anymore lows, the likes of which you will drop to when you realize that, yet again, you have not found your beloved Rebecca." We went up the stairs and to my room, me following behind the ruffling of her voluminous skirts. I unlocked the door and she followed me inside.

"I've been let down enough, after being *so* sure, that I'm not giving in so easily this time."

"Good. I'm glad. You've been hooked on her for hundreds of years, and it's time to move on."

"Evelyn, after the bar tonight, I went to her apartment—on the second floor, and she opened the window for me. Took out the screen. It was as if she knew and welcomed me."

"Of course she was happy to see you—you're handsome. And you had just all but swept her off her feet a few hours earlier at the club."

"You're right, of course. But I don't think that was quite all there was."

"So you were invited in? And now you can enter whenever you like?" Evelyn asked, changing the focus.

"Well, no. Last night she opened the window, took out the screen, and then slammed the window down and dove into her bed. It was the strangest thing. She wasn't surprised, and I was hanging onto her window by just my fingers, and she didn't scream—she just slammed it down." It was all most confusing for me, since at one moment, it was as if she knew me, then she was turning against me. I wondered if we were experiencing all of the same flashbacks.

"So she didn't invite you in, then?" she asked, inspecting one well-manicured hand.

"She was the cop who showed up when I took care of that thief at the convenience store." I poured myself a very old brandy and offered the same to Evelyn, but she waved the bottle away. "That night I showed up at her apartment, and I think she was dreaming about me. I wanted to ask her to invite me in, but I don't want to keep hoping for a Rebecca when she's really just dead."

"Although I am glad you're occasionally finding the chance to enjoy yourself, you must realize that there are others out there, in here, to love. You're fixated on a forgettable woman who died life-times ago."

I flew across the room to grab her and press her up against a wall, my vampire game face on with full fangs. "I've been used. I've done my job. I've serviced and said yes and pleasured. Rebecca knew what I was and still loved me."

She threw me back several feet, so I fell to my knees and she could look upon me with disdain. "Many others have known and loved you."

"It's not the same. She was alive, and willing to die for me. She didn't ask me to change her, but she invited me in and . . ." I turned from Evelyn, not reacting to how easily she tossed me aside. "I was going to change her. Into one of us. Do you know I've never done that—changed someone? Never, ever, but I was going to with her. I loved her enough *not* to change her, and enough *to* change her." There was no way I could explain to Evelyn that I'd come to town expecting to dust myself at the end of the annual reunion of Evelyn's clan. I couldn't go on just hoping to find Rebecca once again. I was tired of my existence. But now this chance that Rhenné was Rebecca was enough to keep me undead long enough to determine if I was right.

Plus, I knew if I told Evelyn a word of my plans, she'd pull everyone either of us knew into the campaign to stop me from doing so. I knew she still had feelings for me, no matter how cava-lier she might sometimes seem about what I was doing. I still cared about her, too, but not as I once had, not since saving Rebecca so long ago on that dirty London street.

Evelyn helped herself to a cigarette and my lighter. "So what's your plan? And I know you, so I know you have one."

"I have no choice but to follow her tomorrow night."

She blew a perfect smoke ring that drifted over my head, very much not a halo. "Prepare to be disappointed."

Evelyn stalked off to her room, and I put out my Do-Not-Disturb sign and zipped up in my body bag, hoping to find sleep quickly.

Instead, my pensive mood refused to leave me, and I remembered the past, exactly as it had occurred. Even when sleep finally came, I remembered.

Modern writers in entertainments from poetry to television submit the idea that vampires are soulless and/or possessed and controlled by demons. The difference between us and regular people is the same as the difference between some folks and others: Some of us are good, others are bad. Some of us think we should turn as many mortals as possible into our kind. Others think humans are a scourge and should be extinguished.

And then there are those like me, who thought from the beginning of this life that the virus infecting us didn't change our moral code. Strength brought responsibility of a kind. Using my strength had brought me the only happiness I'd known in the last century and a half—Rebecca and her love for me.

Rebecca . . . I saw some low-life vamp about to kill someone, and I went to rescue the person about to be eaten. And even while I saved her I sensed the goodness within Rebecca and was convinced of the rightness of my action. But, also, I saw her—heaving bosom, ivory skin, silken locks—and wanted her. And sensed her and all she was and I wanted to mark her as mine.

I saved her and then, when she ran from me, I followed her home. But she didn't really live there, she was just visiting, so she couldn't invite me in. Or so I thought.

Regardless, in the middle of the darkness, I began wooing her. It started under the guise of ensuring she made it home safely, but it grew beyond that quickly, as, night after night, I was drawn to that same window.

Until one fateful night when she did the impossible: She climbed out of bed and opened the window to look right at me. Stare right into my eyes. Right into me.

Her face was so close to mine I could feel her breath on my skin. She gazed into my eyes, as if looking into the soul I wasn't sure I possessed, and then she laid her hand gently on my cheek.

The heat of it shot through me, warming even those parts of me I thought had died when I did.

"Why do you call night after night, always when I sleep? Why do you not come calling during the accepted hours, as would any other suitor?"

I could not believe I was again so close to this lovely creature, nor could I believe that she had known of my visits. I could put any mortal in thrall to me, but I'd not used such powers with her. She had always appeared to be peacefully asleep. "I cannot woo you as would any other suitor."

"Then you are truly a creature of the night."

"Alas, it is true. I am not like you."

"Yet I stand close to you and am not afraid. I gaze into your eyes and feel a warmth coursing throughout me, such as I have never known."

How could I tell her I felt the same? She was fragile, human and perfect. I wanted her, but could give her nothing she could value.

Her voice as soft as her touch, she said, "I have heard that to look into the eyes of one such as you is like unto death. Yet you saved my virtue, if not my life, the first time we met, without ever knowing me." *Rebecca paused, looking into my eyes, then continued,* "Is it true then? Can you really fly?"

I did not answer. Her touch held me spellbound, instead of the other way around. Never before had this happened to me.

She ran her hands gently over my fingers, feeling the tension in them as I held onto the windowsill. "No, I suppose it is like much of what I have heard about your kind."

What had she heard, and from whom? There was nothing available to a girl such as this that didn't paint my kind as the incarnation of evil itself. Yet she really did seem unafraid.

She stepped back from the window then, still locking gazes with me, and took a deep breath. "You should come in."

"Your invitation means nothing here," *I said, finally finding words.* "One must be a resident, must be living within, to give invitation to me. To one like me."

"My hosts have made me as a member of the family. Please, come in."

And it was that easy. That simple. I hefted myself up onto the win-

dowsill, expecting that I would encounter a barrier, but yet, I was able to step into the room.

A single tear ran down Rebecca's cheek as I did so. "I don't know why I am not afraid. It seems my foolish heart does not want to believe you merely saved for yourself what was nearly stolen forcibly from me the night we met." She lowered the collar of her nightgown to expose her lovely, pale neck even further. Her heavy breathing was audible in the silent darkness of the room.

I ran my fingers through her dark, silken locks. I knew I had not merely saved her in order to drain her. I wanted more and yet I did not know what more there could possibly be that she deserved.

Rebecca dropped her gaze, trembling under my touch. "Please, kind sir, just be gentle."

I knew she was offering her blood—but then I knew what I really wanted from her, what I could get from her and no one else. "I am no kind sir."

"Do what you will with me, then. My life is yours."

I leaned down to caress Rebecca's lips with my own, gently touching them for a brief moment.

Rebecca gasped as she pulled away and said, "Sir! I would give you my blood, but I will not be your willing whore."

"Do you not understand, even yet? I am no sir." I took her soft hand in mine. She momentarily tried to escape my grasp, but she gave in, allowing me to place her hand upon my breast so she would have no doubt as to what I was.

Rebecca left her hand where it was, but nonetheless questioned, "Then how can you kiss me in such a way?" She was shivering now.

"If you wish me to do so, I will leave." I stepped from her reach.

"No."

"Are you sure?"

"My life has been yours since the moment you saved me."

"There is no debt to be paid."

"I have been yours since I first saw you. Stay." She stepped toward me, reaching out to grasp my arms beneath my cloak. She leaned up toward my lips, touching them again with her own. The contact was brief and she stepped back. "I am yours. But of the free will you and God have given me, I do want you to stay. Since that first night, I have slept knowing you watched me yet. I have dreamt about the taste of your lips, and the feel of your fingers on my body."

"You give yourself to me, yet I do not even know your name, nor you mine."

"I am Rebecca, and you are my dark lover. My demon lover."

VII: RHENNÉ

The dark woman helped me undress, slowly peeling away layer after layer of my nightclothes, revealing my skin, flesh no one had ever seen before, touching me in ways no one before ever had while making me feel things I'd never known I could feel . . . Making me want her to touch me further, more, as I was revealed inch-by-inch to her.

My body reacted in its own ways, ways unknown to me previously. Sensation was overwhelming. Was this what hid between the lines of the lurid novels I'd found in my host's study? I was heavy with wet. Parts of me were hard and . . . wanting.

She carried me to the bed, gently helping me under the covers to keep me from the cold, English climate in the chilly house. Only my lady's maid had ever seen me so exposed, yet I allowed this . . . dark creature . . . this woman to strip me naked.

I was trembling within and without, feeling heat course through my body with every loving touch this woman gave. A deep boiling was starting inside of me, connecting itself with a point right between my legs, making me long for this woman's touch, making me arch my body so as to entrap those soft, gentle fingers against me, to increase the contact between us.

Perhaps I should have asked for her name, but nothing between us was so ordinary. Once I'd discovered her womanly nature, I was beyond speech and all sense of propriety. I wished that I knew not what was real, but I knew—this was no dream.

The woman softly stroked me, and I longed for her to see me fully. I knew it was wrong and I should not even think about such things, let alone be doing such a thing, but I could not resist. I could not stop. I could not say no.

She gently cupped and stroked my breasts, causing the tips to stand erect, yet I longed for even more. I was gasping for air with every breath, but could not tell her what I wanted. I could not utter such wants, let alone speak such words. I could not admit to such.

But still, the woman knew.

She stripped down to her pants and shirt, then lay on top of me, insinuating her leg between my thighs, which I wanted to close like a proper lady, but couldn't, and not just because she was lying between them.

I arched against the leg, wanting—needing—so much more. I began whimpering with a longing so complete it clouded almost every other thought I had, all except the knowledge that I wanted to become as one with this woman, my demon lover.

She reached between my legs, touching me where no one, including myself, had ever touched.

I couldn't breathe, couldn't think, couldn't tell what was happening.

And then I realized I wasn't a maiden anymore. My surrender was complete. I was filled with the woman, and even then, she took me further, opening my legs even more. Embarrassingly so, but then . . . she was kissing me there, running her tongue up and down, flickering and doing oh-so-many wonderful things to my body, making me writhe across the bed, making me toss the blankets off and expose myself further still.

"I love you, Rebecca."

"Daron! Oh god, Daron!" I screamed.

"Rhenné! Rhenné! Wake up!"

"Yes! Yes!"

"Rhenné! You'll wake the neighborhood!"

Something pulled me from where I'd been, and I popped my eyes open and saw that I was in my room. "What the hell?" Heat was still pounding through my body, and the covers were twisted between me and Paula.

"You were having a nightmare," Paula said, helping me sit up. She wrapped her arms around me, trying to lay my head on her shoulder.

My out-of-control body was having nothing to do with it.

I suddenly realized my T-shirt was shoved up almost underneath my armpits, and my pajama bottoms were practically around my ankles. "I'm all right, really," I said, embarrassed and wanting Paula to leave me alone so I could cover myself.

Paula leaned back, assessing me. "What were you dreaming about anyway? You were yelling some guy's name."

"What was the name?" I asked. The dream was warming me still. The dream, and the night, and the past nights and all that I had missed.

Sunlight streamed through the tightly closed blinds but I wanted to return to the night.

"Daron? Is that some guy you know?"

I shook my head. I didn't know anyone by that name. Except from my dreams. And even then, I had no idea how I knew it. Daron. Demon lover.

VIII: DARON

I'd been a thief. A pickpocket. A criminal.

I couldn't remember my parents. Not even in my dreams. Or nightmares. Why was it, after dreaming of my beloved Rebecca, of the night I claimed her, I had to sort through the earlier memories of when I'd become the creature she had loved? Perhaps because, had it not been for the change, I'd have not known Rebecca's love.

An orphan and street urchin. Then a fine and elegant lady called me out, and as I mucked her stables she taunted me with her décolletage, enticed me with her long blonde curls, intimate gazes and featherlight touches.

I learned how to run a stable, keep up an estate, and how to read and write. I studied mathematics and didn't get my hands cut off for being a thief. I traveled with her. Saw the world. And lived longer than I ought to have.

Before she killed me, that is.

And ever since she started our little annual reunion, I dreamt the same dream every year. She made me, though she'd given me no choice in the matter. I was no longer her creation, but she made me.

I was carrying water up for her bath one eve . . .

"You're looking quite handsome," she said, lounging in her tub as I poured in the final pail of hot water.

"I think I prefer real labor to bein' dressed up in all this finery," said I, indicating my gentlemanly apparel.

"You do like working with your hands, don't you?" She hooked her leg over the edge of her fancy tub—slender, long, white and smooth . . . leading my gaze farther up her body.

"Better'n all this fancy putting-on of airs." I tried, but was unable to keep my eyes off her naked form.

"What if I gave you something more interesting to do with your hands—and mouth—indoors?" She stood up in her tub, revealing herself to me in all her naked beauty. The water glistened along her skin. "Do you like what you see?" She stepped out of the tub. "Do you want to touch me?"

I couldn't resist. I moved toward her. I couldn't not. It wasn't my choice—only later would I know she had mesmerized me. Only later, with Rebecca, would choice matter to me. But for now, I cupped Evelyn's cheeks, ran my thumbs over those full, soft lips she'd licked so often in front of me, and then trailed my hands down her neck and over her collarbone till I . . . God. She stood smirking at me even as I cupped her breasts, enjoying their softness and feeling the need to . . . suck on them.

I knelt before her to do so.

She sat on the tub edge, bringing me with her even as she spread her legs for me and guided my fingers into her heat. "I see it's time I teach you something new," she said, "in order to keep you interested in all I have to offer you."

She was soft and warm and sweet and nice and . . . with her naked and me clothed I felt as if I were in control for the first time in my life. Not until later, much later, would I realize that I was not.

And that she was such a fine lady made everything even more so. That we were both women and she obviously wanted my touch brought up my deepest, most secret desires.

"Yes, please, inside, now," she said, guiding me into her.

I lifted her easily—after all, I was strong, and she was even shorter *than I—and laid her on the bare floor, intent on exploring every inch of the wonderful body I'd so oft admired from a distance. I kissed, licked, suckled and touched. I squeezed and felt her, moving from her breasts to her lips to her thighs.*

"Stop," said she, clenching her legs around my hand, trapping me inside her, even as she held my head against her chest. "Take it slow. Enjoy me." She released my head. "Kiss me."

I leaned down to place my lips against hers. She opened her mouth and gently nibbled on my lower lip, then she slid her tongue into my mouth to dance with mine. She put her hand over mine between her legs.

"Open me up," she said. "Spread me open, like this. And then run your fingers up and down me right . . . like this."

I stirred out of the dream of the first time I had made love to Evelyn and mused again that she had taught me how to pleasure a woman, just like she had me trained on so many things. She made sure I knew exactly what she liked, and how she liked it. It was something I also liked and enjoyed.

After we became lovers—me still playing the part of a man— she had someone teach me more languages, and how to tie a tie, and all the essentials of being a perfect gentleman. It was almost as if she was raising me to be the perfect mate for her.

When she determined I was at my physical prime, she took me to bed for a night of lust that could still bring a shiver to my blood when remembered. After I made her come, she made me come, and then she killed me, sucked out all my blood, and forced me to drink hers.

These days I joked that not even death kept a good butch from making her femme scream.

Were it not the nature of things, I'd resent that she'd given me no warning, no choice and had been greatly upset when I had left her some years later to live a separate life. Perhaps that was why, when I met my Rebecca, I had wanted to give her the choice denied me.

Rebecca had chosen me . . . and I had never recovered from

that. Her love was fatal to my solitude and I had never been happier. Now I found myself centuries later still trying to find that love. All these years of looking only to have one I thought might be Rebecca prove untrue, or die as mortals so often did.

And I really hoped Rebe . . . Rhenné . . . Rhenné was masturbating right now with her mind full of me. Every time I looked at her I knew that no one—man or woman—had been inside her head the way I was and could be. In this modern world she was full of her career and her life. The only place for me was in her bed, and if that was the way to discover if she really was my Rebecca, I'd get to her through her body. I imagined what it would be like . . .

She'd be lying in bed. Unable to stop thinking about me. She'd be wet and wanting and needing.

She'd take off her sleep attire, to experience her own nudity, to feel the bedclothes—the sheets and blankets—against her bare skin. To feel as exposed as I'd make her feel if I were there.

She'd have left the window open. She'd lower the bedclothes, so that if I were perched in the window, I'd see her in all of her beauty—all of her naked, nubile, lush, silky-skinned wonder.

She'd run her hands down her body . . . caressing her breasts . . . feathering lightly over her tummy, slowly opening her thighs, allowing herself to start feeling, *really* feeling and experiencing all I gave her. All I did to her. For her.

She'd moan and writhe, running her fingers up and down her swollen clit, reaching down to coat them in her wet and sliding a finger inside herself. She'd draw that finger up to flick her clit back and forth, then slide it and another back inside, using both hands now while I watched, raising her hips, opening her legs further . . .

She'd be imagining that it was me there, me touching and caressing her. Me fucking her. Me doing things to her.

She'd use her left hand to caress her body, tweak her nipples, squeezing them until she slipped her left index finger up and down herself, getting it lubricated enough to slide it behind her and circle her asshole before shoving it inside.

She'd want to feel me invading her in every way, throwing open her legs as she held in her scream as she gave herself to me entirely, coming harder than she ever had in this incarnation.

I paced my room, only glancing slightly toward the tightly shut curtains, knowing I couldn't even venture toward them yet, no matter how much I wanted to—wanted to go out, into the daylight, find my Rebecca and again claim her.

Sometimes it sucked being so violently allergic to sunlight.

IX: RHENNÉ

Halloween Day

ither it was a terrible nightmare, or some sort of a really hot dream," Paula said over breakfast. "Are you going to tell me which?"

I knew I was probably blushing. "I don't really remember much about it, really."

Paula gave me the evil eye, apparently figuring there was more to it. "So who is Daron?"

This time I didn't have to act. I shook my head. "I really don't know."

"So you up to some fun tonight?" Paula asked, still apparently disbelieving me.

"Listen, Paula, it's a school night. And I gotta get to work now."

"Yo, Leon! Nice job at the convenience store!" Oser yelled at me when I entered the station at the start of my shift. Only thing was, he didn't mean it as a compliment.

"Yeah-huh, Hoser," I said. "At least I'm *in* the action—not standing on the sidelines like the loser you are."

"Hey, partner," Chuck said, punching me in the arm as we

headed into the briefing room. "Ya think maybe we might try something different today and, like, maybe *try to catch the perp?*"

"Chuckie," Stunckel said, "doncha think it's maybe asking a little much for your partner to actually catch one? As opposed to being some sorta half-assed witness?"

I had a feeling that until this was all over, I'd be really glad I just worked four twelve-hour shifts a week. Five days per would've maximized the other cops' chances to harass me. None of them would have caught our vigilantes either, not that their itsy macho brains could believe it.

"Lay off," Chuck said. "She helped pull in two guys, which is more than any of you can say." As I looked at him, he almost seemed to morph into . . . a coachman? During my brief vision he was attired in breeches and a waistcoat and . . . well. Old clothes. Well, not old old clothes—but clothes from olden times—as in, hundreds of years ago by my guessing.

I stopped and briefly had to gasp for air, 'cause the sight hit me like a kick to the gut. I grabbed Chuck's arm to steady me. Who was I? Or was the better question who exactly had I been?

Throughout the rest of the shift it was as if I was shifting between the past and present, reality and dream . . .

During the briefing Sergeant Nichols kept looking so much like a . . . butler. Dressed rather a lot like Chuck had been when I'd hallucinated him in olden clothing.

I'd mentally undressed people—men—before, but this was something different. I had no control over this.

And so we patrolled and pulled folks over, stopped some vandalism, responded to a domestic violence call and it was all the norm.

Except for how I'd look out at the street and see carriages—and horses—going by. Or when the steering wheel turned into reins. A gun turned into a musket. The streets were dirt and waste flowed freely. Just like there were occasional pictures of medieval London or such thrown into the film of my life.

It was rather disconcerting overall. I was a Fruit Loop and

everyone else was okay. The world was normal to them. I had to ignore it all to pass, to keep going with my day-to-day. I'd get locked up if I told a word of this to anybody.

When I got home that night, Paula was brooding and moping. She was also making something wonderful smelling in the kitchen.

"Mmmm," I said. "Something good's for dinner."

"Yes. I'm a very good cook."

"Who's obviously quite pleased with her work today. What's up, Paula?"

"Dinner. Wash up, de-weapon, de-uniform, and it'll be on the table."

Usually I worked out or went for a quick jog after work, but the thought of some good home-cooked food de-motivated me on that—and made me really want to get down to the eating. I didn't even remember what I'd had for lunch. Everything outside the apartment no longer seemed real.

I jumped through a quick shower and changed into sweats. My shirt was over my head when I realized what I'd thought was the radio was a real conversation—an increasingly loud and heated conversation—between Paula and someone else.

"C'mon Paula, you know you want to." If it hadn't been a woman's voice, I probably would've grabbed my gun before going to the kitchen. But it *was* a woman's voice, and I knew I didn't need my gun to deal with this.

"Is there a problem?" I eyed the tall, hard-looking woman who towered over Paula.

"Hey," the woman said, turning to me and quickly changing to a smile before holding out a hand. "You must be Runner. Er, Rhenné. I've heard a lot about you. I'm Jack. Jackie. Paula's girl-friend."

"Ex," Paula said, crossing her arms in front of her and leaning against the stove. "Ow." She stood back up rather quickly.

I, on the other hand, didn't take Jackie's hand. I looked around her at Paula. "Ex. So you want her to go, right?"

"Yes. That would be of the good."

"You heard my sister," I said.

"Listen, just give us a mo', all right?" Jackie said. "It's all just a little misunderstanding. That's all it is. Ya see, me and your sister? We do this, see."

"Uh, no, not so much," I said, stepping forward. "What I heard was my sister saying she doesn't want you here. And since *here* is my apartment, I'm thinking you should go. Now."

"We fight, we fuck, we make up. It's what we do," Jackie said. "But you wouldn't know about that, huh?"

"If I didn't, I would now since you just told me." I had a feeling she wasn't just meaning that I didn't know Paula was gay, but that maybe she was meaning more that I didn't get out much.

"Her home's with me, so I'm here to bring her back *home* with *me*."

"I'm family. I'm her home." We stood toe-to-toe. It was a face-off, but I was used to such things.

"Okay, so you get that I'm her partner—her lover."

"Ex, from what I hear."

"So she finally told you?"

"She came out to me earlier. Funny, she didn't mention you. At all," I said. She really was figuring me for some sort of homophobe.

"Huh. She was always terrified to tell you."

"She got over it. She told me. I heard. I dealt. She's living here now. You aren't. So I suggest you leave."

"Family's only what we make it, you know," Jackie said.

"I'm her blood relation—her sister—and she's chosen me over you. She's welcome here as long as she wants to be here. Now don't make me angry, 'cause you wouldn't like me when I'm angry."

"That sounds like a threat. You think you can take me?"

"You *did* get the memo I'm a cop, right? So what you're doing falls directly into the category of *Not Smart*."

"Oh, what? I piss you off so you put out a warrant on me or something?"

"I can play dirty if I need to," I said. For the first time in days I felt right at home. I knew how to do this. I knew where I stood and what to do.

"Jack, leave, okay—just leave," Paula said.

I stood my ground. "I can play dirty, I can play nasty, and I can be downright mean if I have to. I don't pull punches." This was ever so much easier than thinking about my recent dreams, hallucinations, and strange attraction to Daron.

"But you're so . . . tiny," Jackie said, looking down at me.

"Paula, call nine-one-one," I said. "Jackie, I'm going to tell you one more time. Leave now."

I blocked Jackie when she tried to step around me as Paula went for the phone.

"So you're just too chicken to fight me, huh?" Jackie said. I knew she wanted to grab me and throw me out of the way, but my badge was stopping her.

"I prefer to solve things without violence," I said.

Jackie stared over my shoulder at Paula, then at me. "Fine. But this ain't over. We belong together." She went to the door.

I slammed my hand against the door, pinning it shut for just a moment. "You're not welcome here. You come here again and you'll end up in jail. Know that. Leave me, my sister, and our entire family alone."

"Whatever!" She slammed the door open and left.

I locked the door behind her, then went to the window to watch her leave the premises. Then I pulled my gun out of the back of my sweatpants and put it on the desk beside me. Just because I knew I didn't need it didn't mean I wouldn't bring it. I'd been caught unarmed once too often lately as it was.

"I didn't invite her in," Paula said, coming up behind me. "She knocked. I opened the door. She came in. I guess I should use the peephole from now on."

"Yeah. That'd be good."

☥

Paula fed me beef bourguignon or some such. It was good and my tummy was happy.

"Thanks for that," Paula said, gathering up the plates when we were done. "I'm really sorry for it . . . and, well, I kinda wouldn't hold onto the hope that she won't be back."

"She as fruit loopy as she appears?"

"Uh. Yeah." Paula looked sheepish.

"And you saw what in her exactly?" I was really glad to be talking about someone else for a while—and about somebody else's problems.

"I came out a few years ago. Came out and dropped right into a really bad relationship. Jackie pulled me from that a few years in. She saved me. Plus she was really good in bed."

"TMI! TMI!" This was really becoming a habit for me, but I so knew how she felt about wanting someone to make you scream.

"Rhenné."

"What?"

"I'm really sorry you had to do that."

"I know. I understand. It's not like I've not made some really wrong and bad dating decisions through the years myself." Recently, even, though I'm not sure those could be called *dating* decisions.

"It's just that, well, Jack's kinda obsessive and so . . ."

"So she'll be back."

"Probably."

"So I'm glad you're staying here."

"You don't want me to leave?" She turned from the sink, obviously surprised.

"No, of course not. I can keep you safe here. Protect you from her. And make sure you don't go back to that loon. In fact, maybe we should go back to that bar again tonight—the one you took me to last night?"

"The Rainbow Room?"

"Yeah," I turned away from her, avoiding her gaze. "You should get back on the market—not that you'll have to move out or in with anyone, you can stay here as long as you'd like—but if Looney Tunes sees you moving on, she might be more likely to leave you alone, y'know?"

Paula stared at me for a moment, then, "Holy shit—you wanna cruise for that chick again!"

"What? What chick? No, I just want to help you get over the Evil Ex and, y'know, move on."

"You got a crush on Dracula!" She started dancing around me and pointing. "My sister's got it for another woman! It *does* run in families!"

I will not blush, I told myself. I will not blush. "Fine. We'll just sit at home and . . . and . . . play Yahtzee. Or Dungeons and Dragons."

"Oh, no, no, no! We're goin' clubbin'! I'm gonna take you out, get you drunk, and get you laid!"

"Yo, yo! Straight here!" Dear sweet God, it sounded lame even to me.

"Not for long with the way you were looking at *her* last night. Plus, she *was* mighty fine."

"She's a suspect, okay?"

Paula stopped dancing. "How?"

"I'm pretty sure she's Superdude." I realized I sounded as crazy as Paula's ex. Crazier, even.

Paula, and who can blame her, laughed in my face. "Have you told any of your brethren about this?" I guess my expression spoke volumes because she added, "That was probably a good idea. You don't really believe it, do you?"

"That's why I want to go back—to find out." *How many lies could I tell myself in one night?* All the sanity I'd felt dealing with Paula's ex drained away as I again felt the disconcerting powerlessness I was growing to hate. I didn't know what I believed about Daron. Whenever I thought about her, I simply stopped thinking.

"Well, okay," Paula said. "I think you're nuts. That woman—

even in the costume—didn't strike me as some blood-cult worshipper. What's interesting is your attraction to her. And I'm lovin'
that it runs in families."

"Oh, for chrissake's! I've flirted a bit with a woman—*one*
woman—as in singular. That doesn't mean I'm queer!"

"So is there a problem with being queer?"

"Well, no, but—" Fine. I'd blush.

"So then what is the problem?"

I took a deep breath. "I'm thrown off by . . ." I stopped. I didn't
want to admit anything to her, because actually saying it would
make it all the more real.

"What, Rhenné?" Paula said, breaking into my thoughts.

"That I might be gay. But there are things about Dar—
Dracula—her that upset me even more."

"Did you nearly just say Daron? Dracula is the Daron you were
moaning about last night?"

My little sister was too freakin' smart and that's all there was to
it. There was no telling what else she'd be able to put together. But
I couldn't lie to her. She'd been lying to me long enough for me to
want the truth from her. And to get the truth I'd have to give the
truth. "Yeah-huh."

"Shit."

"Yeah-huh."

X: DARON

Halloween Night

Y ou're looking for her. Again," Evelyn said to me across the table at the Rainbow Room.

"No, I'm really not."

"It's just like a couple of years ago, with that woman you met in London and wasted so much time on. Until you realized she really wasn't Rebecca." Evelyn played with my lighter, a Zippo with a picture of a horned and haloed devil/angel with fangs. "None of them are Rebecca, and they're so fragile, these mortal women."

And they all die, I thought to myself. I grabbed my Zippo from her to light my smoke, then tucked it into my pocket. I didn't like women playing with my lighter, not even my sire. "I think I sometimes convince myself a woman *might be* Rebecca so it's okay for me to have sex. Just so I can get laid."

"Daron, darling, get with the times! You don't need an excuse to get lucky these days—it's not like it was hundreds of years ago. Now you can just go after the candy you want. And you're hot enough that it'll jump out of the case and right into your mouth."

"And either one of us'd be the first in line," Marguerite said, sitting down at our table with her Cosmo. She rightly discerned I wasn't going to light the cigarette she was holding out as she helped herself to my smoke to light up.

I took back my smoke and had a long drag before I sipped my Courvoisier. "So, do we have any special plans or celebrations scheduled for tonight?"

"What," Marguerite said, "getting together and seeing everyone isn't enough anymore? Our annual reunion in the area Evelyn thinks important?"

"Yeah," I said, on the verge of terminal boredom. "It's nice, it's fun, it's all good. Can't complain 'bout gettin' with my peeps again . . ."

"Except?" Marguerite prompted.

"Some of these young'uns are so young and so . . . I can't relate. There's no reason I'm meeting with them. We have nothing in common. I mean—that Teen Vamp who never heard of Old King Cole? I'm too old for this now. I don't know why I'm here." If not for the possibilities Rhenné might offer, I'd end myself right now.

"I understand a lot of what you're saying," Evelyn said. She'd been looking around, disconnected with everything and anything. That was how she was—she was so old, she was beyond it all. I often wasn't quite sure what was going on with my ex-lover, but I supposed that was always the way one was with a parent . . . sire.

"Yeah, but I can do a girl without changing her."

"Oh, baby," Marguerite said, wrapping herself around me, "from what I've heard, you've changed every woman you've ever met."

"Your girl's here," Evelyn said while I rolled my eyes, her gaze never leaving me and the area behind me. I loved how she could sense so much beyond sight—she would always be better at that than I was. I looked over her shoulder and saw Rebecca . . . Rhenné . . . entering with another woman I thought was her sister. Again. Evelyn pointing out Rhenné just went to show that Evelyn was no longer after me, unlike Marguerite, who simply annoyed me with her puppiness.

"My cue," I said, disentangling myself from Marguerite. At the bar I got myself a refill, and drinks for both Rebec . . . Rhenné and her sister. I intercepted them as they came to the bar to get their own drinks.

The sister, whom I wanted to call Providence, took her drink, winked at Rhenné, and went to cruise. I was simultaneously glad that I was still in costume so she'd recognize me, but I also wished I was in something different so I wouldn't be so stereotypical. There were other clothes that better showed off my features and color.

"I . . . uh . . . Thanks for the drink," Rhenné said, toasting me. "But there's something I have to tell you."

I pulled her to the side so we would have some privacy and wouldn't have to scream to hear each other over the music. I popped out my fake vampire teeth. "Sorry, I can't really talk with these things in." I stopped myself from commenting on the irony. "Go on," I said instead.

"I do really love this costume," Rhenné said, almost as if against her will, running her hands along the edges of my cape and drawing it around her, cocooning us together in it.

I held her tight, enjoying the feel of her and the illusion it was Rebecca. I realized she was drawn to me the same way I was drawn to her—no matter what hesitancy we had, it was overcome by the mere sight of each other.

I didn't want to believe she was Rebecca, but I couldn't help it. I reckoned she was under the same sort of spell I was.

I pulled Rhenné into the gaming room, which was a side room from the rest of the bar, and was populated by a mere six other people. Without pause, I pushed her into a corner, further isolating us behind my cape.

"No, listen," she said. "This is the sort of thing that isn't right. It's . . ."

I ran my lips lightly over her neck. I'd expected as much from her. But she felt so good against me, in my arms. And the taste of her was absolutely delightful. If even just her flesh. Her skin. Her outside.

"It's . . ."

I lightly bit on her pulse point.

"I'm straight."

"Are you now, really?" I said into her neck. I had been Rebecca's first awareness of a woman as a bed partner, too.

Her hands were bunched in my cape and I knew she was torn between pulling me closer and pushing me away. The scent of her body filled my head and memory came when I least wanted to live it again.

My large black stallion charged through the cold night air, sweating regardless of the chill and wind. Sweat covered his body while saliva and foam gathered around the bit firmly planted in his mouth. My black jacket, pants, boots, gloves, hat and riding cape would swallow the moonlight as opposed to reflecting it, just as his sleek black coat did.

Even as I pushed my charge ever harder and faster, flowing with his rippling muscles, my senses were on overload. I searched the surrounding landscape. My keen eyes, accustomed to the darkness of night, gazed over the deserted road and surrounding countryside, looking for even the vaguest sign of a disturbance as my ears stood on end, waiting for the slightest word or whisper to come in on the harsh breezes of the cold night air.

Her family thought I was man. I'd wooed her publicly, consistently, charmingly. She was to be mine in all the earthly ways, and mine in every other way as well.

Rebecca should have been safely in my arms yesterday, and we should have performed the ritual last night. We were already deeply bonded, but the eternal tie remained to be woven.

In all reality, we could have performed it—the ritual—any time in the last few months but other plans had caused us to set back the date. I never should have conceded to Rebecca's plan of me going ahead to set up our home in London while she tied up her affairs in the country, and, even now, I could hear Rebecca's voice echoing through my ears, "We shall do it in our new home, so as to start our life together anew in all its entirety."

Normally, an extra day, or even two, on the arduous cross-country coach trip would not have worried me in the slightest, especially not with the rainy season so far upon us, but this time . . . I should have gone to meet Rebecca, instead of vice versa.

I impatiently waited until night broke in all its evil promises before I arose to begin my journey, planning to cover as much ground under cover of darkness as possible. I worried about her though I had no reason to. I did not care how many times I would have to stop to change steeds, I would continue until I found Rebecca, whom I knew, just knew deep within my being through our eternal connection, was dealing with infamous treachery. I would ride all the way to that small country village and back again, regardless of how weary the long trek made me, in order to find my darling Rebecca.

I pushed my hat securely down atop my head and brought my horse to a halt just at the edge of a cliff. As he stood panting, I looked as far as I could, and willed my mind outside of my body, so it could travel on the currents of the night in search of Rebecca. It was as I was taking a long, deep breath that I realized a hint of a familiar scent, the smell of blood. Of Rebecca's blood.

I slowly, fearfully, looked down to the base of the cliff on which I was standing and realized that there, hidden amongst the bramble and overgrowth, was a ruined coach. Without thinking, I willed my horse to stay, and worked my way down the cliff to where the wind had picked up the scent. I carefully navigated the abutments and loose stones.

I had to push and shove and use all of my preternatural strength, but eventually I unearthed the coach from where it had become lodged against the cliff among fallen boulders, vines and trees. The reins and leads were snapped, as if the frightened horses that had once drawn the grand conveyance had broken free either during or after what I could only guess had been a robbery.

The thieves had come on horseback, and willfully dispensed damage and cruelty to the beasts, the coach and its inhabitants. They would pay for their deeds. Of that I was sure. But I still had to determine exactly what those deeds were—and thus, also, the exact nature of their punishment.

And then I opened the carriage door and . . .

. . . and . . .

. . . that was the first and only time in my immortal life that I became ill.

Blood was spattered on the walls and bodies were scattered throughout the shell, tossed about like broken, discarded trinkets and baubles.

My nose led me immediately to Rebeccas's pale, cold, lifeless body, and I knew it was too late to do anything. Anything at all. I couldn't even bring her back now. She was gone. Eternally gone.

Rhenné took advantage of my distraction and fled back into the main bar. She was Rebecca, she had to be. I'd never fallen into memory like that, not while awake. Somehow I knew she'd remembered it too. We'd been dreaming together for a very long time.

If my heart beat, it would've been beating in double-time. I wanted her. I wanted to make her come, scream my name, and writhe beneath and under me. I also wanted to make her mine—take her and bring her over. Every inch of me inside my skin itched for it, but I tried to hold my cool.

Gathering as much poise as I could, I went to the table where Rhenné, pale and drawn, sat with her sister. "I'm Daron," I said, holding my hand out to Rhenné's sister.

"I'm Paula. Thank you for the drink." She reached for my hand, but as soon as our skin touched, she jerked back and looked up at me.

"My pleasure," I said, watching her rub her hand where we'd touched as if she were burned. Or frozen.

"We've met before," she said.

"I've come to this bar, by its many names, around All Hallow's for many years now," I said to Paula.

"No," Paula said, her gaze unfocused. "It's not that. I mean, I might've seen you then, but—I remember you from . . . elsewhere."

I saw the look in her eyes. It was as if she wanted to add "Elsewhen."

"Maybe you met in a convenience store recently?" Rhenné said.

"It's possible," I said. "But not likely. I'm from out of town." I gestured at the empty chair next to Rhenné and sat when neither protested, keeping my body language wide open. "Out of the country, even. You see, I have a castle in England."

"I know I first saw you in a convenience store—a Seven-Eleven," Rhenné said to me. "Just a few nights ago, in fact." Her tone was openly challenging and I realized she remembered that first encounter even though I'd hypnotized her. She should have remembered nothing.

I needed to take charge of the situation. Especially if I wanted Rhenné, whom I was increasingly sure actually *was* my Rebecca. No one previously had passed as many tests as this one.

Rising, I looked at each woman in turn. "I'll be with you in a moment," I said to Rhenné, holding up a finger to her. Thralling her would make things easier, but I was nearly certain she was my Rebecca, and I had never done that to my only true love. Anyway, my thrall had apparently not taken the first time, at the convenience store.

I turned to Paula, having no such compulsions about her. "I'm safe, and you already know this," I said to her. "You like me, in fact."

"Actually, you scare the shit outta me," Paula said, staring at me like I was a lunatic as she inched away from me.

"What the hell?" I said, looking between the sisters. I couldn't thrall *either* of them? If Rhenné was Rebecca—and I believed she was now—I could understand her perhaps being immune to me. But Providence I'd not known nearly so well, even though I'd liked her.

"Rhenné," Paula said. "Let's get gone." She was slowly backing away from me, her eyes wide, her blood pressure up, her heart rate accelerating. When Rhenné didn't automatically go with her, Paula tried grabbing her arm.

"You *are* her," I said to Rhenné.

"God I want you," she whispered, like it had to be dragged from her. They were words I wanted to say myself. My powers didn't work on her, and yet she was offering herself to me as freely and openly as Rebecca had. She was like no woman I'd met in a hundred years. Or even a thousand.

"Let's go, *now*," Paula said, tugging Rhenné's arm.

The woman of my destiny was not going to walk away now. I ran my fingers down Rhenné's cheek, then slipped an arm around her waist to ease her toward me. She tipped her head back naturally when I leaned forward to touch my lips to hers.

We caressed each others' lips, and she pulled her arm from Paula's grasp to come fully to me, both arms sliding slowly up and around my neck.

I gently bit her lower lip, then slid my tongue into her mouth when she gasped. I pulled her tightly against me, fitting our bodies together. Not in a hundred years had I fit so well with another.

"Rhenné, we need to leave, now!" Paula said, yanking her sister from me.

"I know you're turned on," I said to Rhenné. I wanted to woo her all over again, but she was going to let Paula drag her away. I desperately played to her baser urges.

"It was nice, but—"

"I can smell it, Rhenné." I leaned forward to whisper in her ear. "You're wet for me."

She was breathing heavily, and blushing, as she allowed Paula to pull her away. "You can't possibly smell . . ."

One arm around her waist, I pulled her up off the ground so she rode my thigh. She pushed her pelvis into me.

"Runner, we need to get gone," Paula said, trying to pull her sister from my arms. Didn't she understand I would never let go now?

Rhenné pulled away just enough to plant her feet on the ground. She remained in my arms, however. "Why? We're just—"

I tightened my grasp while thinking that in the past Providence had been happy for her sister when she had fallen in love with me.

What was different now? "You brought her here, why are you now so dead set on leaving?" I said.

Paula tightened her hold on Rhenné as well. "I sometimes have feelings about people as soon as I meet them. It doesn't always happen, but it's always right. I know you're . . . well . . . this won't end well. So we need to leave. Now."

"No, you can't get away that easily. Explain."

"You're evil."

Rhenné pulled out of her sister's grasp. "Did you happen to do a lot of coke recently?" she asked Paula.

"I don't know what it is," Paula said to her sister, her voice rising in desperation. "I saw you with Daron and I thought—well, at first—cool. You," she said to me, "were all with the cruising of my sister—while she was all . . . Well, fuck, you two were . . . perfect together."

"So what changed?" Rhenné asked. "Tell me, Paula."

I watched Paula's face for a moment and realized that when she'd touched me, it'd brought the past back to her as well. She'd had no preparation and must've been spooked out of her mind.

"You've been all about me hooking up with a woman," Rhenné said. "Especially—"

She couldn't bring herself to finish her statement, so I did. "Especially me?" I said, keeping my arm around Rhenné.

"Yeah. You," Paula said. "It was you."

"Hold up," Rhenné said. "I didn't think you two knew each other." Carefully, looking increasingly shaken, she removed my hands and arms from her body.

"She's no good for you." Paula's eyes were dilated and I was suddenly afraid she was going to pass out. "She . . . she . . . let you die." Her voice changed. "They come for you and she's never there in time. Over and over again, she's never there when you need her."

"This is wicked *X-Filey*," Rhenné said. "And makes no sense whatsoever."

Nowhere in any of my imaginings had I thought, when I found my Rebecca, that I'd have a hysterical sister to deal with. "She was happy to see you hooking it with a woman, but she's suddenly getting cold feet."

"No," Paula said. "It's *you* giving me the jeebies."

"No. You know Rebe—Rhenné and I belong together," I said.

"What I know is that bad things'll happen, like before. Like every time."

"There's no *before*," Rhenné wrapped her arms around herself, and I felt her shiver as if it had coursed through my own body. "That's just dreams. Nightmares. It can't be true."

"It won't be true again, not if I have anything to say about it." Paula clamped both hands on Rhenné's arm and pulled. Rhenné resisted only a moment, then they were both hurrying for the door.

"Let her go." Marguerite's coy whisper startled me. I hadn't even sensed her near. "Even if she's the same soul, she's not the same person. Stop chasing the dream and live reality instead." She coiled her arms around me. "It can be much more fun, after all."

"You expect me to let her go, now that I'm *sure* I've finally found her again? Now that I know for a fucking goddamned fact that she's come back to me?" I stared at the door, watching as Rhenné and Paula left. I knew where they lived, so I could go there again. See her there, again.

"It's never her. And if it was, why should she come back to you? She's got a different life now and you don't."

I wasn't gentle when I freed myself from her grasp, and I didn't care about her wounded pout. "This time, I'm not wrong. Her soul knows mine and we'll never rest easy, either of us, until we face who we are and have been."

Whatever she snarled in response I didn't hear. Even if I hadn't already known the way to Rhenné's house, my heart would have led me there.

XI: RHENNÉ

. . . meanwhile . . .

I wanted Daron. I knew this. And everything that'd just happened made Paula, my ex-smoker sister, crave a cigarette. I tried to talk her out of it, but she was adamant. In fact, she was scaring me—I'd never seen her so tightly wound. I cruised into a gas station near home so she could buy a pack. She said she wouldn't tell me another thing without one.

Should've been simple enough. But it wasn't. A lot of joints were closed because of the robberies. It was kind of like that sniper deal in DC a few years ago—vulnerable merchants closed up shop early to avoid the risk until the bad guys were caught.

The case, the vigilantes—damn. I had been planning to study my suspect, to find a way to arrest her, even. Sure. Right. I got near her and I couldn't think. I didn't feel like myself. But I liked the way I felt. I wanted to feel that way more. If she was a vampire . . . what was I thinking? Crazy, I was thinking crazy.

Paula walked to the cashier's window. She slid her money through the slot. What had her so spooked? Was she thinking "vampire" too? Thinking crazy, like me?

A car pulled up to a pump, and a short guy with a Richard Nixon mask on got out of it. I watched him without really seeing him as he went to the cashier's window and stood next to my sister. And then he pulled a gun out of his pocket and put it to Paula's gut, wrenching her next to him.

Life went into slow motion. It seemed to take me forever to yank my gun out of the glove compartment. Shortie, holding my terrified sister in an iron grip, glanced about, as if he'd seen my movement from the corner of his eye.

Shortie's car inched forward, as if the driver was noticing that Shortie's attention had been drawn toward my car.

Gun in hand, I froze. I stopped everything and tried to slow my pounding heart to figure out what I should do. I could try to shoot these assholes, but I might miss. Or one of them could shoot before I disabled both of them. Three times in one week I'd been confronted with these kinds of thugs, but now my sister was in the line of fire and I was having a hard time trying to think like a cop.

They never killed anyone, I told myself. But they had tried to shoot at least one person, with intent to kill. Paula was stiff and still, and kept looking toward the car like I was going to arrive in some blaze of glory, but I was thinking that the safest thing in the world right now was for me to let the robbery happen and get those guys the hell out of the gas station where they were never supposed to be in the first place.

The cashier was pushing bills under the window to Shortie. She wouldn't let him in, but she seemed to be doing and giving him everything and anything he wanted, which was exactly what she should be doing.

Given that the last two times, when things went wrong, when Daron and the other vigilante stopped the thieves, the drivers took off, it made sense that if I shot Shortie, chances were the same thing would happen here—his driver would take off, abandoning him and thus be a non-issue.

But it still came down to the fact that this repeat offender was standing there with a gun in my sister's gut and whether or not I wanted to risk her life by acting.

Or was it a greater risk not to do anything?

The clerk was shaking her head, and Shortie became visibly irate. He pulled his gun from Paula's gut to shoot the glass door so he could get in. They'd broken routine to start on gas stations, I told myself. Firing any kind of shots meant attention, and they were acting like they weren't afraid. He fired again and the door shattered. For chrissake's, they were looking ripe to escalate to real killers. I had to act.

I rolled out of the car, keeping low, as he shoved his gun back into Paula's gut.

"Watch out!" the driver yelled to Shortie. He waved a Beretta from the window in my direction. I veered right, his shot missed me, but the loud report left my ears ringing. Had there been another? I couldn't see the driver, but couldn't afford to glance toward the store either.

A car squealed into the lot and the ski-masked vigilante—not Daron, my heart told me—leapt from the driver's seat. With movements so fast they were a blur, she hurtled at Shortie. I thought she didn't see me but even as she closed in on Shortie she snarled at me a bitter, "You!"

I heard a bike closing in, then that roar was drowned out by a shot. Then another. I only noticed I had my gun out and up when I saw the blur of the vigilante rushing right at me. I tried pulling the trigger, aiming at the ski mask, even as I realized Shortie was on the ground, and his accomplice was peeling out of the lot. Paula was on the ground as well.

I was flipped around, lying with my back against the hood of my car and not knowing how I got there. My arms wouldn't obey me and I was helpless to do anything but stare into enraged eyes as the unknown vigilante held me down. The roar of the bike was closer and then it abruptly cut off.

"Just a flick of my wrist," the woman holding me down said, in a vaguely familiar voice, "and Rebecca dies. *Again*." She wasn't talking to me, and I became sure I'd heard her in this lifetime as well as others.

I heard the clatter of a helmet hitting the ground. "But why would you do that to me?" Daron said. "I understand you going after all these assholes—I mean, save humanity and get a good meal, but . . . Rebecca?"

"You think you feel the weight of all eternity on you? I'm a thousand years older than you," the woman holding me said. She didn't seem large, but she was incredibly strong. I couldn't even budge against her. "You have no idea what it's like to live forever. You might have found Rebecca again, but you don't realize I am your only possible lasting companion. I will let you go only so far from me."

"So you started this with this intention—of bringing me back into your fold?"

"No. Actually, I go after these scum because they're scum. I keep thinking about breaking into the White House as well, but . . . You're just an added bonus."

"Makes sense. Up till now," Daron said. "Evelyn, you don't know what you're doing."

"Shall I drain her dry, or just break her neck?" Evelyn increased the pressure against my windpipe as her hands went around my neck. A helplessness invaded me and I stopped all struggling. It was not at all what I felt when in Daron's grasp. I didn't want this and I was powerless to say no.

Two light points of pressure pricked at my carotid artery. "I did it before, got rid of that little fool when you didn't have the sense to. She was the ruin of all I invested in you. She kept finding you and I had to keep getting rid of her. Don't even think about fighting me, Daron, dearheart. I'm stronger, faster and more powerful than you'll ever be."

Daron's voice was laden with old, old pain. "It was you? *You* had her torn to pieces?"

I could feel my heart beating hard and heavy in my chest. I didn't know what was going to happen to me, or what had happened to Paula.

Evelyn continued, "Shall we make her one—"

Over Evelyn's shoulder, at practically the speed of light, I saw a blur, and a splinter of yellow slicing through the air toward Evelyn.

Suddenly, the pressure against my neck was gone. I looked into eyes dark with disbelief, then anger, and then the ski mask dissolved and a skeleton was holding me until I was choking on thick dust. I looked at it on my hands but in moments, the dust too disappeared.

"Rebecca, Rhenné, I thought I'd lost you again!" Daron said, pulling me into her arms.

"What the hell?" I asked, trying to push away from her.

"I staked her. Number two pencil. She's gone, eternally gone." She sheepishly held up the pencil. In a tone caught between horror and relief, Daron added, "She gave me immortality and I just ended hers."

That mattered nothing to me. "Paula . . . Paula . . . where is she?"

"Oh, fuck."

"What? Daron, what?" I whirled around only to see my worst fear: Paula lying on the ground in a spreading pool of blood.

I stumbled toward her but Daron whisked by me, reaching her first. I saw Paula's face. She looked like all the other shooting victims I'd seen who weren't going to make it.

"She's alive, but won't survive long enough for the paramedics," Daron said, from where she knelt next to Paula.

The clerk ran out of the office. "The cops—ambulances—should be here any minute!"

Daron looked up at me. I could see the question in her eyes.

"What are you asking me?" I needed her to put it into words because it was all so decidedly impossible.

Her face morphed right before my eyes into a demonic visage with elongated canines. "I'm asking if you want me to change her. I'm telling you it's her only chance for any kind of life."

"A life like yours? *What are you?*" I just wanted her to say it, name it, or I'd be crazy forever.

"I am an immortal, a vampire. You know this. And I can give your sister immortality."

"I can't choose for her! Only for myself." It was too much, all happening too fast.

Her eyes darkened and she said, "And if you were choosing just for you, Rebecca?"

Yes, I wanted to say. We can talk about it, I wanted to say. No, I wanted to say, then run screaming to an asylum. All my nightmares were true, I realized. The fantasy of love, my love for her, freely given, was true too. I opened my mouth, tasting Yes on my tongue.

Paula coughed weakly.

"She can't make it!" Daron held up a hand to hold off the clerk. "Stay!" She turned back to me. "Yes or no?" she yelled.

"She's my sister!" I screamed. "I can't decide for her!"

Daron glared at me, then dropped her head to Paula's neck. It wasn't even a heartbeat later that she sat up, bit her own wrist, and held it to Paula's mouth, holding Paula's head against her like a suckling babe.

Daron looked at me, her fangs dripping with my sister's blood, and her face morphed back into human form, even as Paula grasped Daron's wrist to her mouth greedily, sucking deep and long.

EPILOGUE

I looked out my window at the apartment building across the street, where Daron perched on the roof, watching me.

She'd made the decision she'd had to, but I wasn't sure if I could live with it. Paula was with her now, with Daron, while Daron taught her all about her new immortality. It took some getting used to. I watched her adapt. I saw how one survived a change so vast.

Paula was still my little sister and I still loved her—how could I not? Even though now I, and the parental units, could only see her at night. We still hadn't told the 'rents about the changes with her, and I wasn't quite sure how, when, or even if we would.

Tonight, after Paula left, I heard a tapping at the window and thought about how I'd made Daron make the choice for Paula, but she was letting me make my own choice. I realized that sometimes choosing love *is* choosing life, so I closed my book, looked at my reflection one last time, went to the window, opened it and said, "Come in."

We Recruit

Julia Watts

CHAPTER 1

Y ou'll be back," Mama said when I told her I was running off to the city. "Everybody always says they're gonna go off to Cincinnati and make good, but they always come back home to their people. Blood calls out to blood."

Mama turned out to be part right, at least. I did come back. But I didn't come back to be with the blood family I'd left. There was one thing Mama was all the way right about, though. "The city," she said, "changes people."

It sure changed me.

I spent all of high school dreaming of Cincinnati. I had been there once with a church group to King's Island. It wasn't the amusement park roller coasters that filled up my mind, though. It was the skyscrapers in downtown Cincinnati—buildings that didn't look like they could go any closer together or any higher up, and all the people—white, brown, tan, young, old—in fancy suits or ratty jeans, all crowding the sidewalks, going about the business of their lives. In a place like that, I thought, nobody would care if your daddy got himself shot in a bar when you were just two or if nobody in your family besides you had bothered to stay in school. In a place like that, you could forget where you came from and just be who you were.

In Morgan, Kentucky, there was no way I could forget where I came from because everybody was always too happy to remind me: I was Billie Jo Scruggs, named after my daddy Billy Joe Scruggs, whose achievements included bootlegging, arson and theft. His skills with a pool cue must not have been up to snuff, though, because when I was just a baby he knocked a guy upside the head with one at the Spot Tavern, and the guy, who was more annoyed than hurt, took out a gun and shot him dead.

Billy Joe Scruggs was the only man my mama ever married, but she sure didn't let her bed get cold after he died. She keeps a boyfriend two or three years and then gets a new one like rich people do with cars. She's been with this one, TJ, for about two and a half years, so I reckon his warranty's about to expire. He draws disability for his nerves, though, which is just enough money to keep Mama in beer and cigarettes without her having to get a job, so she may hold onto him longer than the others.

In Morgan there's a saying used to describe somebody who won't work for a living—"as sorry as a Scruggs." When I was just a little kid, I swore I would prove that saying wrong. I went to school every day and did all my homework and even made some good grades from the few teachers who weren't prejudiced against me on account of my last name. I was the first member of my family to graduate from high school.

But none of that changed the way people looked at me. Everybody was quick to tell me I was "nothing but a Scruggs." And after graduation, when I went around looking for a job, none of the places that paid pretty good, like the greeting card factory and the bandage factory, would hire me because of who I was. The only job I could land was a dead-end part-timer, sweeping and mopping and taking out the garbage at the Burger Hut. The job was as miserable as I had thought it would be, and home was the same misery it had always been, but I knew I couldn't leave Morgan till I'd saved up some money and gotten some wheels.

Of course, there was one other thing keeping me in Morgan. Well, not a thing—a girl. Tara. Tara with her long, dyed black hair and lipstick so dark it was almost black, too. Tara, who was always reading a book about vampires or writing scary but beautiful poems in the purple notebook she carried with her all the time. I spent all four years of high school staring at Tara, sometimes getting up enough nerve to joke around with her, but mostly just staring. One time in chemistry the teacher paired us up as lab partners, and I got so nervous I mixed the wrong things together and caused an explosion that burned off both of our eyebrows. Tara just laughed and came to school the next day with black painted-on eyebrows the shape of upside-down V's. She looked beautiful.

The only reason I could see not to leave Morgan was that I didn't want to leave Tara. Neither of us fit in—her in her black clothes with her vampire books and me being not only a Scruggs but a girl who looked and acted like a boy. My favorite daydream as I mopped the floors of the Burger Hut was that I'd make enough money to buy a used motorcycle—a Harley, if possible. I'd climb on my Harley, Tara would climb on behind me and put her arms around my waist, and off we'd go, bound for the skyscrapers of Cincinnati.

Mama always did say I was bad to fill up my head with notions that were never gonna happen, and I guess this was one of these notions. I would have had to work part-time at the Burger Hut for years before I could afford a Harley, and even if I did get one, there was no way Tara was gonna climb on it and ride with me into parts unknown. She knew me as her goofy tomboy pal from school, not as her Romeo.

But that didn't stop me from dreaming. One day I was wiping spilled ketchup off a table when Tara walked in. She had on a denim miniskirt and army boots. The sun made her black hair shine blue. I stopped in mid-wipe and grinned at her. But I stopped in mid-grin when I saw who was with her—Cody Prewitt, the long-haired, earringed, leather-jacket-wearing-even-when-it's-a-hundred-degrees-outside dumbass who thinks he's a rock star just because he plays in a third-rate bar band.

"Hey, Billie Jo," Tara said, smiling. Her skin was milk white against the black of her lipstick. I took in every detail: her chipped black nail polish, her curvy figure, the dog chain she was wearing for a necklace. If I could have a tape of her saying, "Hey, Billie Jo," I thought, I'd play it over and over.

But then there were the next words out of her black lips: "Did you know that me and Cody are moving in together?"

"Um . . . I've got to take care of something in the back," I said and ran to the restroom just in time to throw up on the floor I'd mopped not ten minutes before. I had no reason to stay in Morgan, and I wasn't sure I had a reason to live.

That night was when Mama told me I'd never make it in Cincinnati, but the next morning I rolled up a pair of jeans and two T-shirts and put them in my backpack. I crammed in what little money I had, along with some socks and underwear, a comb and a toothbrush. I took the backpack with me when TJ drove me to work (he always demanded a quarter of my paycheck—for "chauffeur services," he said), and after he dropped me in front of the Burger Hut, I kept on walking till I reached the interstate. Then I stuck up my thumb.

It was stupid, I know. I could have been raped or beaten or chopped up in little pieces. I knew this at the time, too, but I didn't care. No matter what happened, I thought, at least I wouldn't be in Morgan.

As it turned out, I must have had a case of beginner's luck. I got picked up by a husband-and-wife trucker team who lectured me on how I ought not to be hitching. They shared their sandwiches with me, let me ride in their big semi all the way to Cincinnati, then slipped me a twenty and dropped me in front of the YWCA.

So there I was, surrounded by those skyscrapers at last but with only enough money for a few days' room and board. I had to find a job fast. I walked the streets by day looking for "now hiring" signs in store windows. I must have filled out a dozen applications, and each time the manager would say, "Thanks. We'll get back to you," and I had to bite my tongue to keep from snapping, "But I need money now!"

If I didn't spend any money on food, I decided, I could hold out a little longer at the Y, and maybe by then I would have a job offer. I didn't know how I was going to make it without buying food, but I knew that whatever happened, I wouldn't beg or steal. No matter how bad I felt, I didn't want to live down to the saying "sorry as a Scruggs."

I found a solution to the food problem. At the end of the day, the New York Bagel Shoppe, up the street from the Y, put all their unsold bagels out on the sidewalk in a clean plastic garbage bag so the homeless and hungry could help themselves. I wasn't homeless, but I was hungry, so every day, right after closing time, I'd root through the garbage bag and grab a few bagels. I had no idea how long a person could live on a diet of day-old bagels, but I hoped I'd survive long enough to land a paying job.

One night when I was digging around in the garbage bag, looking for one of the cinnamon-raisin bagels I liked, a shiny black car pulled up beside me. The back window rolled down, and I saw a beautiful redheaded woman in the backseat. Her hair was pulled back in a tight bun that showed off her high cheekbones. Her lips were crimson and glossy, and she was wearing sunglasses even though it was dark. I thought I'd never seen anybody so elegant.

"Hungry?" she asked.

CHAPTER 2

I had never smelled anything as good as the inside of her car. Part of it was the warm scent of the black leather upholstery, but most of it was her. She smelled like a whole garden of the best-smelling flowers in the world. Smelling her made me feel so peaceful I wanted to close my eyes and go to sleep like Dorothy in the poppy field in "The Wizard of Oz."

"We'll get you something to eat," she said. Her skin was so white and clear it was impossible to imagine it with a pimple or a wrinkle. It was also hard to figure out whether she was closer to pimple age or wrinkle age—I could tell she was older than me, but that's all I could tell.

"Are you from a church or somethin?" I asked.

"No," she said, and laughed for a long time.

The driver let us off in front of a skyscraper—an old gray building with lots of curlicues and statues of funny little critters decorating its face. She said nothing, but she let me follow her into the building's lobby which had a marble floor and giant Chinese vases and was the fanciest place I'd ever been. She pushed the button for the gold-doored elevator. "I live on the top floor," she said.

The whole top floor was hers. It looked more like a museum than an apartment. There were big paintings all over walls—the

kind that you can't tell what they're supposed to be pictures of—
and giant statues, some of people that were put together funny,
some of I didn't know what. "The kitchen is this way," she said,
and I followed her.

The kitchen was so shiny and white I couldn't imagine a single
grease spatter on the stove or crumb on the counter. "This is real
nice of you," I said as she tied on a plain white apron. "I just
thought you was gonna take me to McDonald's or something. I
didn't think you was gonna cook for me."

"I wanted to help you," she said. "And nobody is helped by
eating at McDonald's." She opened the big silver refrigerator
which, I was surprised to see, was empty except for a single plastic-
wrapped steak and a bowl of salad. "Sit." She nodded toward the
kitchen table.

The table was set for one. She placed a bowl of salad in front of
me and poured a glass of purple liquid into a stemmed glass and
handed it to me. "Red wine," she said. "It builds the blood."

"I don't really . . ." I began. I had never drunk wine—never
drunk alcohol at all. Too many people in my family are bad to
drink, and I didn't want to give anybody another reason to think
"sorry as a Scruggs" was true.

"Drink it," she said. "You look anemic."

"Are you a doctor?"

She laughed, but not for as long as when I'd asked her if she was
from a church.

The steak sizzled when she threw it in the pan. I ate my salad
and drank my wine. Both of them tasted bitter, but I was so hungry
I didn't care. When I cut into the steak, a pool of blood spilled
onto the white plate. I had never eaten meat so rare—Mama
always cooked meat until it was in the chewy-tough condition she
called "good and done." But I liked it, maybe because I was so
hungry. Or maybe I was anemic. I gobbled down several bites
before I looked up to see her sitting across from me, watching me
eat. "This is real good," I said. "I sure appreciate it."

She said nothing, just stared. Her eyes without the sunglasses were the same green as the wine bottle on the table. "My name's Billie Jo," I said. "You got a name, ma'am?"

"Maeve." She smiled a little, maybe because I'd called her "ma'am," but she didn't say anything else.

My plate was clean, my salad bowl and wineglass were empty, and I was feeling comfortably sluggish from the food and wine. I couldn't get too comfortable, though, because the fact that I had just taken charity gnawed at me. I hadn't begged, but I still felt beholden. "Ma'am," I said, "if there's anything I can do to help you out . . . you know to pay you back, I'd be happy to do it. You ain't got many dishes to wash, but—"

"There is something," she said, rising from her chair. "Come with me."

I followed her down the white hall into a room that was lit by dozens of candles. When had she lit them? I wondered. Did she keep them burning all the time? Wasn't that a fire hazard as bad as TJ passing out drunk with a lit cigarette?

"When I saw you on the street," she said, "I took you for the kind of woman who gives other women pleasure. Is this true?"

All of a sudden, the dangers of candles left burning were the last thing on my mind. I had thought before—okay, I had thought a lot—about "giving another woman pleasure," like she said. I had thought about giving Tara pleasure more times than I could count. But thinking was as far as I'd ever gotten, and I was pretty vague on the specifics. So I had a choice: I could say that yes, I was that kind of woman and let her think that women all over the world were screaming my name. Or I could own up to my own ignorance. My past experiences had taught me that if you try to act like you're not ignorant, people find out almost as soon as if you'd just admitted it in the first place. "I reckon it's true and it ain't at the same time," I said. "I'm the kind of woman who's thought about giving another woman pleasure, but I've never actually done it."

Maeve smiled, but it was a different kind of smile. It spread over her face slowly. "Well, then, you must let me teach you." She looked right at me with those bottle green eyes and started unbuttoning her blouse. I couldn't even imagine looking away, and her aroma filled the room like we were surrounded by a thousand flowers. She slipped her blouse over her shoulders and unzipped her skirt and let it fall into a puddle at her feet. She stood in a lacy black slip, black stockings, and black high heels. The last move she made was to reach up and take the pins out of her hair, which tumbled over her shoulders and back in fiery waves.

I didn't even know this woman, but I knew I couldn't refuse her. Not this, not anything.

Feeling like I was floating on a cloud of her scent, I walked to her. She took my hand and pulled me to the crimson-covered bed which the candles surrounded. I leaned in and kissed her, shyly, but then she kissed back with pressure and passion, her parted lips forcing mine open. It was my first kiss.

But kissing wasn't enough. She grabbed the top of her slip and ripped it, revealing beautiful white breasts with nipples the pink of birthday cake frosting. She pulled me on top of her, and I kissed her from throat to collarbone to breast. Her skin was cool but warmed under my touch as if her body was drawing the heat from mine.

She gasped from my kisses, then took my hand and moved it to the part of her thigh where her stocking ended and her garter began. I moved my hand up, expecting silky underwear but finding silky skin instead. She whispered, "Use your mouth."

I slid down to the sweet nest of orange curls. It was beautiful, and I felt drunk from the scent of flowers, but I was still afraid because I had no idea what I was doing. Now what? I asked in my mind.

Her body answered my unspoken question. All of a sudden, I knew what to do. My tongue found the right spot like a magnet finds metal, and I knew to go slow at first—to use long, slow, gentle strokes until her body told me, just as sure as if it had been spoken out loud, faster. My tongue flickered and danced, and I felt heat pouring from her body, smelled the scent of a million flowers, heard her cry "Ahh!" as her long nails raked my back.

When I flopped on the pillow beside her, I felt as happy as I could ever remember feeling. "Now I know what you are," I said. "You're a teacher."

"And you're a very fine student."

I felt myself blushing. I wanted to put my arms around her, to cuddle her, but something told me not to.

"Lie back," she said. "There's something I want to give you."

She was on top of me, sliding over me like a snake. She kissed me hard, biting down on my lower lip till she drew blood. She licked my lips and let out a low, rumbling sound like a purring cat. I was excited, but I was also scared. If it had been Driver's Ed instead of sex, she would have been shoving me out onto the interstate when I had only just learned how to circle an empty parking lot. "Sweet," she whispered, licking her own lips, then leaning down to kiss my neck.

But it wasn't just a kiss. The points of her teeth entered me, sinking deep into my flesh. And then there was the sucking, rhythmic, insistent. It wasn't like anything I'd ever felt before, but it felt good. Better than good, really. I could feel my blood, the force of my life, rushing toward her. Her scent was everywhere—it was inside me, a part of me, and my whole body was thrumming and rolling with pleasure. Red . . . everything was red, not the red you see when you're angry, but the red of passion, of rose petals, of velvet couches where lovers embrace.

And then it stopped with the suddeness of a slap in the face. Maeve lay beside me, gasping, her chin streaked with my blood. "It's so hard . . ." she gasped, "to make myself stop."

"So why did you?" When her mouth was on me, I had felt like I was hurtling toward something fantastic, something better than anybody had ever felt before. But she had stopped before I reached it.

"Because if I hadn't, you would've died."

"Oh," I said, and I knew that at the time, even if I had known death was the final destination, I still wouldn't have wanted her to stop.

"Now me," she said. She reached onto the table full of candles.

I saw a flash of silver and then a clean gash on the inside of her forearm. When she moved the wound toward my mouth, I felt disgusted, but once it was close enough that the smell of the blood hit my nose, I grabbed her arm with both hands and locked my mouth over the gash. The coppery taste exploded in my mouth, and the sucking and swallowing felt like the most natural thing anybody had ever done. I was a baby at my mother's breast. I had no fear or sadness. I was happy.

When she tried to pull away, I grabbed her arm tighter and sucked harder. With her free hand, she hit me hard across the face and broke the seal of my suction. It felt like all pleasure was over for all time.

"You see what I mean now," she said, "about it being hard to stop."

I nodded and rubbed my aching jaw.

"You can't take much, though, not at first, even though you want to. You'll have to learn your limits, but of course, there's a lot you'll have to learn."

It was a hell of a way to lose your virginity. I licked my lips, tasted a trace of her blood, and felt a small pulse of pleasure. "I'm different now, right?" I said. "I mean, I'll never be the same again."

Maeve smiled and stroked my hair. "But haven't you always been different? Different from the people around you so that they single you out like lions spotting an injured gazelle on the veldt?"

"Yeah, but . . ." I wasn't sure what to say. What was in my head was, but I was human then, and I'm not anymore, am I? But it sounded so crazy I couldn't bring myself to say it.

"Now," Maeve said, resting a finger on my lips, "there is strength in your difference. You are the predator, not the prey."

I didn't like the idea of being prey, but I didn't care for the thought of being a predator either. I'd never killed anything short of a bug, and one time when TJ had gone hunting and come home with a deer, I had cried to see it gutted and hanging from a tree, its eyes open but seeing nothing. I refused to eat any of the meat. "I don't know if I can . . ."

"Of course you can. It's in your blood now. You just need me to teach you how to hunt wisely."

I couldn't understand how fast my life was changing. I felt like crying, but no tears would come. My eyes were as dry as glass. "Why did you do this to me? Why did you pick me?"

Maeve took my hand. "As I said, I wanted to help you . . . to transform your life so you would never again be a street urchin digging through the garbage for a meal. I like to choose people on the margins of society . . . to give them power they would never know otherwise."

I wasn't sure I wanted the power. "But why do you have to do this to anybody?"

Maeve shrugged her white shoulders. "In a way, it's part of my job. Predators are necessary to ensure the balance of nature. The big cats, the wolves and coyotes . . . they attempt to keep their population up by breeding. Our kind, though, can't reproduce." Her bottle green eyes locked with mine. "So we recruit."

CHAPTER 3

Just like anything else you study, vampirism has its own lingo. For example, a vampire never calls a bitten human her victim.

"Victim is such an offensive term," Maeve told me, as she lounged in a filmy white nightgown on the first night of my hunting lessons. "It implies that what's happening to the person is somehow unjust, that the person is being unfairly victimized. When in fact, this isn't the case at all. If a lioness brings down a zebra, do you call her evil? Of course not. She, like us, is only doing what she must to survive, and controlling the overpopulation of the prey as she does it. Prey . . . that's the term we use. Not victim. And we are predators, not monsters. It speaks to the natural order of things, don't you think?"

"I guess so." I thought back to when I was a little thing—no bigger than five or six—and I saw my cat Tigger with a mouse. He held his paw down on the end of the mouse's tail, keeping it trapped, but letting it run around in panicky circles. Sometimes he'd smack it with his free paw, and it would stop running for a few seconds until it would get up again and run and run but never get away. I was too scared to try to save the mouse myself, so I ran into the trailer, hollering, "Mama! Mama! I thought Tigger was nice, but he's mean."

After I explained what my kitty was doing, Mama said, "He ain't mean, honey. That's just the way of nature."

I wondered if Mama would say the same thing about me if she knew what I was.

Maeve had gotten up off the couch and was padding around the living room in her bare feet. "In terms of the frequency with which you'll hunt prey," she said, "don't believe what you see in the movies. A vampire who fed every night would be so bloated you could pop her like a tick. In terms of our dietary needs, the predators we most closely resemble are reptiles. A meal a month is enough to sustain us, and we don't even need to drain the prey completely in order to feel sated. But make no mistake: the prey must die, and its remains must be disposed of with the utmost discretion."

She settled back down on the leather couch, tucked her little white feet underneath her, and then rattled off different ways of disposing of a corpse the same bored way the counter girl at the Burger Hut rattled off the different hamburger toppings: "Dismembering and dissolving in lye; burning; weighing down and dumping in the river—though if you do that, you'll want to destroy the fingerprints and knock out the teeth . . ."

I felt sick. I had felt sick ever since I drank her blood, like something had invaded my body and taken it over . . . a cancer. "But how am I supposed to get rid of a body all by myself?"

Maeve smiled. "You'll be surprised how strong you are. But the first time, I'll help you."

I swallowed hard. "The first time . . . when will that be?"

"You'll know when you're hungry. And when you are, you'll want to jump on the first potential prey you see. But you have to be careful. Just as the lioness singles out the weakest gazelle in the pack, you will single out the type of prey that won't cause too much of a stir if it goes missing. The wealthy, the famous, even the happily married . . . all poor choices for prey."

"And how will I tell if somebody's happily married just by looking at em?"

Maeve laughed a little and shook her head. "But you have to do more than look. You have to talk to them, too."

"Talk? To the person I'm about to kill?"

"Of course. How else can you ascertain if someone is a suitable choice? Plus, you'll have to get the prey to go somewhere alone with you. The act requires privacy. You have to make the prey like you, trust you, perhaps even want you. It's a seduction."

I jumped up and ran for the door, even though I knew there was no sense in trying to get away. Maeve owned the whole building, and the exits were guarded. I looked at the door and looked at Maeve. I tried to imagine pretending to be somebody's friend then killing them. "Well," I said, "you picked the wrong girl. I ain't the kind of person that could do that to somebody."

Maeve laughed. "Wait."

Two weeks passed. I spent my days sleeping in the guest bedroom with the shades drawn—no vampire in her right mind would sleep in a coffin, except for dramatic effect, Maeve said—and my nights with Maeve. She taught me how to wet my tearless eyes with eyedrops and to slather my body in lotion so it wouldn't get dry and papery. But she didn't always talk about vampire stuff. Sometimes she would lecture me on art or literature or put classical music on the stereo. Some nights we'd walk the streets, wearing sunglasses to protect our sensitive eyes from the dazzling city lights.

Maeve never invited me into her bed again, making me think she had seduced me just as a way of getting to a seduction of another kind. But I wasn't hurt. Instead I was amazed that she had ever allowed me into her bed in the first place. And while I always noticed Maeve's beauty, I saw her more like the Bible thumpers back home saw God than how I had seen Tara. Maeve was my creator, and I worshipped and feared her.

One time, I saw a nature program where a mama lion was teaching her cubs to hunt. She brought home some kind of big rat-looking thing, still alive, and let it loose so the cubs could kill it. If it got away from them, she brought it back and laid it at the cubs' feet so they could take another whack at it.

Maeve taught me the same way.

My hunger had started a couple of days before, and it was worse than anything I'd ever felt. As a kid I'd gone to bed hungry more than once—when Mama had cashed in the food stamps to buy beer and cigarettes—but the pain of an empty belly compared to my predator's hunger was like a hangnail compared to a sawed-off hand. My whole body felt like a husk, empty of everything but stabbing pain. The pain was in my head, too, and my brain was empty of everything except the need to make the pain go away. I shook, and I sweated. I bit my lip to taste the blood. I wanted my suffering to end, but I knew that the only thing that would end my suffering would begin somebody else's.

"I'm going out," Maeve said, standing over me as I twisted in my tangled sheets, "to get something to make you feel better."

I had a feeling she wasn't just running to the drug store. Part of me wanted to tell her not to do it, but I couldn't even speak.

"While I'm gone, pull yourself together," she said, slipping on her sunglasses. "Take a shower, put on some clean clothes, and try to locate what little vocabulary you possess. We're going to have company."

Half an hour or so after she left, I managed to drag myself out of the bed and into the bathroom. I didn't have the strength to stand under the shower, so I ran the tub full and lay in it, letting the hot water soak off the sweat and the strange, rotten-sweet smell that seemed to go along with my hunger. After I got out of the tub, I collapsed on the bed again for a few minutes, trying to get up enough strength to dress.

Maeve had given me a whole closet full of clothes—crisp shirts and tailored jackets and pleated pants . . . polished leather loafers and oxfords. I'd never looked right when I'd been forced to dress up in girly clothes, but I looked right in these.

Once I'd put on a clean white shirt and some charcoal gray

pants, I lay back down, exhausted but awake, until I heard the door click open and Maeve say, "I want you to meet my niece." Then she called, "Rebecca! We have company!"

In my addled brain, it took me a minute to realize I was supposed to be Rebecca. It was another rule Maeve had taught me: never use your real name when talking to prey.

And prey was in the house. I could smell it.

I stood, finger-combed my hair, and tried to walk without stumbling or shaking into the living room where Maeve, smiling all over herself, stood next to a pudgy middle-aged man wearing camouflage pants and a T-shirt with a picture of a crucified Jesus on it that said, "God's Gym—His Pain, Your Gain." I looked at the Jesus picture, at the blood dripping from the nail-pierced hands and thought, yum. It wasn't just the picture of the blood on the shirt, though. It was the blood in the guy's veins—I could smell it. I could hear it whooshing through his body, and I wanted it in my mouth and running down my throat. But then there was the side of me that said this is a human being, and good Lord, girl, you're looking at a picture of the bleeding Jesus the same way most people would look at a picture of a Big Mac.

"Rebecca," Maeve said, "this is Brother Jimmy. He, like us, absolutely lives for the Lord."

I looked at Brother Jimmy's piggy eyes and greasy comb-over and wondered how I could feel such blood lust for somebody I wouldn't normally touch for any amount of money. "Is that right?" I said.

"I found him outside of Rumours," Maeve said, "you know, the bar where the sodomites go." She whispered sodomites like it was too dirty to say.

My first instinct was to say, hey, I'm a sodomite, and you've played at least a game or two in that ballpark, but before I could say anything, Brother Jimmy chimed in, "I was there protesting, like I do every Saturday night." I noticed the poster board sign propped against the wall of the foyer. In childishly scrawled magic marker, it read, "Fags, turn or burn," and "Leviticus."

All of a sudden I wasn't feeling so bad about being a predator. Would the world really be a worse place for not having Brother Jimmy in it?

"Saturdays are a busy day for Brother Jimmy," Maeve said, looking at him like he was her best friend in the world. "On Saturday mornings, he protests down at the—what was your clever term for it, Jimmy?"

"The abortuary," he said, flashing a yellow-toothed grin. "And sometimes in the afternoons I go to funerals. I look through the papers, you know, to see if any fags have died of AIDS, then I show up at the funeral with my signs. I've been arrested before, but Jesus was arrested for doing His work, too."

I looked at Brother Jimmy and wondered how somebody so hateful and judgmental could think he bore the least resemblance to Jesus. My hunger and my anger bubbled inside me like lava, and when I looked at Brother Jimmy again, all I could see was the red of his blood. I took a step toward him.

"Rebecca," Maeve said, her voice firm. "I asked Brother Jimmy here because I was telling him about our history of giving generous donations to people who are truly doing the Lord's work. Why don't you go get Brother Jimmy a glass of that lemonade that's in the refrigerator? Then we'll settle in for a nice talk."

The only thing in the refrigerator was the glass of lemonade meant for Brother Jimmy. I took it to him, and he accepted it without thanking me, like a man who expected women to wait on him. He gulped down half the glass, then said, "Now far be it from me to glorify mammon, but a donation from you ladies would sure help my ministry reach more people. I could get me a first-rate Web site and a car so I could travel outside of Cincinnati . . . the world's full of sodomites who need to wake up to their sins."

"So many souls to save," Maeve said, looking at Brother Jimmy like he was a living saint.

"Yep," Brother Jimmy said, draining the rest of his glass. "There's really only two ways to deal with faggots: cure 'em or kill 'em. I figure it's my Christian duty to try to do the first one, and the good Lord created the AIDS virus to help with the second one. Of course, I pray every day that the government will come to its senses and start helping out by executing faggots who refuse to be cured. But you can't expect much from the government when it has to depend on the checkbooks of all those liberals in Hollyweird and Jew York . . ." Brother Jimmy's eyes lost their focus, then rolled back in his head. The lemonade glass fell from his limp fingers and shattered on the floor.

"I don't usually drug prey," Maeve said, looking down at Brother Jimmy's unconscious body, "but since this will be your first kill, I wanted to make it easy for you." She focused her bottle green eyes on me. "Speaking of killing, you're not feeling too squeamish about killing this one, are you?"

"Not really," I said. There was nothing left of me but hunger and anger.

"I thought not. The only positive contribution Brother Jimmy can make is as a food source." She yanked him off the couch and onto the floor, where his head hit the marble with a thud. She squatted beside him and motioned for me to join her. "The carotid artery is right here," she said, running her manicured index finger down the side of his stubbly neck. "The trick is not to bite too hard. You want to pierce the artery, not sever it, or blood will spray all over the place . . . which is a terrible waste. Since this is your first full feed, you won't be able to take too much. I'll pull you off when I think you've had enough."

I was waiting for more instructions, but they didn't come. "So . . . should I just . . . start?"

"Yes," she said, in the same tone that a sulky kid would say, "Duh."

I lay beside Brother Jimmy—something I'd never do for any other reason—and leaned into his sweaty, hairy neck. Once I was that close, though, the sweat and stubble didn't matter because all I could smell was the salt-rich broth of his blood; all I could feel was its pulse underneath his skin. My canine teeth, which extended like a cat's claws, pierced through the flesh of his neck, and a red torrent spurted like water from a fountain. I locked my lips over it, and it filled my mouth and flooded my throat. And ah . . . I had never imagined my body could feel such pleasure. There was the taste, of course, the salt and the tang of iron, but more than that, there was the feeling of the hot fluid pumping out of him and into me, filling me with warmth, with life. The rhythm of it was amazing—the pulse of the blood in time with my sucking and swallowing. It was the song and dance of life.

When Maeve pulled me off, I scratched and hit at her, but she threw me across the room like I didn't weigh more than a bean bag. When I got up, I saw her straddling Brother Jimmy, her head bobbing where mine had just been, her hands spread in the puddle of blood on the white marble.

Even though she was my creator, my goddess, part of me wanted to slap her away so I could have more. But the sane part of me knew I couldn't handle it. I was feeling so warm and woozy from what I had drunk that I found myself climbing over Brother Jimmy's body so I could flop on the couch.

In a few minutes, Maeve, her mouth so smeared with blood it looked like a clown's painted-on grin, flopped down next to me. "There," she panted. "You'll feel sleepier than you normally would after a kill . . . that's because I drugged him."

"I do feel sleepy . . . it feels nice, though."

"Well, you should try to stay as alert as you can. We'll need to dispose of the body."

Strange as it seems, I had kind of forgotten for a minute that the drained shell of Brother Jimmy was right there with us, under our feet like an ottoman. "How will we do that?"

"Well, in this case, it's quite simple, actually. When I bought this building, I equipped it with a first-rate incinerator. So all we have to do is carve him up into manageable pieces, then roast him."

"You sound like you're on a cooking show."

Maeve smiled. "But I bet you've never seen Martha Stewart use a chainsaw."

By the time the chunks of Brother Jimmy had been bagged and burnt and I had mopped the blood up off the floor, the first birds of morning were chirping. To my surprise, Maeve put her hands on my shoulders and kissed my forehead. "You have been an excellent student, Billie Jo. Tonight, when you wake, it will be time for you to leave."

"But I don't think I'm ready yet." I had expected to be pushed out of the nest, but not quite so soon.

"You're ready. You have the skills you need, and I'll be happy to provide you with enough money to negotiate your way through the world of the living. All the clothes in the closet are yours to keep as well. You should be quite well-equipped to survive." She looked at me so hard it was like she was looking into me. "But remember . . . your duty is not just to survive but also to recruit . . . to ensure the survival of our kind. And your recruits must be chosen even more carefully than your prey."

"Yes, ma'am," I said. But the first time Maeve had lectured me about recruiting, I knew who my first choice would be. I remembered watching Tara in high school study hall, amazed by her beauty when she flipped back her curtain of black hair, the better to see her dog-eared copy of *The Vampire Lestat*. I remembered aching with love and thinking that a little white trash dyke like me could never possibly have anything to offer a creature so dark and mysterious and lovely.

But I had been wrong. Now I had something to offer.

CHAPTER 4

I told you you'd come back," Mama said when she opened the
door of the trailer. She was wearing the same NASCAR T-shirt
and pink sweatpants she'd had on the day I left, but now she
also wore the satisfied look of somebody who's been proven right.

Mama thought she had me all figured out when she saw me
standing in the doorway, fresh off an all-night ride on the
Greyhound. I was just one more loser who couldn't make it in the
big city. She didn't know that the suitcase in my left hand was full
of designer clothes and the briefcase in my other hand was full of
hundred-dollar bills, courtesy of Maeve. Mama didn't know that
somebody else's blood was running through my veins.

"I'll just be staying here a few days till I can find a place of my
own," I said, walking past TJ, who didn't even look away from the
TV. It felt good to be out of the morning sunlight; Maeve had told
me that we could stand a couple of hours of daylight before our
skin started to dry out, and I was pretty sure I had hit my limit. "I'll
be sleeping in the daytime," I said. "I got me a job over at the
bandage factory. The night shift."

In a town the size of Morgan, it doesn't take long to track
somebody down. I found out Tara was working at the Kwik-E

Mart out by the interstate, so on my first night back, I walked there to buy a Pepsi I couldn't have drunk if I'd wanted to.

She was sitting at the checkout counter, her nose in a paperback that had something about blood in the title. I was glad to see her reading tastes hadn't changed. I took a deep breath, getting up my nerve. "Hey, Tara," I said.

She looked up. "Oh . . . hey. I heard you went up to Cincinnati."

"I did, but I'm back now. You still living with Cody?" I finally made myself really look at her. It was hard because the feelings she stirred up in me made me tongue-tied.

"Yeah," she said, but she didn't sound happy. She didn't look happy either. Not that black-wearing, vampire-loving Tara had ever been a ray of sunshine, but there was something different about her . . . a kind of lifelessness to her voice and expression. And on her cheek, under the pale makeup she always wore, was that a bruise?

"So . . . uh, what time do you get off? You want to hang out or something?" It wasn't smooth, but it was better than I'd ever done with her before.

"I don't get off till twelve thirty," she said.

"I stay up late."

I still don't know why she said yes—maybe because she was hurting and alone, maybe because she had a feeling I could maybe change things for her. But at twelve thirty, she was waiting outside the Kwik-E Mart, all sultry and smoking a cigarette. "You wanna ride with me?" she asked.

More than anything. I nodded, and she led me to her beat-up Ford Escort.

"So where are we going?" she asked, once we were in the car. "We could drive over the state line and get some beer. Big Joe's never cards me."

"I don't drink beer."

"Oh. Well, I would invite you back to my place, but I don't really want to go back there just yet."

"Why don't we just find a country road and maybe a field where we can look at the stars?"

She laughed. "You sound like a boy wanting to get me alone."

"I'm not a boy."

She laughed again and started the car. "I know that, but I'm glad you know it, too." She drove us to a pasture under a sky that sparkled with stars. We lay in the grass, and she took out a joint. "You want some?"

"No, you go ahead, though." I knew that drugs wouldn't affect me unless I ingested them in somebody else's blood.

"Don't smoke, drink or chew, huh?" she said, lighting up. "Of course, I didn't much either till me and Cody got together. With me, it's just beer and weed, though. Cody does all kinds of crazy shit."

"Like putting that bruise on your face?" I didn't plan to say it; the words just spilled out of my mouth.

She looked down and tossed her hair over the injured cheek. "He didn't mean to hurt me. Sometimes he just gets so mad he doesn't know what he's doing. It's just because of the way he was raised."

"Just because you was raised that way don't make it right. People can change."

"I know." Tara sucked on the joint. "That's why I stay with him. Because I believe he can change."

"That's not what I meant. I meant maybe he should've already changed by now."

"Yeah, well . . ." She rolled onto her side and propped up on her elbow. "Living in Morgan you get used to waiting around for change that's never gonna happen. It's always the same old shit, you know?"

"Not always. I've changed."

"Oh, yeah, how's that?"

"I've changed since I went to Cincinnati. Only one thing about me has stayed the same." I took a deep breath and told her about Maeve picking me up off the street and seducing me and turning me into one of her kind. I told her about the lessons Maeve gave me and about my first kill. The whole time I talked, Tara stared at me, slack-jawed.

When I finished, she said, "Are you fucking with me because I'm high?"

"No, it's true, all of it."

She laughed and shook her head. "Prove it."

Not knowing what else to do, I opened my mouth wide and let my fangs extend to their full length. She screamed, and I clamped my hand over her mouth. "It's okay," I said. "As soon as this happened, all I wanted to do was get to you. I might have changed, but the one thing that's stayed the same is that I love you." I took my hand off her mouth in time to hear her gasp.

"This is . . . this is . . ." She ground out the joint in the grass. "This is too much . . . I mean, this is huge . . . like finding out Santa Claus isn't really your mother and daddy. And then for you to say . . . what you just said . . ." She trailed off and buried her face in her hands.

"I know," I said, "you need time to think. But Tara, if you wanted me to make you like I am, I'd do it in a minute . . . especially if you'd stay with me and keep me company." I reached out to stroke her hair and saw tears streaking her face. "But you need to decide." I stood up. "I'll be over at my mama's trailer on White Pine Road if you want to talk to me." I started on my long walk home, but then turned around to holler at the stars, "I do love you, Tara!"

She knocked on my door three days later. It was just dark, and I'd only been up long enough to dress and shower. When I opened the door, I saw her beautiful, full, lower lip was split and scabby and her left eye was black. "I want to do it," she said. "I want to be like you."

TJ was sitting not three feet away, drinking beer and watching wrestling. "We can't talk here," I mouthed, then I hollered, "TJ,

Tara's gonna give me a ride to work." I let the door slam behind me. "They think I work the night shift over at the bandage factory," I said, then I reached out to touch her face. "Did Cody do this to you?"

She nodded, tears welling in her eyes. "He did it when I told him I wanted to break up with him. He won't do it again, though. I went downtown and got a restraining order against him."

"Mama got one of them one time when some feller was bothering her," I said. "They ain't worth the paper they're printed on. But . . ." I sat down in the passenger seat of her car. "If you really want to make the change, he won't be able to hurt you again. Nobody will."

She nodded, her tears running in black streaks from her eyeliner. "It's what I want. A vampire is all I ever wanted to be. It's just that before I didn't think it was possible. I thought I was gonna have to settle for being a beautician instead."

"From here on out, you won't have to settle for anything. Could you drive us back to that field where we went the other night? It kind of feels like our place."

We spread a quilt on the ground and lay down on it, side by side. I stroked the curtain of her black hair. "I've loved you since I was fifteen years old," I said. "And I don't know if you love me or not, but if we do this . . . I want you to know I'm not doing it to trap you. It's my dream you'd stay with me forever, but if you wanted to go, you'd be free to do it. I'm not Cody. I'm not gonna make you stay if you don't want to."

She smiled and touched my cheek. "Nobody's ever been sweet to me like you, Billie Jo. I reckon if I love anybody in this world, it ought to be you."

It wasn't exactly an "I love you," but it was close enough to make my skin break out in goose bumps. "Can . . . can I kiss you, Tara?"

She nodded. I kissed her lightly, mindful of her hurt lip, but she kissed me back with force, either not hurting or not caring if she did. Soon we were rolled up in the quilt, our arms and legs and tongues entwined, our hearts pounding against each other.

"Will you let me make love to you?" I whispered into her ear.

Tara giggled. "Cody never called it that."

"Cody don't know what making love means," I breathed into her neck. "I do."

There was a catch in her voice when she said, "Show me."

She was meant to spread out under starlight, under me. I kissed her neck, her shoulder, all the way down her arm to her black polished fingernails. She smelled like smoke and cinnamon and the fresh grass in the field, and I couldn't believe I was kissing her instead of the pillow that had served for years as her stand-in. Her skin was even softer than I'd imagined it, and I wanted to seesmelltouchtaste all of it. I slipped her black T-shirt over her head and pulled her long skirt down over her hips and legs so she lay there, looking up at me, in only a black bra, black panties, and black army boots. For the first time, I saw the small blue crescent moon tattoo on top of her left breast. If I had been struck blind right then, it would have been worth it just to have seen her like that, looking up at me with those soft, smoky eyes.

I wanted to be gentle, to touch her in a way so she would never confuse me with Cody. I grazed my lips along her collarbone and could feel the pulse of her blood, but she didn't smell like prey; she smelled like love. My lips brushed over the top of her breast, my tongue flicking out to taste the crescent moon tattoo. Her pulse quickened, and she sat up to unhook her bra. I gasped at the glory of her breasts, so full, so different from my own barely there bumps. She lay back, and I buried my face in her bounty, feeling the rapid drumbeat of her heart. As I kissed and licked and sucked, she gasped and cried out, "Billie Jo!"

Hearing her call my name inspired me to move lower, slipping her panties around her hips. When I settled down between her thighs, she tensed up and said, "You don't have to do this, if you don't want to . . . put your mouth down there, I mean."

I guessed that Cody hadn't been the kind of guy who put his mouth where the money was, or why else would she have gotten so shy? "But Tara," I said, kissing her lightly on the inner thigh. "I've wanted to do this for years."

My tongue flicked to the beat of her blood, matching the pulse of her pleasure to the pulse in her veins. She gasped in the same rhythm, too, and grabbed the quilt in her clenched fists. I matched my own breathing, my own pulse, to hers, and I felt that even before giving my blood, I was already a part of her. Her breath was my breath, her pulse was my pulse, and when she cried out so loud it must have reached the stars, her pleasure was my pleasure, too.

I rested my head on her shoulder, waiting for our breathing to slow down, then asked, "Are you sure you want me to . . . change you?"

She leaned her head back, pulled her hair away from her white neck. "Please . . . do it now."

My fangs extended like a horny teenaged boy's hard-on. I sealed my lips to her neck and took each of her hands in mine, and as gently as I could, sank my teeth into her soft flesh.

There is no blood like the blood of a lover, no taste like her essence, no feel like that essence gushing in your mouth and down your throat. But I knew, even as I drank her in, that I could let myself get lost in the experience. If I took too much, she would die. I had to stop when she was at the edge of death, her heart slowed but not stopped. I knew this, but it was still hard to stop.

I pulled away, licked my lips, and took out the pocketknife I always carried in my jeans. I drew the blade across the inside of my wrist and pressed the wound to her mouth. She sucked and swallowed and grunted with pleasure, and I knew it would be almost as hard to make her stop as it was to stop myself. I wanted my essence inside her, too, wanted it so much it was tempting to let her drink me dry.

When I took my wrist from her mouth, she gasped, "So good . . . so good . . . I didn't know anything could be so good."

I didn't know if she meant the sex or the bite or the blood or all of it together, but whatever she meant, I knew I agreed with her. I laid my head on her breast and whispered, "I know."

Tara and I married each other that night, surer than if we'd stood in front of a preacher and said "I do." Her blood was mine, and my blood was hers. The quilt was our altar, and the stars were our witnesses.

We slept the next day in my bedroom in the trailer, but I knew we couldn't live the way we wanted all squeezed in with Mama and TJ. Besides, I didn't like the way TJ looked at Tara.

I saw an ad in the paper for a one-bedroom house for sale in Black Oak Hollow. I called the number and asked the man who answered if he could show the house in the evening because of my work schedule.

When Tara and I met him, he looked at us suspiciously, maybe because I was boyish and Tara was witchy, or maybe just because a pair of nineteen-year-old girls didn't match his image of home buyers. It was a white frame house, just four little rooms, but it was in good condition and had a little porch with a swing where I could imagine passing many happy evenings with Tara. Using about half of what Maeve had given me, I paid the man the full asking price in cash. I thought he was going to pass out when he saw all that money.

We furnished the house with odds and ends we bought from people advertising in the newspaper, and Tara decorated the place in her style—with candles and statues of bats and dragons and patterned scarves draped over the lamps to give a soft glow. We had a home and a car. We were in love. We were living the American dream.

There was only one problem. I was getting hungry.

This time, I thought, Maeve wouldn't be there to choose my prey and help me kill it. The choice and the kill would be my responsibility. As it turned out, though, the choice wouldn't be that hard.

One night, Tara and I were doing some painting. She had decided that a deep purple would be pretty for the walls and that darker walls would help us sleep better in the daytime. I was up on a ladder, and she was on her knees with a roller when a deep voice outside hollered, "Tara!"

She dropped the roller, splattering the floor with purple paint. "Shit, it's Cody." Her face was a mask of panic. "I knew he'd find me sooner or later."

"Don't worry," I said. "He can't hurt you anymore."

"Tara, I know you're in there, goddamn it!" he yelled. "You thought you'd leave my ass and go off and be a dyke with that white trash Scruggs bitch, didn't you? Her stepdaddy told me all about it over at the tavern!"

I looked out the window to see Cody, standing in the yard next to his motorcycle, a can of Pabst Blue Ribbon in his hand. As soon as he saw me, he hurled the can at the window. It missed.

"Should we call the cops?" Tara said.

I felt the familiar brew of hunger and anger I'd felt the night Brother Jimmy drew his last. Then the heat inside me went cold. "Tara, is Cody close to his family?"

She looked confused. "They kicked him out of the house on his sixteenth birthday. Why?"

"Is there anybody real close to him who'd look for him real hard if he was to come up missing?"

"Well, he pretty much pissed off all the guys in his old band so they won't speak to him." Tara's eyes widened. "Omigod, Billie Jo, are you thinking . . ."

"I'm thinking we should invite him in."

Tara covered her mouth to stifle a giggle, even as Cody kept on hollering her name outside. "Okay," she said, still laughing. "I think I can do this. You just play along, okay?"

"Okay."

She took my hand and led me out onto the porch. "Well, for God's sake, Cody," she said, "if you want to talk, get off my yard and come on in the house."

He squinted, looking confused. "You mean it?"

"As long as you're here, I figure I might as well hear what you've got to say," Tara said.

With another beer in his hand, Cody followed us in and

plopped down on the couch, eyeing the candles and statues of skulls and dragons. "So y'all are dykes and devil worshippers, too?" he said.

"Well, you know, the two things just kinda go together . . . like peanut butter and jelly," I said. Tara nudged me. Apparently being a wise-ass wasn't part of "playing along."

"I don't remember you having a big problem with dykes when we lived together," Tara said. "All them magazines you had with pictures of girls together, sometimes two girls with one guy . . ." Tara sat on the arm of the couch and, to my nausea, played with Cody's long hair. "I bet you'd love to see what me and Billie Jo do, wouldn't you? What if we was to show you? And what about after that, if I . . ." She leaned over and whispered in his ear. A drunk, goofy smile spread over his face. It's a wonder he didn't drop dead from the sheer force of my hate.

"The bedroom's this way, stud," Tara said, dragging Cody off the couch. In the bedroom, she told him to lie back on the bed, then proceeded to tie his wrists to the headboard with the sash to her bathrobe. "What the . . ." Cody said, but he was laughing.

"This is to make sure that at first, it's look but don't touch," Tara said. "Oh, and we'll want to keep you quiet, too." She reached into her underwear drawer, pulled out a pair of black bikini panties, wadded them up, stuffed them in his mouth, and laughed.

I watched Tara in awe. She was a born predator. Whatever it was in her personality that had allowed this ignorant redneck to victimize her had drained out with her human blood.

"Are you ready, baby?" she asked me.

I was. I took her in my arms and kissed her, so the last sight Cody would see was his girl getting loved up by me. I looked down at Cody, and he looked like he was expecting a kiss, too, instead of a fang through the carotid artery. But the fang was what he got, and he jerked and twitched underneath me, letting out muffled grunts around his mouthful of underwear. My first prey, of course, had been unconscious, and I was glad Tara had had the presence of mind to tie this one up. If not, he would've been a real flailer.

But oh God, the blood—the heat and the taste and the rhythm

of it. I wanted to take it all, but marriage is about sharing, so after a few minutes, I rose up to let Tara drink. She leaned over him like a lover, but, I thought with pleasure, she was my lover, not his.

I listened to her suck and swallow until I thought she'd had all she could take. She hissed and clawed at me when I pulled her off him, but I crooned, "It's okay, baby. You can't have anymore yet . . . your body has to get used to the blood."

"Okay," she gasped, seeming to come back to herself. "Okay." But she still licked the blood off her lips and fingers.

Cody was pale, unconscious, barely breathing. I leaned down and finished him off.

"God," Tara laughed, when I'd finished and sat up. "I feel great." Her eyes were soft and dreamy. "I guess maybe I should feel guilty, but he deserved it, the fucker."

"I wasn't gonna let him live after what he done to you," I said. "You reckon we could fit him in the trunk of your car?"

"I think so," Tara said, "if we kinda wadded him up. It's not like we have to worry about him being comfortable." She started laughing so hard she couldn't catch her breath, and so did I. It felt good to laugh and be together, full of blood and love.

We wrapped Cody in blankets and stuffed him in the trunk of the Escort. I knew just where to take him, and I led the way on his bike while Tara followed me in the car. In coal mining country, it's easy to dispose of a body. All you have to do is find an abandoned mining site and dump it into the nearest hole—a hole that's guaranteed to be so deep that nobody can see it or smell what's inside it. We tossed Cody into one of these holes, and then with much regret, I pushed his bike in after him.

In my short ride to the mining site, I had fallen in love with that bike, with its rumbling engine and shiny chrome, with the feeling of all that power between my legs. I tried to figure out a way to keep it, but I knew it was too risky. Nobody was going to miss Cody, but I sure was going to miss his bike.

CHAPTER 5

I t hadn't been dark long. I had been out, doing a little moon-light yard work, and when I came inside, I heard Tara in the bedroom, making a little choking sound in her throat. It was a sound I knew—the noise you make when you want to cry but you can't because your bone-dry predator's eyes don't produce tears. I'd made the sound a few times myself—back at Maeve's when I was feeling scared and alone—but this was the first time I'd heard the sound coming from Tara.

She was lying on the bed, and I sat down beside her. "What's wrong, baby?"

She wiped at her eyes as if there was something there to wipe. "I thought I'd call Jamie and see how he was . . . I've been meaning to call him forever. His mom said he's in the hospital . . . 'same reason as usual,' she said, like he tries to kill himself just to get on her nerves."

"That's rough," I said. Jamie was Tara's best friend in high school. A wispy thin, delicate-featured girly boy, he was as much of a misfit as Tara and me, except high school was even harder for him. Girls talk about or ignore other girls who don't fit in, but if there's a boy who doesn't fit in, other boys will always take it on themselves to beat the crap out of him. From what Jamie said, his life at home was at least twice as bad as his life at school, and by the time he graduated, he had been hospitalized twice for attempted suicide.

"I feel awful for not calling him sooner," Tara said. "I've just been so happy these past couple of months it's like I've cut myself off from everybody else. I feel like one of those bitchy girls that ditches her best friend the minute she gets a boyfriend."

"So I'm your boyfriend now, am I?" I gave her a squeeze. "Well, I hope I'm a damn sight better than Cody. I'll tell you what . . . let me get cleaned up right quick, and then we can drive out to the hospital to see Jamie."

The whole hospital smelled like blood. I'm sure you couldn't have smelled it if you weren't like I am, but to my nose, the smell was overwhelming, intoxicating. When we found Jamie's room, the old man who was his roommate was having a transfusion, and it was hard to look at Jamie because I could barely take my eyes off the vivid red inside the plastic bag.

It was hard to look at Jamie anyway, though. He looked unhealthy and unhappy. His skin was pale, and dark crescents shadowed his blue eyes. His usually styled ash blonde hair was uncombed, and he looked even thinner than I remembered him. He did smile, though, when he saw Tara. "Omigod, it's Vampirella!" he squealed. "And how is my little Queen of the Damned?"

My stomach did a flip-flop until I remembered that Jamie always made up jokey vampire nicknames for Tara.

"Worried about my little queen," Tara said. "You?"

"No need to worry. I never seem to get it right." He seemed to notice me for the first time. "Well, hey, Billie Jo. How you doing?"

"Better than you are, I reckon."

"So what was it this time?" Tara asked.

"Vicodin. Just not enough of them."

"Well, thank god for that," Tara said. She took his hand and held it. "I thought things were going better for you, Jamie. High school's over, and you're working and saving up money for college . . ."

Jamie rolled his eyes. "Well, high school's over, I'll give you that one. But I'm still having to live with my hellacious family because I can't afford my own place and save for college, too. And working . . . well, let's just say the guys over at the greeting card factory are pretty much the same guys from high school. And who's to say college'll be any different from high school either? Who's to say things can change for the better?"

"I can say it," Tara said. "Part of the reason I've been out of touch—and I'm real sorry about that, by the way, is that my life's been going through some big, good changes. Me and Billie Jo are together now."

Jamie's eyes widened. "Really? So you're playing for our team now?"

Tara smiled. "That's one of the teams I'm playing for."

"And that Cody asshole is history?"

Tara glanced over at me. "You could say that, yeah." She smoothed Jamie's hair. "But listen, me and Billie Jo have got this great little house out in the country. When they let you out of here, why don't you come visit and get away from your family a little bit?"

Once we were in the car, Tara said, "I think we should invite him to live with us."

"I don't know," I said. "I like Jamie, but you and me need our privacy."

"Oh, I don't think that'll be a problem. We'll keep the bedroom, and the couch in the living room folds out into a bed . . ."

"I didn't mean privacy for sex. I meant privacy for us to, oh, sleep during the day and be awake at night . . . drink the blood of human prey, that kind of thing."

"Oh, that," Tara laughed. "Well, I don't know . . . I thought maybe we could recruit him."

"Recruit him? The guy's tried to kill himself three times before his twentieth birthday, and you want to saddle him with living forever?"

"But it's just that he's unhappy with the kind of life he's got," Tara said. "If he had our kind of life, he'd be happy. Who wouldn't be?"

"Vampires?" Jamie laughed. We were sitting in our living room. "Okay, maybe you think I'm not mentally all there because I tried to off myself, but that still don't mean I'm crazy enough to believe you're vampires."

"But it's true!" Tara opened her dark-lipsticked mouth wide and let her fangs extend.

"Jesus on a cracker!" Jamie yelped. "That's some good special effects, I'll give you that."

"It's not special effects," Tara said. "Jamie, we've talked about this a lot, and we've decided to invite you to join us . . . to live here as one of us, as a family."

"A family of vampires?" Jamie shook his head. "I think I might ought to call the doctor about adjusting my medication."

"There's nothing wrong with your head, Jamie," Tara said. "Think about it. You'd never be anybody's victim again. You could live your life the way you wanted to, forever. Just think about it."

The next night, Jamie was back at the house, "Okay," he said, "I've decided you girls are probably as nutty as fruitcakes, but I must be, too. Go ahead . . . make me like you are."

I looked at Tara. "Do you want me to do it, or do you want to?"

"You'd better. I don't know what I'm doing, and I'm afraid I'd hurt him."

"Okay." I touched Jamie's shoulder. "Why don't we go into the bedroom? You'll need to lie down."

"Oh, I get it," Jamie said, rolling his eyes. "You girls are just trying to seduce me."

It felt strange to be lying on a bed next to a boy. "Uh . . ." I said, "this is kind of awkward. Tara's the only person I've done this with before, and with her, there was lots of kissing and stuff first."

"Well, with me, you can just skip the foreplay and go straight to the deed," Jamie said.

I sealed my lips around his neck and pierced the delicate skin. The blood came—good, always so good—but I stopped myself before I'd had too much. When I pulled away, I looked at Jamie's eyes, a little glazed, but wide with wonder. "This . . . this is real, isn't it?" he asked, his voice thick and groggy.

"It's the realest thing I know." I drew the blade of my pocketknife over my wrist. I put his mouth to my skin and let him suck, like a mother feeding her newborn baby.

With Jamie living with us, we really threw ourselves into making our house a home. We finished painting the walls and started gardening at night, making beds of night-blooming flowers. And keeping the place clean wasn't hard at all. When you take cooking and dishwashing out of the equation, housework gets loads easier.

I don't think any of us could believe how happy we were. For each of us, words like "home" and "family" had always brought up fear and anger and sadness. But now the three of us were a family with a home, and we loved it. Sometimes I thought of our little house in the country as one of those neat little cottages in fairy tales. We were like the Three Bears.

After Jamie had been with us almost a month, the Three Bears started getting hungry. And not for porridge.

We lay around the house, empty-eyed and aching. "God, I feel awful," Jamie said. "Is it always this bad?"

"Yep," I said. I was lying on the couch on my side, clutching my cramping stomach. The only reason I hadn't acted yet to end my hunger was fear. My first prey had been caught for me, and my second had been delivered to my door like a pizza. But this time, I was going to have to go out in the world and find the prey myself. "So . . ." I said, "who's ready to go hunting?"

With Tara at the wheel, we cruised through downtown Morgan. The few businesses left downtown—the Dixie Diner, Susie's Florist, the Sun Spa tanning salon—were all closed up for the evening. There wasn't a person in sight.

"Lord," Jamie said, "I reckon it'd be easier to be like we are in a big city, not in a little town like Morgan where they roll up the sidewalks at five p.m."

"There was always people out at night in Cincinnati," I said. "Maeve always said the best thing was to hit the nightclubs after people had had time to get good and drunk. 'People with impaired judgment are the ideal prey,' she said."

"It's a sad thing to be a vampire in a dry county," Jamie said. "Where do people go of a night except home to bed?"

"The Super Wal-Mart out by the interstate is open all night," Tara said.

I leaned over and kissed her cheek. "That's perfect! See, I don't just love you because you're beautiful; I love you because you're a genius."

Even though our hunger grew worse by the minute, we decided to wait a couple of hours until the store was less crowded. I also figured the later the hour, the more likely we were to find the kind of wouldn't-be-missed misfits who make the perfect prey.

If you happen to be a vampire and plan on cruising the Wal-Mart, don't forget your sunglasses. Without shades, the harsh fluorescent lighting will sear your light-sensitive eyeballs. The three of us cut quite a figure entering the Wal-Mart in our dark sunglasses and the matching leather jackets we'd spent some of Maeve's money on.

"How are you'uns doing tonight?" a grandfatherly old geezer in a blue Wal-Mart vest asked us.

"Pretty good, sir. How about yourself?" Just because we'd come there to kill somebody was no reason to be rude.

"Can't complain, sonny," he said, mistaking me for a boy like so many old people did.

He pushed a shopping cart toward us, but Tara said, "We don't need a cart. We're just here to pick up . . . an item." We managed not to giggle until we were out of the old man's hearing.

We wandered through the store, pretending to be interested in ugly clothes or automotive supplies, all the while scoping out the customers. Most of them were obviously poor choices. The woman who had run in to buy a package of diapers obviously had at least one child at home waiting for her. The young guy buying Tampax obviously wasn't shopping for himself either; plus, any guy who will go in a store and buy Tampax for a woman is obviously too nice to be singled out as prey.

When we hit the pharmaceutical section, though, I heard Jamie suck in his breath. "What?" I said.

"That guy," Jamie said, nodding toward a grungy man with a scraggly blonde beard and a trucker cap who was reading package labels in the cold and allergy medicine aisle.

"What about him?" I asked.

"He's a drug dealer," Jamie said. "He makes meth. He sold some to my cousin when he was just fifteen years old. Now he's a total addict."

"Yeah," Tara said. "I thought that guy looked familiar. I think Cody used to buy off of him."

"Hm," I said. A known drug dealer who came up missing probably wouldn't get looked for that hard. Everybody would just think he'd gotten killed in a deal that turned ugly. "Prey?" I asked.

"Definitely," Jamie said, and I could hear the hunger and the anger in his voice.

"I'm game," Tara said. "Why don't I go up to him first and make him think we want to do business?"

"Go for it," I said. I figured that having lived with Cody, she knew a lot more about how to talk to a drug dealer than I would.

I watched Tara saunter up to the scraggly man. They talked in quiet voices, and in a couple of minutes, she came back with him in tow. "Guys," she said, "this is Raymond."

"How are you'uns doing tonight?" Raymond said, sounding more like a Wal-Mart greeter than a meth dealer. Raymond's personal hygiene definitely suited a dealer better than a greeter, however. What teeth he had were black and twisted, and he smelled like an unchanged litter box.

"After we check out, Raymond's gonna come with us out to the car," Tara explained. We had picked up a couple of items to buy—eye drops, some of the strawberry-scented bubble bath Tara liked—so we wouldn't look like shoplifters. Raymond followed us out to the Escort, which we'd left in an isolated corner of the parking lot.

"Raymond, why don't you sit in the back with me a minute?" Tara asked in a tone that implied she might be interested in more than just meth.

"I reckon I can do that," he said, flashing his black, twisted grin. Jamie and I got in the front and turned around to see Raymond and Tara. Raymond reached into his pocket and said, "This is some serious shit."

"It sure is," Tara said, and so fast it was hard to follow her motions, she grabbed him by the hair and slammed his head hard against the car window, stunning him, then leaned into his neck. The smell of blood—delicious—filled the car. Tara sucked and slurped and swallowed, then finally came up for air, gasping.

"Your turn," I said to Jamie, who leaned awkwardly between the front seats to reach Raymond in the back. I let him drink for three minutes, then pulled him off because it was his first feed. By the time I got to Raymond the pulse of his blood had slowed—it was nothing like the gush of the just-bitten—but the blood was still heaven on my tongue, and it trickled down my throat like hot, nourishing soup.

When I pulled away and leaned back into my seat, Jamie said, "Well, I guess it's true. You really can find anything you need at the Wal-Mart."

After we dropped Raymond at the same mining site that was Cody's home, we went home to relax. But we couldn't. I guess there must've been traces of meth in Raymond's blood because we were all so hyper we cleaned the house from top to bottom. It was still a couple of hours till sunrise, and Jamie said he was going to go out to try to walk off some of his energy. Tara said she was going to run a bubble bath.

Is there anything more beautiful than a beautiful woman lying naked in a tub full of fluffy white bubbles? As I looked at Tara, her black hair floating like a mermaid's, her beautiful curves decorated by glittering foam, I was sure that nobody was as lucky as I was. I felt great about my life: about Tara, about being a predator.

It was funny . . . back when Maeve had been teaching me, I had thought I'd be tortured by guilt over killing, but I wasn't at all. When I thought about Brother Jimmy and Cody and Raymond . . . killing them had made the world a safer place.

"Come here," Tara said, motioning me with her index finger.

I climbed in and snuggled half beside her, half on top of her, nearly overflowing the tub. "You were fierce tonight," I whispered.

She crinkled her nose. "I didn't scare you, did I?"

"I like it when you're fierce." I kissed her, then glided my lips over her water-slick shoulders and breasts. I could feel the heat of the blood she'd drunk radiating through her skin. My hands slid over the slippery surface of her, her waist, her hips, her buttocks, until my right hand found the part of her that was slick, but not from the bath. The water splashed in rhythm with me as I moved inside her, and she gripped the sides of the tub as her body tensed. I moved faster, letting her body tell me what it wanted, feeling it like a guitar player feels the music, and when she cried out at the height of her pleasure, it was the prettiest song I'd ever heard.

I lay with my head against her breast. "You know," I said, "when I see how strong and powerful you are, it's hard for me to believe that Cody was able to do what he did to you."

"Well, I wasn't strong and powerful then. You changed me, Billie Jo." She stroked my hair.

"Nah, you had the strength and power all along, you just didn't know it. And now . . ." I raised up to gaze at her. "Now when I look at you, you're like a queen."

She laughed. "The Queen of the Damned?"

"No." I thought back to Maeve's lessons, to how she saw our place in the world of nature. "The queen of the jungle."

Chapter 6

Since his first taste of prey, Jamie had been positively giddy. For him, being a vampire was like his new religion. And just like any person who just converted to a new religion, he couldn't stop talking about it. "The next kill I want to be mine," he said, his eyes gleaming. "I want to pick out the person, and I want to be the one who does the bite."

"Sure, okay," I said. Tara was lying on the couch with her feet in my lap, and I was painting her toenails.

"Is that okay with you, too, Tara?" Jamie asked eagerly.

Tara stretched her arms and yawned. "Sure, whatever."

Jamie had started going out alone some nights, which, Tara and I figured, was understandable. She and I were happy most evenings to stay home and cuddle. Since Jamie didn't have anybody to cuddle with, staying home to watch us couldn't have been too entertaining.

One night, after our hunger had hit, Jamie came home early. "Girls!" he called from the doorway. "I've brought somebody for a visit!"

Tara and I looked from our spot on the couch to see Jamie standing beside Tyler Gordon, the former halfback for the Morgan County High School Blue Devils.

"These are the girls?" Tyler asked. Since graduation, some of his muscle had turned to flab.

"I told him there'd be beer and girls," Jamie explained to us. Then he turned to Tyler and said, "You remember Billie Jo and Tara, don't you? And a buddy of ours should be back from the bootlegger's with the beer any minute now."

Once we were in the kitchen, I hissed, "Jamie, if you think we're gonna kill off a football star without anybody noticing, you are sadly mistaken."

"An *ex*-football star," Jamie whispered back. "His grades and his football record weren't good enough to get him in to play college ball anywhere, and now not even his own daddy gives a damn about him. He was telling me the whole sob story on the way over here."

"I don't know," I said.

"Billie Jo, do you know what hell that boy made my life back in high school?" Jamie said, his voice cracking. "He alone was responsible for two trips I took to the emergency room. He also broke into my locker and spray painted faggot on the inside of the door and on every single one of my textbooks."

"He is a total asshole," Tara said. "He used to say, 'Hey, vampire girl, come suck me.'"

"And now you can finally take him up on it," Jamie said, giggling.

"Look," I said, "I know he's an asshole. I've taken plenty of shit off him, too. But we want to make sure he's not an asshole somebody would miss."

"His daddy disowned him when he didn't get a football scholarship," Jamie said. "His little cheerleader bitch girlfriend dumped him. He lives alone and works the kind of shit job where they expect people not to show up for days on end. Billie Jo, if you're waiting for an engraved invitation, I'll be happy to print one up . . ."

"Oh, all right." I felt myself starting to look forward to giving the jock bully his comeuppance.

"But I want to run the show," Jamie said. "I want to scare that fucker the same way he used to scare me."

When we went back into the living room, Jamie chirped, "Our beer should be here any minute. Hey! I've got an idea. While we wait, let's arm wrestle."

Tyler's eyebrows shot up. "Me? Arm wrestle you? I'll break your fucking arm."

"Try me," Jamie said.

They sat on the floor, placed their elbows on the table, and clasped hands. In what seemed less than a second, Jamie brought Tyler's arm down flat.

"What the—?" Tyler said.

Jamie laughed his girlish giggle. "You want to try again in case it was a fluke?" Again, Jamie brought Tyler's arm down. "Nope, guess it wasn't!" Jamie said.

"But that's impossible," Tyler said, rubbing his beefy arm. "I mean, look at you. You're a skinny little faggot . . ."

"That may be, hon," Jamie said. "But this skinny little faggot is way stronger and more powerful than you because this skinny little faggot . . ." He drew back his lips and extended his fangs—". . . is not human!"

"Wha?" Tyler's eyes, which were usually slitty and expressionless, were now wide with terror. I looked over and saw that Tara was baring her fangs, too. I shrugged and bared mine. This scene all seemed a little over the top to me, but I didn't want to ruin the effect for Jamie's sake. This little drama seemed to mean a lot to him.

"I'm not a victim anymore!" Jamie shrieked. "I'm a vampire! But I remember when I was your victim. I remember the bloody nose and the broken wrists and all the terrible things you said to me . . ."

Tyler cowered on the floor, tears pouring from his eyes, snot pouring from his nose. "I'm sorry," he whimpered. "I'm sorry. I know I probably deserve this, but I'm real, real sorry."

"Well . . ." Jamie sounded a little jarred at having received an apology. "Sorry isn't good enough."

"I know," Tyler sobbed. "I know it isn't good enough. You're . . . you're gonna kill me, right?"

"Yup!" Jamie said, as if he'd been asked if they were about to go out for ice cream.

"Well, then . . . I got something to say." Tyler wiped at his eyes with his meaty fists. "You know how they always let the condemned man say his last words? Can I say 'em?"

Jamie looked over at me. I nodded. "Go ahead."

Tyler looked at Jamie, then at Tara, then at me, his eyes shiny with tears. "You kids that get pushed around in high school 'cause you're queer or poor or weird or whatever . . . you think everything is perfect for us jocks just 'cause we're on the football team. But did you know that every time the Blue Devils lost a game, my daddy beat me with a belt? I know that don't make nothing I said or done right, but when you've got your daddy telling you how weak you are, you start looking for ways to feel strong." He wiped away a fistful of snot. "I wouldn't say a word of this if I didn't know I was about to die, but Jamie . . . a lot of that 'faggot' stuff I said to you was me dealing with my own shit. I had these . . . these feelings for Kyle Baker on the team, see, and I thought maybe if I beat up on a faggot, it would mean I wasn't a faggot myself."

"Kyle Baker?" Jamie said, sounding more like a high school gossip queen than a killer vampire.

"Yeah, so go ahead," Tyler said. He sat up on the couch and bared his neck. "I know I couldn't get away from you if I tried, so go on and get it over with." He leaned his head back, and I watched Jamie lean over him. For some reason, though, Tyler's blood didn't smell good to me, and the feeling in my stomach wasn't hunger. It was fear.

Tyler's eyes were squeezed shut, and Jamie's head was against his neck. But after a second, Jamie rose up. "I can't. I can't do it," he said. "You do it, Tara."

"Oh, for God's sake," Tara said, rolling her eyes. She strode across the room, straddled Tyler, then leaned over him. After a few seconds, she said, "Awwgh!" and stood up. "I can't do it either. I don't know why. I would say it's because I know him, but hell, I knew Cody up one side and down the other, and that sure as hell wasn't a problem. Billie Jo, looks like this one's yours."

Walking across the room, I honestly thought I was going to be able to do it. But then, as he lay there underneath me, passively offering himself up, I thought back to Brother Jimmy, of all people. His hateful voice filled my head: "There's really only two ways to deal with faggots: kill 'em or cure 'em."

I had been offended by Jimmy's belief that the people he thought were sinful deserved to die, no questions asked. But at the moment, I didn't feel so different than Brother Jimmy, passing the death sentence on Tyler for his sins. I hadn't hesitated when it came to biting Brother Jimmy or Cody or Raymond the meth dealer, but with Tyler, I didn't feel so confident. He did say he was sorry, and while he might never have said those words under less life-threatening conditions, I couldn't be sure. And he didn't have to tell us about his dad or about Kyle Baker. No matter how hard I tried to be the predator I was supposed to be, Tyler felt like a person, not prey. And I couldn't be sure he deserved to die.

"All right," I said, "I can't do it either."

Tyler's eyes snapped open, and we all just looked at each other for a minute.

"So," Tara said finally, "what do we do now?"

"You could let me go," Tyler offered helpfully.

"Yeah," I said, deciding it was time to regain some control of the situation. "We could let you go, but if we did and you said a word to anybody about us being vampires, what do you think would happen then?"

"Well, shoot," Tyler said, "then you'd have to kill me, wouldn't you? That's why I ain't saying nothing. And . . ." He looked down sheepishly. "If y'all could maybe not tell anybody about me and Kyle Baker, I'd sure appreciate it."

"It won't leave this room," I said.

Tara opened the door, and Tyler ran out with speed that would have served him well on the football field.

The three of us slumped on the couch. "So," Tara said, "what happens to vampires who don't eat? Do we just . . . die?"

"No," I said. "We can't die. But the hunger gets worse and worse and we get weaker and weaker till we can't move. Our skin dries up, our eyes shrivel in their sockets like raisins, but we're still alive, and the ache of the hunger is still there. That's what Maeve told me."

"And in the end?" Jamie asked.

"There's no end to it. We'd stay alive, but we'd be dried up, not moving, just 'a shell of pain' is how Maeve described it. She said it was the saddest thing that could happen to a predator."

"Jesus," Jamie said, shuddering.

"I'm not saying I'll never kill anybody again," Tara said. "But I can't kill somebody if I'm not sure they deserve it. And tonight . . . I wasn't sure."

"Can you ever be all the way sure?" I said.

"Of course you can," Tara said. "You can't tell me you've lost a bunch of sleep over killing Cody."

"No," I said. "I was glad to see him die. But how much of that was because he deserved it and how much of it was because I was jealous of him for being with you?"

"You girls are getting too deep for me," Jamie said. "All I know is when I looked at Tyler, I felt like I was looking at myself. And I couldn't do it."

"Do you think you could ever do it again, to somebody else?" I asked.

"Maybe, but only if I knew they were really, really bad."

"But see," Tara said, "what are the chances we could find one person a month who we could all agree deserved to die?" She put her hands in her head. "God, we're just gonna waste away, aren't we?"

"Anorexic vampires," Jamie said.

"No," I said. "There's got to be a way to deal with this. I just need some time to think."

Tara and I tried to sleep that morning, but we couldn't lie still. Our gnawing hunger made us restless and feverish. We threw off our covers and turned on a fan, but we still soaked our sheets with the rotten-sweet sweat of starvation. My efforts at thinking didn't go any better than my efforts at sleeping. My mind was fuzzy with hunger and moved jerkily, as if the gears and cogs were covered with cobwebs and in need of greasing. Finally, as the sun was going down, I said, "Maeve."

Tara raised up on one elbow and looked at me groggily. "What?"

"Maeve. If we can get to Maeve, she'll know what to do."

We took turns driving, but none of us should've been behind the wheel of a car. My arms and legs and shoulders and jaw ached like somebody had taken a hammer to them, and I was so shaky I had to grip the steering wheel extra tight to hold it steady. Overwhelming all these feelings was the emptiness—the feeling that there was nothing to fill my body, that any minute I could blow away on the breeze like a dried-up leaf.

By the time we got to Cincinnati, it was around 1 a.m.

I pushed Maeve's buzzer outside her apartment building, my stomach knotting. What if she wouldn't see us? What if she wasn't home for the night or if she didn't even live here anymore? We would have nowhere to go, and we were getting weaker and weaker. Tara leaned heavily against me, and it was a strain to support her weight when I could barely support my own.

"Yes?" Maeve's voice sounded cold and neutral over the intercom.

"Maeve? It's Billie Jo. Remember me?" I sounded like a not-so-bright ten-year-old.

"Yes, of course. Come up."

I let out my breath as the buzzer sounded. I felt like I'd been holding it all the way since Morgan. We walked through the marble lobby up to the golden elevators.

"You used to live here?" Jamie said, looking around, wide-eyed. "And you came back to Morgan?"

I squeezed Tara's hand. "I had my reasons."

When the elevator door opened, Maeve was waiting for us. She was wearing an emerald green V-necked dress, and her flaming hair was loose and wild around her shoulders. Her eyes rested on me for a moment, then moved to take in Tara and Jamie. "You're hungry," she said. "I can smell it."

"Yes," I said. "This is Tara and Jamie, by the way."

Maeve nodded but didn't say anything. Tara was giving Maeve a cool once-over; she knew how Maeve first drew me in, and I have to admit I kind of liked that Tara was jealous. Maeve didn't seem jealous of Tara, though. Her attitude toward us was businesslike and slightly annoyed. "You've come for help of some kind?"

She hadn't invited us to sit. My knees were shaking, and Tara and Jamie were leaning against the wall for support. "Would it be okay if we sat down for a minute?" I asked.

"If you like." She nodded toward the leather sofa, but she stayed standing.

Once we'd sat down, I said, "We're having some trouble . . . with prey."

"Finding it or catching it?" Maeve said.

"Killing it," I said. "The last person we caught, we couldn't do it . . . kill him, I mean. Everybody else, they seemed like they deserved it, but him . . ."

"Oh, a crisis of conscience," Maeve said, rolling her eyes. "Honestly, Billie Jo, I never would've expected it of you. The first time I saw you, you were rooting through a garbage bag for food, but you looked as proud as if you'd just stepped out of a limousine. This girl, I said, is a survivor. She'll do whatever it takes to stay alive. But clearly I misjudged you. Or maybe love . . ." She shot a glance at Tara—"has softened you. And you've recruited two more who are as soft as you are." She shook her head. "Not proud additions to my legacy."

"I'm sorry I've disappointed you," I said, though deep down, I wasn't sure how sorry I was not to be as cold as Maeve. "And we won't take up much more of your time. I just thought maybe you'd know what we should do."

Maeve laughed. "What you should do is get out there on the streets and find someone drunk or dissolute enough to lure into an alley. What you *should* do—what you were *made* to do—is kill."

"But, ma'am . . ." It was Jamie. His voice was choked. "What if we can't? Does that mean we just suffer for the rest of time?"

"That's what it should mean," Maeve said. "Unfortunately, I suppose I have my soft side, too. With humans, I know no mercy. But when it comes to other predators . . . well, preys' suffering is momentary, but predators' suffering is eternal. And I can't condemn anyone to eternal suffering, even if their behavior has been woefully disappointing." She picked up a notepad and a golden pencil from the coffee table, wrote something down, then tore off the slip of paper and handed it to me. "Go to this address," she said. "A group of predators there share your problem and have found a solution to it, albeit a rather pathetic one." She shook her head disdainfully. "Race traitors is what I call them. Some predators go so far as to say that their kind should be wiped out, but in my opinion, they're not worth the effort."

"But these people," I said. "I mean, these predators—they'll help us?"

Maeve laughed. "It's a natural mistake. They're closer to being people than they are to being predators. But yes . . . they'll help you . . . if you can call what they do helping."

"Thank you so much, Maeve!" I reached for her hand to kiss it, but she waved me away.

"Off with you," Maeve said. "Just because I refuse to let you suffer eternally doesn't mean that I like you. I despise what you've become, and this is the last time you can expect my door to be open to you."

My creator was casting me out of her garden. I looked at Maeve's chalk white skin, at her fiery hair and icy gaze. She was as beautiful as she was terrifying. "I understand," I said.

The address Maeve gave us was an alley, strewn with used needles and condoms and crushed beer cans, in a neighborhood where only the immortal should walk at night.

"I don't think there's any kind of group around here," Jamie said, wrinkling his nose at the garbage on the ground. "Not any group I'd want to be a part of, anyway."

"Oh, I don't think there was a group in the first place," Tara said. "She just made it up to get us out of there. I'll always be grateful to Maeve for making you, Billie Jo, but that doesn't mean I'd trust that red-headed bitch as far as I could sling her."

Jamie laughed. "Actually, you could probably sling her a pretty good ways . . ."

"Wait," I said. Farther down the alley, I had spotted a flight of concrete stairs that went below street level. At the bottom of the stairs was a door with the letters P.H.T.P. spray painted on it in red. I looked at the door, then at Jamie and Tara. "You reckon I ought to knock?"

Jamie glanced at his watch. "All I'm saying is that if you're knocking on a strange door at two forty-three a.m., you'd better hope there's vampires behind it."

I looked at Tara to see what she thought. Her face was gray, and she was leaning against the filthy brick wall for support. "Knock," she said.

I knocked. The door opened just enough for me to see the face of a tall, willowy guy with spiky hair dyed the same shade as Tara's. "How did you find out about us?" he half-whispered.

"Um . . . Maeve sent us," I said.

"Maeve?" He laughed. "Maeve likes us about as much as the KKK likes the ACLU."

"Well . . ." I said, struggling. "We went to Maeve because we . . .

we can't hunt anymore. She thought we were a sorry bunch and said as much, but then she sent us to you."

He poked his head out the door and sniffed the air. His nose was small and elegant. "You're hungry, aren't you?"

We nodded.

"Okay, come on in."

We followed him down a dark, narrow hallway that opened into a cheaply paneled room, furnished with junk store couches and lit by a single bare bulb. "Welcome," he said, "to the impressive Cincinnati branch office of P.H.T.P." Looking at the white banner hanging above one of the battered couches, I saw, spelled out in red block letters, what P.H.T.P. stood for: Predators for the Humane Treatment of Prey.

Our spiky-haired host held out a slender hand. "I'm Ferdinand, by the way."

"That's an unusual name," Jamie said. And even though I knew Jamie was weak from hunger, when he looked at Ferdinand, his eyes lit up so bright they looked like they could shoot sparks.

"It's my chosen name," Ferdinand said, meeting Jamie's gaze with a look that could shoot some sparks of its own. "A lot of us choose new names to get away from the kind of predators we used to be. I named myself after the little bull in the children's book who'd rather smell flowers than gore matadors."

"Oh, I loved that book when I was little!" Jamie said, and he and Ferdinand shared a smile.

We introduced ourselves, and Ferdinand introduced us to the couple of P.H.T.P. members who happened to be hanging around: Daisy, a young woman in a tie-dyed T-shirt with her hair in long, fuzzy braids, and Garnet, a black-clad Goth girl whose hair color matched her name.

"I know you're hungry," Ferdinand said, "and I don't want you to think I'm like some kind of missionary who's going to try to convert you before I'll feed you. Just have a seat, and I'll be back with your drinks."

"He sounds like a waiter," Garnet said, laughing.

Ferdinand returned carrying three paper cups—the kind that might hold Kool-Aid at a kids' birthday party. But when he handed me mine, I saw it wasn't Kool-Aid. The redness was too deep, too rich, and the salt-copper smell wafted up to my nose, so good it would've brought tears to my eyes if my body could have produced them.

"Before you drink," Ferdinand said, "I want you to know that no humans were killed in the procurement of this blood."

I drank. Without the rhythm of the pulsing vein, the music of feeding was lost, but out of a cup I could gulp greedily, and I felt the blood heating me, filling me, healing me. When I finished, I looked over at Tara and Jamie and saw that they were flushed and shiny-eyed. I put my hand in Tara's, and for the first time in days, she felt warm.

Ferdinand pulled up a chair and sat down across from us. "All the blood consumed by P.H.T.P. members is given willingly by living donors. This office is just one small branch in a huge international network. In hospitals and blood banks around the country, people are secretly donating pint after pint of blood so that vampires can live without killing."

It was a lot to take in at once, and I was still a little loopy from my overdue meal. "So . . . who gives the blood?"

Ferdinand smiled. "Friends and family members of vampires, in some cases. But the vast majority of our donors are fans."

"Fans?" I asked.

"Oh, you know the type," Ferdinand said. "Those folks in black clothes who are always skulking around with some paperback about vampires sticking out of their backpacks . . . young folks, mostly, but there are a few left over from the days of *Dark Shadows*."

"That's like me before I changed," Tara said.

"Me, too," Ferdinand said. "So you know what it's like to be one of them—to want vampires to be real. Well, the founders of P.H.T.P. tapped into selected groups of fans and let them know that we are real—and that a good percentage of us want to peacefully coexist with humans. The word spread, and basically, it's the fans who have been keeping us alive."

"So you can actually get enough blood to live on without having to kill anybody?" Jamie asked.

"Sure," Ferdinand said.

"But," said Garnet, "you're gonna get *just enough* to live on . . . there are no big gorges like when you're an active predator."

"Yeah," Daisy said, hugging her knees to her chest, "but it's worth living on less to know that you're not doing any harm. It's like that bumper sticker that says, 'Live simply so others may simply live.'"

Garnet playfully elbowed her. "You are such a hippie."

"Well, what do you expect?" Daisy said. "I got bitten at a Dead show back in ninety three. Imagine being a life-long vegetarian and then realizing that in order to stay alive, I needed to drink human blood. I was like, can't I just have a Tofu Pup?"

"Which brings us to another key element of P.H.T.P," Ferdinand said. "Recruitment. Daisy here should never have been recruited. She lacks a predator's disposition. Our policy is not to recruit anybody until they've spent a full year thinking over the decision to become a vampire. It's not a decision to rush into on the part of either the creator or the created because once you've stepped onto the path, you can't turn back."

"That's the truth," I said, and I wondered: If Maeve had given me the chance to choose, would I have chosen this life for myself? But then I felt Tara's hand in mind, and when I looked up to see her, my beautiful vampire bride, I knew that if I'd had to choose this life in order to have her, the answer would have been yes.

Epilogue

The city didn't keep me the second time, either. I came back to Morgan, along with Tara and Jamie, this time changed again.

We're still vampires, but we're not predators. P.H.T.P. sends us our supply of frozen blood every month by Federal Express. It's enough to end our hunger but no more, so we're leaner but not meaner.

Our little house has turned into a stopover for P.H.T.P. vampires passing through Kentucky, a safe place where they can grab a day's sleep before they move on. It's also turning into a country retreat for P.H.T.P.ers who need a break from the city. Daisy the Deadhead stayed here two weeks in the spring, going on and on about the fresh air and the feel of the grass under her bare feet. But the visitor we have most often is Ferdinand. He spends every other weekend here, and as lovey-dovey as he and Jamie are getting, it looks like we're going to be converting the kitchen into a private bedroom for the two of them.

Tara and I still love our privacy, too. Tara seems to have turned her old passion for the hunt into an even deeper passion in the bedroom, and I have to say I've got no complaints. We're not hungry for the kill anymore. We're hungry for each other.

CONTRIBUTOR BIOS

Barbara Johnson has always been fascinated by vampires. As a baby dyke, she would rush home from school to watch Barnabas Collins mesmerize the beautiful women of *Dark Shadows*. As a teen, she thrilled as Christopher Lee and Frank Langella seduced their amply bosomed victims in stage and film versions of *Dracula*. As an adult, she realized that beautiful women and ample bosoms were more important to her than capes and fangs, and soon wore out her remote fast-forwarding through the boring parts of *The Hunger* to see Catherine Deneuve and Susan Sarandon bite each other's necks. Barbara's insatiable thirst for hot vampire action even drove her to rent the European cult classic *Vampyros Lesbos* (cheesier than a case of Velveeta). Her current fanged fave is David Boreanaz as TV's tortured *Angel*, whom she admits is her "bi moment."

KARIN KALLMAKER, the author of more than twenty romances and fantasy/science fiction novels, recently expanded her repertoire to include explicit erotica. As Karin says, "Nice Girls Do." Her works include the award-winning *Just Like That, Maybe Next Time* and *Sugar*. Short stories have appeared in anthologies from publishers like Alyson, Bold Strokes, Circlet and Haworth, as well as novellas and short stories with Bella Books. She began her writing career with the venerable Naiad Press and continues with Bella.

She and her partner are the mothers of two and live in the San Francisco Bay Area. She is descended from Lady Godiva, a fact which she'll share with anyone who will listen. She likes her Internet fast, her iPod loud and her chocolate real.

All of Karin's work can now be found at Bella Books. Details and background about her novels, and her other pen name, Laura Adams, can be found at www.kallmaker.com.

THERESE SZYMANSKI is a vampire. She regularly stays up through the night and shuns the light of day. She has pictures of herself with a Watcher and two slayers (one of whom asked her if she flossed . . . while she, the Slayer, leaned so far over a table, Reese had a right nice view down her blouse. To this day Reese insists Kennedy was not flirting with her).

Elsewhen was first drafted in the 90s. Since then, Reese wrote a companion story to it for *Call of the Dark*. She was the main lobbyist for the New Exploits team to do vampires.

Reese has been short-listed for a couple of Lammys and Goldies, a Spectrum, and made the Publishing Triangle's list of Notable Lesbian Books with her first anthology.

You can e-mail Reese at tsszymanski@worldnet.att.net.

As a child, **JULIA WATTS** cut her fangs on *Dark Shadows* and *Bunnicula*. As a black-clad, horror-obsessed teen, she could often be seen carrying around tattered copies of Anne Rice's vampire novels. In college, her first published story was a comic piece about a vampire who offers a woman eternal life but is rejected because the woman isn't ready for that kind of commitment. *We Recruit* is the first time she has revisited the vampire genre since penning that admittedly silly short story in college. Watts's non-vampire-related writing includes the novels *Women's Studies*, *Wildwood Flowers*, *Piece of My Heart*, *Phases of the Moon*, and the Lambda Literary Award-winning *Finding H.F.*

DON'T MISS THESE FABULOUS BOOKS BY THE SAME BESTSELLING AUTHORS:

Bell, Book and Dyke: New Exploits of Magical Lesbians
Once Upon a Dyke: New Exploits of Fairy Tale Lesbians

Barbara Johnson:
• *Strangers in the Night* • *Bad Moon Rising*
• *The Beach Affair* • *Stonehurst*
Edited by: *The Perfect Valentine (with Therese Szymanski)*

KARIN KALLMAKER:
• *Finders Keepers* • *Just Like That* • *Sugar* • *One Degree of Separation*
• *Maybe Next Time* • *Substitute for Love* • *Frosting on the Cake*
• *Unforgettable* • *Watermark* • *Making Up for Lost Time*
• *Embrace in Motion* • *Wild Things* • *Painted Moon*
• *Car Pool* • *Paperback Romance* • *Touchwood* • *In Every Port*
For Bella After Dark: *18th & Castro* • *All the Wrong Places*
Writing as Laura Adams: *Sleight of Hand* • *Seeds of Fire*

THERESE SZYMANSKI
• *When First We Practice* • *When the Corpse Lies*
• *When Good Girls Go Bad* • *When Evil Changes Face*
• *When Some Body Disappears* • *When the Dead Speak*
• *When the Dancing Stops*
Edited by: *Wild Nights: (Mostly) True Stories of Lesbian Desire*
• *The Perfect Valentine (with Barbara Johnson)*
• *Call of the Dark: Erotic Lesbian Tales of the Supernatural*
• *Back to Basics: A Butch/Femme Anthology*

JULIA WATTS
• *Women's Studies (Spinsters Ink)*
Wedding Bell Blues • *Piece of My Heart* • *Phases of the Moon*
• *Wildwood Flowers (Bella Books)*
• *Mixed Blessings (Jacobyte Books, www.jacobytebooks.com)*
• *Finding H.F. (Alyson)*

OUT OF THE FIRE by Beth Moore. Author Ann Covington feels at the top of the world when told her book is being made into a movie. Then in walks Casey Duncan the actress who is playing the lead in her movie. Will Casey turn Ann's world upside down?
1-59493-088-0 $13.95

STAKE THROUGH THE HEART: NEW EXPLOITS OF TWILIGHT LESBIANS by Karin Kallmaker, Julia Watts, Barbara Johnson and Therese Szymanski. The playful quartet that penned the acclaimed *Once Upon A Dyke* are dimming the lights for journeys into worlds of breathless seduction.
1-59493-071-6 $15.95

THE HOUSE ON SANDSTONE by KG MacGregor. Carly Griffin returns home to Leland and finds that her old high school friend Justice is awakening more than just old memories.
1-59493-076-7 $13.95

WILD NIGHTS: MOSTLY TRUE STORIES OF WOMEN LOVING WOMEN edited by Therese Szymanski. 264 pp. 23 new stories from today's hottest erotic writers are sure to give you your wildest night ever!
1-59493-069-4 $15.95

COYOTE SKY by Gerri Hill. 248 pp. Sheriff Lee Foxx is trying to cope with the realization that she has fallen in love for the first time. And fallen for author Kate Winters, who is technically unavailable. Will Lee fight to keep Kate in Coyote?
1-59493-065-1 $13.95

VOICES OF THE HEART by Frankie J. Jones. 264 pp. A series of events force Erin to swear off love as she tries to break away from the woman of her dreams. Will Erin ever find the key to her future happiness?
1-59493-068-6 $13.95

SHELTER FROM THE STORM by Peggy J. Herring. 296 pp. A story about family and getting reacquainted with one's past that shows that sometimes you don't appreciate what you have until you almost lose it.
1-59493-064-3 $13.95

WRITING MY LOVE by Claire McNab. 192 pp. Romance writer Vonny Smith believes she will be able to woo her editor Diana through her writing . . .
1-59493-063-5 $13.95

PAID IN FULL by Ann Roberts. 200 pp. Ari Adams will need to choose between the debts of the past and the promise of a happy future.
1-59493-059-7 $13.95

ROMANCING THE ZONE by Kenna White. 272 pp. Liz's world begins to crumble when a secret from her past returns to Ashton . . .
1-59493-060-0 $13.95

SIGN ON THE LINE by Jaime Clevenger. 204 pp. Alexis Getty, a flirtatious delivery driver is committed to finding the rightful owner of a mysterious package.
1-59493-052-X $13.95

END OF WATCH by Clare Baxter. 256 pp. LAPD Lieutenant L.A Franco Frank follows the lone clue down the unlit steps of memory to a final, unthinkable resolution.

1-59493-064-4 $13.95

BEHIND THE PINE CURTAIN by Gerri Hill. 280pp. Jacqueline returns home after her father's death and comes face-to-face with her first crush.   1-59493-057-0 $13.95

PIPELINE by Brenda Adcock. 240pp. Joanna faces a lost love returning and pulling her into a seamy underground corporation that kills for money.   1-59493-062-7 $13.95

18TH & CASTRO by Karin Kallmaker. 200pp. First-time couplings and couples who know how to mix lust and love make 18th & Castro the hottest address in the city by the bay.
1-59493-066-X $13.95

JUST THIS ONCE by KG MacGregor. 200pp. Mindful of the obligations back home that she must honor, Wynne Connelly struggles to resist the fascination and allure that a particular woman she meets on her business trip represents.   1-59493-087-2 $13.95

ANTICIPATION by Terri Breneman. 240pp. Two women struggle to remain professional as they work together to find a serial killer.   1-59493-055-4 $13.95

OBSESSION by Jackie Calhoun. 240pp. Lindsey's life is turned upside down when Sarah comes into the family nursery in search of perennials.   1-59493-058-9 $13.95

BENEATH THE WILLOW by Kenna White. 240pp. A torch that still burns brightly even after twenty-five years threatens to consume two childhood friends.

1-59493-053-8 $13.95

SISTER LOST, SISTER FOUND by Jeanne G'fellers. 224pp. The highly anticipated sequel to No Sister of Mine.   1-59493-056-2 $13.95

THE WEEKEND VISITOR by Jessica Thomas. 240 pp. In this latest Alex Peres mystery, Alex is asked to investigate an assault on a local woman but finds that her client may have more secrets than she lets on.   1-59493-054-6 $13.95

THE KILLING ROOM by Gerri Hill. 392 pp. How can two women forget and go their separate ways?   1-59493-050-3 $12.95

PASSIONATE KISSES by Megan Carter. 240 pp. Will two old friends run from love?

1-59493-051-1 $12.95

ALWAYS AND FOREVER by Lyn Denison. 224 pp. The girl next door turns Shannon's world upside down.   1-59493-049-X $12.95

BACK TALK by Saxon Bennett. 200 pp. Can a talk show host find love after heartbreak?

1-59493-028-7 $12.95

THE PERFECT VALENTINE: EROTIC LESBIAN VALENTINE STORIES edited by Barbara Johnson and Therese Szymanski—from Bella After Dark. 328 pp. Stories from the hottest writers around.   1-59493-061-9 $14.95

MURDER AT RANDOM by Claire McNab. 200 pp. The Sixth Denise Cleever Thriller. Denise realizes the fate of thousands is in her hands.   1-59493-047-3 $12.95

THE TIDES OF PASSION by Diana Tremain Braund. 240 pp. Will Susan be able to hold it all together and find the one woman who touches her soul?   1-59493-048-1 $12.95

JUST LIKE THAT by Karin Kallmaker. 240 pp. Disliking each other—and everything they stand for—even before they meet, Toni and Syrah find feelings can change, just like that.

1-59493-025-2 $12.95

WHEN FIRST WE PRACTICE by Therese Szymanski. 200 pp. Brett and Allie are once again caught in the middle of murder and intrigue.   1-59493-045-7 $12.95

REUNION by Jane Frances. 240 pp. Cathy Braithwaite seems to have it all: good looks, money and a thriving accounting practice . . .   1-59493-046-5 $12.95

BELL, BOOK & DYKE: NEW EXPLOITS OF MAGICAL LESBIANS by Kallmaker, Watts, Johnson and Szymanski. 360 pp. Reluctant witches, tempting spells and skyclad beauties—delve into the mysteries of love, lust and power in this quartet of novellas.
1-59493-023-6 $14.95

ARTIST'S DREAM by Gerri Hill. 320 pp. When Cassie meets Luke Winston, she can no longer deny her attraction to women . . .   1-59493-042-2 $12.95

NO EVIDENCE by Nancy Sanra. 240 pp. Private Investigator Tally McGinnis once again returns to the horror-filled world of a serial killer.   1-59493-043-04 $12.95

WHEN LOVE FINDS A HOME by Megan Carter. 280 pp. What will it take for Anna and Rona to find their way back to each other again?   1-59493-041-4 $12.95

MEMORIES TO DIE FOR by Adrian Gold. 240 pp. Rachel attempts to avoid her attraction to the charms of Anna Sigurdson . . .   1-59493-038-4 $12.95

SILENT HEART by Claire McNab. 280 pp. Exotic lesbian romance.

1-59493-044-9 $12.95

MIDNIGHT RAIN by Peggy J. Herring. 240 pp. Bridget McBee is determined to find the woman who saved her life.   1-59493-021-X $12.95

THE MISSING PAGE A Brenda Strange Mystery by Patty G. Henderson. 240 pp. Brenda investigates her client's murder . . .   1-59493-004-X $12.95

WHISPERS ON THE WIND by Frankie J. Jones. 240 pp. Dixon thinks she and her best friend, Elizabeth Colter, would make the perfect couple . . .   1-59493-037-6 $12.95

CALL OF THE DARK: EROTIC LESBIAN TALES OF THE SUPERNATURAL edited by Therese Szymanski—from Bella After Dark. 320 pp.   1-59493-040-6 $14.95

A TIME TO CAST AWAY A Helen Black Mystery by Pat Welch. 240 pp. Helen stops by Alice's apartment—only to find the woman dead . . .   1-59493-036-8 $12.95

DESERT OF THE HEART by Jane Rule. 224 pp. The book that launched the most popular lesbian movie of all time is back.   1-1-59493-035-X $12.95

THE NEXT WORLD by Ursula Steck. 240 pp. Anna's friend Mido is threatened and eventually disappears . . .   1-59493-024-4 $12.95

CALL SHOTGUN by Jaime Clevenger. 240 pp. Kelly gets pulled back into the world of private investigation . . .   1-59493-016-3 $12.95

52 PICKUP by Bonnie J. Morris and E.B. Casey. 240 pp. 52 hot, romantic tales—one for every Saturday night of the year.   1-59493-026-0 $12.95

GOLD FEVER by Lyn Denison. 240 pp. Kate's first love, Ashley, returns to their home town, where Kate now lives . . .   1-1-59493-039-2 $12.95

RISKY INVESTMENT by Beth Moore. 240 pp. Lynn's best friend and roommate needs her to pretend Chris is his fiancé. But nothing is ever easy.   1-59493-019-8 $12.95

HUNTER'S WAY by Gerri Hill. 240 pp. Homicide detective Tori Hunter is forced to team up with the hot-tempered Samantha Kennedy.   1-59493-018-X $12.95

CAR POOL by Karin Kallmaker. 240 pp. Soft shoulders, merging traffic and slippery when wet . . . Anthea and Shay find love in the car pool   1-59493-013-9 $12.95

NO SISTER OF MINE by Jeanne G'Fellers. 240 pp. Telepathic women fight to coexist with a patriarchal society that wishes their eradication. ISBN 1-59493-017-1 $12.95

ON THE WINGS OF LOVE by Megan Carter. 240 pp. Stacie's reporting career is on the rocks. She has to interview bestselling author Cheryl, or else! ISBN 1-59493-027-9 $12.95

WICKED GOOD TIME by Diana Tremain Braund. 224 pp. Does Christina need Miki as a protector . . . or want her as a lover? ISBN 1-59493-031-7 $12.95

THOSE WHO WAIT by Peggy J. Herring. 240 pp. Two brilliant sisters—in love with the same woman! ISBN 1-59493-032-5 $12.95

ABBY'S PASSION by Jackie Calhoun. 240 pp. Abby's bipolar sister helps turn her world upside down, so she must decide what's most important. ISBN 1-59493-014-7 $12.95

PICTURE PERFECT by Jane Vollbrecht. 240 pp. Kate is reintroduced to Casey, the daughter of an old friend. Can they withstand Kate's career? ISBN 1-59493-015-5 $12.95

PAPERBACK ROMANCE by Karin Kallmaker. 240 pp. Carolyn falls for tall, dark and . . . female . . . in this classic lesbian romance. ISBN 1-59493-033-3 $12.95

DAWN OF CHANGE by Gerri Hill. 240 pp. Susan ran away to find peace in remote Kings Canyon—then she met Shawn . . . ISBN 1-59493-011-2 $12.95

DOWN THE RABBIT HOLE by Lynne Jamneck. 240 pp. Is a killer holding a grudge against FBI Agent Samantha Skellar? ISBN 1-59493-012-0 $12.95

SEASONS OF THE HEART by Jackie Calhoun. 240 pp. Overwhelmed, Sara saw only one way out—leaving . . . ISBN 1-59493-030-9 $12.95

TURNING THE TABLES by Jessica Thomas. 240 pp. The 2nd Alex Peres Mystery. *From ghosties and ghoulies and long leggity beasties . . .* ISBN 1-59493-009-0 $12.95

FOR EVERY SEASON by Frankie Jones. 240 pp. Andi, who is investigating a 65-year-old murder, meets Janice, a charming district attorney . . . ISBN 1-59493-010-4 $12.95

LOVE ON THE LINE by Laura DeHart Young. 240 pp. Kay leaves a younger woman behind to go on a mission to Alaska . . . will she regret it? ISBN 1-59493-008-2 $12.95

UNDER THE SOUTHERN CROSS by Claire McNab. 200 pp. Lee, an American travel agent, goes down under and meets Australian Alex, and the sparks fly under the Southern Cross. ISBN 1-59493-029-5 $12.95

SUGAR by Karin Kallmaker. 240 pp. Three women want sugar from Sugar, who can't make up her mind. ISBN 1-59493-001-5 $12.95

FALL GUY by Claire McNab. 200 pp. 16th Detective Inspector Carol Ashton Mystery. ISBN 1-59493-000-7 $12.95

ONE SUMMER NIGHT by Gerri Hill. 232 pp. Johanna swore to never fall in love again—but then she met the charming Kelly . . . ISBN 1-59493-007-4 $12.95

TALK OF THE TOWN TOO by Saxon Bennett. 181 pp. Second in the series about wild and fun loving friends. ISBN 1-931513-77-5 $12.95

LOVE SPEAKS HER NAME by Laura DeHart Young. 170 pp. Love and friendship, desire and intrigue, spark this exciting sequel to *Forever and the Night*. ISBN 1-59493-002-3 $12.95

TO HAVE AND TO HOLD by Peggy J. Herring. 184 pp. By finally letting down her defenses, will Dorian be opening herself to a devastating betrayal? ISBN 1-59493-005-8 $12.95

WILD THINGS by Karin Kallmaker. 228 pp. Dutiful daughter Faith has met the perfect man. There's just one problem: she's in love with his sister. ISBN 1-931513-64-3 $12.95

SHARED WINDS by Kenna White. 216 pp. Can Emma rebuild more than just Lanny's marina? ISBN 1-59493-006-6 $12.95

THE UNKNOWN MILE by Jaime Clevenger. 253 pp. Kelly's world is getting more and more complicated every moment. ISBN 1-931513-57-0 $12.95

TREASURED PAST by Linda Hill. 189 pp. A shared passion for antiques leads to love. ISBN 1-59493-003-1 $12.95

SIERRA CITY by Gerri Hill. 284 pp. Chris and Jesse cannot deny their growing attraction . . . ISBN 1-931513-98-8 $12.95

ALL THE WRONG PLACES by Karin Kallmaker. 174 pp. Sex and the single girl—Brandy is looking for love and usually she finds it. Karin Kallmaker's first *After Dark* erotic novel. ISBN 1-931513-76-7 $12.95

WHEN THE CORPSE LIES A Motor City Thriller by Therese Szymanski. 328 pp. Butch bad-girl Brett Higgins is used to waking up next to beautiful women she hardly knows. Problem is, this one's dead. ISBN 1-931513-74-0 $12.95

GUARDED HEARTS by Hannah Rickard. 240 pp. Someone's reminding Alyssa about her secret past, and then she becomes the suspect in a series of burglaries. ISBN 1-931513-99-6 $12.95

ONCE MORE WITH FEELING by Peggy J. Herring. 184 pp. Lighthearted, loving, romantic adventure. ISBN 1-931513-60-0 $12.95

TANGLED AND DARK A Brenda Strange Mystery by Patty G. Henderson. 240 pp. When investigating a local death, Brenda finds two possible killers—one diagnosed with Multiple Personality Disorder. ISBN 1-931513-75-9 $12.95

WHITE LACE AND PROMISES by Peggy J. Herring. 240 pp. Maxine and Betina realize sex may not be the most important thing in their lives. ISBN 1-931513-73-2 $12.95

UNFORGETTABLE by Karin Kallmaker. 288 pp. Can Rett find love with the cheerleader who broke her heart so many years ago? ISBN 1-931513-63-5 $12.95

HIGHER GROUND by Saxon Bennett. 280 pp. A delightfully complex reflection of the successful, high society lives of a small group of women. ISBN 1-931513-69-4 $12.95

LAST CALL A Detective Franco Mystery by Baxter Clare. 240 pp. Frank overlooks all else to try to solve a cold case of two murdered children . . . ISBN 1-931513-70-8 $12.95

ONCE UPON A DYKE: NEW EXPLOITS OF FAIRY-TALE LESBIANS by Karin Kallmaker, Julia Watts, Barbara Johnson & Therese Szymanski. 320 pp. You've never read fairy tales like these before! From Bella After Dark. ISBN 1-931513-71-6 $14.95

FINEST KIND OF LOVE by Diana Tremain Braund. 224 pp. Can Molly and Carolyn stop clashing long enough to see beyond their differences? ISBN 1-931513-68-6 $12.95

DREAM LOVER by Lyn Denison. 188 pp. A soft, sensuous, romantic fantasy. ISBN 1-931513-96-1 $12.95

NEVER SAY NEVER by Linda Hill. 224 pp. A classic love story . . . where rules aren't the only things broken. ISBN 1-931513-67-8 $12.95

PAINTED MOON by Karin Kallmaker. 214 pp. Stranded together in a snowbound cabin, Jackie and Leah's lives will never be the same. ISBN 1-931513-53-8 $12.95